S0-BEZ-279

THE MAN NOBODY KNEW

A NOVEL

GARRETT C. WHITWORTH

WESTBOW
PRESS®
A DIVISION OF THOMAS NELSON
& ZONDERVAN

The Kingdom New Testament. Copyright 2011 by Nicholas
Thomas Wright. Used with permission.

Copyright Faithlife Corporation, Makers of Logos Bible
Software - www.logos.com (interior Temple image)

Author photograph by Stephen Wormser

WestBow Press books may be ordered through booksellers or by contacting:

WestBow Press
A Division of Thomas Nelson & Zondervan
1663 Liberty Drive
Bloomington, IN 47403
www.westbowpress.com
1 (866) 928-1240

ISBN: 978-1-5127-3993-0 (sc)
ISBN: 978-1-5127-3994-7 (hc)
ISBN: 978-1-5127-3992-3 (e)

Library of Congress Control Number: 2016906851

Print information available on the last page.

WestBow Press rev. date: 05/05/2016

For my wife, Colleen, and for our children and grandchildren.

This book is also dedicated to N. T. Wright, whose books have inspired me to write this book. He knows the man.

ACKNOWLEDGMENTS

I would like to thank my wife, Colleen, for encouraging me throughout the writing of the manuscript that became this book. I would also like to thank our daughter, Elizabeth, for patiently listening to my ideas and providing helpful feedback.

My thanks also go to Ted Hamilton and Glenn Aufderhar, both of whom have a deep understanding of and intimate relationship with the book's title character, for spending many hours reading the manuscript; their suggestions were most useful.

I am also indebted to WestBow Press and everyone there with whom I dealt; their support and wise counsel were invaluable.

PROLOGUE

This book was written many years after the events described in these pages occurred. I was a young man then. I am an old man now. I live as an exile on a tiny island in the Aegean Sea. As far as I know, I alone am the survivor among the men and women who appear in this volume with one exception—the man nobody knew.

—John

CHAPTER 1

The first time I saw the man was next to a river that flowed through the desert not far from my home. I had gone there to see another man, a man who was stirring up a lot of excitement—some would say trouble—in my country. Many thought him to be a lunatic, a dangerous man, perhaps even a revolutionary. The political, religious, and military powers watched him closely.

My name is John. At the beginning of the story I am about to tell, I was a lad of sixteen years. My home was in the small but prosperous fishing village of Capernaum, located on the northern coast of a small lake, somewhat grandly called the Sea of Galilee, in the north of the small country of Israel. The Sea of Galilee was also at the crossroads of two trade routes, one going south to Jerusalem, and one going to the east and west. I was born and raised in Capernaum, and my family had always lived there. My father, my older brother, James, and I were fishermen. The best fishing on the lake was in the northern region, which was the main reason why we lived there. Father and two of our friends, Simon and Andrew, owned the business, which was modestly successful. We were not wealthy, but we lived comfortably. We worked hard, usually every day of the week, weather permitting, except the Sabbath. As Jews, we kept that day holy. The Hebrew faith was an ancient religion, thousands of years old. We took it seriously, observing its holy days and festivals and making annual pilgrimages to Israel's capital city of Jerusalem. It was also the home of our holiest edifice, the temple. The Hebrew religion was unlike any other on earth. We believed with all our hearts that it was *the one* true religion. We worshipped a *living* God, not a wooden, metal, or stone idol.

It was a typically hot, dry summer day. I journeyed south by foot from my home on the lake, following the Jordan River, the largest and most important river in our country. My father had reluctantly given me permission to take the day off from fishing with him and James, who was five years my senior. James was not happy, as his workload would double because of my absence. However, I was determined to see the strange man about whom everybody was talking. Simon and Andrew had told me about this man, also named John. They'd heard him speak some weeks before, in another part of our region. Some said he was the Anointed One on a mission from God. Some said he was a prophet, perhaps even an ancient prophet mysteriously returned. Thousands of my compatriots flocked to the desolate places—I'd heard he never visited villages and towns—to see him and hear what he had to say. Word had spread that he was a fiery orator with a powerful message, and that he looked like a wild man. He was an ascetic, living a life of extreme self-denial.

As I approached where he was speaking that day, I saw a large crowd, perhaps as many as a thousand men, women, and children. I had heard he often spoke to twice that number. He stood astride a large, flat rock that elevated him about ten feet above his audience. He paced back and forth, shouting, waving his sunbaked arms. His face, also browned by the sun, was about the same color and texture of the leather belt that girded his camel-hair cloak. His own hair was long and unkempt; his beard was scraggly. (All adult Jewish men wore beards, but I had not been able to produce one yet.) It was said his diet consisted of locusts and wild honey! His back was to the river, and the throng sat in a semicircle around him. They were still and quiet, captivated by him. His voice was clear; it was easy to understand every word he said.

I joined the crowd and got an earful. I caught a glimpse of Simon and Andrew, both of whom were in the audience. The reports about John were accurate. I was riveted; when this man talked, it was impossible not to be. He spoke plainly: It was high time—past high time—for all of us Jews to wake up and realize that we must

2

make serious changes in what we believed about God and in the way we lived our lives. We needed to *repent,* as he called it, to realize we were going in the wrong direction—metaphorically—and to turn around. He was anything but vague, saying it was time to make these changes in every aspect of our lives—the way we related to our Maker, our families, our friends, and also to strangers, even foreigners. We had little interaction with non-Jews, or as we called them, Gentiles. We especially detested our Roman conquerors and occupiers. We even needed to change how we thought about and practiced our religion. Moreover, he said that the time to make these changes was now, because it would soon be too late; our opportunity would pass. The man said the consequence of not repenting would be a severe judgment visited upon us from the hands of the God we acknowledged as not only our Creator but also the supreme judge of our country, the whole world, and its entire population. *Judgment,* especially God's judgment, was a frightening word in our religion.

"Well," the man said, "do not try to imagine what God's judgment is like, for it is unimaginable, and you do not want to experience it."

The reason John accorded so much importance to repentance was that, as he put it, "The kingdom of God is imminent, at hand." He said that God had chosen him to prepare the way for its arrival. To justify the message he preached throughout the region, he quoted the words of a prophet of long ago, still held in high esteem by religious Jews.

A man in the audience shouted a question. "What shall we do then? Tell us more about what you mean by repentance."

John then talked about treating others fairly and being generous toward those in need; he even gave specific advice to tax collectors (do not collect more than you are authorized to collect) and soldiers (do not use your position to intimidate people). He said the one for whom he was preparing the way was greater than he—he was not even worthy to carry his sandals.

He performed an unusual, not to say unknown, ritual that he said was integral to his ministry: he immersed into the river those who consented. The man explained this was an outward manifestation of a person's death to sin and resurrection to a new life in harmony with God's will. When he began to plunge the willing ones into the water, most of the others departed. That gave me the opportunity to move closer to the water's edge. As I did so, I saw Simon and Andrew far ahead of me, awaiting their turns. That day, a hundred or more were *baptized*. That was John's word for the ritual. He was at that particular place so there would be enough water for him to perform this sacrament.

I was one of those John baptized in the Jordan River that day. I was the last in line. Just ahead of me was a group of religious leaders. They were dressed in the type of garments worn by such men from Jerusalem. I had seen many like them on my family's annual pilgrimages to that city. I had always held such men in high regard. My father was a descendant of Levi, the forebear of a family who became, by tradition, priests of our faith. Father was also a cousin of the high priest, Caiaphas, currently presiding over our temple in Jerusalem. I was surprised and pleased that they sought baptism, as it gave me confidence that it was the right thing for me to do too.

When the first of them came to his turn, John did something that surprised me. In the most scathing terms I had ever heard, he denounced as hypocrites this man and all the others with him. I was embarrassed for them. They tried to argue with John, but he cut them off and refused to baptize them. They went away angry, mumbling among themselves.

And then it was my turn. As I came up out of the water, I had a sensation like nothing I had felt before. John had told us that if we repented of our wrongs and were baptized as a sign of our repentance, we would experience a sense of renewal in mind and spirit. I was skeptical but willing to try it. I did feel differently but really did not understand what, if anything, it meant. Had I been duped? My brother had told me many times that I would believe almost anything.

I thought I was to be last one in the river with John that day, but I was wrong. As I stepped out of the water and onto the riverbank, I saw the man for the first time. I had not seen him in the thinning crowd until that moment. He was an ordinary-looking man, probably about thirty years of age. I should say that he looked ordinary except in one way: he had the most penetrating—though not intimidating—eyes I had ever seen. I could not take my eyes off him. He asked John to baptize him too. John seemed taken aback and said the man should perform the sacrament on him, John. However, the man insisted, and John consented.

By this time, there were only a few people, many of them close followers of John, observing what happened next. As the man came out of the water, a white dove descended from above and flew close to him. The sound of a deep voice, almost like the rumble of thunder, was audible, causing the hair on the back of my neck to stand up. There wasn't a cloud in the sky. The sound lasted only a moment, and then it was eerily quiet. I could hardly believe what I thought I had heard.

John also seemed overwhelmed by this event and fell to his knees in an attitude of prayer. He spoke then, and I remember his words exactly: "This man is the Lamb of God. He will take upon himself the sins of the whole world. This is the man of whom I said, 'He who comes after me is preferred before me, for he was before me.'"

Could this man be the one John had spoken of an hour before?

The man thanked John, smiled at him, and walked away, alone.

All who had witnessed this scene were dumbstruck. Nobody said anything or even moved for a few moments.

Finally, I began to recover my composure and looked in the direction the man had walked. The landscape was mostly barren—except for a few trees along the river—and flat, save for some large rock outcroppings, a few quite high, in the distance. I then caught a glimpse of the man. I was sure it was he because of the color of his tunic, dark brown. I cannot explain what I did next: I began to pursue him. I was a strong lad, and I started running, soon beginning to gain on him. My heart was pounding, my legs burning and aching. Just at that moment, he turned to the right and walked behind one of the large rock outcroppings, passing out of my sight. I ran faster, confident of catching up to him. As I rounded the large rock, I expected him to be only a few yards ahead of me. However, he was nowhere in sight, which seemed impossible, as there was no place for him to conceal himself from me, if that had been his purpose. My eyes panned up the large rock. Could he have climbed it? No, that was impossible; it was nearly vertical, and no one could scale it. I looked for him for over an hour, without success. Disappointed, I turned in the direction of home. I had just enough time to reach there before dark.

I had a lot to think about on the way. Just who was this man? What was the meaning of the way John reacted to him, the significance of the descending dove and the voice like thunder that I, and others, had heard? If my ears had not deceived me, what I heard was both more frightening and exciting than anything else I had ever heard before.

I reached home just in time for supper. I could not contain my excitement. I desperately wanted to tell my family—my father, my mother, my older brother, and my three younger sisters—what I had seen and heard. However, I talked so fast, no one could understand me. Finally, I calmed down, and smelling the food reminded me I had not eaten since early morning. I was starving. My mother insisted that we all eat before I told them why I was so animated.

Generally, I was not a very talkative person. I was usually reluctant to speak up in public or even around my own family. This would prove to be a rare exception.

Supper finished, I began my account of the day's events, leaving out no details: the crowd, John's jeremiad, the ritual he performed on dozens of people old and young alike, the religious leaders he had roundly condemned, insulted, and embarrassed (my father winced upon hearing that), and my own baptism. They all accorded me their full attention, listening with obvious interest and without interrupting me. And then I told them about the man. I started talking very rapidly again, and my father told me to slow down. When I got to the part about the dove and the deep, masculine voice that sounded like thunder and seemed to come from the sky, my three younger sisters listened with even greater attention, their mouths agape. However, I could see the skepticism in the expressions of my father, my mother, and especially my older brother. Finally, I told them what I thought the voice had said—at least what it sounded like to me. Their incredulity was palpable; I had lost them. My father, mother, and brother had always thought me naive—ready to believe anything—but this was more than they were willing to accept. My father suggested I'd had too much sun; my mother said I needed a good night's sleep; my brother just looked at me, frowned, and shook his head.

I'd planned to tell them about my pursuit of the man, almost catching up to him before he vanished, but I thought better of it. I felt a little foolish now. I excused myself and went to bed.

My mother was right: I did need a good night's sleep. Perhaps my father was right too. Maybe I did get too much sun and it had affected my ability to think clearly and unemotionally. Even though I was physically exhausted, it took me a long time to fall asleep. My mind kept churning, turning over and over the events of the day. When I did at last drift off, I dreamed about them. And, about the man.

I awoke earlier than usual and was more convinced than ever that I knew exactly what I had seen and heard. But what did it mean? What had become of the man? Would I ever see him again?

The days passed into weeks; the weeks into months. My seventeenth birthday passed as well. I said no more about the events of that day: not discussing them further with my family and not telling my friends about them. Six days each week, I toiled with my father and brother in the family fishing business. As time passed, I began to doubt that the dove and the words like thunder from the sky carried any real significance. Yet, I could not get them—or the man—out of my mind.

CHAPTER 2

One morning, as usual, my father, my brother, two hired helpers, and I were at the lake performing a tedious but necessary task: mending our nets. We always arose three hours before sunrise to take advantage of the best time to catch fish: early morning. We had fished until midmorning and went ashore with a rather meager catch to prepare the fish for market. It was late autumn now and blessedly cooler, several months after the events at the Jordan River.

As we toiled, I looked down the beach and saw a stranger, perhaps a hundred yards away, talking with Simon and Andrew, who had just beached their boat. A few minutes later, I looked up again and saw that our friends had pushed their boat a few feet offshore, and it appeared the visitor had joined them. A small crowd of fishermen had gathered on the shore, and the stranger seemed to be speaking to them. My father noticed that I had ceased my net mending and admonished me to get back to work. I kept my head down for several minutes, but curiosity got the better of me, and I looked up again.

The small crowd had dispersed, and now Simon and Andrew's boat was a few hundred feet offshore. The newcomer was a passenger. Oddly, the brothers were casting their nets over the side of the boat. I say "oddly," because it was noon, the wrong time of day to catch fish. Nevertheless, almost immediately, the net was so full of fish that they were having a hard time hauling it into the boat. Both brothers started waving their arms and shouting frantically for help. My father and brother also heard them yelling and turned to see what was happening. There were so many fish in the nets that it was impossible for the boat to hold even half of them. We immediately threw down our nets, and my brother and I each grabbed an oar and

8

rowed like madmen to their rescue. Arriving aside their boat we—all six of us, including their passenger—began scooping as many fish as possible into our boat. Their boat was already full beyond its normal capacity, and we all feared it might not safely make shore.

We headed for the beach slowly, so as not to capsize the boats. We had all been so caught up in the immediate task of saving the boat, and as many of the fish as possible in the process, that there was little conversation and only brief glances at the stranger. Finally, we reached shore, so physically spent that all six of us fell prostrate on the beach and just lay there for several minutes. Simon and Andrew's hired helpers, joined by ours, began preparing the bounty for market before the fish could spoil.

As I lay sprawled on the sand, thinking about how tired I was and why I was so tired, it hit me: The huge catch! What or who could explain that? In addition to our boat rushing out to help Simon and Andrew, many other boats with hopeful fishermen had also hastily gone out, not to assist their friends in distress, but, rather, to take advantage of an apparent miracle: boatloads of fish for the taking, in the heat of the day.

I raised myself up on one elbow and asked Andrew, who was lying nearest to me, why Simon and he had gone out fishing at that strange time of day. He suggested I ask Simon. I sat up, and as much as I did not want to, I got up and walked over to Simon, passing my father and brother on the way. A few feet past Simon, lay the stranger, flat on his back, with his forearm shielding his eyes from the hot, bright sun. Simon appeared to be sleeping, and I was not about to wake him. He, not unlike my father, could be volatile at times, and I did not want to risk his ire. I sat down quietly and waited for him to awaken.

Simon was nearing forty years of age, tall, with broad shoulders, dark hair, and a dark beard. He was a born leader, a man's man. He was also quite garrulous, usually interesting, sometimes funny, and sometimes annoying. Sometimes his mouth seemed to get ahead of his brain. I liked him, liked being around him; most everybody did.

Within a few minutes' time, Simon began to stir. My brother, our father, and Andrew had already sat up and were talking among themselves about the events of the day. The stranger was still prostrate, covering his eyes. Simon sat up, stretched, yawned, and turned toward me. I asked him why he thought he could catch fish in the middle of the day. He explained that when he had complained to him (he pointed toward the stranger) about his and Andrew's failure to catch a single fish the night before, he had suggested they try again. They both protested the futility of it, but the man had urged them and offered to go out with them. Simon then asked the man if he had ever been a fisherman. The man said he had never fished a day in his life. But there was something about him that inspired confidence, and they took him up on his offer to come along.

"You know the rest," said Simon.

Indeed I did; we all did. Still, the miracle of the fish went unexplained.

Simon and I sat in silence for a few moments; he seemed to be in deep thought. And then the stranger began to rouse. He sat up, stretching and yawning, and opened his eyes. It was a good thing I was still sitting down because if I had been standing, I think might have fallen down. The stranger was *the* man. There was no question in my mind about it. It was his eyes. Simon called my father and brother over and introduced the three of us to the man, telling him our names and that we were from the same village as Andrew and he. Simon added that he had known my father since he was a little boy and that he had known my brother and me from the time we were born.

Simon told us the man's name was Jesus, a rather common and ordinary name for someone who seemed anything but common and ordinary to me.

I nodded to the man, unable to find my voice.

The man smiled and said he was glad to know us all.

Now I knew that the man really existed! There had been times when I thought I had only imagined him. I was relieved to know that was not the case.

It was now late afternoon, and we were all hungry. Simon suggested that we eat some of the fish we had caught, and we all agreed. My father asked me to collect wood for a fire so that we could roast the fish, and I set about the task. Jesus volunteered to help. We worked together in silence, picking up dry branches and driftwood. I tried to think of something to say to him, but words did not come easily.

And then he stopped, looked at me closely with those eyes, and said, "One day last summer, you were in the desert, at the river where John was preaching and baptizing. You were the one who was in line in front of me, and you were baptized by John, just before I was."

"Yes, sir," I timidly replied. "I remember you too, sir. I tried to follow you."

I immediately regretted saying those last few words. What would he think?

"Yes, I know you did," he said evenly. "I had an important appointment to keep, and I had to go alone."

He paused for a moment, still looking directly at me with those penetrating yet inviting eyes. "Tell me, John, are you willing to follow me now? You need not answer right away; just think about it. Let's go build a fire. We're all hungry!"

My mind was spinning. All the way back to the beach where the others were waiting impatiently for us, I kept dropping the wood and stopping to pick it up. I tried to start the fire twice before my brother took over and got it going.

We roasted fish, and everyone but I had a hearty appetite. I had something serious to think about; food did not seem that important right then. However, at the urging of the others, I did manage to eat a small portion of the fish. By the time we finished eating, the sun was going down.

My father, the oldest of our little group, was obviously very tired and excused himself, walking to our house, which was not far away.

It was getting chilly and the five of us remaining—Simon, Andrew, James, Jesus, and I—sat around the fire to keep warm.

Between the fire and the almost-full moon, there was plenty of light for us to converse and see each other.

I was sitting next to James, and I whispered to him that Jesus was the man I had told him and our family about on the evening I returned from my river baptism. Between the crackling of the fire and Simon's booming voice, he could not hear what I said and just looked at me with a puzzled expression.

At last, Simon ran out of breath, and there were a few moments of silence.

Just then, Jesus, looking alternately at James and me, said simply, "Follow me." Two words said without apparent emotion, spoken as an invitation, not as a command.

I supposed he thought the time between the wood gathering and this moment had been sufficient for me to think about what he had said not two hours before, but what about my brother? As far as I knew, James had no inkling that he was to receive such an invitation. Moreover, what about our father? I was sure he knew nothing of this. What would his reaction be? How could he get by without our working side by side with him? We had done so for years and expected to go on doing so for years to come. We would always be fishermen. It was all we knew. I then wondered about Simon and Andrew. Had Jesus asked them to follow him too? If not, would he invite them? However, the most important question of all was, what did it mean to follow Jesus?

All these questions flashed through my mind in a matter of a few seconds. During that time, no one said anything; the only sounds were the crackling fire and the small waves lapping against the shoreline. I glanced at James; his expression displayed confusion mixed with surprise.

Jesus continued to look alternately at each of us, waiting for our answers.

Just then, there was another surprise.

In a firm voice, James said, "Yes, Jesus, I will follow you."

That made it easier for me, and I added, in a feebler voice, "I will follow you too."

Jesus looked at us and smiled.

Simon and Andrew jumped to their feet, and with great excitement made it plain that they were both delighted to have us join them as followers of Jesus.

Simon explained that sometime earlier he and Andrew had both received and accepted the same invitation, just as James and I had done now.

Remember that my family, especially my older brother, had thought me naive. That was certainly true the night I told them about my encounter with the man, the same man who had just asked us to follow him. Knowing that not only my brother, but Simon and Andrew as well, had made the same decision, made me more confident of my affirmative reply to Jesus. We could not all be naive, could we?

Simon suggested that we meet again the next day, share a late lunch, and get to know Jesus better.

Everyone agreed.

CHAPTER 3

James and I walked home together, in conversation the whole way. He asked me several questions.

"Is Jesus the same man you told us about that night you returned from the river after John had baptized you?"

"Yes; I have no doubt. Do you remember me trying to whisper to you after we had finished our meal?"

"Yes, but I couldn't hear what you said."

"I was trying to tell you that he, Jesus, was the man I had seen that day. Unlike me, you had never laid eyes on the man before today. You had not heard a voice like thunder come out of the sky when Jesus came up out of the water after John baptized him. A voice that I understood to say: 'This is My son, the one I love. I am delighted with him,' while at the same time, a white dove descended from the sky and flew close to him. I tried to follow him as he walked away from the river, and just about the time I was catching up to him, he vanished. While he and I were gathering wood for the fire this afternoon, *he* looked at me and reminded *me* that we had encountered each other by the river that day. He knew that I had tried to follow him, but he had an appointment with someone and had to go alone. And then he asked me if I would like to follow him now. He said I need not answer right away, but I should think about it."

James was obviously surprised to hear this.

"Now I have a question for you, James. Why did you say you would follow Jesus? You managed to say yes even before I could open my mouth to answer! Why, James?"

"I don't know," he stammered, and then added, "Wait. I don't remember your saying anything about trying to follow the man that day."

"I didn't. Don't you remember? Father and Mother, and even you, began ridiculing me, making me feel like a fool. Even our sisters laughed at me. That's why I didn't say anything about following the man. I was embarrassed and just quietly went off to bed. … But today! Today, Jesus actually invited me to follow him! It was easy to say yes, even if you did say it first."

We both laughed.

"Look, John, you know Jesus better than I. What do you think following him means? Does it mean leaving our families, our jobs, and our village?"

"I don't really know him at all; not yet. But I want to know him. As far as what following him means, I think we all—Simon, Andrew, you, and I—are about to discover that. We'll need to tell our parents about our decision. The question is, when and how do we tell them?"

"First, we need to know more about what Jesus means by following him," said James. "Let's wait until we've asked him exactly what that means. Maybe we won't have to leave our families and our livelihood."

"Well, even if it does mean leaving home, I'm willing to do it."

"Yes, John. I, too, am willing."

By the time we arrived home, the house was quiet; everyone was asleep.

James and I crept into our beds.

For me, sleep did not come soon. I kept turning over in my mind the invitation Jesus had extended to the four of us, wondering what it might entail. James and I were not married, unlike Simon. The more I thought about it, the more convinced I was that a great and unknowable adventure awaited us all.

Two hours before dawn, Father, James, and I were finished with breakfast and on our way to our boats for the day's fishing.

Simon and Andrew had already arrived and were just casting

off. Simon shouted our names, reminding us of our afternoon appointment with them and Jesus, and then added that our father also was welcome to come.

We explained to our father that Simon had invited James and me to spend some time with him, Andrew, and Jesus, the purpose of which was to become better acquainted with our new friend.

Father conditioned his presence at such a gathering—and by implication, ours as well—saying that all would depend on the day's catch. In other words, a big catch might require all our hands and those of our helpers well into midafternoon.

Hearing this reasonable but disquieting pronouncement, James and I looked at each other anxiously. We did not want miss this appointment.

We need not have worried. Our catch was average at best; Simon and Andrew did no better. We all got back to shore by late morning. With the help of our hired men, including those of our friends, we finished preparing all the fish for market by early afternoon. We were all hungry by this time and ready to eat. But where was our guest of honor?

Just then, Andrew called to us and pointed down the beach. Less than a hundred feet away, Jesus was building a fire over which we could cook our lunch. The five of us selected two or three fish each, the exception being Simon, who scooped up six or seven in his big hands, and headed toward Jesus. Of course, it soon became clear that Simon intended some of his fish for our guest. There were warm greetings all around, with Jesus thanking us for his meal, and the rest of us thanking him for preparing the fire. There was much pleasant conversation among us all during our humble repast: Jesus asked us about our occupation and our families. However, nobody was asking Jesus any questions. I began to worry that no one would ask Jesus to explain what he meant by "follow me."

I was sitting next to James, and leaning over and whispering to him, I said, "Ask Jesus what it means to follow him."

"I will, just as soon as there is a lull in the conversation," he replied.

Briefly, very briefly, the talking stopped; but before James could get the words out, Simon started telling one of his many stories, this one about the time when he was out in his boat alone on the lake at night, and a big storm blew up and almost capsized his boat. Even though I had heard it before—and probably everybody else had, too. Simon was a good storyteller, and nobody seemed to mind. His voice inflections, his facial expressions, and his gestures all contributed to the quality of his tales. I could almost feel the spray of the cold wind-whipped waves on my face, not to mention the terror of drowning, and imagine the grief of my family at my passing. Yes, he was a good talker, all right. Even Jesus listened with rapt attention and delight, along with the rest of us.

The story ended, and before Simon could tell another one, James mustered his courage and blurted out, "Jesus, may I ask you a question?"

"Of course you may, James."

"Well, I—that is, we … John and I—would like to know … would you please explain to us what you mean by your invitation to follow you?"

It got very quiet. The wind rustling the trees stopped blowing; the lake became as glass, no waves lapping the shore; although the fire was still alive, it made no discernible sound. I glanced at my father. His jaw had dropped, and he looked in puzzled amazement at James and me. Perhaps we should have told him what Jesus had said to us the previous evening. But what good would that have done? He would have asked us what Jesus meant by the words "follow me." We could not explain its meaning because *we* did not know what it meant. Perhaps now we would. Everyone looked at Jesus.

"I will answer your question, James, but, first, I want to tell you more about myself and why I'm seeking a few good men to work with me to accomplish my purpose, my mission."

Jesus talked about John, the "voice crying in the wilderness." He spoke of his message that a new kingdom was coming soon, very soon; in fact, it was already here. He told us that he would present

John's message in a way even more revolutionary than John was doing. It was obvious that Jesus held John in high regard, and he made it clear that the Baptist, still actively promulgating his message, would continue to do so in a way that complemented Jesus's own ministry.

"Now, as to your question, James, about what it means to follow me: It means that I can't do this—what I just described—alone. I'll need your help in ways that you, all of you, will learn more about each day we're together. It means you will have to leave your work, your families, your homes, and travel with me throughout—not only in Galilee, but into other parts of Israel. You will not see your families and your friends for weeks, sometimes months, at a time. Following me may cause some of you to be rejected by your families and friends. We will travel almost constantly, going from village to village, town to town, city to city, province to province. My work, and now your work too, will demand your complete attention and commitment. More often than not, we will sleep under the stars. Usually, we will depend on the generosity of others for our food, and sometimes our shelter. Our work will be hard. But it will also be rewarding, though not in a worldly, material sense. In short, we are going to tell the good news of God's new kingdom, which is coming now, and I want you to help me in that most important work. You four are fishermen by trade. Come with me, and I will teach you how to fish for men. Simon and Andrew already know what I've just told you, James. Now that you know what lies ahead, are you still with me?"

James answered firmly, with a loud, clear "Yes!"

"John, because of your age, before I ask the same question of you, I'm going to ask for your father's permission. I will abide by his decision."

My heart sank. I was not at all certain he would agree, and I would be devastated if he did not.

Looking straight at my father, Jesus asked, "Zebedee, is it all right if John comes with me? I promise to look after him."

Father was silent for what seemed to me an eternity. I could not decipher his expression or begin to guess how he would respond.

Finally, he answered. "Yes, Jesus, he may go with you; I entrust his life to you, and may God protect all of you."

I jumped up and ran to my father, throwing my arms around him. Filled with emotion, I brushed back tears of joy. His eyes were wet too, but his tears were probably born of apprehension.

Simon and Andrew spoke words of encouragement to him about the importance of Jesus's mission, which was now our mission too. Simon said that he, too, would keep an eye on me. He would leave the business in my father's charge, and he recommended several fishermen and helpers who might be available to replace not only James and me, but also Andrew and himself.

James and I knew all the men he mentioned, and we heartily agreed that they would be good partners and helpers in the business.

Father agreed, and that was a source of great relief to my brother and me.

"How soon can you be ready to leave," Jesus asked. "As soon as the day after tomorrow?"

We looked at our father, who generously nodded his approval.

Yes, we could be ready by then.

Jesus suggested that we meet early in the morning of the appointed day, at Simon's house, which was not far from our own.

We all agreed.

The three of us made the short walk to our home.

Father told us that he would break the news of our departure to our mother, not that night, but the following evening. He explained two reasons for the delay: First, he had to consider carefully how he would explain our leaving to her and our sisters; and, second, he thought that the less time Mother had to think about it, the better.

Obviously, our father knew our mother better than we did, but we knew her well enough to agree that his plan was the best for all concerned.

James and I shared a sleeping room, and as we lay on our pallets in the dark, our shared excitement kept us talking for at least two hours. We believed we were about to enter into a great but largely unknown, and even mysterious, adventure. An adventure that was of uncertain duration, to places we had never seen, with a man we did not yet really know.

The next morning, as was our wont, we were up well before dawn, eating breakfast prepared by our mother, who obviously had no idea that her sons would be off the next day to … where? The three of us reached our boats and shoved off for another routine day of fishing. Little did my brother and I know that this would be the last ordinary day of our lives; after today, would we ever fish for fish again?

The conversation with our father that morning was easier than we had expected. Although he would miss us, he said that he believed our work with Jesus was important, more important than fishing— perhaps more important than anything else we could or would ever do in our lives. He all but said he wished he were going with us. When James asked him how he thought he and I should explain to our mother what we had determined to do, he told us to let him begin the conversation; he understood our mother better than we did, and he could probably convince her not to discourage us in any way. He believed that our mother could and would trust Jesus to look after her boys, especially the youngest.

"You two can tell her your reasons," he said, suggesting that we closely parallel Jesus's answer to James's question about what following him meant. "His answer convinced me of the importance of his work, enough for me to know that I want you both to be a part of it," he said. "I think your mother will agree. But be prepared for some tears."

He warned us not to bring any of this up until after dinner. "Let's not risk spoiling our dinner," he said with a chuckle.

We had a good day of fishing, with a better-than-average catch.

I felt some sadness, and I think James did too, that we would not be out with Father again tomorrow. We both loved and respected him a great deal, and we were grateful that he shared our enthusiasm for our new vocation.

As was her custom, Mother had dinner waiting on the table. All seven of us sat down in our usual places. As was his practice, along with all the men of our religion, Father said the appropriate prayer of thanksgiving for God's care for all of us during the day now drawing to a close, and for the meal that, by His grace, we were about to receive. There was nothing out of the ordinary during our dinner-table conversation. Mother reported on a few goings-on among our neighbors and nearby relatives; our sisters talked of what they had done to help our mother during the day, especially the parts of the meal their efforts had contributed to; Father, James and I answered questions about the day's fishing successes.

When we had finished the meal, Father said he wanted all of our attention; he had something important to say. What he said was exactly what he had told James and me he had planned to say. Our sisters were excited and started to ask questions. He hushed them, looked at Mother, who sat silently, with an expression I see in my mind's eye to this day but still find hard to describe.

"What do you think, dear?" Father asked softly, looking at her. "Do you have any questions of James and John?"

It took her a moment to gather herself. I did not see any tears, but she did press her sleeve against her right eye.

She asked several questions; under the circumstances, reasonable questions for a mother to ask of her sons, especially a son of my age, still a boy, not yet a man.

Thankful for our Father's advice, James and I took turns describing the nature and purpose of our mission in following Jesus, using many of his own words in explaining that mission to us and our father the previous evening. We spoke of Simon and Andrew, whom our mother knew, liked, and respected, and their commitment to follow Jesus as well. She brightened and seemed to relax a little with this bit of news.

She then asked when we intended to leave; when would "following Jesus" begin?

I could see James's Adam's apple move down, and then up quickly, as he swallowed hard.

"We are leaving tomorrow, Mother. In the morning," he said.

The tears began to roll copiously down Mother's cheeks as she softly sobbed.

Father, James, and I, followed by our sisters, quickly moved close to her side to reassure her that her sons were going to be all right and not to worry.

Slowly, she regained her composure and asked, "Will I be able to meet this Jesus before you leave?"

"I don't see why not," replied Father. "He has asked James and John to meet him at Simon's house. We, all of us, will go over there in the morning, and you and the girls can meet him and see for yourselves what kind of man he is. You are their mother and have every right to be there!"

My brother and I had never held Father in higher esteem than we did at that moment.

"Thank you, dear," Mother said. "That makes me feel much better, much better."

James and I slept well that night.

CHAPTER 4

My brother and I awoke earlier than usual. Hurriedly, we each packed some clothes to take on our journey. Mother, who obviously had arisen much earlier than we, prepared an especially delicious and filling breakfast. The whole family—even our sisters, who rarely rose before dawn—gathered around the table for what was to be our last meal together, for how long we did not know.

Father said the customary prayer of thanks for our food, at the conclusion of which he added, "And, dear Lord, bless our two precious sons, who now leave home to serve you in spreading the great news of your coming kingdom."

He then paraphrased a blessing from an ancient Hebrew writing: "May the Lord watch between us and our sons while we are absent one from another. Amen."

All seven of us brushed a tear or two away from our eyes as he finished.

Mother exhibited remarkable composure during breakfast, speaking positively, even lightheartedly, about the adventure that lay before James and me.

Our meal finished, we all helped Mother clear the table, wash the eating and cooking utensils, and put them all away. We then walked to Simon's house, which was a few minutes away, just outside Capernaum.

By this time, the sun had risen on what promised to be a beautiful day. Arriving at Simon's house, we were greeted by him, his wife, Concordia, her mother, and Andrew, who also made his home there. Simon and Concordia had no children. It was a large house with enough room for all of us to sit in the spacious parlor.

Jesus had not yet arrived. During our wait, we all chatted amiably about various things, but, mostly, we talked about Jesus and what lay ahead for the four of us who would be off with him that day. Where would we go? What would we do? When would we return?

Concordia and her mother had already met Jesus; he had recently dined with them one evening. They said they liked him, believed him to be an extraordinary man, and believed in his mission. They also said they were honored that he had chosen Simon and Andrew to partake of his work. Their words visibly relaxed Mother and seemed to encourage her.

There was a knock at the door; Jesus had arrived. He walked straight to our mother, introduced himself, said he was most pleased to meet her, and that he appreciated the sacrifice she was making, entrusting her sons, especially the younger one, to a stranger.

Mother was practically speechless, unusual for her, managing to say that she, too, was happy to make his acquaintance.

Jesus then went around the circle, speaking cordially to each of us, paying special heed to my three sisters, who seemed most pleased at this extra attention.

We all chatted for another half hour or so, enjoying each other's company.

Jesus then looked at the four of us who were to accompany him, announcing, "Well, men, let's be off. We have a lot to do."

Looking at Concordia and her mother, Jesus thanked them for their hospitality.

"Wait just a moment, please!" said Concordia. "We'll be right back."

Concordia and her mother hurriedly entered the kitchen. They returned shortly, carrying a large basket. "You'll be hungry before sundown; we've prepared food for your evening meal."

All five of us expressed our sincere thanks.

And so, we set forth. By this time, it was midmorning of the sixth day of the week—we called it *preparation day*—the day before the Sabbath, the day God had commanded us to keep holy, separate from the ordinary days of the week, which were the days when we worked. On the Sabbath, we rested from our labors, we went to synagogue (where we worshipped), we read Holy Scripture, and we prayed. How far would we travel this day, this preparation day? It was to be not far at all.

Jesus led the way. He seemed to have a destination in mind, but he did not share it with any of us.

No one asked him where we were going.

We walked northwest, away from the lake. There was conversation among us, mostly led by Simon, but even he seemed less gregarious than usual.

On our way, I moved close to Andrew, telling him I had seen Simon and him in the crowd that day at the Jordan River a few months before, when Jesus and I were baptized.

"Yes, Simon and I saw you, too," Andrew replied. "We tried to get your attention, but you seemed distracted, I supposed by the thunder."

"That wasn't all that distracted me. Did you see the white dove?"

"Yes, we did."

"I can assure you that was no ordinary thunder," I said. "It sounded like a majestic and mighty voice to me."

"Could you understand what the voice said, John?"

"I remember the words exactly, and I'll never forget them: 'This is My son, the one I love. I am delighted with him.'"

"Did you tell James what you heard?" Andrew asked.

"Yes. I told my whole family, that very night, as soon as I got home."

"Did they believe you?"

"Not then, but they do now," I said and then added, "What about you and Simon? Did you understand the voice? Did Simon?"

"Yes, John. We heard exactly what you heard."

"Do you and Simon believe what you heard?"

Andrew stopped, and he looked me in the eye. "Why do you think we're here?"

The farther away from the lake we got, the fewer people we saw, until, eventually, we saw no one else. We reached a grove of sycamore trees, and we headed into it. Jesus announced that this was where we would spend the night.

We had traveled less than a mile. It was still midmorning, and we were somewhat surprised at the shortness of our first day's journey. We were not the least bit tired, but I was puzzled—I think all of us were—that our first day's journey had been so brief. In the ensuing months and years, we would be surprised and puzzled almost daily.

Jesus sat down on the ground and invited us to sit facing him. This was the first of what would become regular sessions in which he would discuss with us, teach us really, what his mission on this earth would be and how we were going to assist him in accomplishing his objectives. His teaching method was simple and direct. He welcomed our questions and comments. He frequently asked questions of us, gently correcting us when our answers were wrong or incomplete, and complimenting us when we were correct. He had an amazing comprehension of human nature, the human condition. In addition, he had a remarkable understanding of the Holy Scriptures of our faith: the Ten Commandments, the laws of Moses, the ancient stories of the patriarchs, the writings of the prophets, and the poetry of the psalmists. His understanding of God and our faith were often surprising and sometimes disquieting. He did not teach as the rabbis in our synagogues taught. He was nothing like them at all.

That first afternoon, Simon asked an excellent question: "Master, why haven't you chosen more learned men, men with more formal training in the Law and the prophets, rabbis and lawyers, to follow you? Why have you chosen us? We are common men with little education, fishermen by trade. Why choose us?"

"I chose you precisely because you are *not* formally educated. Those educated in the rabbinical schools—especially the one in Jerusalem—would find my teachings only puzzling; not only would they resist them, they would reject them out of hand. They would give my positions no thoughtful consideration. My teachings are simple; theirs are unnecessarily complicated. Their minds are closed and set in stone. I cannot succeed in my mission with men like that. It would be a complete waste of my time, and it would lead to failure. Nevertheless, I believe I can succeed in my work with you. That's why I chose you, Simon; you, Andrew; you, James; and you, John." As he said our names, he looked each of us in the eye. "You will have to be good listeners: If you don't understand something I say, ask me to explain. The only exception to that will be when I am speaking publicly, which I will do almost daily, beginning tomorrow. At those times, wait and ask your questions when we are alone. There will be some things—at least for the time being—I want to explain only to you, my closest friends. Do any of you have a question for me now?"

Simon, of course, did. "The sun will set soon, and it will be Sabbath. Because the law allows us to journey only short distances during the Sabbath hours, will we spend tomorrow here?"

Jesus smiled at Simon's question. "No. We will walk back to Capernaum and attend synagogue. It's a short distance, less than the allotted distance for Sabbath travel. None of you need be concerned with breaking the law."

"But, Master," Simon protested. "Why did we leave Capernaum if we're just going to turn around and go back there tomorrow?"

"Now *that* is a good and important question! During our time together, we will often go off to a quiet place such as this so that we can be alone. Those times will be vital to my mission—our mission—and your understanding of it. They will be times of teaching and learning, encouragement, and, sometimes, rest and recreation. Our work together will be taxing, both physically and mentally, and we will all need occasional respites. As to our attendance at synagogue tomorrow, I have something important to say and to do there. But right now, Simon, where is that basket of food Concordia and her mother prepared for us?"

CHAPTER 5

Concordia and her mother, bless them, had packed enough food to provide for our breakfast the next morning! When we finished eating, we walked back to Capernaum to attend synagogue.

A few words about synagogue will assist you in understanding its purposes. Primarily, it was a place of worship where observant Jews gathered each Sabbath to pray, meditate, learn, and hear Holy Scripture, the Torah, read to them by a rabbi or any other literate man. Women were welcome but had to remain silent. In addition, the synagogue could also have a secular purpose as a town or village hall. However, on the Sabbath, the synagogue's purpose was exclusively for the preeminent reason that it existed: worship. There were no fixed times for worship to begin or end. Customarily, a rabbi or a layman stood up to read Scripture; occasionally, no one did. At such times, those in attendance would simply sit quietly and pray, with only their lips moving. Men and boys sat on one side of the synagogue; women and girls, on the other.

When we arrived, we found room to sit near the front of the synagogue. There were perhaps a hundred in attendance. No one was reading or teaching. After a few moments, Jesus rose, stepped up to the lectern, and began to teach—yes, teach—and not read. A slight murmur arose from congregation. This was unprecedented. It was permissible for a rabbi to teach, but not a layman. A layman could read Scripture as long as he read it verbatim, without comment or interpretation. Everyone in attendance knew the local rabbis, and they knew that this man was not one of them. Nevertheless, they seemed to be listening closely to what he said, which was not always the case with the rabbis.

Jesus spoke only briefly, but what he said was powerful. Unlike the rabbis, who spoke in legalistic terms and who prefaced almost everything they uttered with, "Moses said," Jesus taught on *his own authority*, not the authority of Moses or anyone else. I had attended synagogue almost every Sabbath of my life, and I had never heard anyone speak like this. What he said that day was very much like what the Baptist preached, and what Jesus had already told us he would emphasize in his own ministry: God's coming kingdom, and what its arrival would mean. Unlike John, though, Jesus was softspoken; he did not gesture and did not pace. But the way he spoke, the way he focused on those of us there, as if he were speaking to each one individually, was what made his message so powerful.

When he finished, for a few moments, you could have heard a pin drop on the stone floor. And then a slight murmur arose as he stepped down and walked back to where we were sitting.

Suddenly, there was a commotion.

A man jumped up in the back of the synagogue. He ran toward Jesus, shouting, "What are you about, Jesus of Nazareth? Have you come to destroy us? I know who you are. You're the Holy One of God."

He started to say something else, but Jesus stopped him with a stern, resounding command: "Be quiet, don't say another word, and leave this man in peace!"

Immediately, the man fell to the floor, convulsing and shrieking. The incident ended as quickly as it had begun: the man stood up, and then he quietly left the synagogue. This entire episode lasted only a moment.

The onlookers were stunned, silent.

Jesus led us outside and then to Simon's home.

Arriving there, we found Concordia and her mother at home, the latter in bed, delirious with a high fever, passing in and out of consciousness, her daughter anxiously looking after her.

"Simon!" Concordia sobbed. "I've done everything I can think of to relieve the fever, giving her cool water to drink and even a sponge bath. But her condition has worsened."

Recalling what he had just witnessed Jesus do at the synagogue, Simon implored him to do something. He and Concordia accompanied Jesus into the elderly woman's room, and the door was closed. A few moments later, the door opened, and Simon's mother-in-law led the others out of her room. She and Concordia went into the kitchen, prepared the Sabbath midday meal, and invited the rest of us to sit down with them to eat. Andrew, James, and I were speechless. Even Simon was quiet, a look of wonder on his face. His mother-in-law was beaming and talkative, as if she had not been ill at all.

Finally, Andrew asked, "Simon, what happened in there?"

Uncharacteristically, Simon, looking at his mother-in-law, said, "Why don't you tell them?"

"I would be happy to," she said. "As I lay in bed, I felt a hand grasp mine, gently at first, then firmly, pulling me upright in bed. And then I felt perfectly fine, not a hint of sickness or fever. It's a miracle."

I was not sure she meant that last word literally. Nevertheless, I agreed with her.

The seven of us spent the afternoon sitting comfortably, chatting pleasantly, in Simon's parlor.

At one point, Concordia urged her mother to lie down, telling her she needed rest after her ordeal.

Her mother dismissed the idea, saying she felt just fine and was not tired at all.

Shortly after sundown, which signified the end of the Sabbath, we all heard a commotion outside. And then someone knocked at the door. Simon went to the door, opened it, and saw a throng of people in front of his house. Before he could ask what this meant, the man who had knocked asked if Jesus was there. Receiving an affirmative answer, he asked if Jesus would please come outside.

The Master came to the door and asked the man what he wanted.

The man simply replied, "Look."

What Jesus saw—what we all saw, for by this time all of us had gone out on the front porch—was a crowd of perhaps a hundred or more people, many of them obviously infirm and assisted by one or more relatives or friends. Some were lame; some were on stretchers, unable to walk at all; some were without sight or speech or hearing; some were even exhibiting symptoms not unlike the man in the synagogue.

I looked at Jesus. In the dull light of early evening, with the glow of the flaming torches several of the men in the crowd held, I could see the look on his face. To put it simply, he pitied them.

They grew quiet as he waded into their midst, speaking to everyone, gently placing his hands on those who needed physical healing, commanding evil spirits to leave those so afflicted. This went on for hours. The Master restored to health everyone who sought healing. The last ones left near midnight.

Jesus was obviously physically exhausted.

We urged him to come in and rest.

He told us that he was going for a walk.

Simon protested, telling him he must sleep.

Jesus went for a walk. He would take many walks at night during the years we were with him, and it would be some time before I discovered what really transpired during those nocturnal absences.

CHAPTER 6

As I said, Simon had a large house in those days; it could easily accommodate three guests. Rather than spend the night at the home of our parents, James and I shared one of the two spare bedrooms, while Jesus slept in the other.

Shortly after dawn, my brother and I heard stirrings in the main part of the house. We roused ourselves, dressing quickly to join the others. Simon and Andrew were sitting in the parlor, talking quietly; the women were in the kitchen, preparing breakfast.

The door to Jesus's bedroom was closed, and we all assumed he was still sleeping.

James and I joined the brothers and entered into the conversation. Naturally, we talked about the events of the previous day, keeping our voices down so as not to wake Jesus. We all agreed that we had never witnessed anything like that which we had seen the evening before; nor had we ever even *heard* of anything like it.

Concordia began to set the table. She walked over to us, asking if any of us knew what time Jesus had returned from his walk the night before, or if we had seen him this morning.

None of us had heard him come in; none of us had seen him since last night.

Concordia asked Simon to see about him.

Simon knocked on the door softly, then a little louder, and then he called out to Jesus. There was no response. Turning and looking at us with a puzzled expression, Simon opened the door slowly and peered in. Jesus was not there; his bed had not been slept in.

"We're going to look for him, the four of us," Simon commanded with a mixture of concern and bafflement. "I hope nothing bad has happened to him."

We all instantly agreed and straightaway headed out the door to begin our search. It did not take long. Within a few minutes, there came Jesus, walking right toward us. We gathered around him, asking where he had been and if he was all right. Ignoring our questions, he simply said that he had gone for a walk. Of course, we were all relieved to have him back safe and sound.

Breakfast awaited us, and after we finished eating, the five of us adjourned to the parlor.

"Today, we'll begin our travels out into the towns and villages of Galilee. Each Sabbath, we'll visit the synagogues in those towns, and I'll speak and teach about the kingdom of God in order to accomplish my mission. I will preach essentially the same message that you heard yesterday in the synagogue here in Capernaum. In between those synagogue visits, I'll teach you, train you, so that you can become more and more effective in this work of mine, which one day will be your work."

Thus, off we went on what was to become the most exciting time of my life.

Each Sabbath, Jesus taught in different synagogues; there were more than a hundred of them in Galilee in those days. Some towns and villages had more than one. Some, as was the case in Capernaum, received him warmly, some tolerated him, and others were hostile, refusing to let him speak. Other days, Jesus laid out our role in his ministry. With each passing week, however, the time available for these instructional sessions diminished. The reason was the crowds that came to see him in every village, every town, and even in the countryside. After the healings in Capernaum, his fame spread rapidly throughout the region. Word would go out that he was on his way to this village or that town, and the people would be waiting for him. Some of them wanted to hear his teaching. However, the majority came for the healing of just about every possible malady of body or mind. And heal them he did, by the hundreds on some days.

One day, I asked Jesus when he was going to teach us how to heal people and how to cast out demons.

He replied, "Those things cannot be taught; they are gifts from God."

Soon, not only were the crowds waiting for us when we arrived in the villages, but some people were even beginning to follow Jesus, along with those of us whom he had invited to follow him. As their numbers increased, Simon, James, and I expressed our misgivings about these interlopers.

"Are you jealous of them? Do you want me all to yourselves?" Jesus asked.

We never again asked that question, or anything like it.

One day, a group of people from Jerusalem came to hear Jesus speak and teach. They had traveled a long way. We were astonished that anyone living that far south had even heard of him.

A few days later, we were in Bethsaida, one of the towns on the northeast coast of the Sea of Galilee, not far from Capernaum. As usual, Jesus had spoken to a large crowd and healed dozens of sick people.

Suddenly, someone shouted, "Unclean, unclean!"

Everyone knew what that meant. Someone in the throng had the most feared of diseases: leprosy. People started scrambling, trying to get away from the dreaded wretch. Everybody knew that leprosy was the most contagious disease and there was absolutely no cure for it. All people with this awful affliction were required by law to announce themselves loudly, so that others could get out of their way and have no contact with them or anything they touched.

The leper walked straight toward Jesus, the crowd parting like the Red Sea along his path. When he reached Jesus, he fell to his knees and pleaded for Jesus's help.

"If you are willing, you can make me clean," the leper said.

Jesus then did something utterly amazing: He reached down, clasped his hands to the man's hands—hands that were grossly eaten away by the ghastly disease—and lifted him up!

Everyone who saw this, including me, gasped in fear and horror.

And then, with the most tender compassion, Jesus said, "I *am* willing; you *are* clean!"

Instantly, the rotting flesh was healed, fully restored; not just the afflicted man's hands, but also his arms, and even the damaged skin on his face. The man, overcome with emotion, and with tears streaming down his face, sobbed out his gratitude.

Jesus quietly told him that he was to do what was required in such cases: Present himself to a priest, and be pronounced clean by him. The priest would also certify that he was indeed clean and could rejoin society. But Jesus cautioned that the man was not to tell the priest in what *manner* he had been healed. (A note of explanation is required here: Recovery from leprosy, while rare, had occasionally occurred. In such cases, it would happen slowly, without apparent cause, and as far as I knew, not by a simple touch from another human being. In fact, touching someone with leprosy was forbidden because it was believed that the disease was transmitted in that way. When such healing did occur, our laws required certification by a priest.)

The man agreed to this stricture, but it soon became obvious that he had not kept silent. From that day on, everywhere Jesus went, lepers would come to him for healing. He healed them all.

We stayed several more days in Bethsaida. Jesus taught and healed ever-increasing numbers of people, some of whom came only to be healed. Some of them came out of simple curiosity, not to be taught or healed. They were easy to spot because they lingered only a short time and then continued on their way.

It was becoming more common in our travels to be invited to stay in the homes of some of those we met, the ones who seemed to have a deeper interest in Jesus's teaching, not just in his healing. We had many pleasant meals and conversations with such folk, and these demonstrations of hospitality made our itinerate life easier.

While we remained in Bethsaida, we stayed in the home of Philip, another fisherman we had known for years. One afternoon, Jesus explained his work to Philip and invited him to become his follower and journey with us. Without hesitation, he accepted. Immediately, Philip excused himself saying he would return shortly. Within an hour, he arrived with a friend, Nathanael, another fisherman, whom we also knew. Philip introduced his friend to Jesus.

"Nathanael," Jesus said, "you are a true Israelite, a genuine descendant of Jacob! You have no deceit in you."

Taken aback by Jesus's greeting, Nathanael blurted out, "How can you know those things about me? We have never met!"

"Just a few minutes ago, when you were sitting in the shade of your special fig tree, reading the ancient prophecies, I saw you, and I saw Philip when he invited you here to meet me. I also heard what you said about my hometown. Contrary to what you think, not all things that come out of Nazareth are bad."

The color left Nathanael's face. For a few moments, he was silent.

Regaining his composure, he looked into Jesus's eyes, saying, "You must be the Messiah, Israel's coming king."

"What?! Just because I could see you and hear what you said?" Jesus said. "No. Come with me, and you'll see greater things than that."

"I *will* come with you."

As far as I know, Nathanael was the first man to refer to Jesus as *the Messiah*.

Early the next morning, Jesus awakened us, announcing that we would depart Bethsaida straightaway and return to Capernaum. This was to happen from time to time, and it was becoming clear to us that Jesus found rest and relaxation in the home of Simon. James and I were happy that our village was to be Jesus's home base, as this allowed us to spend time with our family. It was to be an eventful visit, and a surprising one too.

CHAPTER 7

A word about taxes. There were three categories of taxes levied on the Jews of Israel at that time. The first and most acceptable to the taxpayers was the *temple tax* that provided for the upkeep of the temple in Jerusalem. Unfortunately, a portion of this tax was also used to support lavish lifestyles of some of the high priests and other temple officials. Generally, observant Jews did not resist paying the temple tax. The second tax, commonly referred to as the *Herodian tax,* was collected and paid to the family of Herod, specifically Herod Antipas, the current king of Israel. His family had "ruled" Israel for many years; that is, the Romans who had conquered and occupied our country for over a century *allowed* Herod to rule. Because most Jews saw him as a traitor and collaborator, this tax for his benefit was despised and only grudgingly paid. However, the most hated tax of all was the *emperor's tax,* which not only supported the occupying forces that ground us under their heels, but also contributed to the lavish lifestyles of the emperor and his acolytes. There were also three categories of tax collectors, one for each type of tax. Jewish tax collectors, respected by most of the people, collected the temple tax. Other Jews, much less admired, collected the Herodian tax. However, worst of all, some Jews collected the imperial tax too. These men were hated. The temple paid the temple tax collectors. The collectors of the Herodian and imperial taxes compensated themselves by charging more than the official tax rates and keeping the overage for themselves. Many of them were among the wealthiest men in Israel, and their wealth served to compound the hatred.

Back to the story at hand, as we approached Capernaum, we came to a tollbooth. These booths were scattered throughout Israel and were the collection points for the Herodian tax. The individual toll was not large, but it was collected from every adult male. The volume was tremendous, especially for a heavily traveled road, as was this one from Bethsaida to Capernaum. The toll taker, a man named Matthew, was probably the village's richest man, and the most despised. A social outcast, Matthew had no wife, no children. The only friends he had were fellow tax collectors and other persons of low reputation. Some of the toll payers mockingly insulted him; most said not a word to him. He was probably the loneliest man in Capernaum.

As the seven of us approached Matthew's booth, which we each had done many times before, we drew out of our purses the small coin required for passage.

Jesus was the last of us to drop his coin into the copper collection pot. As he did, we all were astonished to hear him say to Matthew, "Follow me"—the same words of invitation he had spoken to each of us.

We looked at each other with a mixture of disbelief and amazement. Had we really heard him correctly? How was it possible that he would invite a *tax collector,* of all people, to join with him? The rest of us were fishermen, perhaps not the noblest of occupations, but we weren't hated for what we did; we had friends and families, we didn't cheat people, we were welcome in the synagogues. How could a tax collector be of any use to Jesus in his work? A tax collector would *repel* people, not help them to know Jesus.

Perhaps Matthew would decline Jesus's invitation and that would be the end of it. But he didn't. He did not even hesitate.

"I will," he declared.

At once, he got up off his stool and began walking with us. He even left behind the copper pot with all the money in it! What was to become of Jesus, his ministry? It would be over almost before it began. Obviously, Jesus had not thought this through.

In a way, I felt sorry for Matthew. The six of us formed a tight circle: we were all of the same occupation, the same social status, the same devout religious point of view. How could the tax collector be anything else but the odd man out?

That was to be the first surprise of this visit to Capernaum.

Jesus led us. Matthew and he walked side by side in conversation, and the rest of us trailed a few yards behind, stunned into silence, not hearing what they said to each other. After several minutes, they stopped, evidently waiting for us to catch up.

"I have some good news," Jesus said. "Matthew has graciously invited us all to his home this evening for a banquet, and he's going to invite his friends as well!"

Matthew had a huge grin on his face. In all my previous encounters with him, I had never seen him smile.

"He's going on ahead to issue the invitations and arrange for the catering. We're to be at his house by no later than sunset."

This situation was rapidly deteriorating. A banquet that would include Matthew's *friends!* Other tax collectors, certainly, perhaps even prostitutes, heavy wine drinkers, and sundry other sinners. Jesus's reputation would suffer severe damage, perhaps even be ruined beyond repair. And what about us? What about those of us who had earlier joined him? What about *our* standing in our communities? What about our families? What would they think? What, if anything, could we do to rescue Jesus from this impending disaster, a catastrophe of his own making?

I was shaken out of these miserable musings by the voice of Jesus.

"It is a few hours before the banquet. Why don't you men go and visit your families in the meantime? I'm going for a walk. I'll see you at Matthew's house at sunset." Walking away, he turned and added cheerily, "Don't be late!"

We all stood together, speechless for a brief moment until Simon spoke up.

Pointing to a grassy area in the shade of a sycamore tree, Simon suggested, "Let's all go over there, sit down, and talk about what just happened."

Simon then expressed his concerns, which were almost identical to mine.

The others joined in, agreeing that the invitation to Matthew, whom none of us liked because of his profession, would only harm Jesus's ministry, at best, and, at worst, destroy it. But was there anything we could do about it?

Simon suggested that we confront Jesus and try to reason with him, urge him to withdraw his invitation to Matthew.

Andrew asked Simon if he would be willing to take the lead in that confrontation.

Simon, looking sheepish, said he would not.

None of the rest of us had the courage to challenge Jesus either. We were brave enough to question Jesus's judgment behind his back, but not to his face. We all decided to take Jesus's advice to visit with our families.

Simon and Andrew invited Philip and Nathanael to join them at their home.

It was late afternoon when James and I arrived at our parents' house. The whole family was home and excited to see us. Our mother began preparing for a special evening meal and was disappointed when we told her we had committed to have dinner elsewhere. The whole family was disappointed. They all wanted to know where we were to have dinner, and why.

Father's disappointment turned to displeasure bordering on anger when we told them we were dining at the tax collector Matthew's house.

"Why?" Father demanded.

"How could you do such a thing?" Mother asked.

Of course, we had to tell the whole story.

They were just as puzzled and confused as we were.

At one point, Father even said that perhaps he had made a mistake when he agreed that we could go with Jesus in the first place.

Mother then said softly, "We may not agree with Jesus's choice of a person like that. But I think we need to trust him, at least for now, and see what happens. Maybe Jesus knows something about Matthew that we don't."

Father calmed down.

James and I paused to consider the quiet wisdom of Mother's words. Perhaps, in jumping to an unwarranted conclusion, we had been unfair to Jesus. Maybe he did have a good reason for choosing a tax collector. James and I talked about these things as we walked to Matthew's house, meeting up with Simon, Andrew, Philip, and Nathanael on the way. There was little conversation among us; what more was there to say? We soon came into view of Matthew's house. And what a house it was, especially for a man who lived alone. The lawn and garden were well manicured and replete with beautiful trees, trimmed shrubs, and colorful flowers. As we drew nearer, we saw Jesus and Matthew sitting in chairs on the front porch, amiably chatting. Our host welcomed us warmly, inviting us to sit in the other six chairs he hastily arranged into a circle. Apparently, this was to be a very small banquet, as we eight seemed to be the only ones there, except for the servants we could hear and see through the windows, bustling around a large table in a large dining room.

"The other guests won't be arriving for a while, probably not for an hour," Jesus said. "I thought we could spend this time getting better acquainted with Matthew. You all know that he is a tax collector. But there are some things you *don't* know about him." ("Some things you don't know about him." Didn't my mother say almost those exact words only a short while ago?) "He and I have been talking for the past two hours. First, Matthew is a student, a serious student, of our venerable prophets and their prophecies, especially those concerning the Messiah. Matthew doesn't particularly like to speak in public, but I think he would be willing to share with us what he has learned in his pursuit of the truth."

Matthew, haltingly at first but then with growing confidence and conviction, told us about his study of the ancient Holy Scriptures. It was obvious that he had a keen, discerning mind, a tender heart, and a sincere love of our religion and its eternal truths. He knew much more about the messianic prophecies than I did. We all learned an indispensable lesson that day: a man can't be judged by his occupation, by his appearance, or by the house he owns.

Alas, I forgot this lesson the minute the other guests began arriving.

Matthew had invited his friends. Who else would he invite? Strangers? Well, yes, he would: *we* were the strangers! It was obvious who and what the others were: his fellow tax collectors, known prostitutes, and other sundry sinners, about twenty of them, not counting us strangers.

As is the case with most banquets, we did not sit down to dinner immediately; we mingled. Jesus was the only one in our group who mingled easily that night. The six of us were like fish out of water. Nevertheless, we all tried for Jesus's sake, and for Matthew's.

While we guests were still socializing on our host's huge front porch, several curious onlookers approached, remaining below us on Matthew's lawn. I recognized two of them: they had been among the religious leaders who sought baptism from John several months before, the day I was baptized, the day I first saw Jesus. They were Pharisees, the strictest practitioners of our religion. They could be most unpleasant people. One of them recognized Simon and beckoned to him. He accommodated them, and I strained to hear what was said.

"Why does your Master consort with tax collectors, prostitutes, and other sinners?" one of them asked.

Considering some of *my* recent thoughts and words, I was ashamed.

Jesus, too, had apparently heard the man's question. Before Simon could respond, he was down the steps. He would speak for himself.

The guests, seeing this, suspended their conversations. They gathered along the porch railing, waiting to see and hear what would happen.

Jesus proceeded to reel off a string of one-line parables: people who aren't sick don't need a doctor; don't patch an old garment with new cloth; and don't put new wine into old wine skins.

The Pharisees looked confused.

Another of the Pharisees asked him why his followers did not fast as the disciples of John did.

"Nobody fasts at a wedding banquet," Jesus told them.

The Pharisees looked bewildered.

Jesus suggested that they leave and figure out for themselves the meaning of his words.

As they turned to leave, Jesus called out after them, speaking in a voice that could be heard by all. "For I desired mercy, and not sacrifice."

He was quoting the prophet Hosea, who was quoting God.

It seemed to me that Jesus *had* answered their questions, but they were not of a mind-set to discern, and certainly not accept, what he had said.

I was beginning to understand why Jesus had invited a tax collector to follow him: Matthew would make a valuable contribution to his ministry.

The banquet was a great success. Jesus liked and was comfortable with all manner of people, and he readily made new friends. Some of Matthew's guests would become his followers. Word spread that he was a different kind of religious leader, perhaps the only one, other than John the Baptist, who treated everyone with respect and love, even—perhaps especially—sinners.

That was the second surprise.

We remained in Capernaum a few more days, Jesus teaching and healing people every day. James and I stayed in our parents' home; Jesus stayed with Simon and Andrew; Philip and Nathanael stayed with Matthew.

The evening before we were to journey on, Father and Mother invited Jesus to join us for breakfast the following morning.

As we finished our meal, Father said he had something he wanted to show Jesus.

James and I looked at our mother, who provided no clue as to what was going on.

Jesus agreed.

Father assured us they would not be gone long, and they returned within half an hour.

James and I were brimming with curiosity, but neither of us asked any questions.

We joined up with our other traveling companions and headed south. After we had traveled about two hours, Jesus suggested we stop and rest for a few minutes. As we sat together in the shade of a tree, he said he had something to tell us.

"Your father, James and John, has given me—to us all really—a very thoughtful and generous gift. He has purchased a house, not far from your house, which I will use as my home base when we are in Galilee."

That was the third surprise.

CHAPTER 8

It was spring, my favorite time of year. Spring meant gentle rains, green grass, wildflowers in bloom. It also meant Passover.

Passover was the most significant celebration of the Hebrew religion. Each year, nearly every observant Jew healthy enough to travel made the pilgrimage to Jerusalem to commemorate the deliverance: the exodus of the children of Israel from bondage in Egypt. This would be our first Passover with Jesus. There now were seven of us chosen by him. In addition, many other followers journeyed along with us. Ever since his first miracle in the synagogue, followed by many more that evening on Simon's lawn, Jesus had attracted a general following. Sometimes it would number in the scores, sometimes in the hundreds. Because of Passover, it was in the many hundreds. Members of our own families accompanied us on this pilgrimage as well. We arrived two days before the feast began.

Jesus, accompanied by the seven of us, went to the Pool of Bethesda, very near the temple courts. The pool was beautiful, surrounded by large porches, with handsome columns and a latticed roof which provided welcome shade. Many men, women, and children, all of them infirm, occupied the porches. Some were blind, lame, paralyzed, or otherwise afflicted. They believed that, on occasion, angels would stir up the waters, and when that happened, the first one reaching the water would be healed. Regrettably, this was probably untrue, as reports of actual healings were rare and could often be explained in other ways. Nevertheless, these people were desperate; if there was even the remotest chance of healing, they clung to this hope.

As we walked among this pitiful collection of humanity, Jesus suddenly stopped next to a man lying on a pallet. It was obvious that he was a cripple, and he appeared to be about fifty years old. Jesus looked at him.

"Do you want to walk again?" Jesus asked the man.

"Sir, I have been unable to walk for thirty-eight years, ever since I was a lad! When the water is disturbed, I can't get to it, and there is never anyone to help me. Someone else always gets there first."

"Get up right now! Pick up your pallet, and walk," Jesus commanded.

Instantly, the man obeyed. He walked away, carrying the pallet, with no sign of infirmity whatsoever. Perhaps too stunned to speak, he didn't even thank Jesus.

Because the man had been a fixture at the pool for so many years, his condition well known, those who witnessed what had happened were astonished. Most of his fellow sufferers were delighted for him, rejoicing with him as he passed by them, carrying his pallet. However, it was the Sabbath day, and a pallet was a burden; carrying a burden was considered work, and work was something a Jew could not do on the Sabbath. You would be surprised what we Jews considered to be work in relation to proper Sabbath observance.

Just then, we all saw a man—a Pharisee no doubt—confront the former cripple. Although we could not hear what he said, we knew the healed man was in trouble for breaking the Sabbath.

We followed Jesus into the temple's outer court, where we saw the healed man praising God for His mercies. Jesus walked over to him, admonishing him to sin no more, or something worse than not being able to walk might happen to him.

The man, obviously taken aback, looked around, walked hurriedly across the court. and excitedly began talking to the same Pharisee who had confronted him at the pool. He then pointed toward Jesus, nodding his head as he did so.

Leaving the temple's outer court, we followed Jesus into the large adjacent synagogue. Being the Sabbath, there were several hundred worshippers present. No one was teaching or reading the Torah at that moment, and Jesus proceeded to mount the steps and stand behind the lectern. He stood there silently for a few moments, and then he looked toward a side door, where several robed men were entering. I looked as well, and saw a small band of robed Pharisees enter and take seats near us. One of them was the man we had seen confront the healed cripple. Jesus just stared at them. It was so quiet; there was not even the sound of anyone breathing.

After a few more moments of dead silence, this same Pharisee stood up and challenged Jesus.

"Tell me," the Pharisee demanded, in a tone dripping with sarcasm, "is it lawful or not lawful to heal people on the Sabbath?"

A trap! If Jesus said it was lawful, he would place himself above the Law, and no man was above the Law. If he said it was not lawful, he would condemn himself as a lawbreaker. Jesus had placed himself in an impossible position. This question jolted me and my colleagues.

Jesus stood quietly, with no hint of concern on his face. Directly in front of him, in the aisle seat of the first row, sat a middle-aged man. Jesus looked at him and asked him to stand up, turn around, and face the crowd. He asked the man to lift his right arm. He complied, revealing a mangled, useless hand. Jesus asked the man to lower his arm but to remain standing in place. Jesus then looked directly at the Pharisee and threw his question back at him.

"Is it lawful to heal on the Sabbath? Is it lawful to save life or to destroy life? Which of you, if you had a sheep fall into a ditch on the Sabbath, would leave it there to die? You wouldn't, would you? You would pull it out, even if you had to enlist the help of your neighbors. I have some news for you: people are more important than sheep!" Jesus exclaimed, his voice ringing throughout the synagogue.

He then asked the man to raise his arm again.

It was plain for all to see that the man's right hand had been fully restored. A murmur arose among the audience.

The man himself was clearly astonished, and he held up his left hand beside the formerly withered one, turning them from front to back, not only so that he could confirm the healing to himself but

47

for all others to see as well. Overcome with emotion, he sat down again and wept with tears of joy.

Jesus had masterfully avoided the trap! However, he was not finished with them, not yet. Over the next half hour or so, he said many important things about himself, things that he hoped would help the ordinary people, if not the Pharisees, better understand him and his work.

Here is some of what he said, words that I can vividly remember to this day.

"My vocation is to do the work of my Father. I can do nothing by myself. I simply and faithfully do what my Father wishes. What you witnessed today is just the beginning; you will see greater things than these. The Father resurrects the dead, and the son will do likewise. The Father has delegated judgment to the son. If you don't honor the son, you don't honor the Father. Those who hear my words and believe me, also believe Him who sent me. They will not experience condemnation but will pass from death to life everlasting.

"I don't do anything by myself; I don't seek my own will but the will of the One who sent me.

"I'm telling you the truth: Many of you, even you Pharisees, believed John the Baptist at first. But, soon, his message was more than you could abide; it was inconsistent with your preconceived ideas about God. My message is going to be even harder for you to swallow. When John baptized me, two of you sitting here today were there and heard what John said about me. You thought John might be the Messiah. You were wrong about him, and you are wrong about me.

"You think you are knowledgeable in the Scriptures, exalting your own interpretations. I'm telling you the truth: If you did know the Scriptures and the prophecies concerning the Messiah, you would accept me. But you lack discernment, and, worse than that, you are devoid of love.

"In the past, you and your ilk have accepted false messiahs. You will do so again after I'm gone. But, when the true Messiah comes, you don't recognize him.

"I'm telling you the truth: You honor yourselves, but you don't honor God. Even Moses condemns you, and you are too ignorant to know who stands before you. If you really believed Moses, you would believe me. He wrote of me.

"All you need do is look at the evidence; but your minds are made up, and your hearts are too hard."

Of the several hundred or so people in the synagogue who saw Jesus heal the man's crippled hand and heard him speak these words, perhaps a hundred or so were Pharisees. With each sentence Jesus spoke, several of them left. By the time he had finished, there remained only a few. It was easy to understand why: he had insulted them, embarrassed them, and condemned them in the most scathing terms.

I said earlier that Jesus's manner of speaking was not as forceful as the Baptist's, but it certainly was that day.

The Pharisees hated what Jesus said, but the ordinary people related to it; not one of them left before he finished speaking.

After we departed the synagogue, Simon asked Jesus why he had chosen to heal the crippled man at the Pool of Bethesda on the Sabbath. The man had waited thirty-eight years for healing; he could have waited another day, and the whole Sabbath healing controversy would thus have been avoided.

Jesus's answer was simple: He had purposefully performed the healing on the Sabbath. He wanted to stir up controversy. Part of his mission was to teach the true meaning of the Sabbath.

CHAPTER 9

Passover having ended, we began our journey back to Galilee. The crowd that now followed Jesus from Jerusalem numbered at least two thousand. In addition to the Galileans, who made up the majority, there were now several hundred more from, not only Jerusalem but also regions south of the Holy City, and stretching from the Mediterranean coast on the west to beyond the Jordan River on the east. It was obvious that some of these folk were more interested in Jesus's healing powers than in his message. And there were those who were simply curious or just caught up in all the excitement and controversy that Jesus generated. However, many sincerely believed that Jesus was the promised Messiah.

Simon, Andrew, James, and I had been invited by Jesus to follow him the previous autumn, Philip and Nathanael in the winter, and Matthew just before we journeyed to Jerusalem. Among the larger crowd that followed Jesus was a smaller group, mostly men, who had consistently traveled with us for the past several months. They came along of their own volition; we seven had been *invited*. Seven. That number was significant. We Jews paid particular attention to numbers, numerology. We considered the number seven to be divine, representing completion. For example there were seven days in the week, ordained by God at creation; the temple menorah had seven candlesticks; our calendar was based on seven years, the last of which was the sabbatical year.

As we seven walked along the road back to Galilee, I brought this subject up for discussion—out of Jesus's hearing, of course. I believed we were, and would remain, Jesus's closest friends and confidants during his entire ministry; I boldly predicted he would make no further invitations. The others quickly recognized the logic and intelligence of my reasoning, and they enthusiastically agreed.

As we continued our trek back to Galilee, which took several days, the throng grew larger and larger. The press of people, some of whom could be quite unruly at times, became stifling. Jesus was unable to rest, even at night, continually disturbed by those seeking healing or just wanting to be near him.

At last, we reached the outskirts of Capernaum late one afternoon. Jesus was clearly exhausted, and we urged him to rest. But how was he to find respite among this huge and needy crowd?

James reminded us that Jesus now had his own home, the house provided by our father for his exclusive use. He could find refuge there.

As fast as we could walk, which was not very fast in the press of that multitude, we made our way to Jesus's new home. With Jesus safely inside, and while Simon stood guard at the closed front door, the rest of us went among the crowd, trying to convince them that Jesus needed rest and would be unavailable until the next day.

Slowly, as the sun began to set, the crowd began to disperse.

Simon suggested that we remain through the night, keeping watch lest Jesus be disturbed. One of us would stay awake at all times, while the others rested. He asked me to walk around the outside of the house to make sure all was well and secure.

Fortunately, the sky was clear, and the half-moon was bright, allowing me to see quite well. I was surprised to see that the house had a back door, as most houses, except exceptionally large ones, did not. I then noticed that the door was slightly ajar. This alarmed me; had someone gained entrance? Was Jesus safe? Not sure what to do, I ran back to the front of the house, whispering to the others what I had found.

Simon told the others to remain in place while he and I went to the back door. Slowly opening the door and stepping into the house, he motioned for me to stay outside.

As I peered inside, I could see that it was quite dark in the house, with only a little moonlight penetrating through the windows. I watched as Simon hesitated for a moment, letting his eyes grow accustomed to the darkness. I could barely hear his quiet footsteps as he searched throughout the house. I heard him call out to Jesus in a whisper, and then again in a louder voice. Next, I heard the front door open, followed by the sound of Simon calling the others to come in. I then entered as well.

Someone found and lighted a candle, and we all searched every part of the house. Jesus was not there.

Where could he be? Andrew speculated that Jesus could have been abducted, suggesting, if that were true, that either Herodians or Pharisees were the perpetrators. After all, both factions were threatened by him. The Herodians feared he might overthrow Herod and set up a new kingdom. The Pharisees and their close allies, the scribes (experts in Jewish religious law, whom I will henceforth simply call "lawyers"), hated his theology and feared it would diminish their influence. We all agreed Andrew's abduction theory was plausible, and it deeply distressed us.

Desperate to calm everyone down, including myself, I suggested that perhaps Jesus had gone on one of his walks. We all knew about these nocturnal odysseys of his.

Philip, who had the most logical mind among us, rejected this idea for the simple reason that Jesus had walked many miles in the last few days, was obviously exhausted, and would not have had the strength for such an undertaking. On the other hand, he added that we had heard no commotion from inside the house to indicate Jesus had been taken against his will.

Our agitation would continue through the night, with none of us sleeping. There was nothing we could do until dawn, and we remained on the front porch until morning.

At first light, we saw five men approaching the house. To our relief, we knew and trusted each of them. They were part of the group I described earlier: close and consistent followers of Jesus who had not received an official invitation from him.

Simon informed them of Jesus's mysterious absence. They were as alarmed and confused as we were. Simon suggested—or, rather, commanded—that we all immediately search for Jesus.

Everyone agreed, and Philip suggested a plan as to how the search be organized for maximum efficiency.

At that very moment, the front door of the house opened from the inside, and Jesus emerged, looking rested and refreshed! To put it mildly, we were all stunned and speechless. Before we could recover our wits and ask him questions, he said we were all going to a quiet place where we would not be disturbed; we were leaving immediately, before the crowds arrived. He invited the five men who had been ready to join us in searching for him to come along.

Reaching inside the door, he retrieved a basket full of bread, and, handing it to me, he said, "Let's get going."

No one else was out at that time of morning. The fishermen were already on the lake, and those who did not make their living in that manner were still sleeping. For the first several minutes, no one said anything.

Finally, Simon spoke up. "Are you going to tell us where you were last night? We were all worried sick about you! We even thought your enemies might have abducted you! Are you all right?"

"Yes, I'm fine, and I appreciate the concern for my well-being. I went on one of my walks out into the countryside."

"You went for a walk!" Philip exclaimed. "You had just completed a five-day walk, and you were plainly exhausted!" His words were bold, his tone challenging, understandable given the anxiety we all felt.

Jesus stopped and, looking at us calmly, said, "It's time for me to explain my nighttime walks. I know you all—especially you, John—have wondered about them. They *are* more than simple walks. I go to quiet places to pray, to pray to my Father and your Father. I ask Him to guide and strengthen me, in my work. And I pray for each one of you in the same manner. My work is now your work too. Why do I look refreshed? Communing with my Father restores my spirit and my body."

We continued on, none of us saying anything. I think we were all trying to absorb, to understand, the implications of what Jesus had said. At least the mystery of his nocturnal absences was solved. Moreover, thank God, he was all right.

As my mind cleared, I began to pay attention to our surroundings. I realized we were traveling the same path on which Jesus had led the four of us—Simon, Andrew, James, and me—when we began our journey with him the previous autumn, nearly six months before.

It was not long before Jesus veered off the path and walked toward a grove of trees, their fresh, green, spring leaves would provide welcome shade. I recognized that grove; it was the same place where we had stopped with him last autumn. Jesus asked us to sit down in a semicircle, facing him, just as we had done before. He then proceeded to teach us in the same manner as he had earlier done with us original four. Even though he spoke almost the same words as before, there seemed to be a greater earnestness and urgency in his voice. Of course, we had heard this same lesson before, but it was no less thrilling to hear it again. Jesus had a way of commanding the full attention of his audiences, whether large or small. It was as if he were speaking to each of us individually.

When he finished, he stood up and asked all of us to kneel around him in a full circle. And then, starting with Simon, Jesus placed his hands on each of our heads.

"Simon, are you still willing to follow me?"

"Yes, I am willing," Simon replied.

In the order of our calling, Jesus asked the same question of each of us, while placing his hands on our heads: first Andrew, then James and me, then Philip and Nathanael, and, finally Matthew. He received the same affirmative response from each of us. However, he did not stop there. He continued around the kneeling circle, asking the same question, in the same manner, and receiving the same response from the five other men. He asked us to stand with him.

"Until this day, you have been my disciples," he said. "I now ordain you twelve as my apostles. As apostles, you will have greater responsibilities, and you will be given greater powers."

Looking at me, he said, "John, do you remember asking me when I would teach you how to perform healing miracles and exorcisms?"

I did not see, but I could feel, the others looking at me. Feebly, I answered, "Yes."

"Well, that time has come. Instead of *teaching* you, I'm going to ask the Father to *empower* each of you to perform miracles, in *His* name, not yours. Do not use this power lightly; do not abuse it, as it will be taken from you as quickly as you receive it. You must pray to the Father, asking Him to help you use this power to *His* glory, not yours. I came to lead a revolution whose result will be the establishment of a new kingdom. You will help me do that. But— now listen to me very carefully—it will not be the kind of revolution you expect. I have no earthly ambition. This kingdom will be God's kingdom, not men's. If you listen very carefully to my words from this day forth, you will understand what I'm saying. But, if you don't understand something, ask me to explain. I will make clear things to you that I will not always make clear to others. We will remain here for another day, as I want to define in more detail the mission you will soon embark upon. I will be sending you out in pairs of my making. You will take the gospel message, the same one you have heard me preach since you have been with me. You know it well, and you will preach it all over Galilee."

By this time, it was late afternoon. We'd had had nothing to eat since the bread Jesus supplied as we began our walk, and we were all hungry. Jesus asked me to fetch the basket.

I was surprised that there was still plenty of bread in it and— what's this?—some broiled fish too! I did not remember seeing the fish before. Anyway, we all had a hearty and delicious meal. Everyone seemed excited about our coming mission assignments.

My theory about Jesus limiting the number of us disciples to seven was no longer valid. Now there were twelve of us, and we were apostles, not just disciples. There was even more honor, more prestige, in that title, and, according to what Jesus had just told us, more responsibility and *power* as well.

The newly appointed apostles were Thomas, James (Matthew's brother; to avoid confusion, we all called him James the Younger), Simon the Zealot (we added "the Zealot" because he had been a member of a revolutionary faction called Zealots, and also to avoid confusion with the first Simon, now also an apostle), Thaddeus, and Judas. Each of these men had been followers of Jesus for the past few months.

I awoke the next morning hungrier than usual, but I remembered, just before reaching for the food basket, that it would be practically empty. We had eaten nearly all the remaining bread and fish the evening before. Opening it, I was amazed and bewildered to see enough bread for everyone to have at least two loaves each. Was I losing my mind? Oh, well, the loaves *were* there, and they were still as fresh as they had been the day before. I took the basket around our circle, and everyone had his fill. But it was now completely empty, and there was no village nearby to buy more bread. What would we do for supper?

Our breakfast finished, Jesus announced that we were going on a short walk to a nearby hill.

CHAPTER 10

The hill was only a few minutes' walk. We made our way toward its crest, which afforded a panoramic view of the Sea of Galilee about a mile away. It was a beautiful spring day: blue skies with fleecy white clouds, and a cool, gentle breeze sweeping up from the lake. It was a treeless hill, but the grass, favored by recent rains, was green and lush. In the near distance, we saw a large number of people ascending the mild slope from the direction of the lakeside villages. When we reached the rounded peak of the hill, Jesus asked us to sit down, facing him; he remained standing. Within a few moments, the multitude—there must have been five thousand men, women, and children—arrived, and he motioned for them to sit behind us. Unlike some of the unruly crowds Jesus had attracted since our Passover visit to Jerusalem, these people were orderly and quiet; even the children and babies were hushed. I wondered what could have induced them, en masse, to come to this particular place at this particular time. Because the hill sloped away from him, Jesus was clearly visible to all.

What happened next remains, to this day, one of the most remarkable and meaningful experiences of my life.

Jesus began to speak, his clarion voice easily heard by the far reaches of his audience.

"I have wonderful news for you. God blesses the poor in spirit; He will give them the kingdom of heaven.

"God blesses those who mourn; He will comfort them in their sorrow and loss.

"God blesses the meek; from Him they will inherit the earth made new.

"God blesses and feeds those who hunger, and gives drink to those who thirst for Him and His righteousness.

"God blesses and will cause those who weep to laugh and rejoice with Him.

"God blesses those who are merciful; He will pour out His mercy upon them.

"God blesses those who are pure in heart; they will spend eternity with Him.

"God blesses the peacemakers; they are His children.

"God blesses those who are persecuted for the sake of His righteousness; He has prepared for them a special place in heaven.

"God blesses those who are reviled by others, persecuted, lied about, rejected by others for His sake, and He says to them, 'Rejoice, be exceedingly glad, because your reward is in heaven, where you will celebrate with those who were treated in the same manner.'"

However, not everything Jesus said that day was easy to hear; some of his words constituted serious warnings.

"Misery to the rich who have been consoled by their riches.

"Misery to those who eat more than they need to eat to sustain life; they will go hungry.

"Misery to those who rejoice in evil; they won't be able to rejoice in anything good.

"Misery to those who, when others speak well of them, praise them more than they praise God."

And then he began to teach. Teaching was at the heart of his message that day. He taught using parables and common illustrations from everyday life, and he was masterful.

"You—you people sitting here today—are the salt of the earth. Don't lose your flavor! What good is salt if it isn't salty? It's not good for anything, so it's thrown away.

"You are the light of the world, like a city on a hill which can't be hidden, like a lighted candle on a candlestick that gives light to the whole house. Let your light shine before others, that they may see your good works and glorify, not you, but God."

And then he taught the Ten Commandments in a way that was nothing like the way the rabbis taught them, or the lawyers and Pharisees interpreted them. He also spoke of the ancient prophets and taught their prophecies.

"I did *not* come to destroy the Law or the prophetic writings. I came to *fulfill* both the requirements of the Law and the ancient prophecies.

"The Ten Commandments are the cornerstone of our faith, and those who teach them conscientiously will be called great in God's kingdom. The sixth commandment forbids murder, but it has a deeper meaning than that. Don't hate anyone; you will murder him in your heart. When you go to the temple to make the required sacrifice, if you remember an unresolved conflict with anyone, leave your sacrifice at the temple gate; go and find that person, and be reconciled first. Go, then, and make your sacrifice with a clear conscience. The seventh commandment condemns adultery, but adultery can be committed in your heart as well as in your body. The third commandment prohibits taking God's name in vain, but the common oaths some of you use violate that commandment. The first commandment demands that we worship only the one true and living God. The second commandment prohibits the worship of idols, as is the habit of most pagans. However, anything—money, houses, land, clothes, position, fame—can become your idol if you value it more than you value your relationship with God.

"The last six commandments can be summarized as simply this: Treat other people the way you want other people to treat you. If you do that, you are fulfilling the requirements of those commandments exactly as God demands."

Next, Jesus, in quick succession, spoke of other things that separate those who honor God and relate to their fellow man in ways that are consistent with His commands from those who do not. There were many surprises in what he said, especially what came first: how we Jews should act toward our Roman conquerors.

"When a soldier commands you to carry his burden for a mile, offer to carry it for a second mile." (Roman law allowed its occupation forces to compel Jewish men to carry their military equipment for one mile but no farther. Every day, all over our land, Jews were humiliated by this practice.)

"If someone slaps you on the cheek, let him slap you on the other cheek too.

"If someone wants the shirt off your back, offer him your tunic as well.

"If someone wants to borrow money from you, let him have it.

"If someone sues you, offer him a settlement.

"You love your friends. Love your enemies too. Bless those who curse you, do well to those who hate you, pray for those who take advantage of you. Why? Because you are children of God, your heavenly Father! He makes the sun to shine on the just and the unjust; He sends rain on the righteous and the wicked. Don't give salutations just to those you love. What's so great about that? Even tax collectors do that. No, greet everyone with courtesy. In short, be perfect, even as your Father in heaven is perfect.

"When you give alms to the poor on the street corners, or offerings to God in the synagogues, don't make a show of it, drawing attention to your generosity. Do it quietly, discreetly.

"When you pray, don't make a show of that either. Pray quietly, preferably alone, inside your house. Don't use vain repetitions; don't be verbose. Let your prayer to God be something like this: 'Our Father in heaven, we honor Your name. May Your kingdom come, and may Your will be done, on earth as it is in heaven. Give us the bread we need for today. Forgive us our trespasses against You as we forgive those who have trespassed against us. Keep us from being led into temptation, and rescue us from evil. Your kingdom is true, Your power is great; all glory is Yours, now and forever. Amen.' Pay special attention to the word *forgive*. If you are not willing to forgive others for the wrongs they have done to you, you will not receive forgiveness from God for the wrongs you have done to Him.

"When you fast, don't make a show of it. As with prayer and almsgiving, do it discreetly, in private. Remember, you are fasting to honor God, not for the recognition of men.

"Don't accumulate earthly treasures. They are here today and gone tomorrow. Your treasures should be in heaven, where they will be safe. Where your treasures are, that's where your heart will be too. It's impossible to serve two masters. You can't serve your possessions and God too. Keep focused on God.

"Don't worry about your life in this present world: what you eat or drink or the clothes you wear. Life is much more than that. Look at the birds: they don't plant seeds, and they don't harvest crops. They know that God will take care of them. You are far more precious to God than they are. As to clothing: Look at the lilies of the field: They don't toil or spin. They are dressed by God more handsomely than even King Solomon was in all his majesty. Take no thought about food or drink or clothing. Instead, seek first God's kingdom and His righteousness, and He will provide all that you need. Do not worry about tomorrow; tomorrow will take care of itself. Sufficient for the day is the evil thereof. Do not condemn others, or they will condemn you. Judgment is God's domain, not yours; you are not qualified to judge."

Next, Jesus began a series of parables to illustrate various lessons he was teaching. Parables were a common device in our culture and religion, and we loved them.

"Can a blind man lead a blind man? Of course not; they will both stumble and fall. Don't worry about a speck of dust in your friend's eye, when you have a plank in yours. First, remove the plank from your own eye, and then you will be able to help him remove the speck of dust from his eye.

"Don't give what is holy to dogs; they won't appreciate it. Do not cast pearls before swine to be trampled under their feet.

"Which of you fathers, if your son asks you for bread, would give him a stone? Or, if he asks for a fish, would give him a snake? Of course you wouldn't. But if you, being an imperfect father, know how to give good things to your children, just think how much more your heavenly Father knows how to give good gifts to you.

"The gate to eternal life is a narrow. and only a few will choose to enter it. The gate to eternal death is very wide, and many more will choose it.

"Beware of false prophets: they disguise themselves as gentle sheep but are really ravening wolves. Men are like trees, the good ones produce good fruit; the bad ones produce bad fruit. What is in a man's heart determines what he says and whether it is true or false.

"There once was a man who built a house. He was careless in choosing the location: the ground was sand, at the top of a hill, and near a precipice. It was a beautiful house, admired by all who saw it. And then a sudden storm came: the rain came down in torrents, and the wind blew mightily. The sand gave way and the house tumbled over the cliff to the valley below. Oh, foolish man! At the same time, another man built another house on the same hill, near the same precipice. However, that man built his house on solid rock. It, too, was a beautiful house admired by all who saw it. The same rain and winds assaulted it at the same time. But this house stood firm; it was safe, warm, and dry. Oh, wise man!

"Some of you here call me *Master.* Not everyone who calls me that will become a part of the new kingdom. However, those who do the will of my Father are secure. On that day, some will say to me, 'Have we not prophesied in your name, cast out demons, and performed other miracles?' To them I will sadly reply, 'I never knew you; go your own way.'"

Jesus spoke for about an hour. During that time, no one had stirred or spoken. When he finished, a score or more of them came up to where he was standing and spoke softly to him. Most of them told him that they had never heard a message like that before and never heard anyone speak with such authority. A few others, who appeared more taken with, or perhaps shaken by, what he had preached asked him to elaborate on or explain some of the things he had said. In the crowd there were many others, some of whom had been in his broader circle of adherents and had followed him intermittently over the past few months. Most of them remained in the background, allowing the first-time listeners the opportunity to know Jesus better. Regrettably, some of them we never saw again.

About an hour after Jesus finished speaking, only a few people remained. Our father, mother, and three sisters had been in the audience, but neither James nor I had seen them until now. Concordia and her mother were there too. Simon, Andrew, Philip, Nathanael, and Matthew joined in, and Jesus introduced our five new colleagues to the families. Things got even better when our father handed James a basket. We would have something to eat after all!

Jesus then suggested we all walk the short distance to our special grove and all enjoy the meal James's and my parents had so generously provided.

My mother, not knowing there would be five additional mouths to feed, and with a look of concern bordering on panic, whispered to me that there would not be enough for thirteen, let alone twenty-four people, if everybody stayed. I don't know how, but Jesus must have heard what she said to me, or read her lips, because he walked over to her and whispered something in her ear. She looked bewildered, and I asked her what Jesus had whispered. She said he had told her not to worry; there would be enough food for all. There was.

Later that day, after our families had departed, as well as in the days that followed, I contemplated the things Jesus had said that morning. My eleven colleagues and I all agreed that he had gone far beyond anything he had previously said in public, or in private to us, and it changed the way we thought about him and his ministry.

The twelve of us were not formerly educated men. None of us had been to rabbinical schools (one of the reasons Jesus had chosen us in the first place), but we could all read and write. Our fathers and mothers had taught us all the precepts of our faith from early childhood. We all kept the Sabbath, observed Jewish food regulations, faithfully attended synagogue, read the Law and the prophets, celebrated feast days, prayed, fasted, and made the required sacrifices at the temple in Jerusalem. In short, we were all deeply observant Jews. Jesus had said things that were not only revolutionary, they seemed upside down, the opposite of what we had believed all our lives. Here is some of what he said.

God blesses the poor in spirit. Most Jews considered the poor—in whatever manner they were poor—as *un*blessed by God.

God blesses those who mourn. How could mourning be a blessing?

God blesses the meek. Wasn't meekness a sign of weakness? Wasn't Israel's meekness the cause of the Roman occupation and the humiliations it brought?

God blesses the peacemakers. We would never rid ourselves of the Roman bondage by being peacemakers.

God blesses those who are persecuted. How could persecution be a blessing?

God blesses those who are reviled. None of us thought of being reviled as a blessing.

Misery to the rich. How could being rich make a man miserable?

Misery to the man others speak well of. How could that be a misery?

Matthew suggested we ask Jesus, who at that moment appeared to be napping a few yards away, to explain these seeming contradictions.

Within a few moments, Jesus sat up, yawned, stretched, and called for us to come and join him.

Simon said we had questions about Jesus's teachings that morning, and then proceeded to reiterate the six *blessing* and two *misery* statements, asking him to explain their apparent contradictions.

Jesus said he would be happy to answer our questions, that he expected us to have questions and would have been surprised if we hadn't.

I was beginning to notice that Jesus *never* seemed to be surprised by anything.

"Simon, you are remembering only part of what I said," Jesus mildly chided.

He then repeated the eight statements, including the phrases we had not remembered, not noticed, or misinterpreted.

"Does that clear things up?"

It did. We all looked at each other with sheepish grins.

I determined to be a better listener.

"I'm glad you asked those questions. It is vital that you understand exactly what I'm about—my mission, that is—because it's your mission too. Now, I know you have other questions, and right now nothing is more important than dealing with them. Please ask, and I will answer."

Simon the Zealot, one of the five apostles appointed by Jesus the previous day, asked the next question. Remember, as I mentioned earlier, that a Zealot was not simply an enthusiastic person. The Zealots were an extreme political faction in Israel. They hated the Romans, hated the Herodians, and hated the tax collectors who collaborated with them, extracting money from ordinary Jews and transferring it to the vile empire and the equally evil Jewish royal family, controlled by imperial Rome. Many, but by no means all, Zealots had gone underground, and both the Roman army and the Herodian palace guards hunted them. The most violent of them were murderers who would stop at nothing to kill the Herodians and drive the Romans out of Israel. Remember, too, that all five of the new apostles were known to and trusted by us before their appointments. It was obvious to everyone who knew him that Simon was no longer a practicing Zealot, in the political sense; he had left that behind. This will help explain his question.

"Master, I was surprised by your statement about going the second mile. I've observed over the past few months that you sometimes speak in parables, or use exaggeration or figures of speech to make a point. Did you mean that literally?"

"Yes."

A few uncomfortable moments passed before Nathanael asked the next question.

"Master, the lawyers and rabbis have always taught that the commandments regarding killing and adultery and idol worship were to be interpreted in a literal sense. You said that hating someone or lusting after someone or making an idol out of anything also violates those commandments. Have we been misled by those teachers and lawyers all these years?"

"Yes."

Two long questions rejoined by the same one word answer.

Another pause ensued.

Matthew then spoke up. "Master, you said, and I think I remember your exact words, 'I did not come to destroy the Law or the prophetic writings. I came to fulfill both the requirements of the Law and the ancient prophecies.' Could you expand on that, please?"

"Matthew, you have not only accurately quoted me, but the Father has also given you a degree of spiritual discernment the significance of which you don't yet know. I *will* elaborate on those words. Their deeper meaning will unfold in the course of our time together. If you all listen carefully, very carefully, to what I say, what I do, the meaning of not only those words but also everything else I say will become transparent. Whenever I say or do something that you find perplexing, ambiguous, or mystifying, do not be timid; speak up. It pleases me to hear and to answer your questions. The more you ask, the better. Unless you understand my message, you cannot understand me. If you cannot understand me, you cannot know me ... you will not really know me at all."

CHAPTER II

I awoke with a start the next morning, immediately realizing that we would have nothing to eat for breakfast. I knew our food basket was empty, and the basket James's and my parents had brought us the day before had been emptied and carried back home upon their departure. Everyone else was still sleeping. I reached for our basket, which I kept close by, but it was not there. I looked around; it was nowhere in sight. I noticed that Jesus was gone. I assumed he had left during the night to pray in a secluded place. I then saw him coming through the trees; he was carrying our basket. By that time, the others were beginning to stir.

Jesus walked up and set the basket down beside me, telling me he had gone into a small village not far away and purchased bread for our breakfast.

I was beginning to realize what a surprising man he was.

After we finished breakfast, Jesus announced that we were returning to Capernaum.

As we neared the village, a group of elders from the local synagogue—the same synagogue where Jesus had healed the demon-possessed man several months earlier—advanced rapidly upon us, in a state of urgency and excitement.

One of them approached Jesus. In a manner that betrayed desperation, the man said, "Master, the centurion who commands the local garrison has sent us to ask that you come and heal one of his servants who is very ill, paralyzed, and in terrible pain. This servant is an older man who is very dear to him."

All of us were shocked at the request.

Judging from his response, so was Jesus.

"A *Roman centurion,* did you say? Why would you want me to heal a *Roman's* servant?" Jesus demanded.

"You must come because this centurion is our friend. He paid for the restoration of our synagogue, the synagogue in which you have taught. This man has great authority and power, but he has been fair, even kind, in his treatment of our people. Please, Master, you must come at once; the servant is near death," the elder begged.

"I will come. Please lead the way."

By this time, a crowd of about five hundred people had joined us.

We almost ran the nearly quarter-mile to the centurion's house. He must have seen us coming because, as we approached, he came out to meet Jesus. He was a young man to occupy such a position of authority, not more than thirty years old. He would have been imposing even without the uniform, which made him look all the more impressive. However, the look on his face revealed great distress.

"Sir, I am not worthy that you should come under my roof. But I know if you just speak the word, my servant will live."

"Your servant is well; he will live," Jesus assured him. "Go into your house, and see for yourself."

Hearing this, the centurion offered Jesus his profound gratitude and ran back into the house.

A moment later, he *and* his servant emerged, both beaming with joy.

Earlier I said I had never seen Jesus surprised by anything, that he seemed incapable of being surprised. He was about to prove me wrong. He turned around to face the crowd, and us. The look on his face was one of total astonishment. He began to speak, the tone of his voice matching that look. What he said surprised not only us, his disciples, but the onlookers as well.

"That man, a man we call a Gentile; that Roman centurion most of us call an enemy; *that* man has today manifested a greater faith than I have seen anywhere else in Israel."

Some of the onlookers were not just surprised, they were embarrassed, even insulted by Jesus's words. How could anyone not of our religion have faith? We Jews had a monopoly on faith; faith was our heritage, the foundation of our life.

In the coming days, we noticed that several of those who had been consistent followers were no longer with us. Nevertheless, the general trend continued: As Jesus's fame spread throughout Galilee, and beyond, more and more people came to be healed, came to be taught, or both.

It was now late afternoon, and Matthew invited us to his home for supper. He had also invited James's and my family, Simon's wife, Concordia, and her mother to join us as well.

After we had finished our evening meal, the servants had cleared the table, and the visiting family members had departed, Jesus asked us to remain seated around the table, explaining that he wanted to delegate two ongoing administrative responsibilities and had observed that two of us were well suited to perform them.

I am ashamed to admit that my first thought was this: *Jesus is going to honor only two of us with very important positions, and I want one of them.*

"Philip, I've noticed that you are a good planner, careful of details, very organized in your thinking, and efficient in all you do. I want you to be in charge of logistics: figuring out what we need, when we need it, and where we can get it, and then procuring it for us. Will you do that?"

Philip answered in the affirmative.

"Good," Jesus replied.

He then continued. "Judas, I want you to be our treasurer. You will be responsible for keeping the purse, and, when Philip needs funds for our food or other needs, supplying it to him. Will you do that?"

Judas agreed.

"Good," said Jesus.

The next morning, we were off again, this time to the nearby village of Nain. I found it interesting, and so did my fellow disciples, that Jesus always seemed to know exactly where we should go next.

He usually announced our next destination either the day before, or sometimes the morning of, our departures. Wherever we went, something challenging, amazing, or wonderful always awaited. I can remember no exceptions to this phenomenon. The village of Nain was not to be disappointing.

As Jesus and the twelve of us, accompanied by a large crowd of several hundred that included a few dozen of his regular and faithful followers, neared the small village, we saw a large funeral procession slowly proceeding to a place of burial. Jewish burial sites were not underground, but, rather, in natural caves or chambers hewn into the sides of hills or mountains. We had passed such a place about a quarter mile from the village, just a few minutes before. The remains of the deceased, a young man, were on a bier. Several mourners were following close behind, bearing embalming spices and grave clothes (linen sheets) in which to wrap the body after its placement into the burial chamber. Beside the bier was his grieving mother who was, as we would learn, a widow. She was inconsolable. All of us—Jesus, his disciples, the whole crowd—pitied her.

But Jesus did more than that; he walked beside her and consoled her.

"Don't cry anymore," he said.

He then touched the bier.

The pallbearers abruptly stood still, the whole procession came to a sudden halt, the mourners fell silent, and so did the throng. Jews were forbidden to touch a dead body or even the bier on which it is conveyed. Pallbearers used poles attached to the bier, so as not to touch it.

Jesus then shattered the silence that had ensued, by uttering these simple words: "I say to you, young man, arise!"

Spontaneously, the young man sat up and asked Jesus what was happening.

The Master did not answer. Rather, he took the young man by the hand and escorted him to his mother, who had been, just a moment before, incapable of consolation; now her joy could not be contained. (*God blesses those who mourn; He will comfort them in their sorrow and loss.*)

We did not know what illness or accident had taken the young man's life, but whatever it was, no sign of it remained. He appeared healthy and robust, albeit understandably confused.

I heard fearful murmurs ripple through the onlookers around me. One man whispered something about an evil spirit being at work. That kind of talk ended as quickly as a flash of lightning, when a great majority of the silent multitude, who could no longer remain silent, burst into shouts of jubilation, praising God for His mercy.

Quickly, the enthusiastic crowd surrounded Jesus. Some spoke to him, several of them calling him a prophet. One woman said that God had visited His people that day, through Jesus. Others desired to touch Jesus or just to brush against his clothes. But, as usual, the great majority who sought out Jesus following this fantastic miracle either wanted physical healing for themselves or someone they had brought with them. And, as usual, Jesus healed these infirmities. I do not think he could help himself. Regrettably, far fewer of them were interested in his teachings: his kingdom message, his calls for repentance. For the first time in his ministry, he rebuked a crowd in the sharpest words I had heard him speak up to that time. I was standing close to Jesus as he spoke, and even though his words were critical, there were tears in his eyes and in his voice; he did not relish what he had to say. He began by denouncing two nearby villages we had recently visited and where some of his greatest works of mercy had been accomplished.

"Misery to you, Chorazin and Bethsaida! You gladly accept my healing powers but reject my call for your repentance. If these works had been performed in Tyre and Sidon, *they* would have repented in sackcloth and ashes. It will be more tolerable for them than you on the day of judgment."

Next, he censured the village that was home to five of his disciples, including me, and it was now his home too.

"Misery to you, Capernaum! You exalt yourself to heaven, but you will descend into hell! It will be more tolerable for Sodom on the day of judgment than for you!"

Hearing these words, the crowd was stunned into complete silence. None of them, and none of us, his disciples, had ever heard Jesus speak in this manner before.

And then he spoke softly, solemnly. Looking up to heaven, he prayed.

"Father, all my praise I give to You, You who are Master of heaven and earth. In Your wisdom, You have hidden heavenly things from the wise and intelligent of the earth and revealed them to innocent children. You, Father, have given me everything. Nobody knows the son except the Father, and nobody knows the Father except the son and anyone the son reveals Him to."

Lowering his head, he now spoke again to the multitude, neither in anger nor sorrow, but in earnest invitation.

"Is life a struggle for you? Are you carrying large, unmanageable burdens? Then come to me! I will give you rest! Take my yoke, and wear it; learn the lessons of eternal life from me. I will be gentle and kind to you; I will make your life easier, not harder. You need rest, and with me, you will have it. My yoke is easily worn, and my load is easily carried."

In the crowd that witnessed what happened in Nain that day were two of John the Baptist's disciples; we all knew and recognized them. After the multitude dispersed, one of them, Timon, approached Jesus and asked to speak with him. He agreed, and we walked a short distance to a nearby grove of trees that would provide not only quiet and seclusion but also welcome shade on that warm afternoon. Some weeks earlier, on the orders of Herod, the Roman Empire's puppet ruler of Israel, the Baptist had been arrested. The counterfeit king was threatened by John's stirring up his subjects, especially what John had preached about a new kingdom that would arrive soon. The corrupt monarch had taken his brother's divorced wife for his own. This was a gross violation of the seventh of our Ten Commandments, and John had boldly condemned him for it. The Baptist had not only threatened his rule, but he had embarrassed Herod, who had him thrown into prison, effectively ending his ministry. Once we had all sat down on the grass, Timon told Jesus that they had been sent by John to ask him a question.

"Master, John would like to know if you are the One, or should we look for another?"

"Go and tell John what you've witnessed today: A dead man risen to life; lepers made whole; those who were blind and deaf now see and hear; those who could not stand now walk; those who were demon possessed are now free. And, most important of all, tell him the good news of God's kingdom was preached."

That should have been enough to convince them and the Baptist that Jesus was the One.

But Jesus was not finished.

"John has doubts about me because I'm not exactly what he expected me to be. I'm not the fiery orator that he is; I preach everywhere, not just in the desert; I don't baptize people; I don't fast; I don't dress or eat or drink the way he does. I don't prepare the way for God's kingdom. That was John's task, and he did it well—so well that he has become Israel's greatest prophet. However, his work is done; he has passed the torch to me. God's kingdom is no longer coming; it is here now, standing right in front of you."

We were all taken aback by those last few words, John's disciples especially so.

"Yes, go and tell John—and no one else—not only what you saw today but also what I just said to you. And tell him that I love him; tell him I am praying for him. Blessed is he who is persecuted for my sake."

Not many weeks after this, John was dead, his execution ordered by that pretender, Herod.

Jesus said many things of great importance that day in Nain. But one phrase in his prayer stuck in my mind: *Nobody knows the son.* It was clear from the context of his prayer that when he said "the son," Jesus was referring to himself. But *we*, his disciples, knew him! *I* knew him!

CHAPTER 12

After our brief but momentous time in Nain, we returned to Capernaum. One of the local residents, a Pharisee named Simon, invited Jesus, the twelve of us, and a few of his friends to his home for supper. Some of us knew him slightly, and we were surprised by the invitation. Since joining Jesus, we had become increasingly aware that Pharisees were not pleased with, and certainly not receptive to, his teachings. Many of them were openly hostile. Could Simon be a different kind of Pharisee?

Jesus accepted the invitation, and we accompanied him to Simon's house. When we arrived, something unusual happened, or, rather, did not happen.

It was customary in our culture for the host to offer a small basin of water to each guest so that he could wash his hands and even his feet upon entering the house (everyone wore sandals, and the roads were dusty). If the host were wealthy, which was certainly true in Simon's circumstance, his servants would perform this custom. Depending upon the importance of the guests—or at least the guest of honor—the host himself would often anoint their heads with a small quantity of fine oil. Simon ignored these customs, which was considered an insult, most likely a deliberate one, I suspected.

Simon bid us all to his table. For more formal meals, as this one was meant to be, guests did not sit on chairs, but, rather, reclined on cushioned benches, raising themselves on one elbow. It was a large table, and there was room for all of us. Shortly after we had positioned ourselves around the table, a woman appeared and, kneeling behind Jesus and crying softly, began bathing his feet with her tears. Everyone stopped talking; the only sound was that of her barely audible weeping. I had never seen anything so shocking in my life. Everyone present was embarrassed by her behavior.

Everyone but Jesus, that is.

The woman's tears flowed copiously, thoroughly wetting Jesus's feet. She had no towel with which to dry them, and neither Simon nor his servants provided one. The woman then added to her shame by letting down her long hair and using it to dry the Master's feet! No decent woman would do such a thing in public. I did not recognize her, but several of my colleagues seemed to.

"Her name is Mary Magdalene," my brother whispered to me, adding, "She is a sinner."

The word *sinner,* when used to describe a woman, was code for *prostitute.*

I gave James a puzzled look.

Next, Mary Magdalene did something else remarkable: she opened a jar and began anointing Jesus's feet with expensive alabaster ointment.

The expression on our host's face was one of utter disdain and condemnation. He remained silent, looking alternately at Jesus and this unwelcome intruder.

Jesus looked straight at our host.

"Simon, I have something to say to you."

Pausing and looking a little uneasy, our host replied, "All right, Rabbi, go on."

Jesus then uttered one of his parables.

"A creditor had two debtors; one owed him five hundred denarii, the other owed him fifty. Neither debtor could afford to pay him, so he forgave them both. Which of the two do you think loves him the most?"

"I suppose the one whom he forgave the most," Simon replied.

"You are right."

Jesus looked at the cowering woman.

"Did you see what she did?" Jesus said.

Turning back toward Simon, Jesus continued. "When I entered

your house, you gave me no water for my feet; she washed my feet with her tears and dried them with her hair. You gave me no kiss of greeting; she has not ceased kissing my feet. You did not anoint my head with oil; she has anointed my feet with ointment. Her sins, which are many, are forgiven because she loves much. Those who receive only a little forgiveness only love a little."

Looking at Mary and taking her by the hand, Jesus helped to her to stand.

"Your sins are forgiven," Jesus told Mary.

The expression on Mary's face turned from sorrow, shame, and fear to joy and peace. (*God blesses and will cause those who weep to rejoice with Him.*) Not so with Simon and his friends: They murmured disapproval; one asking how this man dared to forgive sins, something only God can do. They immediately and indignantly departed.

Our host stood up, an unmistakable sign that we were to leave as well. The dinner, not yet begun, was over.

Throughout this episode, I watched Jesus closely. I was amazed by his self-control, his poise: He spoke evenly, without passion. He appreciated the woman's gesture and was not offended by the rudeness of his host.

From that day on, Mary Magdalene was a faithful follower of Jesus. Joanna, the former wife of Herod's steward, took Mary under her wing, the two of them ministering lovingly and effectively to women of the same unhappy background. Many of them turned away from their former lives and became believers. When Joanna first became a follower, some of us suspected her of spying for the corrupt king, but that was not to be the case. Her husband had divorced her, taking their children, when she told him of her decision to follow Jesus. My mother, Salome, also often joined us on our travels. She, too, would prove to be an excellent addition to Jesus's ministry, taking charge of meal planning and preparation, assisted by several other women. She worked closely with Philip. (Remember that Jesus had put him in charge of the logistics and administrative details of the ministry, which included provisioning our company with sufficient foodstuffs. Philip in turn worked with Judas, appointed keeper of the purse by Jesus, and therefore in charge of supplying the money for all our provisions.)

We remained in Capernaum for several more days.

One day, Jesus cast a demon out of a man who was both blind and dumb. When the evil spirit left him, at the Master's command, the man was able to both speak and see.

One witness to this miracle, an elderly man, referring to Jesus, shouted out, "Is this not the son of David?"

David was Israel's most well-known and beloved king. Only someone thought to be the long-awaited Messiah could be called his son.

A Pharisee, who was also a lawyer, heard this proclamation and shouted back, "This man casts out demons by the power of Beelzebub!"

Beelzebub was, of course, another name for Satan.

Jesus's reply was a delightful example of his quick wit and superior reasoning.

"What? Your logic is flawed! Why would Satan cast out Satan? Do you think Satan is at war with himself? A kingdom divided against itself cannot stand. No! I cast out demons by the Spirit of God, whose kingdom has come to you. You Pharisees are a generation of snakes, you are incapable of speaking the truth, your hearts are evil, and only evil comes out of your mouths."

Murmurs of both approval and disapproval rippled through the crowd.

The same Pharisee then sought to defend his slander by further challenging Jesus.

"If you are truly bringing us God's kingdom, show us a sign from heaven. Give us proof."

Jesus calmly replied, "No sign or proof will be given to you except the sign of Jonah, whom God sent to Nineveh to warn the people of that city that His judgment was coming upon them. They repented, but you are incapable of repentance. The queen of Sheba traveled a great distance, seeking Solomon's wisdom. She believed and received that wisdom, and she will condemn this unrepentant generation. One greater than Solomon stands before you today."

A woman in the crowd shouted, "Blessed is the mother who bore you!"

To which Jesus replied, "Blessed are those who hear the word of God, and keep it."

The timing of the assertion about Jesus's mother was interesting, in light what happened next.

Someone in the back of the large crowd called out, "Master! Your mother, your brothers, and your sisters are here! They want to speak with you but can't find a way through this multitude!"

"My mother, my brothers, and my sisters are those who hear the word of God and do it," he responded, turning and looking at us, and then adding, "These here are my mother, my brothers, and my sisters. Whoever does the will of God are my mother, my brothers, and my sisters."

A gasp went up from the crowd, followed quickly by the buzz of indignant chatter among them.

With that, Jesus motioned us to follow him, and we walked away from the throng, which had already begun to disperse. Usually at such times, a score or more people would follow us, wanting to speak to Jesus. Not this time. It was just Jesus and the twelve of us. He did not seek out his family, and they did not attempt to pursue him. As we walked along with him, there was no conversation among us. We were too shocked to speak. We were all bewildered at his treatment of his family. Our religion, as well as our culture, required great respect for our families. We were taught to love and esteem them. The fifth commandment demands we honor our mother and father. Jesus had emphasized the importance of the Ten Commandments and our obligation to them in word and deed. Now it seemed as if he were ignoring one of them.

I had not considered the possibility of Jesus having a family. Of course, I knew that he must have had a father and mother; everybody had parents. However, he had never spoken of them, and none of us had asked him about his family. I suppose we assumed his parents were dead, and we had not even thought about his having brothers and sisters. We all knew he was from Nazareth, one of the few villages in Galilee we had not visited. Why? If he had living family members there, why hadn't he visited with them? Why hadn't he introduced us to them? I was unnerved by this incident. The way Jesus treated his family disturbed me, and doubt began to insinuate itself into my mind. Perhaps Jesus was right when he said that nobody knew him, not even his closest friends.

Twilight was coming on as we walked to—where were we going? We were walking in single file, unusual for us, as we normally walked side by side in groups of two, three, or four, conversing with each other. Jesus was still in the lead, joined now by Matthew, the two of them the only ones speaking. They stopped and waited for the rest of us to catch up.

Jesus announced that we would all stay the night at Matthew's home, the only one of our houses large enough to accommodate all of us. Somehow, Matthew's servants knew we were coming, as supper had been prepared and was on the table. It was the quietest meal we had ever shared together; even Simon was silent. When we had finished eating, Jesus announced that tomorrow morning we would walk down to the Sea of Galilee, to a well-known inlet, a small bay. He would have some important things to say there, he told us.

After what had happened that afternoon, I wondered if we would be his only listeners.

CHAPTER 13

Early next morning, we all ate breakfast around Matthew's large dining table, the same table at which we had eaten the banquet meal with him and a number of his friends a few months before. That had been a noisy, happy gathering. This one was rather quiet, even somber. The conversation was perfunctory: please pass the bread, please pass the fish, and so on.

Of course, Jesus noticed our melancholy mood, and he could abide it no longer.

"I know what's troubling you men," he said. "You are shocked by what I said about my family yesterday, and you deserve an explanation. My family and I are estranged right now. They don't believe in, or even understand, my ministry. Both of my brothers think I'm insane. They came to try to reason with me. They want me to abandon my work. Don't misunderstand. I love them all dearly, and I long for the day they will believe in me and support what I must do. However, I will not let them interfere in my mission—*our* mission. You see, God is inaugurating a new family of common spiritual values that will transcend traditional family bonds. You and I, together, are that new family. Our mission is to grow that family, not just here in Galilee, not just in Israel, but throughout the whole world!"

He paused momentarily and then added, "Are you still with me?"

Without hesitation and almost with one voice, our unanimous answer was a resounding *yes.*

The dark mood of just moments before evaporated in an instant. Our enthusiasm was rekindled. We were ready to rededicate our lives to Jesus and his mission—*our* mission. Each of us, one after the other, spoke up enthusiastically, reconfirming our undying commitment to Jesus, our friend, our Master.

"Let's go!" Jesus said. "This is a very important day, and we must be off."

We all followed, without reservation or hesitation.

On the way down to the lake, there was a lot of conversation among us. Simon asked Jesus about his father, who had not been among his family the day before. Jesus explained that his father, Joseph, had taken ill some years before, and died. His two brothers and four sisters looked after their mother, Mary; the brothers continued in their father's carpentry business after his death, providing her financial support; the sisters looked after their mother's personal needs. He spoke tenderly of them all.

We went to a cove, a small inlet on the Sea of Galilee that would become known as the Bay of Parables. It was in the shape of a horseshoe, its sides sloping moderately up from the lake. It was a perfect natural amphitheater. As we neared this beautiful spot, I looked over my shoulder, and to my surprise and delight, saw a crowd of several hundred people following us. At its head were probably fifty or so of our more faithful outer-circle followers; the rest appeared to be local folk, some of whom had been in the audience the previous day. This encouraged me; it encouraged us all. There was a fishing boat tied up to the shore, and as the people pressed closer and closer, Jesus had no choice but to board the boat, cast off a few yards, and drop anchor. It was a beautiful day, sunny and warm, with just a hint of a cool breeze. The water in the bay was as smooth as glass. The natural curvature of the inlet, together with the grass-covered slope, provided the perfect setting. Jesus, ideally positioned, projected his voice so that everyone could hear him perfectly. He then began to teach, once again in parables.

The Sower

A farmer went out to sow his seed. As he was spreading the seed, some of it fell on the pathway, where passersby trod on it and birds came and ate it. Some of the seed fell on stony ground, and when it sprouted, it quickly withered, because the sun scorched it and there was not enough soil for it to take root; it produced nothing. Other seed fell among weeds, and when it started to grow, the weeds overwhelmed it so that it yielded nothing at harvest. But other seed fell into good, rich soil, and flourished, producing a bountiful crop. If you've got ears, listen.

The Mustard Seed and Leaven

What shall we say God's kingdom is like? How can we picture it? It is like a mustard seed. When the farmer throws it on the ground, it is the smallest of any seed on earth. But, when it grows, it springs up and becomes a tree. Its branches are large enough for the birds to make their nests in it. It's also like leaven that a baker hides in three pounds of flour; it spreads throughout the flour until it leavens all if it.

The Weeds

The kingdom of God is also like this: A farmer sowed good wheat seed in his field. While he and his helpers were asleep, an enemy sneaked into the field, sowed weeds, and sneaked away. When the wheat crop began to grow, the weeds came up too.

His servants discovered the weeds, came to him, bid him look at the field, and asked, "Master, didn't you sow only good wheat seed in your field? Where have all these weeds come from?"

"This is the work of my enemy," he replied.

His servants asked him if they should uproot the weeds.

"No, he said, "if you do that, you'll uproot and destroy the wheat as well. Just let them grow together until the harvest. Then I will instruct the reapers to gather the weeds first, tie them into bundles, and burn them. The wheat will be gathered into my barn."

The Hidden Treasure

The kingdom of God is like a treasure trove hidden in a field. A man walking through the field stumbles upon it. He buries the treasure, then goes off and sells everything he has to get enough money to buy that field. The kingdom of God is also like a merchant trader looking for fine pearls. He finds one that is perfect, priceless. He, too, goes off and sells everything he owns, and buys it.

Jesus's last parable that day contained an ominous warning.

The Fishing Net

God's kingdom is also like a fishing net thrown into the sea, which collects every kind of fish. When the net is full, the fisherman brings it to shore and separates the good fish from the bad fish. He keeps the good ones and throws the bad ones away. That's how it will be at the end of the age: God's angels will separate the righteous from the wicked who will be cast into outer darkness. There will be much weeping and bitter regret among them.

Now you know why this place came to be called the Bay of Parables.

These parables had delighted and entertained the assembly. Their settings—farming, baking, and fishing—were scenes of everyday life, and so they were not difficult to comprehend, even for the unschooled. Nevertheless, all of them were allegorical, symbolical, containing deeper meanings. The last one about the fishing net had a disturbing ending, which may have been the reason why the crowd quietly dispersed after hearing it.

When only Jesus and we twelve remained, he asked us if we had any questions, or if he needed to further explain any of these parables.

Simon asked Jesus to elaborate on the first one, about the sower.

"The seed that fell on the pathway that the birds came and snatched away is like a man who hears the good news of God's kingdom, and yet does not understand it," Jesus said. "Satan comes and snatches away the seed that was sown in the man's heart, and he doesn't even realize it. The seed that fell on stony ground is like a man who hears the word and receives it enthusiastically, but it never really takes root in his heart because he is distracted by his troubles. The seed that fell among the weeds is like a man who hears the word of God, but the material things of this world—for example, the seduction of wealth—distract him from the word of God, and so it doesn't come to fruition in his life. However, the seed sown on good soil is like a man who hears the word of God, understands it, accepts it, and, most important of all, lives it. Someone like that will bear much fruit. Do you understand it now?"

Yes, we did!

"Could you explain the parable about the weeds in the wheat field?" asked Judas.

"The one who sows the good seed is the Son of Man," Jesus replied. "The field is the whole world, not just Israel; the good seed are the children of God's kingdom; the weeds are the children of the Evil One; the Enemy who sows them is Satan. The harvest is the close of the age; the reapers are God's angels. His angels will gather the children of the Evil One and cast them into outer darkness, where they will forever be separated from God. But the children of God's kingdom will shine like the sun and be in His presence for eternity."

"Master, who is the 'Son of Man'?" Andrew asked. "I have never heard you say that before."

"I'm the Son of Man, Andrew. Sometimes I will refer to myself in that way."

Jesus then asked if we had questions about any of the other parables he had spoken that day.

"Master," said Simon the Zealot, "I have a question, not about any of today's parables, but, rather, why do you explain the parables to us and not to the crowd? If we can't comprehend some of these things, they may not be able to understand them either."

"I speak in parables because the time is not right for others to understand all of the things I say. There will come a time when they will understand, but that time is not yet. You, however, must know and understand these things now, not later. I will impart to you the secrets of God. You already know the wisdom of the ages; you are steeped in the Law and the prophets, and that is good. Now, you must be immersed in the secrets of God's new kingdom; you must know and fully understand the old and the new."

"The secrets of God"—those words made the hair on the back of my neck stand up.

It was late afternoon, and we began the short walk back to Matthew's house, where we would enjoy a pleasant evening meal together—much more so than that of the previous evening—and a good night's rest too.

CHAPTER 14

The next morning, we followed Jesus back down to the Sea of Galilee, to the same bay where he had spoken his series of parables. The *same* boat was tied up, just as we had left it. No one followed us, and there was no one else in sight. Whose boat it was remains a mystery to this day. Jesus got into the boat, and so did we. Fortunately, it was large enough to accommodate us all. He bid us to push off and proceed in an easterly direction to the opposite shore. We rowed out of the inlet into the open waters of the lake, hoisted the sail, caught a favorable wind, and proceeded eastward the several miles to the other side. Within minutes, Jesus, lying on a cushion in the stern of the boat, was fast asleep. We all looked at each other in puzzlement and began conversing quietly, so as not to wake him. Our consternation was palpable: Why were we going to the eastern shore, of all places? That was the region of Gadara, also known as Decapolis—the ten cities—which were really just small villages. No Jews lived there, only godless heathens who hated Jews, and Jews were none too fond of them either.

We sailed for about half an hour. When we left the western shore, the skies were clear, and the winds favorable. Andrew pointed to the east. Angry storm clouds were rapidly forming; the winds were shifting and gathering force, now blowing directly against us. Six of us were experienced fishermen. We had sailed and fished this lake since we were children. We were used to rapid weather changes; we had been in countless gales, and successfully navigated them all, always returning safely to shore. We tried to lower the sail, but there was not enough time, the tempest was upon us before we could act. This storm was fiercer than any of us had previously witnessed. We were all terrified, even Simon, the most experienced and toughened boatman among us. Lightning bolts blazed, and thunder, the likes of which I had never heard before, nearly shattered my ears. The waves were enormous, and the accompanying rains were blinding, so hard that their impact stung my face. Between the heavy rain and the waves now beginning to wash over the bow of the boat, I did not know how we could stay afloat. It was so dark, I could barely see my friends' faces, but their expressions, and mine too, betrayed a fear for our very lives.

I crawled to the back of the boat, and what did I see? Jesus still *sleeping!* How could he, how could anyone, sleep through this?

I shook his arm roughly and screamed at him. "Wake up! Don't you care that we're all about to drown?!"

Jesus looked at me, and the serenity of his face was quite a contrast to my own expression of fear. He stood up—I don't know how he kept his balance—and in a voice that was louder than the beating rain, the howling wind, and the constant crash of thunder all in combination, shouted three simple, single-syllable words: "Peace! Be still!"

I did not even have time to think how impossibly foolish those words sounded in the circumstances. In an instant, the winds died, the rain stopped, the clouds disappeared, and the thunder ceased. There was a dead calm, the lake as smooth as glass. The sun shone as bright as ever. Standing up, I backed away from Jesus and moved toward my colleagues. I think I was more frightened in that moment than I had been at the height of the storm. What man had that kind of power, that kind of authority over the world's physical elements? Of course, he had manifested power over sickness and evil spirits; he had even a restored a young man to life on his way to the tomb. Those feats were rare but not unheard of in the history of our people. But this! What explanation could there possibly be? I looked at my friends; they seemed as terrified as I.

Walking toward us, Jesus asked, "Why are you afraid? Don't you have *any* faith at all? Let's get going; we don't want to be late."

Late! Late for what? I wondered.

By some good fortune, our sail was intact, and the mast was undamaged. A gentle breeze came up from the west and pushed us on our way. Soon, the region of Gadara came into view. I had never been there; none of us had, not even Jesus. It looked desolate: no town or even village in sight, just a narrow beach and a vertical cliff rising perhaps a hundred feet above it. At the top of the cliff, a gently sloping, practically barren, plain ran away, toward the interior of the region. A large herd of swine was grazing, a few herdsmen tending them, one more reason not to get out of the boat. We arrived on shore presently, secured the boat, and disembarked. None of us—except Jesus—knew why were in this pathetic, forsaken place.

We then heard a bloodcurdling scream. A naked man was rapidly descending a narrow winding pathway from the top of the cliff to the beach, all the while shouting incoherently as he came closer and closer to us. All of us—even big, strong, manly Simon— were afraid for the second time within the past hour. We had all seen demon-possessed men, and even women, many times, even more of them since our sojourn with Jesus began; he was a magnet for them. But this man was without doubt the most violent, threatening, and frightening of them all. In addition to being naked, his hair and beard, and even his fingernails, were long and unkempt. Had he ever in his life had a bath? We backed out of his path as he ran straight toward Jesus, who stood his ground, looking directly at the man. It appeared he was going to run right into the Master and knock him down, but then, just before reaching him, the man dropped to his knees and started shouting.

"What do you and we have to do with each other, Jesus?" he screamed. "You are the son of the highest God! Please don't add to our torment!"

How did this devil-possessed man know Jesus's name?

"What is your name?" Jesus asked.

This made no sense to me. The man knew Jesus's name, but Jesus didn't know his name.

"Our name is Legion," answered the man, in a completely different voice.

And then, in yet another voice, he added, "For I have many personalities."

Hearing this, Jesus commanded the evil spirits to depart from him. At first, the evil spirit (spirits?) resisted, yet again in a different voice. He then consented but begged that Jesus send the demons into the herd of swine grazing on the plain above the cliff. Jesus honored his request, and, immediately, we heard the thunder of hooves above and about a hundred yards north of the beach where we stood. With amazement, we witnessed the entire herd, hundreds and hundreds of swine, plunging over the cliff into the lake, where they drowned.

The man, freed of his torment and realizing he was naked and dirty, ran into the water and began to wash himself.

Jesus, turning to me, told me to go to the boat and retrieve a small bundle.

"What bundle?" I asked.

"You'll see it," he said.

And sure enough, there was a bundle.

"Open it," Jesus said.

I did. There was a tunic inside.

"Give it to the man," Jesus told me.

The man's hair, beard, and fingernails were still too long, but at least he was clean; and now he was also clothed. However, most remarkable, he was in his right mind: calm, coherent, and speaking in a single, controlled voice. He thanked Jesus profusely for delivering him from his unspeakable pain and misery. He had cuts and scars all over his arms and face. Simon asked him how he got them. He was not sure, but he speculated they were self-inflicted because of his own self-loathing. He told us he had been living in burial caves for the last several years—he did not know how many. The demons that possessed him had somehow imbued him with superhuman strength, increasing his menace. Everyone living in the area feared him. From time to time, some of the braver of them had successfully crept up on him while he was sleeping, binding him with iron chains. He had easily broken them. He had no friends, no family to care for or even acknowledge him. Because of his lunatic behavior, everyone he encountered recoiled in fear and disgust. Everyone but Jesus.

By this time, it was early afternoon. Philip, our logistics man, had brought along a basket of bread and broiled fish. We were hungry; the man was ravenous. While eating our meal, we heard voices from above. Descending the path to the beach were about a dozen men who, as it happened, were the owners of the swine herd, which they claimed to be two thousand in number, now all lost. They were not happy. Their spokesman asked which of us was responsible for this economic disaster. Before any of us could make a reply, one of them apparently recognized the formerly demon-possessed man. He tugged at the sleeve of their leader, and they all went into a whispered conference. Their anger quickly turned into fear. They had feared the man as a lunatic, but seeing him in his right mind was somehow even more frightening to them. What black magic was this? Rather than seeking compensation for their loss, they begged our hasty departure. Turning tail, they hastily retreated up the pathway.

We finished our dinner, after which Jesus and the man walked down the beach, sat in the shade of an overhanging rock, and conversed for over an hour.

The rest of us discussed the astonishing events of the day not yet over. We agreed it had been the most surprising, fear inducing, albeit exciting day of our lives. We also agreed that we hoped there would not be another like it. We needed peace and quiet and rest.

When they returned from their private talk, Jesus said it was time for us to return to Capernaum. The man entreated Jesus to let him come with us. He was afraid to stay in his own region, and who could blame him? What would become of him? Would the evil spirits that had dogged him for years return? Jesus assured him they would not. Would his countrymen kill him? The Master said no harm would come to him.

"I want you to go to your people and tell them what God has done for you this day," Jesus said. "You are a different man now. They will listen to you; they won't fear you anymore. Will you do that for me?"

Smiling, the man replied, "Yes, Lord, I will!"

He certainly was a different man. All of us gathered around him, shaking his hand and wishing him well in his newly restored life.

We got into the boat and blessedly headed west, back to familiar territory. It was late afternoon; the breeze had shifted, now coming out of the east and speeding us back to civilization.

On the way, Simon asked Jesus what he and the man had talked about during their sequestered conversation.

Jesus simply replied that he now had a follower in Gadara.

The man was a Gentile! How could a *Gentile* be a follower?

I thought I understood Jesus and really knew him. After the events of this day, once again, I was not so sure.

We arrived back in the quiet, deserted bay just as the sun was setting, tied up the boat, and made our way the short distance back to Capernaum. Jesus would go to his house, Simon and Andrew to theirs, James and I to our parents' home, and the other eight to Matthew's house. We were all exhausted—a life-threatening storm and an aggressive, demon-possessed lunatic can have that effect—all but Jesus, that is. He seemed energized by the day's events. The first home we came to was Jesus's. Bidding us good night, he asked us all to meet him there in the morning, an hour after sunrise.

Our father, mother, and sisters greeted James and me with looks and words of joyful relief. They knew about the storm, of course; its fury had driven our father and probably all the other fishermen off the lake earlier than usual. Thanks be to God, there had been no casualties.

During supper, James and I took turns telling them about the momentous events of the day: how incredibly fierce the gale had been; how we had feared for our lives; *and* how Jesus had saved us. They were astounded, to say the least, especially our father who had sailed and fished the Sea of Galilee for nearly forty years. Their reactions were the same as ours: how could anyone, other than God Himself, exercise that kind of power and authority over the world's physical elements?

And then, again leaving out no details, we told them about our across-the-lake odyssey into Gadara.

"Gadara!" Father gasped, asking why Jesus would want to go there.

We then related the equally hard-to-believe story of the demon-possessed man. The expressions on their faces betrayed understandable skepticism, but our adamant earnestness convinced them in the end.

We asked our mother to wake us an hour before sunrise; we were so exhausted that we feared waking too late to make our appointment with Jesus.

CHAPTER 15

James and I arrived at Jesus's house at the appointed hour. Simon and Andrew were already there, sitting on the front porch; within moments, the other eight joined us.

Jesus opened the front door and smiled broadly.

"Good morning, friends! Let's be on our way."

What surprises awaited us, I could not begin to imagine—in Jesus's company, there were always surprises.

We had not even reached the street in front of Jesus's house, when a man ran up to him and fell at his feet. This phenomenon was happening more and more frequently. Those of us who lived in Capernaum recognized the man immediately. His name was Jairus, a leader in our synagogue, and something was terribly wrong.

Through uncontrollable sobs, he blurted out, "Master, my twelve-year-old daughter lies sick in my house, at the point of death. I beg you to come with me to her side. If you lay your hand on her, I know she will live."

Jesus agreed, and we all followed the distraught father as he hurriedly led the way to his home. I found this episode remarkable because, while Jesus was quite popular among the ordinary folk of Capernaum, most of whom attended synagogue, he was not looked upon with favor by the synagogue leadership, including Jairus. However, desperate men do desperate things, and Jairus was a desperate man now.

Within minutes, a large throng pressed in upon us, slowing our progress. Everyone wanted to be close to Jesus, it seemed; this usually happened wherever we went.

This increased Jairus's anxiety, and he began shouting, pleading for the crowd to get out of the way.

It did not work. The multitude pressed even closer—men, women, and children reached out to touch Jesus or even just his tunic.

Suddenly, Jesus stopped and stood still, and the crowd became quiet.

"Who touched my clothes?" he asked.

Simon, who was standing nearest to him, replied, "Who touched you? People are pressing up against you all around, and you ask who touched you?"

"I know that a particular person has touched me, because I felt power flow out of me. Now, which of you was it?" Jesus asked, passing his eyes over those nearby.

The silence continued for a moment, no one confessing, no one saying anything.

And then a middle-aged woman slowly, timidly approached Jesus, fell down at his feet, and acknowledged she was the one. She seemed embarrassed, reluctant to say more, at least within earshot of the crowd.

Jesus, sensing this, bent down, lifted her up, and whispered something to her; she whispered something to him.

Jesus then spoke in a voice everyone heard. "Young woman, your faith has made you well! Go in peace."

An expression of great relief and quiet joy adorned what had been, just moments before, a troubled, forlorn countenance. Some women in the crowd, apparently those who knew her and whatever her affliction had been, gathered around her, praising God.

I loved moments like this.

In the meantime, Jairus had been standing by impatiently, beside himself, fearing for the life of his child.

"Please, Master, let's go to my daughter as quickly as possible," he implored.

Just at that moment, one of Jairus's servants ran up to him, panting, and said, "Your daughter is dead. There is nothing to be done; there is no reason for the Master to come now."

Before Jairus could react to this devastating news, Jesus put his hand on the distressed father's shoulder.

"Don't be afraid. Only believe, and she will live."

It was obvious Jairus wanted to believe; what loving father would not? However, wanting and doing are two very different things.

We continued on, arriving at the synagogue official's home in a few minutes' time.

It was a large house. The mourners were already gathering on the spacious lawn. Jairus, accompanied by Jesus, led the way to his front door, closely followed by the twelve of us. The larger following remained in the street. And then something unexpected happened. Jesus turned to us and asked Simon, James, and me to come with him into the house. Jairus escorted us through the main room, where there must have been at least thirty people, probably close family and friends, all in a state of shock, many of them weeping. We came to a closed door, the little girl's room. Jairus opened it. Inside were his wife and several other people, including two physicians. The daughter's lifeless body lay on her bed. James, Simon, and I hesitated at the threshold, reluctant to follow. Jesus turned toward us, motioning that we were to enter.

"Everyone is to leave this room except the child's mother and father, my three friends, and me," Jesus said.

There was an audible gasp. The physicians, especially, seemed incredulous and made no move to leave.

Jairus told them to get out; he then told everyone else in the house to leave immediately.

Jesus walked over to the child's bedside and bowed his head for a moment.

The five of us who remained with him, even the mother, who had been softly sobbing, were perfectly still and quiet.

"Young girl, I say to you, arise!" Jesus said.

We were all looking intently at the child.

She opened her eyes, raised her head, sat up, and stared—first at her parents, then at Jesus, and then at the three of us. Of course, she clearly recognized her mother and father, but who were these strange men? She climbed out of bed and stood up, looking the picture of health and vitality.

As their grief turned to rapture, her parents flew to her side, throwing their arms around her, their tears of sorrow now tears of joy. The girl asked her mother what was happening, but she was too overcome with emotion even to try to explain the events of the past several hours to her daughter now. Her father simply said that this man, gesturing toward Jesus, had saved her life.

The girl looked at Jesus, smiled, walked over, and embraced and thanked him. She then asked him who we were.

"Those are my closest friends," Jesus said. "Simon, James, and John."

She was pleased to make our acquaintance, and we chatted with her for a few moments.

While we were speaking with her, I heard Jesus ask her parents to keep confidential what had occurred and to give her something to eat.

Despite his request, word of this event spread throughout the region within days.

These two incidents happened on the fifth day of the week. Tomorrow, the sixth day—preparation day—we would journey to Nazareth. Jesus was going to speak in the synagogue in his hometown on the Sabbath. This surprised us. It had only been a few days since the unfortunate encounter with his family. I wondered why he would go there.

James and I spent the night with our family. As you will recall, we share a bedroom. Shortly after we had blown out the candles and gotten into our beds, I asked James what he thought about Jesus asking Simon and the two of us to accompany him into the room of the once-dead child—leaving the nine others behind. Moreover, what did he make of Jesus introducing the three of us as his closest friends?

James took so long to reply that I wondered if he had fallen asleep and had not even heard me. Finally, he responded by saying that he considered it a great honor and a sign of Jesus's recognition of our value to his ministry.

That was how I had interpreted his words and actions too. I told James I agreed with him, adding that I thought we would both have important positions in his new kingdom.

We would be live to regret those words.

Nazareth was about twenty miles southwest of Capernaum. Walking at a normal pace, stopping every few miles to rest and once for a midday meal, would take about eight hours. That meant we could leave after sunrise and comfortably reach our destination before sundown. Between the inner and outer circle of Jesus's followers, there were about forty of us in all. There were not many villages on our route, and their inhabitants did not seem to notice us. Because Jesus was not on good terms with his family—or, rather, because they were not on good terms with him—we would not be staying the night in their home. Instead, we slept under the stars, at the edge of the village.

At midmorning, we walked the short distance to the synagogue. On the way, I observed the village; it was the first time I had been to Nazareth. It was not nearly as clean or prosperous looking as most of the other towns and villages I had seen in Galilee, and it was certainly no match for Capernaum. I did not wonder at Jesus's choosing to live elsewhere. It was not an inviting place—no one we encountered had spoken to us or even acknowledged our presence. I hoped we would not be here long. We arrived at the synagogue, a building that was just about as attractive and inviting as the rest of the town. It was nearly full; we could not all sit together, but we were able to find enough available seats here and there. I looked around and saw Jesus's entire family—mother, brothers, and sisters—sitting together. No one was at the lectern. The congregants were sitting quietly, some praying, some reading.

Jesus, the last of us to locate a seat, spied one on the front bench.

As he made his way down the center aisle, an unfriendly murmur rose from the audience. Jesus sat down and bowed his head in prayer. The commotion ceased. When he stood up and walked to the lectern, the angry grumbling resumed. He stood there quietly, passing his eyes over the congregation, which, after a moment of that determined gaze, fell silent.

He then began to teach. We had heard him teach the same message many times, and I never tired of it. God's new kingdom has arrived. He quoted Moses and the prophets, Scriptures that promised a renewal, a new beginning for Israel and her people. He taught with authority, not timidity; boldness, not caution; power, not frailty; hope, not despair. His listeners that day were impressed but not convinced; stirred but not changed.

When he sat down, the murmurs started up again.

One man, in a voice heard above the clamor, asked, "Isn't this man the *carpenter's* son?" Pointing to Jesus's family, he said, "Aren't they his mother and his brothers and sisters?"

No one answered.

Looking at Jesus's family, the man then added sarcastically, "You must be very proud of him!"

Jesus stood up and turned around.

The spectators fell silent again, waiting to see how he would respond to that insult.

"A prophet is not without honor—except in his own country—in his own village—and among his own family."

Hearing these words, especially the word *prophet* in that context, the boorish crowd turned into an angry one.

There was nothing to be gained by lingering, and we departed at once.

Neither Jesus nor his family attempted any contact that day.

No one followed us as we departed Nazareth; it was just Jesus, the twelve of us, and the small band of faithful followers who had accompanied him from Capernaum. We all walked a short distance from Nazareth to a pleasant grove of trees and ate our midday meal in peace and quiet, among trusted and pleasant friends. It was a relief to be out of Nazareth; I never wanted to see that place again.

Andrew, who was probably the least talkative of the disciples—no wonder, his brother Simon usually dominated every conversation, except when Jesus was talking—had a question.

"Master, no one in Nazareth came to you for healing. Why not?"

"Because there is so little faith in Nazareth. I cannot heal those who lack faith. Faith is a prerequisite for healing, both physical and spiritual; they go hand in hand."

"That's very sad, isn't it?"

"Yes, it is tragic. That's why I have often commented on the faith of those I have healed."

Andrew's question reinforced my observation that he was one of the more sensitive, thoughtful, and caring of our number. Simply put, he loved people. He seemed genuinely distressed about human suffering, and he rejoiced in the healing touch of Jesus in relieving that suffering.

It was a little more than a year since I had met and become a follower of Jesus. During that time, I'd had the privilege of seeing him in a variety of widely different circumstances dealing with all types of people. Some loved him, some hated him; some praised him, some condemned him; some accepted him, some rejected him, even his own family. How did he respond to these vicissitudes? I never saw him in a state of elation or dejection. He was the most steadfast, even-tempered man I ever knew.

CHAPTER 16

The next day, we returned to Capernaum, arriving in the early evening. Jesus asked us to meet him the following morning, at Matthew's house. By this time, I considered the reformed tax collector one of my best friends. Whenever we were in my hometown and Jesus wanted to meet with us privately, he chose Matthew's home—the only one large enough to accommodate us all.

That morning, Jesus, together with our host and fellow disciple, welcomed us.

The Master then asked us to all to sit around the large dining table. He said he had an announcement to make.

"For a while now, we've been together, traveling throughout Galilee and announcing the good news of God's kingdom," Jesus began. "We also went to Jerusalem last spring for Passover, and, more recently, across the lake to Gadara. However, for the time being, the epicenter of my work—our work—is here in Galilee. There remain many villages and towns in our province which have not yet heard the good news. It is time for you twelve to go out and take that good news to those who haven't heard it. You will be heralds of God's kingdom. You are to exhort them to repent of their sins and prepare for the kingdom of heaven. You will receive the power to heal people's afflictions, even leprosy, and to cast out evil spirits, in the Father's name. This is to be a journey of faith: You are to make only the most basic provision for your needs. Don't take money or extra food or clothing; rely on the hospitality of good people everywhere you go. When you enter a town or village, make inquiries as to which are the God-fearing families in that place. Find them; they will invite you in and provide your food and shelter, but don't ask them for money—the gospel you bring is free! If you enter a town or a house that is not receptive to you, leave it, and shake the dust off your feet. It will be worse for that place than it was for Sodom and Gomorrah. Your mission is to preach to the lost sheep of the house of Israel, not to the Gentiles—not now. You are to talk to people individually, in households, and in small groups and large. If the town has a synagogue, go there and teach on the Sabbath. I'm sending you out as sheep in the midst of wolves, and you will encounter some wolves; they will a treat you with contempt. Do not let that worry or discourage you. You are to be as harmless as doves and as wise as serpents."

The Master then gave us our assignments. We were to go in pairs, each pair visiting four towns or villages, places we had not heretofore visited; or, in some cases, places we had just passed through. This is how he paired us: Matthew and Simon the Zealot; Simon and Thaddeus; Andrew and Thomas; James and Philip; Nathanael and James the Younger; Judas and me.

He asked if we understood his instructions and if we had any questions.

"When do we leave?" Philip asked excitedly.

"Tomorrow morning."

"That soon!" Philip gasped.

"Yes. Are there any other questions?"

Thomas spoke up. "Master, are you sure we're ready for this? I certainly have doubts as to my ability to accomplish the mission you have described. Don't you think we need more time, more training?"

"No, Thomas, I don't. All of you have been with me for many months now. I believe you *are* ready. If I didn't, I wouldn't send you. You and the kingdom message you preach will be accepted by some and rejected by others, just as has happened with me. As you know, even my own family does not yet accept me. Don't let that dishearten you. I urge you to pray earnestly to the Father, for strength, for the right words to say—the ones that will have the most beneficial impact on those you meet. He will answer your prayers. Again, that doesn't mean you will always have success in every village or with every person to whom you present the good news. Remember, you are all not only my disciples, my followers; you are also my apostles, those I send out. Be back in Capernaum no later than six weeks from now. God go with you."

I'm not sure why the Master paired us the way he did. I thought he might send my brother and me together; perhaps Simon with his brother, Andrew; and Philip and Nathanael, since they were good friends. To me, the most surprising pairing was that of Matthew and Simon the Zealot. Although Simon had shown no bitterness toward Matthew, the former tax collector and his natural enemy, I still thought it odd. However, Jesus had so far demonstrated that he knew us well, perhaps better than we knew ourselves.

We all left the next morning on our mission journey. The four towns and villages assigned to each team were geographically convenient; the distance between one place and the next was usually just a few miles. I liked Judas; he and I worked well together. Our successes and failures were what Jesus had predicted: the successes exhilarating, the failures disappointing. I was thankful that he had prepared us for these vicissitudes. I kept thinking about how even-tempered Jesus was, and that helped me to stay focused on our task and weather the disappointments. We always found some family in each location who welcomed us into their home, feeding us and providing shelter and encouragement. And God did give us power to heal and cast out demons. However, as the Master had told us, the healings and exorcisms depended on the recipients' faith.

Our most memorable experience happened in the village of Cana. The family with whom Judas and I stayed had a son who had been married a few months before we met the Master. When the father learned that we were disciples of Jesus and it was he who had sent us on this mission, with great delight he told us an amazing story. At his son's wedding reception, he had miscalculated the quantity of wine that would be needed, and his steward informed him that the wine supply was exhausted. He panicked; this was an unforgivable oversight. What was he to do? Among the wedding guests was a family from Nazareth. Their widowed mother overheard this conversation and went to find her eldest son. She brought him to the father and the steward, and suggested that they do whatever he told them to do. The son asked if there were any large jars available, and, if so, to bring them to him. Several such jars were brought to him, and he asked that they be filled with water. He then touched each of the jars and asked the father to sample their contents.

The man finished the story by exclaiming, "It was the most delicious wine I ever tasted! That man saved the reception, and I avoided great embarrassment! His name was Jesus."

We all arrived back in Capernaum within a few days of each other, no later than the appointed time.

Matthew invited Jesus to join the twelve of us at his house for supper.

After our meal, Jesus asked us to tell him about our missions. We enthusiastically reported on the successes and also related what we had learned from the failures. Jesus listened attentively and asked many questions.

Judas and I decided not to bring up the water-into-wine story, thinking it might make Jesus feel sad about his estranged family.

After our stories were told, Simon asked Jesus what he had done during our absence.

Jesus replied that he had visited some of the villages that he had not assigned to us, but he provided no details. He finished the evening by asking us to meet him at his house an hour after sunrise the next morning.

The following morning, Jesus led us down to the lake and the now-familiar bay. Once again, the same boat was waiting for us. I had discussed this mysterious boat with my colleagues on more than one occasion; none of them could explain the regularity of its presence either. We cast off, put up the sail, and caught a light but favorable breeze.

Simon, who was piloting the boat, asked Jesus where he wanted to go.

I hoped it would not be back to Gadara!

"Set the sail for Bethsaida," the Master replied.

I breathed a sigh of relief. Our destination was up the coast about five or six miles, and our course kept us near the shoreline.

Andrew pointed toward land and told us all to look. Several hundred people were keeping pace with us, and with every step, they were joined by many others. There was little doubt they knew Jesus was in the boat, and they wanted to go wherever he was going. By the time we neared Bethsaida, there were thousands of them. I felt sorry for Jesus. He had probably wanted to get away from the crowds that now followed him almost everywhere he went, waking him early in the morning and keeping him awake late into the night. But his compassion always exceeded his exhaustion. When we landed and tied up the boat, the multitude was waiting.

Jesus led the throng to a hill that gently sloped up and away from the village. As was his wont, he began to heal those who needed healing, whatever their afflictions. He then ascended a little higher, asked the multitude to sit, and began to teach them.

He finished speaking in the early afternoon, past the usual hour of the midday meal. I was hungry; Jesus and my fellow disciples and the crowd were surely hungry too.

The Master turned to Philip and asked him where sufficient food could be obtained, not only for us but for the throng as well.

When we had departed Capernaum that morning, Philip, not knowing what Jesus's plan for the day was, had made no provision for a meal for us, let alone thousands of others.

"Master, we have no food," he said. "I would need to return to the village to buy some. We have enough money to provide for ourselves, but not for this crowd. That would take thousands of denarii!"

Judas confirmed that the treasury would not support such an expenditure.

Andrew spoke up. "There is a lad here who has a small basket with five barley loaves and two fish; but that would feed only two or three people. You should send them away so they can buy their own food."

"No, Andrew, we will feed them," Jesus said. "Bring the boy's basket to me. And then, have the people sit down in groups of fifty to a hundred; the rest of you can assist with this task. Ask as many of our regular followers as you need to help you."

We were stunned by this fantastic demand; but we did as Jesus said. Fortunately, there were nearly a hundred additional regular followers in the audience that day, and we were able to quickly assemble the large crowd into smaller, more manageable groups. I glanced at Jesus once during this time and saw him holding the lad's basket, looking up to the heavens, his lips moving. Our work completed, the twelve of us returned to the Master's side. There were more than a hundred separate groups—well over five thousand people—waiting to eat. How would this be possible? But, what's this?! Where there had been one basket before, there were now scores of baskets filled to the brim: half of them with barley loaves, the other half with fish! Jesus's regular followers joined us in distributing the bounty. When we had finished, they all—men, women, and children—had had their fill. (*God blesses and feeds those who hunger and gives drink to those who thirst for Him and His righteousness.*)

That day, Jesus fed both their physical and spiritual hunger. He asked us to gather up any uneaten food so that it could be given to those in need in Bethsaida. As the twelve of us passed through the crowd, we heard many people speaking excitedly about Jesus being be the One, the longed-for Messiah—who else could perform such a miracle? They also said that Jesus would lead the rebellion and drive the hated Romans out of Israel. This kind of talk excited me; excited all his followers. We would be an integral part of his coming kingdom! What glory, what honor would be ours!

My fanciful thoughts were interrupted by the sight of a score of men—perhaps even more than that—shouting excitedly and rushing toward Jesus, who at that moment was standing alone. Simon, James, and Andrew also saw what was happening, and the four of us ran to Jesus's side. These men, speaking loudly and acting aggressively, were insisting that Jesus be made king immediately, and, if he did not acquiesce, they would take him by force to accomplish their purpose. I thought Jesus should be made king too, but not like this.

Jesus did not say a word; he simply turned around and walked away, over the brow of the hill.

Simon, who could be intimidating when he chose to be, took the lead in dissuading these firebrands from pursuing Jesus. Sufficiently cowed, they turned around and retreated down the hill with the rest of the multitude. The four of us then walked in the direction Jesus had taken, quickly reaching the hilltop. He was nowhere in sight; what were we to do? Simon said that Jesus knew how to take care of himself, and suggested that we should follow his instructions and distribute the leftover food to the needy in Bethsaida. We all agreed. The other disciples, after Simon had explained what had happened, agreed as well.

You will recall that early in Jesus's ministry, more than a year before, there had been three incidents regarding food baskets: one completely empty, one nearly empty, and one with too little food to feed a larger number of people than anticipated. What happened on that hillside near Bethsaida was like those incidents, only on a much larger scale. Each was a miracle: Three of them small, one very large; but, nonetheless, all miracles.

When we had finished distributing the surplus food, we went to where we had left the boat, half-expecting Jesus to be there waiting for us; he was not. James suggested we wait for him until sunset, adding that even if he had not arrived by then, there was a full moon, the sky was clear, the distance short, and we could easily navigate our way back to the small bay. We agreed. Even with Simon's assurance that Jesus could take care of himself, it was clear that we were all apprehensive for his safety. It was winter, and the sun would set within an hour. Alas, he did not return; reluctantly, we left without him.

CHAPTER 17

We cast off, hoisted the sail, and caught a very light breeze that provided only minimal assistance on our journey to the southwest toward Capernaum. Rather than the route along the coast we had taken earlier in the day on our way to Bethsaida, we chose the more direct open-water course on the way back, but we were never more than a mile from shore. Within a few minutes, the breeze was gone; the sail, no longer of any use, was lowered, and we took turns pulling the oars. In another few minutes, the wind returned but this time against us, making for slow going. The headwind stiffened and grew stronger, more forceful, until we were making little, if any, forward progress. The attendant waves made things even more difficult. This was a minor gale compared with the one described earlier, so we did not fear for our lives; nevertheless, we were quickly becoming exhausted. We debated among ourselves if we should head for shore and wait until conditions were more favorable, but we decided to keep going. We rowed for more than five hours, and I doubt that we progressed even halfway to our destination, the Bay of Parables. At one point, we were within a hundred yards or so of the shoreline, as it turned out in the area of Gennesarat, about three miles short of Capernaum. The sky was still clear and the moon full, and we could see someone walking along the shore, going in the same direction as we. His pace was quicker than ours was; we could have walked home by now!

Thaddaeus was the first to see this, exclaiming, "That man is walking *toward* us! He appears to be walking *on top* of the water!"

Judas and I, who were manning the oars at that moment, turned to look. We stopped rowing, and I almost dropped my oar in the water. He, or it, *was* walking on the water. I say "it," because some of us believed the figure to be an apparition. We were scared out of our wits. What we supposed to be a ghost was now about fifty feet from our boat and walking straight toward us. I was not the only one shaking in fear.

And then we heard a familiar voice. *It was Jesus!*

"Be of good cheer!" he said. "It is I; don't be afraid!"

"If it's really you, ask me to come and join you," replied Simon. "Come on, then!"

Simon really was the bravest of us all! He stepped gingerly over the gunwale and—*walked . . . on . . . water!* We were all dumbfounded. The winds were still blowing and the waves were still white capped as he made his way toward Jesus, who stood waiting for him.

Suddenly, there was stronger gust of wind. Simon, who had kept his eyes steadily on Jesus up until that moment, looked down. He began to sink into the water!

"Lord, save me!" Simon cried desperately.

As he was going under—only his big right hand visible above the water—Jesus reached out his own hand and, taking firm hold of Simon's, lifted his body completely to the surface. The two now stood face-to-face on top of the water.

"Why did your faith fail you? Why did you begin to doubt?" Jesus asked him.

Simon, usually at no loss for words, could not find any.

Immediately, the winds ceased, and there was a dead calm.

Jesus and Simon stepped into the boat together. Nobody said anything.

I was still shaken by what I had seen. For the second time in two weeks, Jesus had mastered the earth's physical elements. How was it possible for a mere man to have this kind of power? There was only one plausible explanation: Jesus was *not* a mere man; he was something else, something more—but what, or who?

Within a few minutes, we had drifted to the shore at Gennesarat—only halfway to our original destination, but we were too tired to go any farther. We beached and tied up the boat. Our mental excitement overwhelmed by our physical exhaustion, we all quickly fell asleep in the boat.

The inviting aroma of broiling fish awakened us. Jesus had somehow acquired several fish and was roasting them over a fire. None of us had eaten anything since the miracle meal of the previous day, and we were famished. The nocturnal event was not discussed; no one asked Jesus how he could do what he did. We all made small talk. That is, all but Jesus. He said that the boat had come ashore exactly where he wanted us to go.

After breakfast, we followed Jesus into the village. It was as if the entire population knew he was coming: All over Gennesarat, everywhere we walked, the lame and otherwise afflicted were out—some on beds or cots—waiting for him to pass by and heal them, which he gladly did. Many of them, just in touching his tunic, were instantly healed.

As we walked along, observing Jesus ministering to these suffering ones, Nathanael and I fell into conversation. You will recall that Nathanael was a serious student of Israel's ancient writings, our Holy Scriptures. He had deep knowledge and clear understanding of the texts of our patriarchs and prophets. He quoted from the first chapter of the first book written by our most honored prophet, Moses: the book of Genesis, the creation story. Every Jew knew these words by heart. The relevant passage that he wanted me to consider, in light of the miracles of Jesus that pertained to his power over nature—calming the storms, walking on water—was this: "God blessed Adam and Eve and said to them 'Be fruitful and multiply: fill the earth and *subdue the earth and have dominion over the fish of the sea and the birds of the air and over other living things on the earth.*'"

"If God gave that kind of power to Adam and Eve, the first humans," Nathanael said, "don't you think He could give it to any human He chooses to have it?"

"Yes," I replied. "But that was in the garden of Eden, before Adam and Eve had sinned. Would God give that kind of power to a human being in this sin-filled world?"

"Well, he gave it to Moses, who parted the Red Sea, allowing the children of Israel to cross over on dry land. John, I believe it's possible that, with Jesus, this power is innate."

"So, you think he was born with it?"

"I do."

Reports of the feeding of the five thousand spread like wildfire throughout the region. Jesus was more popular, sought out by more people, than ever before.

Early the next morning, we sailed the short distance home to Capernaum, leaving the boat tied up in the Bay of Parables, where perhaps fifty people were waiting for Jesus.

Several men ran up to him, one of whom exclaimed, "Rabbi, we finally found you! We thought you might come here."

I recognized some of these men as having been on the hillside near Bethsaida the day before, one of those who had wanted to crown Jesus king.

Jesus said to the man, "I'm telling you the truth: You searched for me, not because you believed my teaching, but because you were fed. You hunger for the bread that satisfies your physical needs; it keeps you alive for a few hours, and then you are hungry again. Why don't you hunger for the bread of heaven that endures to everlasting life, which I will gladly give you? That is the true work that God the Father has given me."

"Rabbi, how can *we* do God's true work too?"

"It's very simple: believe in the one God has sent."

With that, the man and the others turned and walked away.

Only the twelve of us followed Jesus the short distance to Capernaum.

It was the preparation day, and we spent it with Jesus, in Matthew's house.

Jesus said he had something to tell us. His demeanor was solemn.

"Tomorrow, we are going to the synagogue here in Capernaum," he began. "I have some things to say to the people there, and to you as well. Some of what I say will shock and confuse them, and it will shock and confuse you too. Neither they nor you will understand much of what I say. For the present time, that's the way it must be. My ministry has reached a point that some of my teachings must be cryptic in the same way some of my parables have been. I have explained those parables to you, but, for the time being, I will not explain to you or to anyone else what I will say tomorrow. I ask you to trust me in this."

None of us asked questions; his last few words had foreclosed any.

Jesus asked us to meet him at his house the next morning, from where we would depart for the synagogue. It was a quiet walk, just the thirteen of us. Entering the building, we found it completely filled and completely silent; there was not a single place to sit. No one was at the lectern. The twelve of us stood in the back. Jesus walked up the center aisle, mounted the steps, moved behind the lectern, and stood there quietly, looking out over the audience. The silence was deafening. He stood there for several moments, saying nothing.

And then the same man who had confronted Jesus near the bay the day before stood up and, in a voice heard by all present, challenged him.

"What sign do you show us that we may believe that the Father has sent you?" His tone was both sarcastic and skeptical.

What sign! I thought. *Jesus has provided* hundreds *of signs: healings, exorcisms, feeding the multitude just two days before!*

Jesus answered this question in a way that most might not have considered an answer at all.

"When Moses and the children of Israel were wandering in the desert with nothing to eat, manna—bread from heaven—was provided for them, and it saved and sustained their physical lives for years. Moses didn't provide that bread; God did. My Father gives you the true bread from heaven. That bread is he whom God has already sent: the one who gives his life for you."

"Master, give *us* this bread!" someone shouted.

Several others seconded this request.

"*I am* that Bread of Life! Those who come to me shall never hunger, and those who believe in me shall never thirst. You have seen me, and you still don't believe. However, those who do believe will come to me and will forever be with me. I came from heaven, not to do my will, but to do the will of Him who sent me. No one has seen the Father except the one He has sent. All those the Father gives me will gain everlasting life; they will rise up on the last day. God invites all to his kingdom, but his invitation must be accepted."

Jesus then paused.

At this point, the murmuring started. I could not understand what people were saying, but I was sure the words "I am" and "I came from heaven" angered them. *I am* was one of the ways in which God referred to Himself, and *I came from heaven* could be interpreted as a claim to divinity. Frankly, these words shocked me, too.

Immediately, several people walked out of the synagogue.

"Stop murmuring; if you've got something to say, say it to me," demanded Jesus.

Those remaining quieted down, and Jesus continued.

"The bread I give to you is my flesh, my blood, my very life. I give it freely, without reservation, for the life of the whole world."

The muttering started again, and Jesus paused.

"How can you give us your flesh, you blood, and your life? How can that save us?" someone near the back shouted.

"I'm telling you the truth: If you don't eat my flesh, the flesh of the Son of Man, and drink my blood, you have no real lasting life within you! However, if you do, you will have everlasting life; you will rise up at the last day. You will live in me, and I will live in you. The Father has sent me; I live in the Father. Those who accept me will live in me."

Those words about his flesh and blood stunned everyone into silence. Those words, in particular, must have been what Jesus had warned us about the day before.

113

The synagogue emptied quickly. No one approached Jesus; no one followed us.

Jesus and the twelve of us went to Matthew's house.

Judas and I were walking side by side several paces behind Jesus and the others when he whispered a question to me.

"What do you think about what Jesus said regarding eating his flesh and drinking his blood?"

Before I could answer, Jesus suddenly stopped, turned to us, and spoke as earnestly as I had ever heard him speak about anything up to that time.

"Does what I said offend you? What if you see me ascend up to where I came from? It is the *spirit* of the man that is important, not the flesh. The flesh is nothing. The *words* that I speak to you are life. But many don't believe my words, especially what I said in synagogue today. They have left me; most of them we will never see again. Will you go away too?"

Simon wasted no time in answering him.

"Lord! To whom shall we go? *You* have the words of eternal life! You are God's Holy One! We all know it! We all believe it!"

I thought Simon's heartfelt and emphatic declaration would reassure and cheer Jesus, but it did not.

"Have I not chosen you twelve? Yet, one of you is an accuser."

Did I hear Jesus correctly? Did he just say that *one of us*—his chosen *apostles,* his closest *friends*—was an *accuser?* "Accuser" was another name for Satan—the Devil, Beelzebub, Lucifer! How could that be possible? We were all reduced to silence. I quickly glanced around at my eleven colleagues; we were all looking at each other, looks of bewilderment on our faces. I knew them all, some better than others, admittedly. *One was my brother, James!* It was beyond my understanding that *any* of us could be remotely like Satan. Some of us had known one another for years. In the last year, we had spent almost every waking hour in each other's company. We had been through good times and bad times together: thrilling times, terrifying times, and heartwarming times. We had learned so much from Jesus: how to pray, how to heal, how to preach, how to trust, how to share, how to love. Now we learned from him that there was an *accuser,* a *traitor,* among us. Jesus had never been wrong about anything, but I hoped he was wrong about this.

CHAPTER 18

We spent the next week in and around Capernaum. Every day, there seemed to be more Pharisees and lawyers (*Judeans,* as we came to call them) from Jerusalem, who shadowed Jesus, looking for opportunities to catch him in some inconsistency or—in their minds—prohibited behavior. There were even more of Herod's spies about too. We knew this because Joanna, the former wife of his steward, recognized them.

One day, as we were about to eat our midday meal, several of these Judeans accosted Jesus, demanding to know why he and his followers did not perform the required ceremonial hand washing before eating meals. Strictly observant Jews, especially Pharisees and legal experts, went to great lengths in ritual hand washing and the cleaning of eating utensils. Not doing so, they taught, made the food eaten unclean in God's sight. The majority of the Galilean common folk did not observe these strictures, however.

"Why do you and your disciples ignore the tradition of the elders?" the spokesman of the Judeans wanted to know.

There were several dozen curious onlookers standing about, waiting to see how Jesus would handle this thorny situation. His response at first confused and then infuriated the Judeans, to the great delight of the bystanders.

"You men are hypocrites!" Jesus said. "Isaiah prophesied about you when he wrote, 'You honor God with your lips but your hearts are far from Him. You worship God in vain, replacing His commandments with the commandments of men. You elevate your traditions above God's holy Law.' I will give you an example: The fifth of the Ten Commandments says, 'Honor you father and your mother that your days on the earth may be long.' Nevertheless, you've found a way to get around that. Rather than providing for their old age, you dedicate that money to the temple, absolving yourself from further obligation to them. You have not only abandoned your parents in their time of need, you have broken the plain commandment of God in the process. As to the ritual of hand washing: What goes into a man's mouth does not defile his body. However, the words that come out of his mouth—if they are prideful, wicked, deceitful, envious, treacherous, or slanderous—the *words a man speaks* make him unclean. If you have ears, then hear."

From the looks on their faces, the Judeans were horrified at hearing what they must have considered gross insults to themselves and the way they practiced their faith. But, for the time being, they had no rejoinder, and simply walked away.

That evening at Matthew's house, before we sat down to supper, we were all out on the porch discussing the confrontation with the Judeans. Simon spoke up, directing a question to Jesus.

"Master, you must know you offended the lawyers and Pharisees today. Why did you do that?"

"Every plant that has *not* been planted by my Father will be uprooted," Jesus replied. "Have nothing to do with the Pharisees or the so-called legal experts. They are blind guides, and those who allow themselves to be led by them are blind too. You know what happens when the blind lead the blind, don't you? They both fall into a ditch. Stay as far away from them as you can."

After supper, Simon and Andrew departed to their house, James and I to our parents' house, and Jesus to his own house; the rest stayed with Matthew.

Before going our separate ways, Jesus asked us to meet him at his house late the following morning. It was the Sabbath, but he told us we would not be attending synagogue in Capernaum.

I was relieved; our last synagogue experience there had been both tense and unpleasant.

Jesus went on to tell us that, instead, we would travel the short distance—less than a Sabbath day's journey—to the same grove of trees we had twice visited earlier in his ministry.

We arrived at Jesus's house at the appointed hour. Standing perhaps a hundred feet away in the street were the same lawyers and Pharisees Jesus had embarrassed the day before. What were they doing here? I supposed they had recovered from their humiliation and were not giving up their quest to discredit Jesus among his countrymen.

Jesus soon came outside, and we began our journey up the gentle slope away from the Sea of Galilee. The unwelcome Judeans followed us, maintaining the same distance interval as usual for them: close enough to observe us but not to hear our conversations.

"I suppose you know we're being followed," James the Younger said to Jesus.

"Yes," Jesus replied. "By the same men I chastised yesterday."

"What do you think they're up to?"

"We'll soon find out."

We walked perhaps a few hundred yards. Just off our path was a grain field with some stalks of ripened wheat, unusual so early in the growing season. It had been a few hours since breakfast, and my brother, James, suggested we help ourselves to some of the grain, eating it to tide us over until dinnertime. We were friends of the field's owner, and knew he would not mind. Besides, such small-scale harvesting—called *gleaning*—was legal and proper in our culture, especially for travelers and the poor. Several of the other disciples joined James and me. We rubbed the stalks between our hands and ate the delicious grain. While we were thus lingering, the lawyers and Pharisees caught up to us and made a beeline toward Jesus.

"Why do you let your disciples break the Sabbath by harvesting and threshing grain on God's holy day?" demanded their mouthpiece, the same man who had confronted Jesus the previous day.

Jesus answered by telling them a story.

"What? Haven't you read the Scriptures? I'm speaking about the story of David and his men when they were fleeing from King Saul's henchmen. On the Sabbath, tired and hungry, they went to a priest and asked for bread. The only bread available was the holy bread of the Presence, eaten only by the priests. Nevertheless, the priest gave them the sacred bread, which they ate. What David and his men did was clearly unlawful, but it was not a sin because it achieved a greater good. It is the same with the Sabbath! Don't you know that the Sabbath was made for man? Man was not made for the Sabbath. Therefore, the Son of Man is Lord also of the Sabbath."

The Pharisee had no comeback for that. He and his fellow travelers turned around and walked back toward Capernaum.

For the second time in as many days, Jesus, using the plain words of Scripture, had demolished their arguments, based as they were on man-made traditions. These were enjoyable and remarkable sights to behold, and we were all smiling broadly. My admiration for Jesus was greater than ever.

"Come on, men," Jesus said. "You see those trees up ahead. That's our special place. We're going to have our dinner there, and we'll talk about the events of yesterday and today."

We walked the remaining quarter-mile or so to the grove. It was a pleasant Sabbath afternoon: the grass was green from the spring rains, and the new leaves on the trees provided just enough shade for a relaxing respite, away from the noise and the crowds of the villages, away from the Judeans. Jesus seemed happy to be in this quiet place, happy to be with us. We enjoyed a hearty meal of bread and dried fish. Nearby, there was a spring with plenty of cool water.

"Do any of you have questions about my response to the lawyers and Pharisees, their criticism of us for not following their rules in ceremonial hand washing?"

"Aren't the Pharisees and the legal experts the only ones who make an issue of such practices?" Simon asked. "I was not raised to perform those rites; most other ordinary folk in Galilee weren't either. I have not seen you washing your hands in that manner."

"The Pharisees and the lawyers and many other Judeans who are influenced by them do perform those rites; you'll notice it when we return to Jerusalem for Passover. There is nothing intrinsically wrong with those ceremonial hand washings. A problem arises when those external cleansings become more important than, and a substitute for, keeping the heart clean. It is much more important to have a clean heart and a clean mind, and to have pure thoughts and motives, than to have clean hands. As I told the Judeans yesterday, their man-made traditions, which they jealousy guard and adhere to in every minute detail, pale to insignificance when compared with the commandments of God, which they have found ways to distort or ignore," Jesus said, pausing before asking, "What about their criticism of some of you men harvesting and threshing grain on the Sabbath? What do you think of that?"

My brother, James, spoke up. "It was my idea, so if there was any Sabbath breaking, it was my fault."

Jesus chuckled. "James, I defended what you did! Do you think I would have done so had I agreed with those stiff-necked hypocrites? Look, the purpose of God's Sabbath is not to burden us; its purpose is to remind us of His creation, and also to provide us with a day of rest from the cares of this world. Speaking of the cares of this world, we're all going to take a few days away from our usual work. We are on our way to a place where nobody knows us. Somewhere they have never even heard of me. Let us all get a good night's rest, and we will be on our way in the morning. We'll make a stop in Cana on the way, and then we'll journey on to the Mediterranean coast."

The Mediterranean coast! I had never been there. There were few, if any, Jews there; certainly no Pharisees or lawyers to harass us. Jesus was right: no one there would know him or us. This would be a real change, and a welcome one, indeed.

We set forth the next morning. It was fifteen miles to the village of Cana, and Jesus said he wanted to be there at midday; our trek took about five hours. You will recall that Jesus had sent Judas and me to Cana as one of the stops on our mission tour several weeks before. Of the four places where we taught and healed, Cana was our favorite.

The people there were friendly and receptive, especially the family that hosted us. Entering the village, Jesus led us straight to their house. Of course, they knew Jesus, and they remembered Judas and me. The family received us warmly, inviting us to share their midday meal and to stay the night. Jesus accepted both these generous offers.

At supper that evening, our host, Reuben, retold the story of Jesus turning water into wine at his son's wedding two years before. Our fellow disciples were surprised. (You'll also recall that Judas and I had decided not to share our knowledge of this event with them or with Jesus.)

The next morning, we headed west, toward the Mediterranean coast. On the way, I saw Mount Carmel, whose ridge, about five miles to the south, paralleled the road we were taking. We reached the small Syrian city of Ptolemais in the early afternoon. As I mentioned, this was my first time on the coast of the Mediterranean Sea. It was beautiful! The water was a shimmering blue-green color, and there was a gentle, most pleasant breeze coming off it. Except for the sea, Ptolemais was nothing special, quite similar in look to many towns in Galilee and Judea. After seeing the vastness of the Mediterranean Sea, I wondered why our comparatively small lake was also called a sea.

We ate our midday meal right on the beach. There was joviality and banter among us all, including Jesus. This really was a holiday. In late afternoon, as it got cooler, we built a fire out of driftwood and waited for the sun to set. I had never before seen a sunset over such a large body of water, and I enjoyed every minute of it.

Ptolemais had one public inn, near the boat dock. We ate supper there, and, fortunately for us, no boats were in port. The small establishment, which only had three rooms, was therefore able to accommodate all of us.

After breakfast the next morning, we continued north along the coast for the twenty-mile journey to the city of Tyre, on the indistinct border separating Syria from Phoenicia. Tyre was a real city, of perhaps a thousand or more inhabitants; it had a bustling port with several ships at anchor. I had never seen such large vessels. Since leaving Cana two days before, we had come upon only a few people on the road or along the beach; even in Ptolemais, we had encountered no more than two or three score of men, women, and children, not one of whom had recognized Jesus! In Tyre, our holiday came to an abrupt halt.

As we entered the city at midafternoon, Philip suggested we find an inn that could accommodate us for the night; he was concerned that if we waited until later, we would have to sleep outside.

Jesus agreed.

As we approached the first inn we came to and were about to enter its door, a middle-aged woman came from out of nowhere and tried to block our way. There ensued one of the most remarkable dialogues I have ever heard in my life.

Falling at Jesus's feet, she cried, "Have mercy on me, oh Lord, son of David! My daughter is grievously vexed with evil spirits, and I'm afraid they will kill her!" Her accent and appearance betrayed her Greek heritage.

Jesus did not even look down at this desperate mother. Completely ignoring her, he walked around her and proceeded toward the inn's front door. That in itself was surprising; I had never seen him ignore anybody.

The woman would not relent and continued to aggressively implore his help.

We were all embarrassed for her; obviously, Jesus did not want to be bothered. Neither did any of the rest us, and we urged him to send her away.

He ignored our advice, and she continued to beg his help.

Finally, he spoke to her.

"I have been sent *only* to the lost sheep of the house of *Israel*," Jesus told the woman.

I cringed. This was true, but harsh.

Nevertheless, her persistence was stunning, and she kept harassing him.

There then came another stinging rebuff from the Master.

"I will feed the children first, because it's not right to take the children's bread and give it to dogs."

This was not at all like Jesus!

We wanted him to send the woman away, not humiliate her like this, calling her a *dog!*

Nevertheless, she refused to be insulted or put off.

"Yes, Lord," she continued. "But the dogs eat the children's leftover crumbs which fall from their master's table."

My heart ached for her. I wanted to slink into a dark corner.

Jesus then dramatically reversed this distressing situation.

"Oh, woman, great is your faith! I will do what you asked. Go home to your daughter. She is healed."

While all this was happening, a crowd had gathered. They were very confused by this exchange, and when it was over, they dispersed and moved on.

We secured our rooms and had a good meal together.

After the meal, James and I, joined by Nathanael, went to the beach to experience another gorgeous sunset. While we were sitting there, talking about the woman's request and the puzzling things Jesus had said to her, Nathanael asked us a question.

"What if the real purpose of this journey is Jesus's conversation with that woman and what *we* might learn from it; not just the healing of her daughter or getting away from his tormentors or a restful holiday? What if, by his words to her, he wanted to teach *us* an important lesson?"

"You mean about salvation not just being for Jews only, but for Gentiles too?" James said.

"Yes," Nathanael replied. "What else could he have meant?"

The three of us pondered in silence for a few moments.

Nathanael then asked us another question. "Which do you think is the most important part of Jesus's ministry: healing people or teaching people?

"I think they go together," I replied.

They both agreed.

By this time, I had recognized Nathanael as perhaps the most thoughtful and insightful among us, and I could not resist asking him what he thought about Jesus's statement of a few days ago: that one of us twelve is an accuser, a traitor.

Nathanael did not reply immediately; he seemed to be in deep contemplation.

At last, he said, "I don't think Jesus would have ever said such a thing if it weren't true. As to which one of us he was referring to, I have no idea. But I think it's possible, even probable, that whoever the traitor is, he may not yet realize it himself."

"In other words, Nathanael, it could be any one of us," James said.

"Regrettably, I think it could."

The next morning, we continued our odyssey, walking north up the coast another twenty or so miles to the port city of Sidon. Nothing unusual happened that day, and the day after that, we would return to territory more familiar.

CHAPTER 19

From Sidon, we trekked southeast, thirty miles to the city of Caesarea Philippi, twenty-five miles north of the Sea of Galilee. This was my first visit to that region—the first visit for all of us, actually. It was a beautiful and prosperous area: fertile farmland irrigated by numerous springs whose waters flowed from Mount Hermon, the highest peak in Israel, fifteen miles to the north. The springs, which formed the headwaters of the Jordan River, converged in Caesarea Philippi. This was a beautiful city deriving the first half of its name from the Roman emperors, and the Romans had built, at the epicenter of the town, a pagan temple to honor each of their Caesars.

We arrived there in the early afternoon of the preparation day. Apparently, word of Jesus had not penetrated this region, as no one recognized him; the crowds, so common to the south, did not materialize. No one sought out Jesus for healing, and when we went to the local synagogue on the Sabbath, he did not teach. The following day, we headed farther south.

On the way, Jesus told us we were going to the Decapolis region, specifically to the town of Hippos. You will recall that it was in this general area that we had encountered the demon-possessed man whom Jesus had put to rights. In that instance, the locals had angrily insisted that we leave and not come back. Jesus assured us that we would pass to the east of that specific location on our way to Hippos, situated on the southeastern shore of the Sea of Galilee. As it was nearly a forty-mile walk, we left Caesarea Philippi at sunrise, reaching Hippos at sunset, exhausted.

The next morning, after breakfast, Jesus led us about a mile to the brow of a hill that sloped gently down to the lake. As we walked along, to our surprise—I mean to say to the surprise of the twelve of us, not Jesus, who seemed to be immune to surprises—we were joined by a large number of people. By the time we reached the spot where the Master wanted to go, the crowd had grown to several hundred. Jesus asked them all to sit down. Many, perhaps most, had come for healing, or brought their friends or relatives for that purpose, and Jesus spent most of this time ministering to them. Nevertheless, some of them wanted to hear what Jesus had to say, and he obliged them, announcing the good news of God's kingdom. Up to this time, the overwhelming majority of Jesus's listeners, including those he healed, had been Jews. This multitude was different. Owing to the ethnic makeup of the area, perhaps one in four of them were Gentiles of Greek descent. I began to further ponder whether the incident in Tyre, with the Gentile woman and the healing of her daughter, had been a preview of what was now happening in Hippos? In any event, Jesus treated everyone, Jew and Gentile alike, the same: teaching and healing everyone, without prejudice.

More and more people arrived throughout the day. By late afternoon, there were at least two thousand in the crowd. Some went home for the evening, but many stayed the night, sleeping on the grass; fortunately, the weather was mild. The next day, the number quickly grew: most of those who had departed the evening before returned in the morning, joined by a large number of newcomers. Philip estimated there were at least three thousand on this second day. Jesus continued to teach and heal well into the evening. Once again, many stayed the night, and even more people arrived the following morning, bringing the total to well above four thousand. Most of these people had brought food with them on the first day, and some of those who returned home at night brought food with them the next morning. But many of them had no food at all. Of course, Philip had supplied our needs; he was good at that. However, we did not have enough to share with this huge throng.

"I'm concerned about these people," Jesus said to us. "Some of them have been here for three days, and many have had little or nothing to eat during that time. They won't have enough strength to get home. We need to do something for them. Do we have enough food to feed them?"

"We don't even have enough food for our own needs, let along theirs," Philip answered. "I didn't plan on our staying in this one place for three whole days! I don't know what we can do for them."

Now, you are probably thinking, *What is wrong with these disciples? Have they forgotten that Jesus miraculously fed even more people than this just a few weeks ago?* And you would be right!

Jesus echoed what he had said less than a month before.

"Have the people sit down in manageable groups, and bring our food basket to me."

He prayed over its meager contents.

"Get some helpers from among the crowd, and pass the food around."

After they'd had their fill, Jesus asked the people to return to their homes, which they did, many praising God as they left.

There had been more than enough food for everyone.

Jesus and the twelve of us ate the leftovers.

The reaction of the people on the hillside near Hippos was the same as that of those on the hillside near Bethsaida not long before. This miracle feeding astonished them; they were astonished by Jesus's healing powers, and they were astonished by his kingdom message.

It was early afternoon when the last of the massive crowd departed; soon afterward, we finished our dinner. Jesus then led us down to the lakeshore, and there it was again, tied up and waiting for us: the mystery boat. We were no longer surprised by this; I think we would have been surprised if it had *not* been there.

"Set the sail for Magdala," the Master commanded.

Magdala was a small fishing village on the western shore of the Sea of Galilee, just a few miles south of Capernaum and a few miles north of Tiberius. We would be back in our home area, and I was happy about that.

On the way, Jesus said something that puzzled us.

"Be wary of the leaven of the Pharisees, the Sadducees, and the Herodians."

A brief explanation is required here. Leaven, or yeast, has a special meaning for Jews. When our ancestors fled the bondage of the Egyptians two millennia before, they had to leave in such haste that Moses told them to bake bread *without leaven* for the journey. It takes longer to bake leavened bread, and time was of the essence. It followed that leaven became a symbol of impurity. Our annual celebration commemorating the flight from Egypt was often called the Feast of Unleavened Bread. This should have given us a clue as to what Jesus meant by his warning, but it did not; hence our confusion, which he quickly ascertained. (By the way, Sadducees were another sect of ultrareligious Jews. They were not normally allies of the Pharisees, but their mutual hatred of Jesus had brought them together.)

"I'm not talking about literal bread," Jesus explained. "I'm talking about how the Pharisees, Sadducees, and Herodians pervert the plain words of Scripture, burdening it with all their man-made rules, substituting their own interpretation of the Holy Word of God. That's what I mean by *leaven*."

We then understood. Moreover, his warning was timely, considering what happened next.

In less than an hour, we had crossed to the other side of the lake, making landfall at Magdala. Before we could beach and tie up the boat, about a score of Pharisees and Sadducees, and even a few Herodians, descended upon us. How they knew we were coming, I cannot say. They looked angry, ready for confrontation, and they asked, once again, for a sign from Jesus. Who, exactly, was he, and what was the purpose of his kingdom-of-God-is-here message.

This is how Jesus answered their impudent questions.

"When it is evening, if the sky is red, you say it will be fair weather tomorrow. When it is morning, if the sky is red, you expect foul weather. *You hypocrites!* You can discern the signs in the sky but not the signs of the time! You are a wicked generation! You look for a sign, but none will be given to you except the sign of Jonah the prophet."

They had no reply to this searing denunciation, and so they walked away in silence.

Another note of explanation: Jonah was a famous prophet of God in the ancient Hebrew Scriptures. God sent him to the pagan city of Nineveh to warn its inhabitants that if they did not repent of their evil ways, His judgment would come upon them, in the form of the destruction of their city. The people of Nineveh did repent, and the city and its inhabitants survived.

We spent a few quiet days in our homes in nearby Capernaum, and then we were off again. Even though we had only recently been in Caesarea Philippi, Jesus told us we were returning there. We easily traversed the distance—under thirty miles—in a single day, but what a memorable day it was.

We stopped for our midday meal about halfway to our destination. When we had finished, Jesus asked us a question.

"You men have met and spoken with hundreds of people over the course of our time together. Tell me: who do those people think I am?"

"Some of the people I've spoken with think you are John the Baptist come back to life," Judas said.

"I've heard many people say they think you are Elijah come back to earth," Thaddaeus added.

I spoke up, saying, "An old woman in the crowd at Hippos thought you were Jeremiah arisen from the grave."

"All right," Jesus said. "But who do *you* say I am?"

Simon who, surprisingly up to this point had not said anything, blurted out in a strong, confident voice, "You are the Christ, God's anointed King, and the Son of the living God."

For a moment, there was complete silence; even the birds chirping in the nearby trees went mute.

As for me, Simon's declaration sent chills up my spine and made the hair on the back of my neck stand up.

"Blessed are you, Simon!" Jesus replied. "What you just said did not come from inside you or from any other man; those words came from my Father in heaven. From now on, your name will be Peter, and we are all going to call you by that name. I'm going to build my church upon the truth that you have just spoken, and the gates of hell shall never prevail against it! And I will give you the keys to the kingdom of heaven: whatever you bind on earth shall be bound in heaven; whatever you loose on earth shall be loosed in heaven."

Jesus paused and then added, "For the time being, I want you all to keep what both Peter and I just said to yourselves."

The Master was going to build his church on the *truth* of Peter's utterance: that he, Jesus, was the Christ. Just as the wise man in one of his parables had built his house on a rock, in order to prevent its destruction from wind, rain and floods, so would the Master build his church on the rock-solid foundation of Peter's confession.

Up to this point, whenever we spoke about Jesus among ourselves, it was clear that we all believed him to be a prophet, perhaps one of the greatest prophets of Israel. We had even entertained the idea that he might be the promised Messiah, God's anointed King, as Peter had just proclaimed him to be. It was now clear that Jesus, too, believed he was the One. If Peter believed it, and, especially, if Jesus believed it, so did I! It was immediately evident that we all did. *Jesus was the Messiah!*

For hundreds of years, Jews had expected the Messiah. Alas, there had been many men who claimed to be the Anointed One, only to prove themselves imposters because they did not accomplish what the ancient prophecies promised they would do. What were our expectations? We believed the Messiah would achieve three things. First, he would rebuild and cleanse the temple. The temple had been rebuilt, but by the wrong man: Herod. Second, the Messiah would expel the Romans, driving them out by means of an army of patriots he would recruit and lead. Third, he would establish and rule a just kingdom, not only in Israel, but also throughout the whole world.

Just as our fervor was about to explode, a somber expression shadowed Jesus's face, which quickly dampened our mood.

"I know what you men believe about the Messiah—and not just what you believe, but what most Jews believe. Some of what you believe is true; much of it is not—at least not in the sense of *when* and *how* the Son of Man will accomplish the purposes for which he is sent. It won't happen the way you expect it to, and I want you to be prepared."

Jesus was obviously speaking of himself, and he was right: we were *not* prepared to hear what he said next.

"The Son of Man will go to Jerusalem, where he must suffer. He will be rejected by the elders, the chief priests, and the lawyers. He will be killed, but he will rise the third day."

We were stunned into silence—all of us but Peter. He jumped to his feet, grabbed Jesus by the arm, and pulled him away from the rest of us. Nevertheless, they were still close enough for us hear what he said to Jesus and what Jesus said to him.

"This will not happen to you! I won't stand for it!" Peter declared in an emphatic tone of voice.

With equal force, and while looking Peter straight in the eye, Jesus said, "You get away from me, Satan! You speak the words of man, not of God! You are offensive to me! You have earthly understanding, not heavenly!"

Peter turned white as a sheet and looked as if he might faint. Within the space of a few minutes' time, Jesus had commended him for his understanding of who he—Jesus—was, telling him he would build his church on the truth of Peter's confession, and now, he was calling Peter *Satan,* the *accuser!*

We all looked at each other in disbelief mixed with sympathy for Peter. He pledged his loyalty to the Master. He would protect Jesus; save him from death at the hands of his enemies. I was sure we all agreed with Peter and would do the same. Why would Jesus censure him for that?

There followed several moments of discomfort for all of us, and, I'm sure, especially for Peter.

Jesus then put his arm around Peter's shoulders and led him several yards away, out of our hearing.

Peter never told us what Jesus had said to him. However, when the Master and he rejoined us, Peter's color had returned, and he looked relieved.

Jesus then continued.

"I have more to say to all of you. Much of it will be incomprehensible, mystifying. But, listen carefully, because someday you will not only remember what I say now, but it will make sense to you, and that will be a great encouragement in your kingdom work, especially in times of trouble.

"You are not only my disciples, you are my apostles; you are my closest friends, and I love each one of you. I have chosen each of you, and you each have chosen to follow me. I want you to understand what following me requires of you. Any man who follows me must deny himself, take up his cross every day, and be prepared to die for me, as I am prepared to take up my cross and die for him. Any man who seeks to preserve his own life will lose it, and any man who loses his life for my sake and the sake of the gospel will preserve his life. What does it profit a man if he gains the whole world but loses his own soul? The man who is ashamed of my words and me, I, the Son of Man, will be ashamed of him when I come in glory with my Father and the holy angels. I'm telling you the truth: some of you here today will not die until you see the kingdom of God come with power."

Jesus was right. We would remember what he said; every word of it, but it would be many months, and in some cases, many years until we understood it fully.

CHAPTER 20

We stayed one night in Caesarea Philippi. The next day, we traveled farther north, fifteen miles to Mount Hermon, the highest mountain in Israel. We arrived at the base of the mountain late in the afternoon.

Jesus asked three of us—Peter, my brother, James, and me—to go with him up the mountain; the other nine were to wait there for our return. As I have previously said, I was not sure why Jesus had chosen us three, to the exclusion of the others, to accompany him at certain times. It took three hours for us to ascend the winding and sometimes very steep trail, and we were exhausted when we neared the peak as the sun began to set. We had seen no others going up or coming down the mountain, and we were alone near the summit. It had been warm when we started our ascent, but it was quite cold at this elevation. We had food enough to last through the next day. A cool, clear stream near the crest would supply our need for water. We had stopped in a meadow covered in grass and encircled with trees. Jesus said we would stay the night there. We sat down and rested for half an hour before eating our supper. None of us had ever been at this great an altitude before, and we all fell asleep soon after we had eaten.

I awakened perhaps two or three hours later, and in the light of a nearly full moon, I noticed that Jesus was not with us. I supposed he had gone off alone to pray, and I quickly went back to sleep.

Suddenly, a light, seemingly as bright as the sun, awakened the three of us. At first, we thought the sun had risen, but that was not the source of the light. No, it was coming from perhaps a hundred feet away, a little farther up the meadow. It took a few moments for our eyes to adjust to the brilliance, and when they did, we recognized Jesus. He appeared to be deep in conversation with two other men we had never seen before; we could not hear what they were saying. The radiance emanated not only from their dazzling white clothing but also from their faces. *They* were the source of the light, which was almost impossible to look at.

We stepped closer to the light.

Just at that instant, something like a fog came over us; it was so thick, I could not see my hand in front of my face. We were terrified and cast about for each other, to no avail.

Next, we heard a booming voice, like thunder from above—very like the voice I had heard more than a year before on the banks of the Jordan River: "This is My son, the one I love. Listen to what he has to say."

Instantly, the fog lifted; Jesus was standing in front of us, telling us not to be afraid. His clothes were no longer shining, but an otherworldly glow was still visible on his face. His two visitors were nowhere in sight.

Sunrise was two hours away; the only remaining light was that of the moon.

We walked the few feet to our campsite; it was cold, and the three of us were trembling.

Jesus bid us to sit down while he rekindled the fire to warm us.

We slowly regained our composure, while Jesus sat quietly poking at the fire with a stick.

James was the first to speak.

"Master, who were those two men you were speaking with?"

"Moses and Elijah." His mention of their names was as casual as if he had been speaking of ordinary men.

"Moses and Elijah!" Peter exclaimed.

"Will you tell us what you were talking about?" I asked.

"They came to encourage me, to strengthen me for the ordeal that lies ahead."

Peter excitedly proposed that as soon as it was light, he, James, and I would build three monuments: one each for Jesus, Moses, and Elijah, to commemorate this stupendous event.

"No, Peter, you're not going to do that. In addition, you are not to say a word about what you saw tonight—none of you shall speak of it until after I rise from the dead. After breakfast, we are all going back down the mountain to rejoin our colleagues. But, right now, we're going to get a little more sleep."

Once again, Jesus had spoken of his rising from the dead. We were not sure what he meant by that, and we were reluctant to ask.

This was the first time I had been up and down such a high mountain. I thought it would be easier coming down than it had been going up. It was not. We reached bottom about midday, and, unlike the day before, there were a hundred or so people gathered around our fellow disciples. We surmised they were from the nearby village we had passed through the previous day. One of them, a Judean lawyer certainly not from that village, was harshly questioning our friends. Someone in the crowd recognized Jesus, and everyone converged on him.

"Why are you bothering my disciples with your pointless questions?" Jesus demanded of the legal expert.

Before the lawyer could answer, a desperate man fell at Jesus's feet, begging that the Master heal his demon-possessed son who was writhing on the ground several yards away.

"Master, my son is possessed of a demon that has taken away his speech and causes him to foam at the mouth and gnash his teeth. He has been driven to lunacy and is greatly vexed; sometimes the satanic force casts him into fires where he is burned or pools of water where he nearly drowns. I asked your disciples to help him, but they couldn't do anything. I am desperate and fear he will die."

"Go get him, and bring him here to me," Jesus said.

I was standing next to Jesus while the man went to bring his son to the Master, and I heard him say something half under his breath and to no one in particular: "You faithless and perverse generation! How long must I put up with you?"

The young man was about my age. The father practically dragged him to Jesus, where he fell on the ground, foaming at the mouth and in obvious pain.

"How long has he been in this condition?" Jesus asked the father.

"Since he was a small child. If you can do anything for him at all, *please* help him."

"Do you *believe* I can help him?"

"Lord, I believe. *Help me to believe!* Rid me of my unbelief!"

"Evil spirit, come out of this young man, and *never* enter him again!"

The son, who, according to his father, could not speak at all, suddenly jumped to his feet, screamed out, and fell to the ground, as if dead. He lay there showing no sign of life. Jesus reached down, took the young man's hands in his, and raised him to a standing position. Not only was he alive, but he appeared in perfect health.

Jesus turned to the young man's father and said simply, "Here's your son. He's well now; take him home."

Everyone in the crowd was astounded. Few of them even knew who Jesus was; certainly, they had never seen him perform a miracle.

After the crowd had dispersed, we twelve gathered around Jesus.

Matthew and James the Younger asked why none of them had been able to cast out the young man's demon, considering that all of us had been able to do so when we were on our missions a few months before.

"That's because your belief alone is not always enough. Remember, I once told you that the people you are endeavoring to heal must have faith, not in your ability, but in God's power. When they don't, healing is impossible."

"So, that's why you asked the boy's father if he believed you could heal his son?" Matthew asked.

"Yes. His faith was necessary in his son's healing. There is one more very important thing to remember: You must earnestly pray that the Father will increase *your* faith in these situations. Prayer is essential."

We stayed the night at the base of the mountain.

The next day, on our way south to Galilee, we passed through the small nearby village. Nearly all its inhabitants were in the street, waiting for us. Some wanted healing, but most wanted Jesus to teach them—to hear his kingdom message, the good news of the gospel. Many believed.

CHAPTER 21

We passed through Caesarea Philippi on our way back home. Word of Jesus's healing the demon-possessed young man, as well as his other healings in the village near Mount Hermon, had obviously preceded us, as hundreds of people lined the main thoroughfare that bisected the heart of the city and skirted the Roman temple. Among the throng were dozens who sought healing, and Jesus was pleased to accommodate them. Opposite the temple was a tree-shaded park, and he was urged by many in the crowd to speak to them there. Of course, there was a Roman garrison in the city, adjacent to the temple, and, seeing the unusual gathering, the Roman commander sent a small contingent of soldiers to watch over the crowd and to suppress any potential unruly behavior. He needn't have been concerned. Jesus spoke and answered questions for about an hour. His kingdom message did not arouse any adverse reactions from the soldiers, who probably failed to understand its implications for them or their empire. There were a few Pharisees and lawyers in the audience but they kept curiously quiet. One of Jesus's hearers invited us to have supper with him and his family, and to stay the night with them as well.

The next morning we continued on to Capernaum. The thirty-mile walk took us all day, as in every village we passed through, people were waiting for Jesus to heal or speak to them. On the way, Jesus said he wanted to spend a few quiet days with us, as he had some things to say for our ears only.

Matthew proposed we all stay with him, and we arrived at his home after dark. Perhaps we would have a few days of peace and quiet.

Unfortunately, our seclusion was cut short early the next morning. We had just finished breakfast when there was a knock at the front door.

Matthew asked Peter if he would see who it was.

Peter opened the door, stepped out on the front porch, and closed the door behind him.

We heard but could not understand a muffled and short conversation.

Peter reentered the house and closed the door. He told us the visitor was a temple tax collector who asked him if Jesus paid the temple tax.

We all bristled.

As I have previously mentioned, most Jews resented the temple tax, not because we were reluctant to pay for the upkeep of the temple, but because the priests, elders, and lawyers spent much of the taxes collected in support of their own lavish lifestyles.

Addressing Peter, Jesus asked, "Well, what did you tell him?"

Peter hesitated and then said somewhat sheepishly, "I told him you did. He asked me to go get it from you and bring it to him."

None of us twelve was pleased with Peter's uncharacteristically timid answer.

Jesus said with a wry grin, "Go out and tell him you'll bring it to him, but he will have to wait awhile."

Peter complied. When he returned, Jesus gave him a task.

"Take a fishing pole, a line, and a hook, and go down to the lake. Cast the hook into the water, and open the mouth of the first fish you catch. You will find a coin inside that will be enough to pay both your tax and mine. I don't like this tax any more than you do, but no good will come of refusing to pay it."

This whole episode seemed odd to me. We had enough money in the treasury to pay the small but offensive tax. Why did Jesus choose to pay it this way? We were supposed to be fishers of *men*, not literal fish.

Peter did as Jesus said, returning within minutes, bearing a shiny coin that he promptly gave to the waiting tax collector, who had been impatiently pacing back and forth on the front porch.

We'd had time to contemplate this strange event, and we all, including Jesus, had a good laugh. The poor fish had paid the tax, not Jesus and Peter. The Master's humor was both subtle and droll.

After our midday meal, Jesus proposed we go for a walk along the lakeshore. We were the only ones out that afternoon, the fishermen having finished their work for the day. For once, the religious fanatics always asking for signs from Jesus did not hound us. As usual, the Master led the way, but his pace was quicker than ours that afternoon, and we fell several yards behind him.

Judas asked a question of all of us: Who did we think would be the greatest in Jesus's soon-to-be-established kingdom? Would it be Peter, in light of what Jesus had recently said about his future leadership position? Or would it be one of the rest of us?

Without noticing it, we had slowed our pace to the point of stopping, and Jesus was now far enough ahead of us that he could not hear what ensued.

We began to debate the question. The only ones who did not join in the dispute were Peter and his brother, Andrew.

I suggested that Peter, James, and I should have high places, because Jesus, on three separate occasions, had asked us to accompany him at critical junctures in his ministry, excluding the other nine.

The conversation got heated. Some of my colleagues suggested we would all be equal in the Master's kingdom; others said that they deserved honored places too.

The argument came to a sudden halt when Peter pointed out that Jesus, perhaps two hundred feet away, had stopped and was looking at us.

We caught up to him and walked in complete silence back to Matthew's house.

By now, it was late afternoon, and Jesus sat down on Matthew's lawn and invited us to sit with him. He was silent for a few moments, and none of us said a word to him or each other.

"What were you men disagreeing about?"

Nobody answered; we all just looked down, staring silently at the grass in silence.

Finally, Andrew, the least talkative of our company, spoke up.

"Master, who will be the greatest in the kingdom of heaven?"

"Thank you, Andrew. I'm glad one of you has the courage to say something," Jesus said. He then paused and added, "If any man desires to be the greatest, he will be the least in God's kingdom, the servant of the others."

There were a few followers in the outer circle standing or sitting at the edge of Matthew's property. One of them, a young woman and a cousin of James's and mine, was there with her three-year-old child. Jesus asked Andrew to go over and invite her and her daughter to join us. Jesus rose to meet them, picked up the child, hugged her, and sat her down in the midst of us. She sat there quietly, looking alternately at each of us.

"*You* must become like a little child, or you'll never see the kingdom of heaven. You won't need to concern yourselves with your positions there because you won't be there. He who humbles himself will be the greatest in the kingdom. He who receives one of these children in my name receives me, and then he also receives the One who sent me. The least among you will be great. Whoever offends one of these children who believe in me, it would be better for him if a millstone was hung around his neck and he was cast into the deepest ocean. Does that answer your question, Andrew?"

"Yes, Master, it certainly does."

The sun had set, and we moved inside Matthew's house and sat down to supper, during which I broached a subject with Jesus. It was something that had been bothering me since he had sent the twelve of us out on our own missions several months before.

"Master, when Judas and I were in Magdala, we encountered a man who was casting out demons in your name. We had never seen him before, and we told him that because he was not one of your disciples, he had no right to perform miracles in your name."

"John, I understand why you and Judas said that. You thought you were standing up for me, looking out for my reputation. But understand this: any man who performs a miracle in my name is not against me; he is for me and for my kingdom."

After supper, we moved into the sitting area, and Jesus told us another parable.

The King and the Debtor Servant

The kingdom of heaven is like a certain king who wanted to test one of his servants. He had lent a great deal of money—ten thousand talents—to the servant, and the man had made no effort to repay him. So, the king demanded that the money be paid back. The servant had squandered it all on high living and bad investments, including a small loan he had made to one of his fellow servants. The profligate servant told the king that all the money was gone, and he couldn't pay it back. On hearing this, the king became angry and threatened to have the man and his family sold into slavery, with the proceeds of the sale applied to his debt. The servant prostrated himself before the king and asked that he be given time to raise the money for repayment. The king took pity on him and canceled the debt. Then this irresponsible servant went to the man to whom he had lent a very small amount, took him by the throat, and demanded that he repay it immediately. The man could not pay it. He begged for mercy, for time to raise the money. The ungrateful servant refused and threatened to have the man thrown into debtors' prison. Some of the other servants went to the king and told him about this.

The king was livid and summoned the thankless servant. "I forgave your huge debt, and you won't even forgive your fellow servant's tiny debt? Get out of my sight. You'll spend the rest of your life in debtors' prison."

"Your parable reminds me of a phrase in the prayer you taught us over a year ago, Master," Nathanael said. "'Forgive us our trespasses against you as we forgive those who have trespassed against us.'"

"You have a good memory, Nathanael."

"Well, just how many times *should* we forgive those who wrong us; as many as seven times?" Peter asked.

"How many times has God forgiven you, Peter? More than seven times, I should think. Look, I'm not trying to embarrass Peter. My point is that God is always willing to forgive our trespasses, our debts, *if* we seek His forgiveness, whether it is seven times or seventy times seven. His mercy and forgiveness are limitless; He doesn't keep count, and neither should you.

"If a shepherd has a hundred sheep under his care, and one of them goes astray, he will leave the ninety-nine and go in search of the one that's lost. And when he finds it, he will rejoice. You have heard me say that I have been sent to preach the good news to the house of the lost sheep of Israel. I'm their shepherd, and you are my under-shepherds. We have a lot of work left to do, and so little time left to do it."

Jesus paused and then continued.

"Let's talk about resolving disputes among the sheep, God's people. Suppose a brother—a fellow believer—sins against you. The first thing you are to do is go to that brother and seek reconciliation. If the two of you can work it out, let that be the end of it. There is no need to involve others. If that does not work, take two or three witnesses with you, and try again. If that also fails, tell it to the church, and let the congregation decide. If the brother repents, that is well and good. If not, he is to be separated from the church family unless and until he sees the error of his ways and confesses them. He then can return to the church."

It had been a tension-filled day, except for the comic relief of the fish story. Jesus asked us to be ready for a long journey in the morning.

CHAPTER 22

It was early winter. Our winters were not severe—snow, except at the higher elevations, was unusual—but winter was also our rainy season, making travel more challenging. Jerusalem was our destination. During our time with Jesus, we always attended Passover in the spring, but we were now on our way to the Feast of the Dedication, instituted nearly two centuries before to commemorate the expulsion of Antiochus Epiphanes, leader of a horde of Syrian invaders who had defiled our holy temple. At that time, Judas Maccabaeus drove the Syrians from Israel, purged the temple, and rebuilt its altar, thus becoming a national hero.

In addition to Jesus and the twelve of us (the inner circle), about a hundred of his regular followers (the outer circle) and perhaps two hundred more pilgrims accompanied us.

The most direct route between Galilee and Jerusalem was through Samaria. The Samaritans were a mixed race—Hebrew and Assyrian—and their religion contained elements of both Judaism and paganism. They had their own priesthood, temple, and sacrificial system. We considered them inferior in race and religion, and they felt the same way about us. Because of this mutual dislike, Samaritans seldom traveled beyond their region, and we seldom traveled through it. Rather, we would skirt Samaria by traveling down the east side of the Jordan River valley. This added twenty miles to what would have been an eighty-five mile journey by the more direct route through Samaria. Apparently, Jesus was anxious to get to Jerusalem in four days instead of five, because he led us straight to the Samaritan frontier. We arrived late in the afternoon of our second day on the road.

Jesus asked my brother, James, and me to cross over to a small village to ascertain if so many Jews passing through their midst would arouse hostilities among the local populace. If our party had been smaller, we would have been less noticeable and less likely to encounter resistance, and, perhaps, even violence. It did not take us long to find out. From their village, the inhabitants could see three hundred Jews poised to traverse their town, and they made it clear we were not welcome. My brother and I were greatly offended, and we made it equally clear to them that we could not abide their dirty little hamlet for one more minute. Turning on our heels, we made a display of shaking the dust from our sandals, and then we hastily stalked away.

On our short walk back to the waiting company, James and I became even more agitated at this insult. By the time we returned to where our party waited for us, our anger was about to boil over. After telling Jesus what had happened, we asked him if he wanted us to call down fire from heaven to consume the entire village, in the manner of the prophet Elijah, who had done the same thing with an unrepentant town in Israel centuries before.

"You don't know what you're saying! I have not come to earth to *destroy* lives but to *save* them," Jesus replied. "We are going to continue our journey, just not through this part of Samaria. We'll head over to the Jordan River valley first thing tomorrow morning."

We stayed the night, in a spot about ten miles away from the Jordan River. In the morning, we walked toward the river, where we turned south and continued on for another fifteen miles before reentering the unfriendly region. Fortunately, the level of animosity we encountered during the rest of our trek through Samaria was of a milder variety: unpleasant looks and grumbling from some, but mere avoidance from most. There was, however, one heart-warming incident.

On the outskirts of one village, we saw ten men standing together about a hundred feet from us. They could not approach us because they were lepers.

As was required, even by Samaritan law, one of them called out in a loud voice, "Unclean, unclean!"

But then, another one of them also cried out, "Have mercy on us!"

Did these men know who Jesus was? If so, how did they know?

"Go and show yourselves to the priest, so that he can certify that you are clean," Jesus shouted back.

The men looked at themselves and then at each other. They all shouted for joy and walked quickly away; all but one, who ran to Jesus, fell at his feet, and thanked him profusely.

"Where are the others?" Jesus asked.

The man did not know.

"Go on your way," Jesus told the man. "Your faith has made you whole."

As I mentioned earlier, on this journey to Jerusalem were perhaps two hundred pilgrims: men, women, and children who traveled with us for the purpose of attending the Feast of the Dedication. Shortly after Jesus had healed the ten lepers, three men, none of whom I recognized, approached him individually. The first stated he was ready to become a full-time follower of the Master. However, there was a condition: His father was old and had perhaps only a short time yet to live. Because of this family obligation, there would be an indefinite delay in his joining us.

To me, that seemed reasonable, but not to Jesus.

"Life is for the living," Jesus said. "Let the dead bury the dead."

The man, looking downcast, turned and walked away. We never saw him again.

I thought Jesus's response was harsh; at best, it seemed perplexing.

A second man came to Jesus—a Judean lawyer, as I would later learn.

"Rabbi, I would like to become one of your disciples," he said.

"Are you sure about that? Jesus responded. "My life is not an easy one."

The second man also turned and walked away.

The third man approached.

"I'll follow you, Master, wherever you go," he said. "But I want to return home first to bid farewell to my family."

"No man who sets his hand to the plow and then looks back is fit for the kingdom," Jesus said.

Looking sad, the third man departed as well.

Here were three men who asked to follow Jesus, and he had rejected them all. Could it be that on some level they had rejected him by the conditions they imposed? We had never before seen the Master do such a thing. His responses to the first and third man were difficult for me to understand. As to the lawyer, good riddance.

On that same day, Jesus walked among the outer circle of his regular followers as well as the pilgrims who were traveling with us. He selected seventy of them and asked these men to follow him and the twelve of us a short distance away from the others. There, he separated them into thirty-five pairs and charged them with going ahead of him into every village, town, and city in Judea (except Jerusalem and its immediate vicinity). Because there were thirty-five two-man teams, each pair was to have only one place to go. Otherwise, his instructions to them were identical to those he had given to us twelve a year before when he had sent us throughout Galilee. They were to teach, preach, and heal, to prepare the people for his own visits to those same places, which would follow in the coming weeks. These seventy would not be going on to Jerusalem to the festival, as Jesus explained that there would be no time for that. The seventy men were to meet us in Bethabara, on the Jordan River, in two weeks' time.

These were Jesus's parting words to the seventy men: "The harvest truly is great, but there are too few workers. Pray that more will join you."

There was no doubt in my mind: Suddenly, Jesus's ministry had taken on a greater urgency. Events from this point forward would move rapidly.

The seventy left for their missions the next morning, and the rest of us pushed on toward Jerusalem, passing out of Samaria late that afternoon. That evening, after we had finished our supper, several dozen of our fellow travelers gathered around Jesus, some of them asking questions. One of them, a lawyer—not the same one who had claimed to want to follow Jesus the day before—asked what he needed to do to inherit eternal life in the age to come.

"Well, you're the legal expert," Jesus replied. "What does the Law say? How do you interpret it on that point?"

"Love the Lord your God with all your heart, all your soul, all your strength, and all your mind, and love your neighbor as you love yourself," the man responded.

"Excellent! You have answered correctly," Jesus said. "Do those two things, and you'll have life everlasting."

"But," persisted the lawyer, "*who* is my neighbor?"

To answer this question, Jesus told one of his parables.

The Good Samaritan

A certain man, a Jew, traveled from Jerusalem to Jericho. On the way, thieves beat him, robbed him, stripped him of his clothes, and left him for dead by the side of the road. A while later, a priest came along, saw him, and passed by on the other side of the road. A few minutes later, a temple assistant stopped briefly, looked at the man, and continued on his way. And then a Samaritan riding a donkey came by, stopped, got off his donkey, went to him, and poured oil and wine into his wounds and bandaged them. He put the man on his donkey, and when they arrived in a small village, he took the man to an inn and cared for him through the night. The next morning, this Samaritan not only paid for the night's stay but also gave the innkeeper extra money to care for the man. He said he would be coming back through the village on his return from Jericho, and would then compensate the innkeeper for any additional costs for lodging and care while he was away.

After the parable, Jesus asked, "Now, which one of these three passersby do you think was the injured man's neighbor?"

"I suppose the one who showed mercy," the lawyer replied weakly.

"You go and do likewise."

We arrived in Jerusalem the next afternoon; the Feast of the Dedication, which lasted eight days, began that evening. We would spend those days in and around Jerusalem. Jesus stayed with friends, Lazarus and his sisters, Mary and Martha, whose acquaintance he had made on one of his earlier Passover visits several years before we knew him. They lived in Bethany, a small village just two miles east of Jerusalem. The rest of us stayed with friends or relatives who lived in or nearby the Holy City. Before parting for the evening, Jesus asked us to meet him the next morning at Solomon's Portico adjacent to the temple.

Within minutes of our arrival, a dozen or more Judeans—Pharisees and lawyers—surrounded us, demanding, yet again, that Jesus offer proof of his identity. (They always called such proof a "sign.") Most of them we had seen before, on more than one occasion; they had been among the Judeans who had shadowed Jesus in Galilee during the past months.

"How long are you going to keep us in suspense? Are you, or are you not, the Christ? Tell us plainly," one of the Pharisees insisted angrily.

"I have told you repeatedly who I am. But you didn't believe my words or my works, which I do in the Father's name. Those works are all the proof you need, and they are all you are going to get. You don't believe me because you are not sheep of my flock. My sheep hear my voice; I know them, and they know me and follow me. I give them eternal life; they will never die, and no man can take them from me. My Father, who is greater than anyone else, gave them to me. I and the Father are one."

Those last few words were the excuse they were looking for. Their anger turned to fury; they picked up stones and were on the brink of letting them fly at Jesus.

Just then, he asked them a question that induced a momentary reprieve.

"I have shown you many good works from my Father. For which of those works do you stone me to death?"

The Judeans looked at one another, drew close together, and quietly conferred. The conference lasted mere moments, and then they turned toward Jesus, their faces contorted in murderous fury. They gripped the stones tightly, ready to throw with all the force they could muster.

"We're not going to stone you for your good works but for blasphemy, for making yourself equal with God!" one of them shouted.

As he articulated this rationalization, his eyes scanned the twelve of us.

A moment before, Jesus had been standing in our midst; now he was nowhere in sight.

My fellow disciples and I had been looking intently at the Judeans and had not seen Jesus depart, but somehow he had. Where he had gone, we could not say.

When we were sure the Judeans had no interest in us and were not following us, we began to search for Jesus. We quickly concluded he most likely would not be in the immediate vicinity of the temple, so we looked elsewhere in Jerusalem: the Amydalon Pond, the Pool of Siloam, and, knowing Jesus's affinity for quiet places where he could pray in solitude, the Mount of Olives, and within it, the garden of Gethsemane. He was in none of those places, and we began to worry.

As we were leaving the garden, a man approached us. He was Lazarus's servant and had been sent by him to fetch us to his master's home for supper. He told us Jesus was already there. Bethany was less than a mile away, on the eastern slope of the Mount of Olives.

Jesus had often talked of Lazarus and his sisters and was obviously fond of them all. It was easy to see why.

Lazarus greeted us warmly and made us all feel welcome. He led us to the sitting room, where we found Jesus unharmed.

We were surprised to see a woman, Lazarus's sister Mary, sitting at Jesus's feet, listening attentively to his every word. We could hear someone in the adjoining kitchen, busily preparing the evening meal. It was Martha, the older sister.

Shortly thereafter, Martha entered the room, looking flustered and perturbed. She walked right past the rest of us, straight to Jesus.

"Master, don't you care that my sister just sits around doing nothing, while I'm slaving away in the kitchen, trying to prepare a large meal, with no help at all? Tell her to get up and help me."

"Martha, Martha," Jesus responded, "You are full of the cares of this world, and trouble yourself about many things. But there is something else more important. Only one thing really matters, and Mary has chosen it."

Jesus said these words with much tenderness; he was not being offensive, and Martha seemed to relax and quietly returned to the kitchen.

The meal she served was excellent, and we all, especially Jesus, complimented her homemaking and culinary skills. This seemed to please her immensely.

We would have two more meals at Lazarus's house in the days that followed, and, on those occasions, Mary did help her sister.

The Feast of the Dedication had ended, but Jesus chose to stay a few more days in and around Jerusalem. We then we traveled east through Jericho, to Bethabara, a small town on the Jordan River, just north of the Dead Sea. There, we met the seventy, who were eager to tell us of their mission activities during the past two weeks. Their enthusiasm and the stories they told—of teaching, preaching, and healing—echoed the ones we twelve had related to Jesus when we returned from our own similar missions the year before. Hundreds of those they had met had come back with them, anxious to meet and hear—and, in some cases, be healed by—the Jesus about whom the seventy had told them. In addition, many hundreds had followed us from Jerusalem as well.

CHAPTER 23

Even though it was winter, the weather in Bethabara was quite moderate. By some accounts, the Dead Sea, just a few miles to the south, was below the level of the Mediterranean, making for extremely hot summers and mild winters. This was fortunate, as there were few accommodations in the village, and with Jesus's arrival, the population had swollen by at least a thousand. Most of the visitors slept under the stars.

Jesus spent the first few days teaching and ministering, not only to the local residents, but also to the hundreds who had accompanied the seventy from their hometowns and villages and the few hundred more who had followed us from Jerusalem. And then he called the seventy and the twelve of us apart, leading us to a quiet place to prepare us for what lay ahead.

He began with his favorite teaching device, a parable.

The Loaves

Suppose an unexpected visitor, a friend or relative, arrives at your house at midnight, knocks loudly on your door, and wakes you. He is hungry, but you have nothing to feed him. So, you go to a neighbor; you knock at his door, wake him up, and ask if you may borrow three loaves of bread. He does not even open the door, tells you that his family is already in bed asleep, and demands you go away and leave them alone. But you keep knocking and asking to borrow the bread. Eventually, he will get up and give you the bread, just to get you to go away and stop bothering him. In a way, God is like that. Ask, and it shall be given to you; seek, and you shall find; knock, and it shall be opened to you. If your son asks you for bread, will you give him a stone? If he asks for a fish, will you give him a snake? If he asks for an egg, will you give him a scorpion? Of course, you won't. If you, ordinary, sinful people, know how to give good things to your children, how much more will your heavenly Father give good things to you if you ask for them?

Regrettably, several Pharisees and lawyers had also followed us from Jerusalem and more than a few of them had pursued us to this place apart from the crowds. Some of them were among those who had harassed and attempted to stone Jesus to death on Solomon's Porch. Their lavish apparel and haughty manner betrayed them. It was only a matter of time before they would once again accost him.

Jesus did not wait for that to happen; he went on the offensive.

"Woe to you Pharisees! You are scrupulous about tithing, which is fine as far as it goes. However, you ignore God's requirements that are more important: to love Him and your fellow man.

"Woe to you Pharisees! You love the choice seats in the synagogues and recognition in public places. Your pride is remarkable!"

The lawyers standing with the Pharisees were offended not to be included in Jesus's condemnation.

One of them shouted out, "In condemning the Pharisees, you also condemn us!"

Jesus was not one to play favorites.

"Woe to you lawyers! You burden ordinary men with grievous rules and regulations that you, yourselves, ignore! Your hypocrisy is exceptional!"

He was just getting started.

"Woe to you Pharisees *and* lawyers! You erect monuments to the prophets, the same prophets your ancestors killed! The blood of the prophets shed from the foundation of the world shall be required of *your* generation, from the blood of Abel to the blood of Zacharias; it shall be on *your* hands!

"Woe to you lawyers! You've hidden the key to the door of truth, a door you've never entered, and you don't want anyone else to enter it either!"

The whole lot of them, Pharisees and lawyers, began to taunt Jesus. I was convinced they were trying to goad him into saying something they could use as an excuse to bring a capital charge against him. However, he would not take the bait. The seventy had enough of this, and they forced these intruders to leave.

Jesus and the eighty-two of us (the seventy and we twelve apostles) remained.

Jesus spent the rest of that day and the next imparting further truths, encouragements, and instructions to us, in order to prepare us for the remainder of this sojourn in Judea. Our time there would last through Passover, a little more than three months away. It would be our longest absence from Galilee thus far.

Jesus continued his instructions.

"Don't be afraid of those who kill the body. After that, there is nothing left for them to do to you. Fear the one who throws you into hellfire, the eternal death. But remember this as well: Five sparrows sell for two pennies, and God forgets not one of them. You are priceless to Him; He even knows the number of hairs on your head! So don't be afraid. If you are my advocate to men, I will be your advocate to my Father. But, if you deny me to men, I will deny you to my Father. If you speak words against me, God will forgive you. However, if you speak words against God's Holy Spirit, there is nothing left for you. Do not speculate about the future or about my mission, because you will get it wrong; wait and see what actually happens. In short, I'm asking for your absolute loyalty, whatever happens.

"Listen to me carefully: There will come a time when you will be summoned to appear before synagogue officials, magistrates, and other high officials. Don't worry about how to respond to their questions or accusations, because God's Spirit will put just the right words into your mouths."

At that moment, one of the seventy interrupted Jesus to ask an improper question.

"Master, I want you to speak to my brother and tell him he has to divide his inheritance with me."

This man's question was thoughtless and out of context, but as he had so often done before, Jesus turned the question into a great truth-teaching moment.

"Man, who made me a judge over such a trivial matter? You are too concerned about material things. Your life doesn't consist of the things you own!" he said, and then he told us another parable.

The Rich Fool

There was a wealthy farmer whose land produced a bumper crop one year.

He said to himself, "My barns are not big enough to store up all this grain. I'll tear down my little barns, and build more and bigger ones. I will have enough to last for years! I can take it easy: eat, drink, and be merry!"

But, God said to him, "You fool! This night, you're going to die, and what good will your riches do you then?" He who lays up treasure for himself is poor in God's sight.

Jesus continued in this vein.

Take no thought for yourself: what you eat or what you wear. Your life is more than the food you eat or the clothes you wear. Think about the ravens: they don't sow, they don't reap, and they don't store up food in barns. God takes care of them. How much more will He care for you! Can you add even one single inch to your height? If you are unable to do that, why do you worry about food or clothes? Look at the flowers in a spring field. They don't spin thread or weave cloth. Even the finest king is not clothed as beautifully as they are. No! Seek first the kingdom of God, and He will take care of your material needs. Do not be afraid: it is God's pleasure to give you His kingdom. If you have more than you need to sustain your life, sell the excess, and help those who are in need. Your real, lasting treasure is in God's kingdom, where nothing can be taken away from you. I'm telling you the truth: where your treasure is, that's where your heart will be too.

The Waiting Servants

Make sure you're alert, dressed, and with your lamps trimmed for the Master's return. Listen for his approaching footsteps, and open the gate when you hear him coming. Blessed are those who watch for him, even if his return is delayed into the small hours of the morning. He will increase your blessing as a reward for your perseverance. The Son of Man will return at an hour you are not expecting him.

Peter asked a question: "Master, is this parable just for us twelve, or is it for the seventy as well?"

Jesus's answer, though oblique, suggested it applied to all his listeners.

Who, then, is a faithful and wise servant whom the Lord will make ruler over his household? The one who is ready at any time. If the servant says that the Lord has delayed his return and in his disappointment takes out his frustration on those servants under him, eating and drinking to excess, the Lord will deal harshly with that servant, consider him an unbeliever, and severely punish him. To whomever much responsibility is given, much faithfulness is required. I came to send fire on the earth; I have a baptism to be baptized with; I'm constrained until that is accomplished. Do you suppose that I have come to give peace on the earth? From now on, there will be five in one house, and that house will be divided: father against son; son against father; mother against daughter; daughter against mother; mother-in-law against daughter-in-law; daughter-in-law against mother-in-law.

It had been less than one month since Jesus had upbraided James and me for suggesting that we call down fire from heaven to destroy a Samaritan village and its inhabitants for insulting our company, refusing to let us pass through. At that time, Jesus said that he had come, not to destroy life but to save it; to bring peace to the earth, not strife. Now he seemed to be saying just the opposite. It would be a long time before I would understand these apparent contradictions.

By this time, it was near sunset, and Jesus said we would spend one more day in this quiet place near Bethabara before moving on. We ate our evening meal, and then went to sleep.

The next morning, a few but different Pharisees and lawyers were in the audience, and the Master's first words were clearly for them.

"When you see a cloud rise out of the west, from the Mediterranean Sea, you say rain is coming, and you're right. When you feel the south wind blow from the Negev Desert, you expect heat, and, again, you are right. You hypocrites! You discern the signs of the sky and the earth; why don't you discern the signs of the time?"

One of the lawyers reacted, but in a more respectful, less confrontational manner than had been the case the day before. He asked Jesus's opinion about two recent tragic events that had occurred in Jerusalem. One was the collapse of the Tower of Siloam, which had killed eighteen people. Because Jews did not believe in accidents, according to our logic, this must have been a judgment from God, and those killed must have been great sinners to deserve this ghastly fate. The second incident could not have been an accident, as Pontius Pilate, Rome's recently appointed prefect of Judea, deliberately instigated it. Several pilgrims from Galilee, one of whom I knew, were slaughtered by his soldiers in the temple courtyard, and their blood was then mixed with the blood of the animals they had sacrificed to God. This was a gross defilement of our holy temple, and Pilate knew it. (He had earlier committed several other outrages against our people and our faith, including the placement of pagan symbols in our Holy City and using temple money to build an aqueduct.) The lawyer wanted to know if Jesus agreed that these events were judgments of God.

Jesus replied, "Don't think that those people were greater sinners than you or anyone else just because of the way they died; they were not. Everyone, including you, your fellow lawyers, and your Pharisee friends, is in need of repentance. You have a simple choice to make: repent or die."

Jesus illustrated this truth with another parable, but, from the looks on their faces, I do not think that either the lawyer or his Pharisee companions fully understood it; I do not think the Master wanted them to.

The Unproductive Fig Tree

A certain man planted a fig tree in his vineyard. After three years, it hadn't produced a single fig. He told his gardener to cut it down; it was wasting space and water. His gardener urged him to give the tree one more year, and, in the meantime, he would give it special care: loosen the soil around it, fertilize it, and prune it. The man agreed. However, a year later the tree had still not produced a single fig. He ordered his gardener to cut it down, dig up the roots, and burn it. It was good for nothing.

The next day was the Sabbath, and that morning, we twelve (there was not room for the seventy) accompanied Jesus to Bethabara's synagogue.

As we approached the entrance, we saw a woman of middle age walking very slowly, entering the door just ahead of us. There was something wrong with her back, as her body was bent forward severely; her head and torso were almost parallel to the ground. I could hear her groaning softly, probably from the pain. Upon entering the synagogue, the woman turned to the right, seeking a seat on the women's side of the synagogue.

Jesus, breaking tradition, followed her. Reaching the woman before she sat down, he touched her, and, instantly, she stood erect and without pain, a look of wonder on her face as she gazed into the Master's eyes. She couldn't thank him audibly, as women must remain silent in synagogue; however, the expression on her face was gratitude enough.

Murmurs swept through the male side of the building as Jesus made his way there to sit with us.

As no one was speaking at the lectern, it soon grew quiet, but only for a moment.

The synagogue president, whose apparel was that of a Pharisee, hurriedly approached Jesus and accosted him in a voice shrill enough for the whole assembly to hear.

"How dare you violate the sanctity of this place by entering the women's section! Worse than that, by healing someone on this holy day, you have also violated the sanctity of the Sabbath, an even greater sin! There are six other days in the week for you to heal people, and yet you chose this day, in this synagogue! You, sir, make a mockery of God's holy day!"

We had been with the Master long enough to know that he would make short work of this arrogant man.

Jesus rose slowly to his feet, stared the man in the eye, and put him in his well-deserved place.

"You hypocrite! If your donkey fell into a ditch on the Sabbath, you would get a rope and pull it out! You would not think it a violation of the Sabbath to perform an act of kindness for an animal! Yet, that woman, a daughter of Abraham no less, you do not want to be released from her pain and suffering on God's holy day! Go home, and think about that!"

The man's face turned a bright shade of red—whether from embarrassment, anger, or both, I could not tell. He left the synagogue immediately, not speaking another word.

You may think that Jesus spoke such words in anger; he did not. To be sure, he spoke with boldness and great conviction, but also with deep-felt sorrow, even regret.

CHAPTER 24

Jesus, we twelve, and the seventy departed Bethabara the next morning, heading west to visit as many of the villages, towns, and cities in Judea as possible before Passover, now less than three months away. As I have said before, there seemed to be a greater urgency in Jesus's ministry now, as if he must accomplish certain objectives before Passover. Everywhere we went, the number of people who came to hear him preach, teach, and heal continued to grow. The populations of entire towns came out to see him, and the throng following us from place to place increased every day. Jesus not only taught the people; he continued to teach us as well. Every time we ate a meal together, or stopped to rest during the day or in the evenings before going to sleep, or in the early mornings before we resumed our journey to the next town, he would take us a little distance apart from the throng to answer our questions, expand on his teachings, or just give us encouragement for what may be in our future, short and long term.

During one of these sessions a few days after we had left Bethabara, one of the seventy gestured toward the multitude, which was well more than a thousand in number.

"Master, will there be many saved, or just a few?"

"Struggle diligently to enter the narrow gate," Jesus said. "Many will try, but only a few will be successful. That's because only God knows exactly when the gate will be locked. Those who find it locked will knock, shouting, 'Lord let us in!' But the Lord will answer, 'I don't know you.' They will plead, 'But we have eaten and drunk in Your presence; You have taught us about Your kingdom,' only to hear the Lord reply, 'I tell you, I don't know you! Depart from me, all of you who work only iniquity. You will weep and gnash your teeth. You'll see Abraham, Isaac, and Jacob, and all the prophets, in my kingdom, but you won't be there.' God's people will come from all over the world, not just Israel, and sit down with Him is His kingdom. The first shall be last, and the last shall be first."

This was a hard thing to hear in two ways. First, Jesus's words were, at least to me at that time, not fully comprehensible, even cryptic. Second, they were foreboding: The future for Israel looked uncertain and tenuous, a prospect I had not theretofore considered. Based upon subsequent conversations with my fellow disciples, most of them agreed with me.

From what Jesus had said about Pharisees, you may have come to believe they were all hypocrites of the first order. However, that was not always true. From time to time, a Pharisee would seek him out to ask a question or engage in a dialogue that indicated an open mind. Usually, this happened in one-to-one conversations with Jesus, which he would later relate to us.

One day, a small group of Pharisees approached and warned him that Herod was looking for an excuse to have him arrested and executed. They appeared genuinely concerned for his safety.

Jesus answered them calmly, "If you see Herod, you tell that fox what you've seen me do today: demons cast out, and people healed of all sorts of maladies."

He paused, and then, in words we did not understand at the time, he added, "Today, tomorrow, and then the third day, I'll be perfected. I cannot perish outside Jerusalem."

He paused again and said with great sorrow, "Jerusalem, oh Jerusalem, the city that kills the prophets and stones those sent to you. How often I would have gathered your children together as a hen gathers her chicks under her wings. But you would not have it. Your house is left to you desolate. I'm telling you the truth: you will not see me again until the time comes when you shall say, 'Blessed is he who comes in the name of the Lord.'"

Jesus told many parables during this three-month-long Judean tour: some to general audiences that always included several Pharisees and lawyers, and, sometimes, Herod's spies; and, occasionally, some to the twelve of us and the seventy, or even to smaller gatherings.

One Sabbath, Jesus and the twelve of us were invited to a Pharisee's house for dinner. He seemed to be one of the more open-minded, or at least less close-minded, of their lot. One of his other guests was an elderly man who was afflicted with edema, which manifested itself in his legs and feet, making it impossible for him to walk without pain.

Jesus noticed his condition and asked our host a question.

"Is it lawful to heal on the Sabbath?"

The Pharisee did not respond.

Jesus walked across the room to where the man was sitting, laid his hands on him, and asked him to get up and walk.

When the man stood, the swelling was gone, and he walked pain-free around the room, beaming with joy, praising God, and thanking Jesus.

Our host remained silent, although *speechless* would probably be a more accurate description.

At this point, Jesus told the same donkey-in-the-ditch-on-the-Sabbath story I related earlier.

The Pharisee maintained his silence but listened carefully. Perhaps the Master had caused him to reconsider the true purpose of our holy day.

After dinner, the Jesus told a parable, although at first it did not sound like a parable to me; recognizing it for what it was would take further reflection on my part.

The Invited

When you are invited to a banquet, don't sit in the best seat. Someone more honorable than you may arrive later, and you will be asked to give up your seat for him and be sent to a less desirable place. Rather, sit in the lowest seat. Maybe you will be invited to move and sit in a better place. Whoever exalts himself shall be humbled; whoever humbles himself shall be exalted.

My first thought on hearing this story was that Jesus was advising our host—and, perhaps, us too—on a point of social etiquette. However, I came to believe that it had a much broader, more important spiritual application: pride and arrogance versus humility.

A few days later, in another town, Jesus spoke to a crowd of at least two thousand, which included an even larger number of Pharisees and lawyers. In addition to delivering his kingdom-of-God message and performing many healings, he told several more parables.

The Great Banquet

A certain man planned a great feast and sent his servants out with invitations, instructing them to invite all his friends to the banquet. The servants returned and told their master that everyone had declined his invitation, most making lame excuses. The man was angry and ordered his servants to go throughout the town and invite everyone they saw, including the poor, the halt, and the blind. A good number of those people accepted the invitation, but not nearly enough to fill the banquet hall.

"All right, go out into the hinterland and invite as many as possible; I want every seat at the table to be filled," he said. "And if any of the ones first invited show up—the ones who rejected my invitation—don't let them in."

I was beginning to understand the deeper meanings of Jesus's parables. It was clear that the first invitees were the priests, rabbis, Pharisees, and lawyers, almost all of whom had already rejected Jesus. It would then follow that the second group of those invited were the typical Jews of Israel, many, but by no means most, of whom had accepted his kingdom message. (Jesus frequently referred to these first two groups as *the lost sheep of the house of Israel*.) That would make the last group the Gentiles. Except for isolated instances—the Syrophoenician woman on the Mediterranean coast, the Gadaran man possessed by many demons, and a small number of Gentiles occasionally among the multitude of Jews in the region of Decapolis—Jesus had not taken his kingdom message to Gentiles.

The Prodigal Son

A certain man, a wealthy farmer, had two sons. The younger son came to his father one day and announced that he was leaving the farm and wanted immediately the inheritance that would someday be his. With considerable sadness, the father complied, giving the son a great deal of money. The son traveled to a far country, where he wasted his entire inheritance on riotous living. A famine came into that land, and with no money or friends to help him, he was desperate and starving. Finally, he found a job: a farmer hired him to take care of his pigs; the only food available to him was the slop the pigs ate.

In this state of despair, he finally remembered his father and the comfortable life he had foolishly left behind. He said to himself, "The lowest of my father's hired servants have plenty of decent food to eat, and here I am, starving to death, with only the husks the pigs leave behind. I will go home to my father, tell him that I have sinned against heaven and him, ask his forgiveness, and beg him to take me back, not as a son, but as the lowliest of his hired men."

He started for home, and when he was just in sight of it, his father saw him and came down the path, running toward him.

As his father drew near, the son began his rehearsed speech: "Father, I have sinned against heaven and you. ..."

His father would not let him finish. Throwing his arms around his son and weeping for pure joy, welcomed the wayward son home. He called several of his servants and ordered them to prepare a great banquet for his returned and beloved son.

"Kill the fatted calf," he said. "And fetch the best one of my robes and a fine pair of shoes, and put them on him; invite all his friends to join in the celebration."

The father removed the signet ring from his own finger and placed it on his son's.

With great emotion, the father shouted for all to hear, "Let us eat, drink, and be merry! For this, my son, was dead and now is alive; he was lost, and now he is found! Let there be unbounded happiness in our home!"

Just at that moment, the father's elder son returned from the fields, heard the raucous music, and saw the lively dancing. Confused by all this, he called out to a servant, asking the meaning of this commotion. The servant told him of his brother's return and his father's reaction.

The older son sought out his father and angrily demanded to know why his rebellious brother's return was cause for celebration. "Ever since your son left with his full inheritance," he said, "I have not only done all my work but his too! I have followed all your rules, faithfully executed all your orders, and been loyal to you in every way. Yet, you never invited *my* friends to a banquet honoring *me!* And now your wayward son, who squandered his inheritance, is treated to a glorious homecoming!"

"Son," the father replied, "you are always with me; everything I have is yours! It was only right that we rejoice, because your brother who was dead is now alive."

Upon hearing this, the father's elder son turned and walked away.

The Rich Man and Lazarus

A certain rich man lived in a lavish house, clothed himself expensively, and ate sumptuously of the finest foods, wines, and delicacies. A sick beggar named Lazarus sat outside the rich man's gate every day, and begged. He would often ask the rich man's servants for the crumbs that fell from their master's table. This wretch had sores all over his body, and the neighborhood stray dogs would lick them, which provided little relief from the pain they caused. One day, the beggar died, and the angels carried him to Abraham's bosom. Shortly thereafter, the rich man died; he went to hell, where he was greatly tormented in both body and spirit. He then saw Lazarus at a great distance, in paradise, which served only to increase his misery.

He called out to Abraham, entreating him to send Lazarus with a little water to cool his tongue. "I'm in agony," he cried.

Abraham rebuked him. "Remember on earth how you lived in luxury and Lazarus lived in poverty? Now he is comforted, and you are tormented. In addition to that, there is a great gulf between Lazarus, and me, and you; no one can travel from here to there, or from there to here."

The rich man was devastated by this condemnation, and he begged Abraham to send Lazarus to warn his brother so that he would not suffer the same fate.

"He has the warnings of Moses and all the other prophets of God; let him read and heed them, so he won't end up like you."

"No, father Abraham! But if one such as Lazarus returned from the grave, my brother would repent and not perish like me!"

"Not so," Abraham rejoined. "If he won't believe Moses and the other prophets, he won't be persuaded even by someone raised from the dead!"

It was obvious to the twelve of us and to the seventy that these four parables, in fact many of Jesus's parables, were aimed directly at the Judeans, specifically the Pharisees and lawyers among them. By this time, most of Jesus's ardent followers no longer asked him to explain the underlying meanings of the parables. Occasionally, he would ask us if we had any questions about them, or if we needed further enlightenment as to their deeper significance. There had been fewer and fewer of such requests. Sometimes, he would ask us to tell him what *we* thought their intrinsic meanings were. All twelve of us participated in these exercises, and from time to time, some of the seventy did as well. When we were alone with Jesus—that is, when the multitudes had departed in the evening, or early in the morning before the crowds came—he would discuss matters with us that he did not share with the multitude, and certainly not with the lawyers and Pharisees who were a growing presence in the larger company.

Here are some of the things he told us.

"Those who follow me must give up everything: family, possessions, and sometimes even their own lives. There is an urgent task ahead of us, with life-and-death issues at stake. Whoever refuses to carry his own cross cannot be my disciple. Before you continue with me, count the cost. Are you willing to pay it? Do you have what it takes to finish this task? Whoever among you does not forsake all he has cannot be my disciple. He is like salt that has lost its flavor and is good for nothing.

"Do you know what the word *repentance* means to the Pharisees and lawyers? To them, that word means accepting *their* interpretation of the Law and the writings of the prophets. Their interpretation is a perversion of the Law and the prophetic writings. They have burdened the truths of each with myriad rules and regulations of their own devising, not of God's. The lawyers and Pharisees think themselves as above repentance. But they need it more than anyone else does! Do you remember all the 'woes' I pronounced against them? I might as well have been talking to a stone wall. But *you!* You understand what repentance is, because it is very simple; it's exactly what John the Baptist and I have said it is: Accept God's kingdom, accept me, because, through me, His kingdom is here. And then follow me—wherever that leads."

As I have said, each day of this grand tour of Judea would see more and more people joining the ever-increasing throng of Jesus's followers. Most were ordinary folk, but there were exceptions— one type I have already mentioned: Pharisees and lawyers, almost all of whom were there to make trouble. However, there was one other faction of followers: tax collectors. Their number had grown considerably, and it was because of Matthew. Most tax collectors in Israel either knew each other or knew of each other. Because most people generally hated them, they found comfort and support, even friendship, in each other. Of course, when Matthew became a follower of Jesus, he gave up his former way of life. Nevertheless, he had made it his special mission to witness to his former colleagues, and in the process, many of them had renounced their way of life, and some were counted among the seventy. Many others, perhaps dozens, became faithful fellow travelers and would accompany us all the way to Jerusalem.

CHAPTER 25

Everywhere we went on this long and slow journey to Jerusalem, the Pharisees and lawyers continued to shadow and hector Jesus. Not a day passed that they did not attempt to provoke him into saying something they could use against him in their desperate crusade to discredit him among his followers, those he healed, or those he invited into God's coming kingdom. One afternoon, a group of these Pharisees and lawyers demanded to know just when the new kingdom Jesus talked about would arrive. It was the same question they had been asking him since the beginning of his ministry, and he answered it the same way he had done all along.

"God's new kingdom isn't something you can watch for and see coming. Open your eyes! It is here now, and it is yours for the taking. Reach out and grab it. When you do, it will be inside you; it will be a part of you, and you will be a part of it. Look around you! Many of those you see have already received this kingdom. That's the one and only answer to your question, no matter how many times you may ask it.

"I have something to say now to those of you who have already received God's kingdom: One of these days, the Son of Man will no longer be with you in the flesh, and you'll desire to actually see him in the flesh. You will look for him, but you won't find him. People will tell you that he is in one place or another, but you will search for him in vain. Like lightning that flashes across the sky, that's what the Son of Man is like. However, before he departs, he must suffer many things: This generation will reject him. As it was in the days of Noah, so shall it be in the days of the Son of Man: The people ate, drank, married, and attended wedding parties. Life went on as usual until Noah entered the ark, and then the great flood killed all but him and his family. Something similar happened in the days of Lot: The people ate, drank, bought, sold, planted, and built. At God's command, Lot left Sodom, and fire destroyed that city and everyone in it. That is what will happen when the Son of Man is revealed. Do not forget Lot's wife: She looked back and she, too, perished. If you try to save your life by yourself, you will lose it; but if you lose your life for my sake, you will save it. Be prepared to meet God at any time! Don't delay your preparations; don't let anything else distract you. Two will be sleeping together: one will be saved, the other lost. Two will be working together: one will be saved, the other lost."

Once again, Jesus was talking about his rejection and suffering. This disturbed and confused not only the twelve of us but the seventy as well.

Jesus then told two more of his parables.

The Persistent Widow

A certain judge had no respect for God or regard for people. A widow came to him, asking that he judge a case against her and rule in her favor. 'Avenge me of my adversary,' she begged. The judge refused to even hear her side of the story. She persisted and pestered the judge, who finally grew weary, heard her case, and decided in her favor. Likewise, God will bring justice to those who serve Him and vigorously seek it from Him. When the Son of Man comes, will he find such faith on the earth?

The Pharisee and the Tax Collector

Two men went up to the temple to pray.

One, a Pharisee, standing in a prominent place, looked up to heaven and said, "God, I thank You that I'm not like other men: extortionists, unjust, adulterers, and, especially, not like this tax collector. I fast twice each week, and faithfully and scrupulously tithe."

The other man, the tax collector, stood in the back of the temple, trying not to be seen. He bowed his head, silently smote his breast, and quietly said, "God, be merciful to me, a sinner."

This man, the tax collector, not the Pharisee, returned to his home, justified in the eyes of God. Those who exalt themselves will be abased; those who humble themselves will be exalted by God.

Early the next morning, we traveled on to another Judean village a few miles away and a little closer to Jerusalem. The number of people following Jesus continued to grow daily, but the cadre of Pharisees and lawyers dogging him remained the same small number.

Later that same day, one of the lawyers tried yet again to entrap Jesus with another loaded question.

"Is it lawful for a man to divorce his wife for any reason he chooses?"

"Well, now. What did Moses say about that?" Jesus replied.

"Moses allowed for it."

"You're right, he did. But do you know why he did?" Jesus did not wait for the lawyer's reply. "Because of the hardness of the people's hearts—a hardness you and your ilk share to this very day! That is why he allowed it. However, that is not the way it was from the creation! Not the way God originally intended marriage to be! No! God created man and woman. When a boy becomes a man, he leaves his father and mother, and then he marries a woman; he is joined to his wife, and they are no longer two but one. God has joined them together! In addition, what God has joined, no man is to separate! *That's* what God intended from the beginning."

Immediately, the lawyer and his cohorts left, to our delight and to the delight of the multitude. If only they would leave for good! Nevertheless, we knew they would be back the next day, with yet more questions, all in their attempt to disrupt Jesus's ministry. They, too, would follow him all the way to Jerusalem.

That evening, when just the twelve of us were alone with Jesus, Peter asked him the question that I supposed was on all our minds.

"Master, I love my wife and have never even thought of divorcing her, so please don't misunderstand my question. Is there any justifiable reason, in the eyes of God, for a man to divorce his wife, or for a woman to divorce her husband?"

"If a man commits adultery, his wife has a justifiable reason to seek a divorce. In addition, if a woman commits adultery, her husband has the same right. Now, that does not necessarily mean they should divorce. There can be repentance, forgiveness, and reconciliation in such circumstances. However, if there is no confession or repentance by the offending party, or no forgiveness by the party offended, then divorce is permitted. In that case, remarriage of the injured party is also allowed. You remember what happened to John the Baptist: He lost his life because he correctly condemned Herod for marrying his brother's wife, Herodias. In that matter, each of them was guilty of adultery in God's sight, and John was correct to denounce both of them."

"Maybe it's not a good idea to marry in the first place," Judas commented.

"That is true for some," Jesus replied.

Among the ever-increasing crowds that now followed Jesus, there were many families and, among those families, a large number of children. That afternoon, several of these parents brought their children to Jesus and asked him to lay his hands on them and bless them. One of the seventy, not one of us twelve—we had learned our lesson—tried to prevent this intrusion by telling them that the Master was too busy to receive them or their children.

Jesus, just as he had done on the previous occasion, reproached this follower, telling him that children were of immeasurable importance to God's kingdom. Jesus then took the children in his arms, touched their heads with his hand, and blessed them.

"Those who don't receive the kingdom as these little children do will have no part in that kingdom," he said.

The next morning, Jesus leading the way, we continued our sojourn. He never seemed in doubt about where we would go to next, and it was not always the most direct route to Jerusalem. Sometimes we would travel in a direction that took us farther from the Holy City, but there was never any doubt about our ultimate destination. On that particular day, something rather unusual and surprising happened. A young man—he could not have been much older than I was—emerged from the crowd and approached Jesus. He was finely dressed, handsome, and well spoken. He had a small entourage with him consisting of servants and other retainers. His wealth was obvious, which made what he did next unexpected and remarkable: he knelt at the Master's feet!

"Good teacher, what must I do to inherit eternal life in the coming age?"

"You called me 'good teacher.' Why? Only God is good." Jesus did not wait for an answer. "But, if you want eternal life, keep the commandments."

"Which ones?"

"Don't commit adultery, don't murder, don't steal, don't lie, and don't defraud anyone. But, *do* honor your father and mother, and *do* love others as you love yourself."

"I've always kept God's commandments, ever since I was a child. Is there anything else I can do?"

Jesus looked at him intently and then said earnestly and warmly, "Yes, there is one more thing you can do: Sell your possessions and give the proceeds to the poor. Become one of my disciples and, with them, take up your cross and follow me."

The young man's face fell; he looked desolate. He turned around and silently walked away, followed closely by his retinue, and disappeared into the crowd. None of us ever saw him again.

Jesus turned, looked at us, and said with great sorrow, "It's hard for the rich to enter into the kingdom."

Everyone who heard this pronouncement was astonished, including us twelve. It was a common belief among our people that wealth was a blessing from God, and that, therefore, He favored those who possessed it. However, Jesus had seemed to contradict this notion. He must have perceived our confusion, because he invited just the twelve of us to follow him to a nearby quiet place, away from the crowds.

As the sun went down, we sat together in a circle.

"You were surprised at what I said about it being difficult for the wealthy to enter into the kingdom, weren't you?"

"Yes, we were," Peter replied. "I have believed all my life that wealth is not only a blessing from God but also a sign of his approval. So, I'm confused by what you said about it being hard for the rich to enter the kingdom."

Jesus replied, "First of all, God does bless some of His people with material wealth, and that is an indication that He *trusts* them to do the right thing with their riches. In other words, He wants them to use their wealth to bless those in need and to advance His kingdom, *not* hoard it all for their own benefit. But the notion that all rich Jews are assured of a place in the kingdom is false. That's because many wealthy people put their trust in material possessions, not in God's mercy. Not only that, but wealth distracts them from seeking a close and dependent relationship with God; they worship money and not God. It's easier for a camel to pass through the eye of a needle than for the rich to get into heaven."

"Then how can there be *any* rich people in heaven?" Matthew asked.

"With mortals it is impossible; but with God, all things are possible."

Matthew had been rich when he joined us, but all that remained of his wealth was his large home, which Jesus encouraged him to keep, as it often served as the one private abode that would accommodate all of us. The former tax collector had, of his own volition, given everything else away, either to those he had defrauded, to the poor, or for the support of Jesus's ministry.

Peter spoke up again. "Look, we've all given up everything to follow you. What will be our reward?"

"In the earth made new—God's kingdom—you will sit on thrones of his glory: twelve thrones for judging the twelve tribes of Israel. I'm telling you the truth: The man who has left home or brothers or sisters, father or mother, wife or children, for my sake and the gospel's will receive one hundred times what he has lost in the present age, and eternal life in the age to come. Do not store up treasure on this earth; let God store up treasure for you in heaven. Many who are first on this earth will be last in God's kingdom."

Jesus illustrated these points with another of his parables.

The Laborers in the Vineyard

The kingdom of heaven is like a landowner who went to the marketplace at sunrise to hire laborers to harvest the grapes in his vineyard. He offered them the standard wage of one denarius to work until sundown, and several accepted. At midmorning, he decided he needed more laborers if the job was to be completed that day. Returning to the marketplace, he hired several more men, promising to pay them a fair wage; they, too, agreed. At noon, and again one hour before sunset, he observed that he still needed more laborers and returned yet again to the marketplace, where he made the same offer and hired more men. The work was completed just as the sun was setting, and he called the men and began to pay them, beginning with those hired last. He gave them each one denarius—as if they had worked the entire day. He did the same with those who had worked three hours, six hours, and nine hours. The ones who had worked from dawn till dusk—twelve hours—began to speculate that he would pay them more than the others, but he paid them the same amount: one denarius.

They began to murmur against the landowner, and when he asked them what they were complaining about, one of them pointed out his unfairness to those who had toiled all day, as compared with those who had worked less: "We deserve more," the man said.

"Didn't I pay you what you agreed was a fair wage?" the landowner responded. "Why are you complaining? I decided to compensate everyone the same. It is my money, and I can spend it as I choose. You may not agree, but that is for me to decide. Take your money."

The first shall be last, and the last shall be first.

Jesus paused and then explained the parable further.

"Now, just in case you don't see how this parable applies to you twelve, let me enlighten you: All of you have been following me for more than two years, some of you for nearly three; the seventy, only a few months. The reward—life eternal—will be the same for all of you. Are there any more questions?"

I was puzzled by the last part of Jesus's invitation to the rich young man we'd seen earlier. Jesus's words, "Take up your cross, and follow me," spoken twice in the past few days, were alarming, and I was surprised that none of us had asked him to explain what that meant. Death by tying or nailing condemned men to a cross, especially those considered enemies of the empire, was the preferred method of execution employed by the Romans, and it was a slow and gruesome way to die. They fashioned two planks of strong and heavy wood, one about fifteen feet in length, the other about six feet; when assembled, it formed the shape of a T. The executioners sank this four feet into the ground, and then they hung the criminal on it, where he would die an agonizing death. Though I was one of the most reluctant in his inner circle to ask Jesus questions, I asked him to explain what he meant by that phrase. His answer made me wish I had kept silent. For the third time in recent weeks, he predicted his own impending death.

"When we get to Jerusalem, the Son of Man will be delivered to the chief priests and lawyers. They will condemn him to death and deliver him to the Romans, just as the prophets of old have foretold. He will be mocked, scourged, spat upon, and then killed. But, on the third day, he will rise again."

Of course, we knew what Jesus meant by the term *Son of Man*. He was referring to himself. However, we could not—or, I can now say in hindsight, would not—fully comprehend what he said about his death.

Peter blurted out, "Then *why* are we going to Jerusalem? Do you *want* to die?"

"I'm going because I must go. My choice to go was made long ago, and I go willingly."

My mother, Salome, had been among the regular female followers of Jesus for more than a year now. She and the other women willingly, happily, looked after our temporal needs: preparing our meals, mending our clothes, bandaging our minor cuts and scrapes, and so on. We all appreciated the contribution that she and the others made.

The next morning, shortly after we had finished breakfast and just before we continued our journey to Jerusalem, Mother looked at James and me.

"I think this would be a good time for me to ask Jesus about your future in his kingdom."

We enthusiastically agreed.

The three of us approached him and asked to speak with him privately. We walked a short distance away from the others, who looked at us curiously.

"Master," she said, "I want you to do something for me."

"What is it you want me to do for you, Salome?"

"Grant that these two sons of mine may sit, one on your right and one on your left, in your kingdom."

Alas, this was not our mother's idea. James and I had put her up to it. We thought that if she made this request, Jesus might be more inclined to grant our wish by making it appear to be hers.

He was not fooled. With a look of disappointment, he turned to James and me.

"You two don't know what you're asking of me! Are you able to drink from the cup that I drink from? Be baptized with the baptism I'm baptized with?"

"Yes!" my brother and I replied in unison.

"And you will. Both of you will. However, to sit on my right and my left is not mine to grant. Those places of honor will be given to whomever my Father chooses; He will decide."

Yet again, we had embarrassed not only ourselves, but our poor mother as well. We felt sufficiently chastised as we walked back, with our heads down, to rejoin the others, who seemed to know what had transpired. Neither they nor our mother spoke to us the rest of the day.

Jesus soon called us twelve together. He had something to say to his closest followers.

"The Romans have a hierarchy of authority: the highest to the lowest, starting with Caesar at the top, to those at the bottom, the ordinary soldiers. It is not going to be like that with you. Whoever among you seeks the highest place shall be the servant of all. Even the Son of Man came to serve, not to be served by others. Do not aspire to be like the rulers of this world: arrogant and grasping. Remember what I said about such things during the Sermon on the Mount."

Unfortunately, we *had* forgotten, especially James and I. We still believed Jesus was going to Jerusalem, not to die but to be crowned king of Israel. He would gather a tremendous army and drive the hated Romans out of the Holy Land, restoring our country to its former greatness. We were sure the other ten believed the same thing. We wanted this journey to the Holy City to be a march to glory: his glory and ours.

CHAPTER 26

With Jesus in the vanguard, we set off for the city of Jericho. The throng of followers grew larger by the day, now numbering in the thousands. Jericho was a walled city that had been inhabited by Philistines two thousand years before, when Joshua led the children of Israel to its gates and demanded the fortress surrender to his troops. They refused, and for seven days, Joshua, following the Lord's command, marched his thousands of soldiers around the city: one time on each of the first six days and seven times on the seventh day, whereupon the walls collapsed and the recalcitrant inhabitants perished. God's people were at last completely in possession of their Promised Land.

On the outskirts of the city, we encountered two blind beggars: one appeared to be in his fifties, the other several years younger. Each sat upon his outer cloak, as the day was sunny and warm. Somehow, they knew it was Jesus approaching, probably because, more often than not, word of his impending arrival now preceded his actual coming. The older man began to shout very loudly.

"Jesus, Lord, you son of David, have mercy on us!" he cried.

He repeated this phrase over and over, each time louder than the time before.

Some of the men in the throng ran toward the beggar, telling him to be quiet, but his shouts only increased in volume.

The old beggar obviously annoyed these followers, but not the Master; he remained calm and was clearly concerned for these unfortunates.

"Peter," Jesus said. "You and Andrew go over and lead those men to me; I'd like to know what they want."

Without hesitation, the brothers went to the men, helped them to their feet, and led them to Jesus.

I heard Andrew reassure them both that they need not worry; everything would be all right.

The older man quieted down, telling Andrew that his name was Bartimaeus and his friend's name was Jude.

Bartimaeus and Jude then came to the Master.

The crowd instantly grew silent.

"What do you want me to do for you?" Jesus asked.

"Please, Lord, we would like our sight to be restored."

Without speaking, the Master gently placed the fingers of his hands on each of their eyes, first Bartimaeus's and then Jude's.

"Son of David, I can see you clearly; praise God!" Bartimaeus cried.

Jude, knelt at Jesus's feet and gazed up at him.

"Is it really you, the Promised One?" he asked. "Oh, that your face should be the first I have ever seen! Thank God for His mercy!"

"It is your faith that has restored your sight. Come now, and follow me."

Bartimaeus and Jude looked at each other. These men had been friends and companions for years but had never known what the other looked like until this moment. They, too, would follow Jesus to the Holy City.

The crowd, which had been mute during the past few minutes, burst forth with shouts of praise to God—all except the dozen or so Pharisees and lawyers, who maintained a cold, stony silence.

Word of the healing of the blind men, both well known in Jericho, spread before us, and the crowds grew larger as we passed through the city. Although the main thoroughfare bisecting the city was a scant mile long, it took hours to traverse, as Jesus paused often to minister to those who sought his healing touch.

As we were about to pass out of Jericho, Jesus suddenly stopped and peered up into a large sycamore tree. It was early spring, but the tree's branches were already fully covered with leaves. I could not see what he saw or understand what he could find of interest in an ordinary tree; we had passed dozens of such trees as we made our way through the city. And then, strangely, he started talking to the tree!

"Zacchaeus, come down from there! Today, I must visit your house!"

The sun was hot; the crowd had pressed close to Jesus all day; he had eaten nothing since breakfast. Was he all right?

I then saw a pair of small legs, followed by an equally small body, emerge from the canopy of the tree. What appeared to be perhaps a five-year-old boy climbed down the trunk of the tree. He landed on his feet, hitting the ground with a slight thud. However, seeing his face, I realized he was not a small boy; he was a man, and an older man at that! He could not have been more than three feet tall—half the height of Peter! I did not know that a grown man could be that small.

Utterly confused and astonished, I blinked and glanced at Peter.

Peter moved close enough to me to whisper in my ear.

"Haven't you ever seen a dwarf before?" he asked.

Dwarf. I'd never heard the word.

"A dwarf is simply a small person," Peter continued in a whisper. "Nobody knows why, but some people never grow to the stature of most other men and women."

"When they're born, are they smaller than most babies?" I asked, also in a whisper.

"Maybe a little smaller, but usually not much. Dwarfs are rare; this man is only the second or third one I've ever seen."

The reason Zacchaeus had ascended the tree was simple. In the large crowd that surrounded Jesus, he was too short to even get a glimpse of the Master, so he climbed the tree to see him. He had heard of Jesus and his kingdom message; earlier that day, he had learned of the Master's imminent arrival in Jericho. His curiosity was aroused, and he had to see this man.

As it happened, Zacchaeus was well known in Jericho, and he

was also well hated: He was the chief tax collector, not only in the city but also in the surrounding region. Dozens of other tax collectors worked under him, collecting levies for the Romans, the temple, and Herod. He took a portion of all the taxes these men collected, making him easily the richest man in Jericho. Jesus had asked if he could visit Zacchaeus's house—rather, he'd told Zacchaeus that he was going to visit his house that day.

The Pharisees and lawyers in the crowd were irate that Jesus would stoop to such a level and honor such an obvious sinner with his presence. As usual, they grumbled among themselves and spread their slanders among the people, some of whom agreed with them and stalked off.

Zacchaeus was thrilled about entertaining Jesus, and the little man eagerly led us to his magnificent home on a hill overlooking Jericho. You will recall that Matthew, a former tax collector and now our colleague, had a large and beautiful home in Capernaum, but it was nothing like this. The grounds and furnishings were exquisite.

Zacchaeus had many servants; he needed them for such a large estate. It was evening now, and Zacchaeus ordered his butler to have the kitchen servants prepare a banquet for Jesus and the twelve of us. The dinner was sumptuous; the food and wine excellent.

Afterward, we all withdrew to a large and comfortable sitting room. Zacchaeus had heard some of Jesus's kingdom message secondhand, but he wanted to hear it from the Master's lips.

Jesus was happy to oblige him. He spoke for over an hour, telling the same story that he had told to countless thousands during the course of the past two-plus years. I never tired of hearing it; none of us did. Jesus was a marvelous raconteur, whether he was speaking in parables or teaching the gospel message, and it made no difference to him if the audience was small or large. His voice was clear, almost musical, and pleasing to the ear. His quiet passion for the gospel narrative was certain and absolute. What he said manifestly and deeply affected even many of those who could not quite bring themselves to accept the truth of his words. The exceptions were the Pharisees and lawyers; their hearts and minds proved to be impenetrable in most cases.

Zacchaeus—and the rest of us—listened intently to what Jesus had to say, and when the Master finished, the receptive tax collector was clearly overjoyed.

"Rabbi, I want to become one of your followers. Wherever you go, I want to go with you. First, I want to make things right with those I have wronged. I'll give half of what I possess to the poor, and if I've defrauded anyone—and I know of several that I have cheated—I will restore to them four times what I've taken wrongly. I understand that you are going to Jerusalem for Passover. I haven't attended Passover for many years, but I will join you and your other followers there. First, however, I will do what I have committed to do."

"You, Zacchaeus, are a son of Abraham too. The Son of Man has come to seek and save the lost; this day, salvation has come to your house."

By this time, it was late in the evening, and Zacchaeus invited us to stay the night with him.

When we left the next morning, the crowd that joined up with us was noticeably smaller. To be sure, the seventy all were there; the faithful outer circle of followers all were there; but many of those who had joined us in recent weeks were gone. I supposed they could not abide Jesus's consorting with the likes of a sinner such as Zacchaeus.

The huge throng of followers from the preceding day had dwindled to a few thousand as we continued up the main road between Jericho and Jerusalem. I say "up," as there is quite an elevation rise between these two cities. It was fifteen miles from Jericho to the Holy City, and because of the large number in our company, the going was slow.

After we had paused for our midday meal, Jesus asked everyone to sit and listen carefully to something he wanted to say to us; it was another parable, and its deep meaning was lost on his listeners, even us, his twelve apostles. All but one of us, that is.

The King, the Servants, and the Money

A certain nobleman went into a far country to receive a royal authority and return to rule his kingdom. However, before leaving on his journey, he called his highest-ranked servants and entrusted to them money—one hundred denarii each—to invest in any manner they chose until his return. But many others who were to be his subjects hated him and sent a delegation to the far country to oppose his being given sovereignty over them. This delegation was rebuffed, and the royal commission was bestowed. When he returned to his home country, he called his retainers and asked them to give an accounting of how they had invested his money and what returns they had achieved. The first one had turned the one hundred denarii into one thousand.

The newly crowned king was pleased and commended him. "Well done! You are a good and faithful servant, and because you have been dutiful over a small matter, I'm making you ruler over ten of the cities in my kingdom."

The second man came forward and stated that he had increased his one hundred denarii fivefold. He, too, was commended and given charge of five cities.

The third servant approached the king hesitantly, saying that he had hidden the one hundred denarii because he was afraid that the money might be lost or stolen. There had been no increase in its value.

"I know you are a hard man," the man said to the king, "taking what is not yours and reaping what you didn't sow." He handed the one hundred denarii back to the angry king.

"I will judge you by your own words, you evil man!" the king said. "Why didn't you at least put my money in a bank, where it could have earned interest? That way I would have had some return on my money!"

The king then handed the one hundred denarii to the servant who had achieved a tenfold increase.

"But, Lord, he has one thousand denarii already," protested those who had observed this scene.

The king answered them, "To everyone who has much, more shall be given; but to him who has little, even that will be taken away from him. As for these enemies of mine who didn't want me to be king, bring them here and slaughter them in front of me."

To me, this was the most cryptic of all the parables Jesus had uttered thus far. I was not alone. I looked at my fellow apostles; I looked at the seventy and those who had been followers for months or even years; I looked at the more-recent followers. All were silent, with looks of bewilderment on their faces; again, all but one. Parts of the story made sense, but when combined with other parts of the parable, well, it just did not seem to fit together. In all of Jesus's previous parables, *king* referred to God, and *servants* referred to the children of Israel. However, the subjects hated the king in this story. Although Israelites had repeatedly disappointed, disobeyed, and defied God, we did not hate Him, and we always turned to Him in the end, after we had tried everything else. Weren't we, all of us, eagerly awaiting the Messiah, the Promised One of God? The great majority of those in the crowd who heard this story believed Jesus to be the Messiah! Moreover, what was the meaning of the delegation that followed the nobleman to the far country to oppose his coronation?

We continued on our way, and that evening, about three miles away from Jerusalem and very close to one of its small suburbs, Bethany, we stopped for the night. The sun was setting, and everyone was tired, especially the children and the elderly in our caravan. We all were ready for a meal and a good night's respite.

After supper, Jesus excused himself. Those of us close to him understood what that meant: He was going to a quiet place to pray.

The twelve of us were alone, and it was not long before Simon asked if anyone understood the parable. Everyone said he did not, except Nathanael. You will remember that Nathanael had a deep understanding of Hebrew Scripture. He had become James's and my close friend, and several of us considered him to be the theologian of our group—aside from Jesus, of course.

We were about to discover that Nathanael was also a historian.

"About two hundred years ago," he began, "when Israel once again rebelled against God and went into exile, God left instructions for those few who remained faithful to Him, telling them what to do until their return from exile. They and their descendants were to do more than just preserve our faith: they were to proclaim it and increase the faithful during that sad period of our history. I think that is what Jesus was referring to when he spoke of the nobleman and the servants he had entrusted the money to, for which he expected an increase. At first, I didn't understand why he seemed to veer off that line of thought in the part of the story that has this same nobleman going to the far country to receive 'royal authority' and to return and rule his people, most of whom hated him and sent a delegation to the far country to demand that he not be given this 'royal authority.' But then, I remembered something that happened when most of us were children; in fact some of us were not even born yet." He looked at James and me at that last part and then continued. "When Herod the Great died about thirty years ago— Jesus was a child then—his eldest son, Archelaus, was next in line to become king, but first he had to travel to Rome to receive authority from the emperor to assume the throne. Most Jews hated him, and they actually sent a delegation to Rome to oppose his coronation. They failed, and he became the puppet ruler of Israel, completely under Roman control and serving at the pleasure of the empire. About ten years later, he was recalled to Rome to defend his grossly ineffectual administration—in the emperor's mind—and his grossly evil rule—in the eyes of the Jews. Again, a delegation of Judeans, and even some Samaritans, followed him, and they convinced the Romans to remove him, replacing him with his younger brother,

Herod Antipas, who seems to be pleasing Rome but is no less hated by us than his brother was."

We were so fascinated by Nathanael's history lesson that we did not hear Jesus's approach, but suddenly, there he was, standing in our midst.

"What Nathanael has told you is correct."

That was all Jesus said, and then he immediately lay down on his blanket, covered himself with another one, and fell fast asleep.

Early the next morning, two men awakened us. The men were close friends of Lazarus and his sisters, Martha and Mary, all three of whom I have previously mentioned. They had received advanced word that Jesus was on his way to the area and had come from Bethany with an urgent message for the Master.

"Lord, he whom you love is very ill, and his sisters implore you to come at once!"

"Don't worry, and tell Martha and Mary not to worry. This sickness will not end in death, but in God's glory, so that the Son of God might be glorified."

This was the first time Jesus ever referred to himself as the *Son of God*. Heretofore, in such contexts, he had always called himself the *Son of Man*. I was shocked by this and happy there were no Pharisees and lawyers nearby to hear it; there were plenty of stones available, and they would not have hesitated to use them.

The couriers were stunned, and so were the rest of us. Lazarus was one of his dearest friends. Why would Jesus delay one minute in hastening to his side?

The disappointed messengers departed.

So did Jesus. He told us he would be gone for an unspecified period of time, and we were to wait right where we were until he returned.

After he walked away alone, the twelve of us looked at each other in bewilderment. Jesus often did surprising and unexpected things, but this was different. His best friend might be dying, and Jesus was walking in the opposite direction!

Jesus was gone for two full days, returning early in the morning of the third day. He never told us where he had gone or what he had been doing.

Upon his return, Jesus said we would continue on to Jerusalem.

The twelve of us were conflicted about going there. On the one hand, we believed—perhaps *hoped* is a better word—that the Master would be crowned king of Israel in the Holy City and somehow miraculously expel the Romans from our country. On the other hand, Jesus had talked of dying there, but we had rationalized that away as being some sort or code language or metaphor. However, our fear of the latter destiny had increasingly made us wary of going.

Speaking for us all, Peter said forcefully, "Master, the Pharisees and lawyers tried to stone you to death the last time we were in Jerusalem! Are you sure you want to go there again?"

Jesus's response was puzzling.

"There are twelve hours in the day. If a man walks in the sunlight, he will not stumble. If he walks in the darkness of night, he will stumble."

Ever the pessimist, Thomas said, "Let's go with Jesus so we, too, can die."

We set forth immediately, traveling in the direction of Jerusalem, which, at a distance of only about three miles, we could reach before noon. Jesus had a different intermediate destination in mind, however, and we turned off onto a side road that would take us into Bethany. So, he was going to see about his friend Lazarus after all.

Once again, Jesus seemed to read our thoughts.

"Yes, we're going to see Lazarus first. He's sleeping, but I'll wake him up."

"Isn't it good that he's sleeping, Master?" Andrew asked. "He's been ill, and sleep is what he needs; he'll get well quicker."

"Our friend Lazarus is dead. It is a good thing for your sakes that I wasn't there when he died. Now you're really going to see God's power."

Dead? Jesus had said his sickness would *not* result in death. Moreover, how did he *know* Lazarus was dead?

As we approached the village, we saw Martha hurrying toward us. She was weeping profusely and close to collapsing as James and I rushed to steady her. Several of Lazarus's friends had accompanied her, and they, too, were grieving.

"Jesus, if you had been here, my brother would not have died," Martha sobbed. "But I believe now, even after my brother has been in the tomb for four days, that whatever you ask of God, He will do."

"Your brother, my good friend, will rise again."

"I know he will rise again, in the resurrection at the last day."

"*I am* the resurrection and the life. Anyone who believes in me will live, even if he dies. Do you believe this, Martha?"

"Yes, Lord. I believe you are the Christ, the Son of God. The one the prophets promised would come into the world."

"Where's Mary?"

"She's in the house."

"Go and tell her to come; I want to see her."

Martha, accompanied by James and me, went to her brother's house, which was only a short distance away. We returned quickly, with Mary and several more of Lazarus's friends, now his mourners.

The grieving Mary fell at Jesus's feet, her tears falling on them.

"If you had been here, my brother would not have died."

Jesus looked at Mary, then at Martha, then at Lazarus's mourning friends, and then at the twelve of us. The grief among us all was palpable, and it was too much for him to bear. I had never seen him so sad. He, too, wept copiously. I heard several among the fifty or so mourners who observed this melancholy scene quietly remark on how much Jesus must have loved Lazarus. But I also heard a few criticize him for not coming sooner and healing Lazarus so that he would not have died.

I had seen Jesus exhibit many strong emotions: joy, laughter, deep caring, tenderness, concern, even anger, in the time I had known him. However, this was the first time I had seen him weep.

It was a few moments before Jesus recovered his composure and was able to speak.

"Where is my dear friend's tomb?" he asked.

"Come and see," said Martha, brushing the tears from her face.

Jesus and the rest of us followed Martha and Mary to the place of burial. On the way, I could hear him groaning quietly, deeply affected by the death of Lazarus and the broken hearts of his friend's sisters. It was a short distance to the burial chamber, Lazarus's family tomb, hewn out of solid rock in the side of the mountain. As was the common practice, a large disk-shaped stone stood in front of its entrance. Jesus asked Peter, Andrew, Judas, and Thaddaeus to roll the stone away from the opening. Hearing this command, Martha and Mary were horrified, and so were most of the mourners.

"Master, he's been dead four days! His body is already decaying. Please don't do this," Martha pleaded.

"Didn't I tell you that if you believe, you will see God's glory? Carry on men."

The heavy stone was rolled away, revealing an opening about three feet in width and six feet in height.

Jesus looked up to heaven and said, "Father, I thank You for hearing me; I know You always hear me. But I'm speaking out loud so the people who are standing nearby may believe that You have sent me."

Everyone became very quiet; even the moaning and the soft sounds of weeping ceased.

Jesus riveted his eyes on the chamber entrance.

In a voice easily heard by all present, he shouted, "Lazarus! Come out!"

Instantly, Lazarus did come out! Because his body, of necessity, had been bound with strips of linen, he emerged slowly and awkwardly. Nevertheless, he walked out of the death chamber of his own volition.

"Peter, you and Andrew go and unbind him so he can see where he's going and walk freely; and put this tunic on him."

Where Jesus got the tunic, I do not know.

Everyone was overwhelmed with joy and thanksgiving. The somber mood evaporated instantly.

Martha and Mary were speechless, but the looks on their faces— relief mixed with ecstasy—was something to behold.

Ironically, the first person to speak, other than Jesus, was Lazarus himself. He was confused and asked what was happening. When Martha told him, he fell at Jesus's feet, filled with gratitude.

Although no Pharisees or lawyers witnessed this event, I did notice a few men at the back of the small crowd whom neither my colleagues nor I recognized. They quickly left, taking the road that led to Jerusalem. Later, we would learn the purpose of their errand.

Lazarus and his sisters invited Jesus and the twelve of us to their house, where Martha *and* Mary prepared a special meal to celebrate the return from the grave of their beloved brother. It was a most joyous occasion.

Of course, Lazarus was not the first person Jesus had raised from the dead. You will recall the young girl and the widow's son. Although I, along with most other close observers, was convinced that they both had been truly dead and not merely in some sort of unconscious state, there were those who had reasonable doubts. However, in the case of Lazarus, there could be no doubt whatsoever. His return from death to life is now considered Jesus's greatest miracle.

Two days later, we attended the local synagogue in Bethany. There was quite a stir when Jesus, Martha, Mary, and—in perfect health— Lazarus entered the building. Of course, everyone present had heard of the recent miraculous event, but it was quite another thing entirely to see him in the flesh, alive and well.

CHAPTER 27

The next morning, the first day of the week, Jesus said he was going into Jerusalem. We knew it was just a matter of time before he would go to the Holy City, and while we were uneasy about it, we were certainly not willing to let him go alone; we would go with him, regardless of the danger. It was the beginning of Passover, a weeklong festival. The city would be crowded with tens of thousands of pilgrims from every province in Israel, and even beyond, as not all Jews lived in our Promised Land. For the past several days, we had seen hundreds of them pass nearby—sometimes singly but more often in family groups—on the road leading from the Jordan River valley to Jerusalem.

Many of the seventy had already gone into the Holy City, or its surrounding villages, to find lodging. The same was true of Jesus's outer circle of followers, and also of the few thousands more who had recently joined the larger company. James's and my father had come down from Capernaum, arriving two days before, and, along with our mother and sisters, had departed for Jerusalem earlier that morning. Ever since I was a small boy, our family had rented the same modest house for our annual Passover visits; it was not far from the temple.

Jesus told us that we would return to Bethany and the home of our friends each evening of that festival week.

My colleagues and I were relieved to hear this as the thought of staying day and night in Jerusalem, where we believed Jesus would be in constant peril, was unsettling.

As we emerged from Lazarus's house, a large but quiet crowd had already gathered, ready to follow Jesus wherever he should lead. Most of them probably presumed he was going to Jerusalem. This was a rational assumption, considering it was the beginning of Passover week, and they were correct.

It was a short walk to the Temple Mount, not more than two miles from Bethany. We were traveling on foot, as we always did, and it seemed that with every step we took, the following throng grew larger. As we approached Bethpage, near the gate to the garden of Gethsemane—at the very the crest of the Mount of Olives that looked out over the Holy City—Jesus stopped.

The Master sent Nathanael and me into the tiny village, bidding us to do an errand.

"A short distance from the village gate, you will find a donkey that no man has sat upon tied to a post," he said. "Untie it and bring it back here to me. If anyone asks you what you're doing, say that the Master needs to borrow the donkey and that it will be returned later today."

Nathanael and I complied. We had not walked far when we saw a donkey tied to a post, just as Jesus had described. We untied the beast, and as we were leading it away, a man standing nearby—I supposed he was its owner—did indeed ask us what we were doing. Nathanael repeated the explanation Jesus had given us. The man seemed satisfied, asked for no elaboration, turned, and walked into his house.

As we were returning to where Jesus and the others were waiting for us, I asked Nathanael what he thought Jesus was going to do with this animal.

"Ride him."

"Why would he do that? In the nearly three years I've been with Jesus, I've never seen him go anywhere except on foot."

Nathanael answered my question by quoting one of our ancient prophets, Micah. "You tell the daughter of Zion not to fear: Look! Your king comes meekly, sitting on a donkey."

Before I had time to think about or react to this passage from Scripture—with which I was not familiar—we were back with Jesus and the others.

Nathanael was right again: Jesus *was* going to ride the donkey into Jerusalem. Judas and James the Younger removed their outer cloaks, placed them on the animal's back, and then helped the Master mount him.

Realizing what was about to happen made the hair on the back of my neck stand up. If there were any doubts that Jesus was indeed the promised Messiah—and, more than that, the rightful king of Israel—those doubts were now put to rest. I felt honored to be one of his closest friends!

Within the few minutes that Nathanael and I had been gone to fetch the donkey, the crowd had grown larger still. They remained quiet, but their expressions betrayed curious excitement. Perhaps some of them were thinking of the same prophecy.

In another few moments' time, we entered Bethpage, and the first person to greet us was the owner of the donkey, standing in the company of his family. I then saw that the entire street leading through the village was lined with an excited multitude—men, women, and children— many more people than could possibly inhabit that small town.

The people began to lay cloaks in Jesus's path.

Waving palm branches, they shouted, "Hosanna! Blessed is the king of Israel who comes in the name of the Lord. Peace in heaven and glory in the highest."

There was no doubt: this was a reception reserved *exclusively for royalty.*

Among the exultant throng were many we recognized: several of the seventy and the long-time outer circle followers, including James's and my father, mother, and sisters. There were hundreds now out in front of Jesus, heralding his coming. As we passed those standing along the road, most of them joined the procession and followed us down the hill toward Jerusalem.

I had not noticed them earlier, but there were a few Pharisees in the crowd too, and they now made themselves known by approaching Jesus, one of them angrily demanding that the Master put a stop to this "outrageous display" by rebuking the multitude.

Jesus quickly dismissed them.

"If my followers were to hold their peace, the very rocks would cry out!"

Immediately, they left in a huff, refusing to be any part of this welcoming celebration.

Just as we were passing out of Bethpage, we came to a place that afforded the most magnificent view of the Holy City and the temple. The day was clear and mild, and the late-morning sun made the temple's golden dome gleam.

The donkey stopped, which caused the crowd to halt and then go silent.

Jesus had something to say, but he spoke so quietly that only those closest to him could hear his ominous lament.

"Oh, Jerusalem, Jerusalem, if you had only known the things which belong to your peace! But, it is too late—now they are hidden from your eyes, your understanding. For the days will come upon you that your enemies will build a trench around you, surround you on every side, entrap you, and lay you to the ground, you and your children. And not one stone of this city will be left on top of another, because you did not know the time of your visitation."

He spoke these apocalyptic words with great sorrow, punctuated with deep, barely audible groans.

I was confused, and I was not alone in my confusion. Here he was, about to enter the Holy City as a beloved prince—surrounded by thousands of his cheering fellow countrymen—on his way to what I believed, or at least hoped, would be a glorious coronation. Rather than acknowledging the accolades of his subjects, he condemned his own capital city to unspeakable destruction. I believe that if the larger throng had heard his words, the processional would have been over. However, as they had not heard it, we began our descent into the City of God, the crowd's excitement undiminished. It would take four hours to traverse the road from Bethpage, where the spontaneous celebration had begun, to Jerusalem, a distance of less than two miles.

When we reached the gates of the Holy City, the road narrowed to a street lined, not with people welcoming Jesus, but with houses and other structures closing us in to the point that the larger company began to disperse. By the time we reached the temple, the Master's entourage had dwindled to just us, his twelve apostles.

There would be no coronation that day.

Jesus dismounted the donkey and asked a young boy standing nearby to look after him until our return.

We followed Jesus into the temple courts. All he did was look around for a few minutes, not saying a word. As we emerged, Jesus instructed Judas to give a small coin to the boy. Instead of mounting the donkey for our uphill journey back to Bethany, Jesus chose to lead it. If the beast—which must have been tired—had been capable of emotion, it certainly would have appreciated this kindness.

Jesus led the donkey and the twelve of us back toward Bethany, to Lazarus's house, where we were to spend the next four nights of our Passover stay.

On the way, Nathanael, James, and I fell back a little distance from the rest. We were anxious to hear Nathanael's thoughts on the day's events.

"What do you think about the way Jesus was received by the crowd, the way he was treated like royalty?" James asked. "They seemed ready to crown him king right then and there!"

Nathanael, looking contemplative, took time before responding.

Finally, he said, "I think we—all twelve of us, and probably hundreds more of Jesus's followers as well—have been expecting him to be crowned king sometime soon, and Passover week seems to be the perfect time for that to happen. Certainly, in our eyes, Jesus embodies what we have been taught, and what we believe, about the Messiah, God's chosen one. I believe Jesus is a king, all right. But I think he may be a different kind of king than we have been expecting. He seems to have no desire to recruit and lead a great army to expel the Romans from Israel. For months now, he has been trying to prepare us for something very different from a coronation. In fact, he has, on more than one occasion, talked of dying in Jerusalem, not of assuming the throne of an earthly king here. Just as we were to descend the hill to the city, we were all standing close to Jesus when he uttered those sad words about its rejection of him, and the judgment of God that would come upon it because of that rejection. I think we all should prepare ourselves for some difficult days ahead and pray that God will strengthen us so we can weather them."

Neither James nor I was shocked by Nathanael's interpretation of the day's events, but we found no comfort in it.

Our conversation with Nathanael had caused us to fall well behind Jesus and the others, and we were now passing through Bethpage. Suddenly, we caught up with our colleagues, who had stopped on the road.

Jesus was handing over the reins of the donkey to its owner—the same man who had questioned Nathanael and me when we first borrowed the animal. He and the Master spoke quietly for a few moments.

We stayed with Lazarus and his sisters, who had prepared an evening meal for us. It had been an eventful day, and we all were ready for a good night's rest.

Not long after we retired, I awoke; someone was moving around, and I looked about to see who it was. Jesus was just passing out of the house. His nocturnal absences had ceased to be a mystery long before, and he was to repeat this practice every night for the next four nights.

The next morning, we headed back to Jerusalem. It was just the thirteen of us this time: no leading or following throng, no greeters shouting hosannas to hail the coming king or strewing cloaks in his path or waving palm branches in his honor. Jesus had wanted it this way; he had told the seventy and the outer circle of faithful followers that he wanted only his closest disciples—we twelve apostles—to accompany him the rest of this Passover week.

On the way, Jesus said he was hungry and pointed ahead to a fig tree by the roadside. This was curious because, as it was spring, there would be no figs; they ripened in late summer and were picked in the early fall. We watched as Jesus walked to the tree, looked up among its branches and thousands of green leaves and, of course, saw no figs.

"Let no fruit grow on you again forever!"

This time, Jesus was talking to the tree and not someone in it. It was a strange thing he did, cursing that tree. Once again, there was a deeper meaning, and we would have to wait a little while to understand it.

No one seemed to recognize or even notice Jesus as we continued on to the Holy City, and when we entered Solomon's Portico, no one there paid him any mind either—at first. As we walked about, we encountered the usual merchants who inhabited that area on a daily basis. There were many more of them, as this was Passover week, and their services were in great demand. (Such services included moneychangers converting denarii into temple coins required for tithes and offerings given by the pilgrims and sellers of unblemished sacrificial animals and birds.) There was a lot of haggling between sellers and buyers, some of it quite unseemly. It was a bustling, noisy place, sometimes even chaotic, and from the look on his face, the Master did not like it.

Suddenly, Jesus became the center of attention.

"Is it not written: 'My house shall be called by all nations the house of *prayer?* But you have made it a den of *thieves!*"

The Master spoke these words with more force and more anger than I had ever heard emanate from his mouth. Even though I was not the object of his scathing denunciation, it almost made me cower as if I had been. He now commanded the attention of everyone within hearing: Hundreds of people—most of them sincere pilgrims, many of them Pharisees, priests, and lawyers, and a small number of them the moneychangers and merchants who were the primary target of his wrath. I say "primary target" because the Pharisees, and especially the priests, were the ones who had permitted and even encouraged these tawdry practices. In addition, the priests benefited from them, receiving a portion of the merchants' and moneychangers' profits—most of this went toward the upkeep of the temple, but some of it was siphoned off to the priests themselves, to support their lavish lifestyles.

Jesus's verbal denunciation soon turned physical. He proceeded to overturn the moneychanger's tables, scattering coins all over the stone floor of Solomon's Portico. These men fled in a panic, not even stooping to gather up their money. Next, he turned on the sellers of sacrificial animals and birds, using a whip to drive these men out of the place. (Where he got the whip, I do not know.) They ran as if fleeing for their lives.

There were still hundreds of people in the area, but none of them made a sound; even the priests, lawyers, and Pharisees held their peace. For those who remained—even those who did not know who Jesus was—word spread quickly as to his identity, and he was soon surrounded by pilgrims who had heard of his healing powers: the blind and the lame prominent among them. Jesus made them whole. The enemies of Jesus observed all this silently. What could they say? What could they do?

After he had finished ministering to the afflicted ones, many of the children present gathered around the Master and began singing praises to him.

"Hosanna to the son of David!" they exclaimed.

This was too much for the priests, who considered such a demonstration to be blasphemous.

One of them broke his silence, demanding, "Do you hear what these ignorant children are saying? Put a stop to it!"

"Yes, I hear them," Jesus said. "Have you not read: 'Out of the mouths of babes God has perfected praise'?"

If they had read it, they had either ignored or forgotten it. Their focus on the Scriptures was upside down: emphasizing *their* man-made rules and regulations, and neglecting what really mattered. One of their number quietly asked Jesus to leave the temple, but he refused, and so *they* left.

Word had spread around the city of Jesus's presence in the temple courts, and hundreds of other pilgrims poured in to see him. The Master stayed for several more hours, healing the afflicted and, once again, proclaiming the good news of God's coming kingdom.

We left the city late that afternoon and returned to Bethany, where we would have supper with our friends and be their guests for the night. As we approached the fig tree that Jesus had cursed that morning, we were astounded to see that all its leaves had fallen off and its branches and trunk were rotted and gnarled. Its appearance was transformed from that of a healthy-looking tree to one that had been dead for decades.

The Master noticed our astonishment.

"I'm telling you the truth: If you have faith and don't doubt, you'll not only be able to do this to a fig tree, but you'll also be able to say to this mountain"—he pointed to the Temple Mount—"'be lifted up and cast into the sea,' and it will happen. Whatever you ask when you pray, you will receive it, *if* you believe."

The Temple Mount cast into the sea! Why any God-fearing Jew would say such a thing, do such a thing, was beyond my understanding.

CHAPTER 28

It was now the third day of Passover week, and, once again, we returned to the temple courts with Jesus, where he continued to heal and teach those who desired either or both. The same chief priests, Pharisees, and lawyers were there as well, usually in the background, but listening carefully for anything the Master might say that they could use against him. It was clear to anyone with eyes to see and ears to hear that they were jealous of Jesus's influence over the pilgrims, an influence that far exceeded their own. They regularly taunted him in a pathetic attempt to discredit both his healing powers and the truths of his kingdom-of-God message. At this, they largely failed, as many of the ordinary people hung on the Master's every word.

Late in the morning, a small delegation of Greeks arrived at the temple. It was not uncommon for Gentiles to visit Jerusalem during Passover. Most were merely curious about what, to them, was a strange religion. However, some were sincere in their desire to know more about the God we worshipped in comparison with the wood, stone, and metal gods in whom they put their faith and to whom they pledged their allegiance. But this visit by these men was different: they had heard about Jesus and had come to learn more about *him*.

One of the Greeks approached Philip and, not wanting to disrupt the Master's teaching, whispered to him that they desired an audience with the man they had traveled more than seven hundred miles to see. Philip told Andrew and, when Jesus had finished his discourse, Andrew passed the word to him.

The Master approached the Greeks and spoke earnestly to them.

"The time has come that the Son of Man will be glorified. I'm telling you the truth: If a grain of wheat falls into the ground and doesn't die, it remains all by itself. However, if it does die, it will bring forth much fruit. He who loves his life will lose it; he who loses his life shall keep it unto eternal life. If any man serves me, let him follow me so that wherever I am, he will be with me."

Judging by the looks on their faces, the Greeks, understandably, were baffled by this statement. The culture in which they were born and bred was one of high philosophy, and their use of metaphors, allegories, and parables was well known and admired by the educated classes of every other culture, including our own, although with some justifiable suspicion. Their language, considered by many to be the most cultivated, had spread everywhere; Jesus himself spoke Greek fluently and was speaking to them in their native tongue.

He continued. "If any man serves me, my Father will honor him. Now is my soul troubled, and what shall I say: Father, save me from this hour? No! For this purpose, I came to this hour. Father, glorify your name!"

"I have glorified My name, and I will glorify it again."

Everyone in the temple court stood stock-still and in complete silence. I understood exactly what was said by the voice like thunder, and my mind flashed back to my experience on the banks of the Jordan River three years before. Over time, I had come to believe that what I'd heard then was the voice of God. I was equally convinced now that I had just heard God's voice again. Later, I confirmed with my colleagues that they, too, had understood what was said. This was not true of the other Jews present: the consensus among them was of hearing the sound of ordinary thunder or perhaps an angel speaking in an unfamiliar tongue.

The Master looked directly at his Greek visitors, and what he said to them next indicated that they had understood the voice as well. That was odd, because the words my colleagues and I heard were in Aramaic, the language, along with Hebrew, that Jesus and most other native Jews spoke.

"This message did not come for my sake but for yours," Jesus said to the Greeks. "Now is the judgment of this world; now shall the ruler of this world be cast out. And if I am lifted up from the earth, I will draw all men to me."

By now, we knew what Jesus meant by "lifted up," and it pained us to hear these foreboding words again.

The Greeks, however, were confused, and one of them asked Jesus a question.

"We have heard that Jews believe their Christ—their Messiah—will live forever. Who is this 'Son of Man' of whom you speak, and what does 'he must be lifted up' mean? Is he the Christ, the Messiah?"

There were a number of priests and lawyers lurking nearby and listening intently to see how the Master would answer this question, so Jesus's response was necessarily cryptic.

"Yet a little time the light is with you; walk while you have the light, before the darkness comes upon you: For he who walks in darkness does not know where he is going. While the light is with you, believe in the light."

The crowd pushed close around Jesus, the Greeks, and us, his disciples. He melded into the throng, and when we tried to follow him, it was in vain: he was nowhere to be found.

Because this had happened before in the same place, when the Pharisees had tried to stone him, we were not surprised or overly concerned for his safety.

The Greeks wanted to search for him, but Peter was able to persuade them otherwise. He led us out of the temple courts and guided us a short distance away, to a quieter, more private place.

We all sat down. It was midday, everyone was hungry, and Martha—bless her—had packed two baskets of bread and dried fish for our noon meal. She always prepared more food than could be eaten in one meal, and this time her generosity paid off: there were twenty of us, not the thirteen she had anticipated. There was plenty to eat, and everyone had his fill. When we finished eating, our foreign guests asked us to tell them more about our religion and, especially, more about Jesus and the strange things he had said to them today.

Philip, whom they had initially asked to introduce them to the Master, asked Nathanael to explain the prophecies Jesus had alluded to in his response to their questions.

First, Nathanael spoke of our ancient Holy Scriptures, with which the Greeks were somewhat familiar, and then he talked generally of Israel's prophets and their prophecies. He quickly focused on one prophet in particular.

"Isaiah authored one of the longest books found in our ancient Scriptures," Nathanael began. "His prophecies focused primarily on the *Christ,* sometimes referred to as the *Messiah,* the *Anointed One,* and various other names meaning the same thing. Jesus often refers to these prophecies in his kingdom message. (Here, Nathanael gave a brief explanation of the gospel, with which the Greeks were already familiar.) Jesus has preached this message all over Israel, and once to an audience in which there were many Gentiles in a region east of our land. However, his primary focus has been to proclaim the good news to, in his words, 'the lost sheep of the house of Israel.' Nevertheless, he has implied on a number of occasions that when the time is right we, his followers, are to take the gospel to the *world.* Now, let's talk about what Jesus said to you today.

"Jesus frequently refers to himself as the *Son of Man.* We have come to understand—believe, really—that this is his humble way of saying he *is* the Messiah, the Anointed One of God. Over the past few centuries, there have been other men who also claimed to be the Messiah, some as recently as a hundred years ago. They all proved to be counterfeits. Jesus, alone among them, has the weight of the messianic prophecies on his side. Before I met the Master, as we sometimes call him, and ever since I was a child and learned to read, I have studied the writings of all our prophets—especially those prophecies that concern the Messiah. For years now, I have hoped he would come in my lifetime. *And he has. His name is Jesus.* Every prophecy about the Messiah fits Jesus perfectly, to the last detail. We don't have time to go into the particulars today, but I will be happy to spend time with any of you who would like to know more."

Our new friends expressed their thanks to Nathanael for the knowledge he had shared with them.

It was now midafternoon, and we continued to wonder what had become of Jesus. Peter suggested we go back to the temple to see if he had returned there. Indeed, he was there, and at least two hundred pilgrims had gathered about him and were listening intently to what he was saying.

"He who believes in me also believes in Him who sent me," Jesus said as we approached. "I have come into the world as a light so that those who do trust in me don't have to live in darkness any longer. In addition, I will not judge those who hear my words and do not believe them, because I didn't come into the world to judge anyone, but to *save* everyone. However, those who do reject my teachings and me *will* be judged. On the last day, God will judge them by my words. I have not spoken of myself, but of the Father who has sent me; He has commanded me to speak certain things, and I know that those things I speak lead to life everlasting. Everything I say, the Father has given me to say."

"Who is this 'father' that you speak of, the one who tells you what to say? We demand an answer!"

The man who shouted this question was one of the chief priests. His rich, well-tailored ecclesiastical robe betrayed his position. Several of his cohorts stood with him.

"I've got a question for you, and if you answer it, I'll tell you who my Father is," Jesus replied. "The baptism of John: was it from heaven, or was it of man's invention?"

We had seen this little drama before.

The priests gathered into a tight circle and began whispering among themselves. Their question was meant to trap the Master into responding in a manner that would give them cause to stone him to death, then and there.

Nevertheless, Jesus, with his counterquestion, had set a trap for them, and they were trying to avoid it. If they said John's baptism was from heaven, then why had they not accepted him as God's true prophet? On the other hand, if they said it was of man's invention, it would not go down well with this crowd of ordinary pilgrims, most of whom still held John in high esteem.

The silent onlookers waited for the priests' answer.

"We're not sure; we can't tell," one of the priests said. His "answer" was an obvious guise, and everyone who heard it, knew it.

"Then neither will I tell you who my Father is."

The crowd was openly delighted with the way Jesus had handled the priests and quietly disdainful of these religious leaders.

This incident provided an ideal opportunity for one of the Master's parables—the shortest one he ever told—that perfectly fit the moment. And there was a surprise at the end of it.

The pilgrims gave him their full attention.

The Two Sons

A certain man had two sons.

He asked the elder, "Son will you go into the vineyard and work today?"

"No," the elder son replied. But, later, he changed his mind and did go to work.

The man then asked the younger, "Son, will you go into the vineyard and work today?"

"Yes," the younger son answered. However, he later changed his mind and didn't go to work.

Which of these sons obeyed the will of his father?

It did not seem like a trap, but it was; and the priests fell into it.

"The first son did," their spokesman replied.

Of course, this was the obvious and correct answer, but the

priests had unwittingly provided Jesus with the opportunity for a scathing denunciation of them. He fixed his gaze upon them.

"I'm telling you the truth: The tax-collectors and prostitutes will get into heaven ahead of you! John came to you, in accordance with God's covenant plan, and you didn't believe him. You didn't repent; you didn't think you needed to repent. But you do. You and your ilk need repentance more than anyone else!"

I expected them to stalk out after this condemnation, but they stayed in place and heard another similarly themed parable.

The Landlord and the Tenant Farmers

A certain man planted a vineyard, surrounded it with a hedge, and built a watchtower in the midst of it. He then leased it out to tenant farmers and left on a long trip to a far country. When harvesttime came, he sent a servant to ask the tenants to pay him the agreed-upon rent out of the proceeds they had received from the sale of the grapes. The farmers refused to pay and beat up the messenger. The injured servant returned to the landlord and told him what had transpired. The owner sent another messenger, and the same thing happened. He then sent two of his strongest servants, but the farmers beat up one and killed the other. What was the landlord to do?

"I'll send my son," he said. "They will respect him."

But, when the son arrived, the farmers plotted among themselves. "This is the heir! Let's kill him, and his inheritance will be ours."

So, they cast him out of the vineyard and killed him.

What shall the lord of the vineyard do about this? I'll tell you what he'll do: he'll come and crush those wicked farmers and give the vineyard to others, who will render to him the fruits of it in their season.

"God forbid!" shouted one of the priests.

By now, if you have been reading this book carefully, you well know the symbolism in this parable. The landlord is God; the tenants are the religious leaders; the servants/messengers are God's prophets; and the landlord's son is the Messiah. I can assure you that is how the chief priests understood this parable.

And this is how Jesus responded to their "God forbid!" outburst.

"Haven't you read the Scriptures? Isaiah wrote, 'The stone which the builders rejected has become the chief cornerstone of the building! Whoever falls on that stone shall be broken; but on whomever that stone falls, he shall be crushed to powder!' I'm telling you the truth: the kingdom of God shall be taken away from you and given to a people that will bring forth fruits."

Hearing this enraged the chief priests, and some of them began to advance on Jesus, with murder in their eyes. Their spokesman, obviously the senior among them, wisely checked them. He knew this crowd, friendly to the Master and believing him to be at least a prophet and perhaps the Messiah, would turn on them physically if they attempted to stone or even silence Jesus.

In speaking of the cornerstone, Jesus was relating a historical fact. When the original temple—designed by King David and built by his son, King Solomon—was under construction, the architects and engineers discovered a large stone among the building materials that did not seem to fit anywhere, so they set it aside. As time went by, they finally discovered where it fit perfectly. It was *the* crucial component of the entire structure: the chief cornerstone; without it, the temple could not have been completed.

There were perhaps two hundred people in the temple courts, and we were in an area that allowed women but no Gentiles. We heard a commotion behind us and, turning around, we saw perhaps a dozen Pharisees and lawyers encircling a woman and walking toward Jesus. One of the lawyers, speaking loudly, made a serious accusation against her.

"Teacher, this woman was caught in the very act of adultery!

Moses commanded that a woman such as this be stoned to death. What do you say?"

Once again, a lawyer had distorted the Law. In matters of adultery, the accusers were to bring *both parties,* the woman *and* the man, before a priest, and the testimony of *two witnesses* was required for the stoning of *both, not just one of them.*

Jesus did not answer the question. He squatted down and began to trace his finger in the thin coat of dust on the stone floor. He was writing something, but I could not see what it was. While he was doing this, the lawyer continued to condemn the woman, whose head was bowed in shame, and to demand that the Master answer his question.

Jesus stood up and looked at him and the rest of her accusers.

"Any of you who is without sin is free to cast the first stone," he said.

The lawyer stopped talking. The woman cowered in fear.

The Master crouched down again and continued tracing his finger in the dust.

The woman's chief accuser walked closer to Jesus to see what he was writing. Seeing it, whatever it was, visibly disturbed him, and he walked away quickly.

The rest of the accusers approached one by one, looked at the floor, and then they, too, left.

The Master stood up, looked about and then at the woman.

"What has happened to your accusers? Where are they? Has no one cast a single stone at you in condemnation?"

"No one, sir," she replied, her head still bowed.

"Well, then, I don't condemn you either. You may go too. And don't sin again."

Just at the moment, a gust of wind blew through the temple courts. We disciples tried to see what Jesus had written, but the wind had erased completely whatever it was.

CHAPTER 29

Up to this point, I have been remiss in not describing our temple, a beautiful edifice, and I will now correct this oversight. There were many components of this, the holiest of buildings in our Holy City. The temple was approached by first entering Solomon's Portico, so named in honor of the third king of Israel. As I have already written, Solomon's father, King David, designed the original temple, but it was left to his son to supervise its construction. From that time until its destruction by the Babylonian army over five centuries before I wrote these words, it was known as Solomon's Temple (or simply the temple). Its reconstruction began during the reign of Herod the Great, about forty years before the events described in this book. From the portico, you would ascend steps to the Gate Beautiful, which was usually open, allowing free passage into the temple courts, which consisted of several areas, the Court of Women being the largest of them and the first one entered from the portico. It was so named because it was the only area in the temple courts (other than Solomon's Portico) where women were allowed. It and the exterior portico were the places where Jesus and the twelve of us spent most of our time that week: it was where he confronted the merchants and moneychangers; it was where he challenged the chief priests, Pharisees, Sadducees, and lawyers. The temple treasury, the depository of monetary gifts, was located in a corner of this court. There was a second set of steps leading up to the Nicanor Gate, which was usually closed and bolted. Behind it were the Court of Priests, the Court of Israel, and the Altar of Sacrifice. These areas were for the exclusive use of the temple priests in the performance of their sacred duties. Beyond that was a third set of steps ascending, first to the Altar of Incense, then to the Holy Place, and, finally, to the curtain behind which was the Most Holy Place. These last three components of the temple were the only ones protected by a roof to keep out the elements, and only designated priests and the high priest himself were allowed under that roof. The curtain separating the Holy Place from the Most Holy Place was about four inches thick. Only the high priest entered the Holy of Holies, and even he only did so once each year: on the Day of Atonement, in the early autumn. The only areas of the temple that ordinary Jews or visiting foreigners, including Gentiles, could enter were the unroofed ones—primarily, the Court of Gentiles, Solomon's Portico, and the Court of Women. As previously mentioned, during this Passover week, Jesus did most of his healing and teaching in these three places. It was there that we spent much of the third day of Passover.

On the this day, Jesus began his teaching with a parable—one that he had told before, but to a much different audience. He varied it slightly that day, but the essential story was the same.

The Marriage of the King's Son

The kingdom of heaven is like a certain king who made a wedding feast for his only son. He had already sent out invitations sometime before, and on the special day, he dispatched many of his servants to call the guests to the celebration. The servants returned and told the king that everyone to whom he had sent an invitation had refused to come. Therefore, he sent the servants out again for a second appeal.

"Tell those invited that I have prepared a great banquet for them: roasted oxen and fatted calves, with all the trimmings. Everything is ready and waiting for them. That will certainly get their attention, and they'll be happy to come."

However, this did not work, either: Those summoned made light of the invitation and went about their business. In addition, they beat up the servants and even killed some of them.

INSIDE THE HOLY PLACE

(cutaway view)

1. Priests' rooms and storage
2. Holy of Holies
3. Veil
4. Altar of Incense
5. Table of Shewbread
6. Lampstand
7. Porch

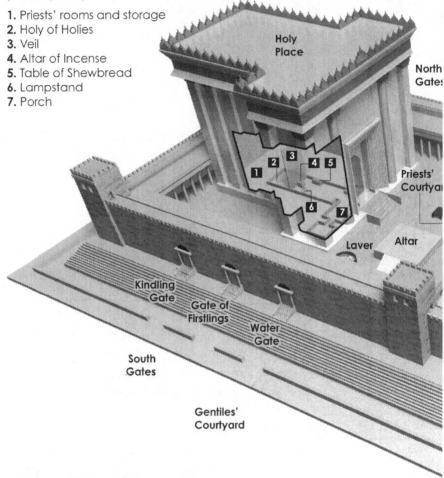

Holy Place

North Gates

Priests' Courtyard

Laver   Altar

Kindling Gate

Gate of Firstlings

Water Gate

South Gates

Gentiles' Courtyard

Herod's Temple

The inner courts of Herod's Temple were accessible by
10 gates, through which only Jews could enter. Once inside, there were
several chambers and a courtyard where sacrifices were made. At one end
was the Holy Place — a two-room sanctuary used by Jewish priests.
Herod's Second Temple and Temple Mount expansive building project was
completed in approximately 62-64 AD, only to be destroyed by the Romans
in 70 AD.

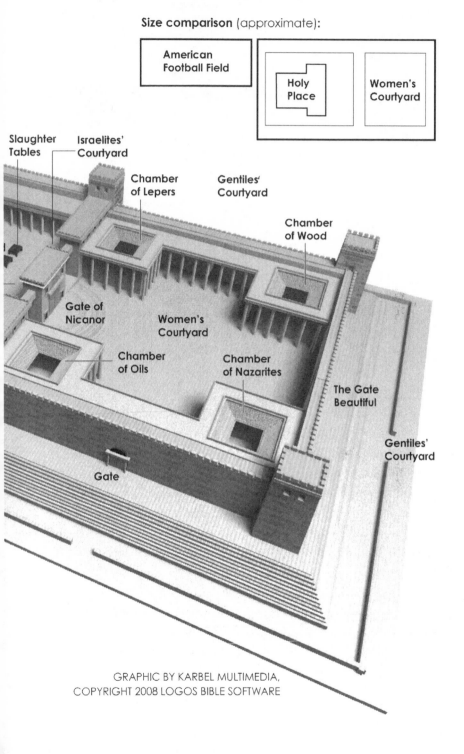

Size comparison (approximate):

American Football Field

Holy Place

Women's Courtyard

Slaughter Tables

Israelites' Courtyard

Chamber of Lepers

Gentiles' Courtyard

Chamber of Wood

Gate of Nicanor

Women's Courtyard

Chamber of Oils

Chamber of Nazarites

The Gate Beautiful

Gentiles' Courtyard

Gate

GRAPHIC BY KARBEL MULTIMEDIA,
COPYRIGHT 2008 LOGOS BIBLE SOFTWARE

When the king heard about this, he was angry and sent his soldiers out to punish those ingrates and destroy their houses and lands.

And then he said to his servants, "The wedding feast is ready, but those invited were not worthy. Go out to the highways and byways and gather all—as many as you can find, and make no distinction among them—so that the wedding may be filled with guests."

And so, it was done.

When the king entered the great banquet hall to greet his guests, he saw a man who was not properly dressed and said to him, "Friend, how did you get in here without appropriate clothing?"

The man was speechless.

The king then said to one of his servants, "Bind him hand and foot; take him out of here and throw him into outer darkness where there shall be weeping and grinding of teeth. For many are called, but few are chosen."

The audience that day, as it had in the previous three days, consisted of mostly pilgrims, but, of course, there were the same familiar faces of the lawyers, chief priests, leaders of the Pharisees, and a few Sadducees as well. All these men opposed Jesus for one reason or another, and they were anxious to discredit him among the people if they could—so far, they had failed miserably in all their attempts to do so. They knew that this latest parable was aimed directly at them, and it made their blood boil. They were not stupid men: All were well educated in the Law and the prophets, insofar as they interpreted those oracles. However, their interpretations were consistently wrong, or at least incomplete, and Jesus had consistently proved this, much to their chagrin. In short, they were spiritually blind. They made yet another attempt to trap the Master into saying something—anything—that would alienate him from the people, get him into trouble with the Roman authorities, or, better yet, do both.

A small cadre of Pharisees and Herodians approached Jesus. They had wisely chosen a Pharisee to pose a question to the Master.

"Master, we know you are truthful and teach God's way honestly. We also know you are impartial in how you treat people, and you don't use flattery to impress or influence them. You don't seem to be concerned about what people think of you. Now, we have a question for you: Should Jews pay tribute to Caesar or not? What do you think?"

This question was the equivalent of a double-edged sword: If Jesus said yes he would be in trouble with the pilgrims; if he said no he would be in trouble with the Romans, and the Romans would consider any Jew who told other Jews not to pay the tribute tax to be guilty of sedition, a crime punishable by death. As I've said, we Jews hated the tribute tax. First, the Romans conquered and occupied our sacred land, and then they demanded we pay taxes for the privilege of being subjugated by them! Around the time my brother, James, was born, a man named Judas led a revolt against the tribute tax, and he and hundreds of other Jews who refused to pay it were rounded up and executed—hung on crosses all over Israel and left there for days as a ghastly warning to all.

Everyone listened expectantly to hear how Jesus would handle this dilemma.

"Show me a tribute coin," he said to the spokesman of his detractors.

The man looked shocked. He turned and counseled quietly with his colleagues. Somehow, he produced the hated coin. (I say "hated," because the tribute coin contained not only the image of Augustus Tiberius, the incumbent Caesar, but on the reverse side it carried the inscription "Son of God and High Priest." Most Jews would not even touch this piece of money, considering it blasphemous to do so. There was only one true God, and it was not Caesar! Moreover, the second of the Ten Commandments forbade the inclusion of images of any personages on anything. The shekel, our national coin, had only the likeness of a stalk of wheat on it.) He looked sheepish as he placed the coin in the Master's hand.

A murmur arose from the crowd.

Jesus looked carefully at the coin, turning it over to examine both sides.

"This image and this inscription, whose are they?" he asked.

"Caesar's," the man replied hesitantly.

"Give to Caesar what is owed to him. Give to God what belongs to Him."

Notice the distinction the Master made between Caesar and God: "Give to Caesar what is *owed* to him. Give to God what *belongs* to Him."

The pilgrims were astonished and delighted by the way Jesus managed to respond to this seemingly impossible question. The Pharisees and Herodians were mortified and confounded, but only the Herodians chose to leave. As you will recall, they benefited from the collection of the tax to support King Herod, a tax that was almost as unpopular among the general populace as the imperial tax.

And then came yet another special interest group: the Sadducees. Historically, they were considered the aristocracy of our faith's priesthood. However, the Pharisees had displaced them many years before. Unlike all other Jews, the Sadducees rejected the idea of a resurrection unto eternal life at the last day. As someone not interested in their theology, I neither knew nor cared why they took that position. They proceeded to present to Jesus a ridiculous scenario that, I supposed, they thought would justify their belief, or more precisely, lack of belief in the resurrection.

Their spokesman stepped forward.

"Moses wrote that if a man's brother dies and had no children, the firstborn of the surviving brothers has an obligation to marry his deceased brother's widow and father her children, in order that her dead husband's legacy may survive into succeeding generations. Now, suppose the deceased brother had seven brothers and she married the first of them, but he died without leaving any children, and then the second brother married her but he, too, died before leaving any children, and so she married the third brother, and he also died before leaving any children, and so on, until all seven of them had perished without producing any children. Suppose, then, that the widow died. In the resurrection at the last day, whose wife will she be?"

My head was spinning from just listening to the convoluted tale. These people did not even believe in the resurrection in the first place, so the only purpose of this query was to set a verbal trap for Jesus in the hope of discrediting him. This absurd attempt—just one of many tried on the Master—would fail as the others had.

Once again, Jesus proved that he knew the Scriptures better than any of his adversaries did.

"I reject the premise of your question, and, if you knew the Scriptures and had an appreciation of God's power, you would have never posed it. Look: The men and women of this present age marry. However, this is not true in the age to come, where they will be resurrected to eternal life. In that new age in the earth made new, there will be no death. And, because there will be no death, there will be no reason for marriage; people will be like the angels. Out of the burning bush, God said to Moses, 'I am the God of Abraham, Isaac, and Jacob.' They are gone from this world but not forever. They will be resurrected and will live forever in the earth made new.' God is not the God of the dead but of the living. So, you are utterly wrong and don't know what you're talking about."

The Sadducees were speechless, completely deflated, but not so the Pharisees, lawyers, and priests. They were in rare agreement with Jesus on this matter and were happy to see their rivals humiliated.

One of them, a lawyer, actually complimented him.

"Well said, Master! I would like to ask you a question. Which is the greatest, the most important, of the commandments in the Law?"

It was obvious this legal expert was not just speaking of the Ten Commandments, but about the entirety of Jewish law as added to over the centuries. There were more than six hundred such laws or regulations.

"This commandment," replied Jesus, "is the first of all: 'Hear, oh Israel: The Lord our God is one Lord.' And this, too, is part of it: 'You shall love the Lord your God with all your heart, with all your soul, with all your mind, and with all your strength.' That is the first and greatest commandment. And, the second is, 'You shall love your neighbor as yourself.' There are no other commandments greater than these two. All the Law and all the writings of all the prophets hang on these two commandments."

"Well, Master, again you have said the truth," the lawyer conceded. "For there is only one God and no other. To love Him and to love our neighbors as we love ourselves means more to Him than all the burnt offerings and all the sacrifices anyone can give."

"You are not far from the kingdom of God," Jesus responded.

This lawyer had said something astonishing. The fundamental purpose, the only purpose of the temple in which he stood, was to receive the sacrifices and burnt offerings of the children of Israel as atonement for their sins. Had he taken leave of his senses? And, Jesus had commended him for saying it.

The pilgrims were stunned into silence, but the lawyer's cohorts, judging from the looks on their faces, were, to say the least, not happy with their colleague.

"Now, I have question for you," Jesus said to the legal expert. "What do you think of the Messiah? Whose son is he?"

"He is the son of David."

"Then why does David, in one of his psalms, call the Messiah 'Lord'? If the Messiah is David's Lord, how can the Messiah also be David's son? God said to the Messiah, 'Sit on my right hand, and I will make your enemies your footstool.' David also called the Messiah his 'Master.' What is your answer to my question?"

Neither the lawyer nor his colleagues could answer the Master's question, and, henceforth, they asked him no more questions.

The pilgrims, however, were visibly elated with the manner in which Jesus had disconcerted them.

In the late afternoon, we walked back toward Bethany. When we reached the gate to the garden of Gethsemane at the Mount of

Olives, Jesus took his leave of us. We did not question his departure: we knew he would spend the night there, praying.

We arrived at Lazarus's house in time for supper. Of course, he, Martha, and Mary asked about the Master's whereabouts, and when we told them, they understood and required no further explanation. There was little talk during the meal. It was as if we all had the same quiet thoughts of what might lay ahead for Jesus as the Passover week ended. Tomorrow, the fifth day of the week, we expected to return to the temple; the next day, preparation day, we would eat the Passover supper. But where? Would we return to the home of our friends? Did Jesus have some other plan for the meal? We did not know because he had not told us.

As we finished our supper, Martha expressed the hope that the Master and we twelve would celebrate the special meal in her brother's house.

We made no commitment, and she understood.

CHAPTER 30

The next morning, we said good-bye to Lazarus and his sisters, not knowing if we would return with Jesus that evening—or, for that matter, when we would see them again. The road from Bethany to Jerusalem led right past the gate to the garden of Gethsemane, and Jesus was waiting for us there. All thirteen of us walked to the temple and entered Solomon's Portico, where there was a larger-than-usual throng awaiting Jesus's arrival. The pilgrims were pleased to see him. This could not be said of the Pharisees, chief priests, and lawyers, all of whom stood off to one side, scowling.

It was about the lawyers that the Master first spoke, and his words were a damning denunciation.

"Beware the lawyers, many of whom are full of pomp and pretension. They walk in long robes, and love recognition and salutations wherever they go. They always seek the highest places in the synagogues and the best seats at banquets. These lawyers also use their legal skills to acquire legacies from widows, of whom they take advantage for their own personal gain. For show, they utter long and insincere prayers. Their reward will be greater damnation. These lawyers, and the Pharisees too, sit in Moses's seat, bidding you to faithfully observe the law, and you are obligated to do so. But do they also abide by the law? They do not! They say, but they don't do. Don't be like them. They bind you with heavy loads, but they refuse to carry the same burdens themselves; they don't lift a finger. They weigh you down with all sorts of rules and regulations—more than six hundred—while they ignore most of them. They perform good works not to honor God, but to be noticed by men. As an outward show of piety, they carry large prayer boxes and attach long tassels to the four corners of their long robes. They love to be called 'rabbi,' 'teacher,' or 'master,' but you are not to call them by any of those titles. For only one deserves those names: the Messiah, the Christ. You are all of one family. Call no man on earth 'father,' for only one is your Father, and He is in heaven. In addition, don't call any man 'Master,' for only one is your Master: the Christ. Of men, he who is greatest among you shall be your servant; whoever exalts himself shall be abased. But he who shall humble himself shall be great."

His followers, many others, and the twelve of us all called Jesus *Master*. He never objected to this title, and we now considered that proof he was the *Messiah*.

Up to this moment, Jesus had directed his comments to the general company of pilgrims. Now, he aimed his words squarely at the lawyers and Pharisees. He had previously used similar language in a different setting.

"Woe betide you lawyers and Pharisees, for you are hypocrites! You lock out the people from the kingdom of God. You will not enter that kingdom, and you don't want anyone else to enter it either.

"Woe betide you lawyers and Pharisees, for you are hypocrites! You will go to great lengths to make of one Gentile a Judean, and when he is made, you both become the children of hell.

"Woe to you, you blind guides who say, 'Whoever swears an oath by the temple swears not at all; but whoever swears by the gold on the temple, swears a valid oath.' You sightless fools! Which is greater: the gold or the temple that sanctifies the gold?

"You also say, 'Whoever swears by the altar, swears not at all; but whoever swears by the gift that is on the altar, swears a valid oath.' Once again, you miss the truth. Which is greater: the gift or the altar that sanctifies the gift? Whoever swears an oath by the altar swears not only on the altar but by everything on it as well. Likewise, whoever swears by heaven, swears an oath by the throne of God and He who sits on it."

(Jesus was speaking of the sacred judicial oath, not common oaths, which, when they invoked God's name or holy things, were considered blasphemy.)

"Woe betide you lawyers and Pharisees, for you are hypocrites! You pay tithe on mint, anise, and cumin—tiny earthly things— but you completely ignore the serious things that matter to God: justice, mercy, and loyalty. These more-important things you ought to have paid attention to while not neglecting the others. You blind guides! You filter out a gnat and swallow a camel. You make clean the outside of the cup and the dish; but inside you are full extortions and excesses. You blind Pharisees! First, cleanse what is inside the cup and the dish, that the outside may be clean too. You are also like whitewashed graves that are beautiful to look at on the outside, but inside are full of dead men's bones and corruption. You appear virtuous and law-abiding on the outside, but inside you are full of hypocrisy and iniquity. You are weak and self-serving.

"Woe betide you lawyers and Pharisees, for you are hypocrites! You build monuments for God's holy prophets, and you adorn their graves. You even say, 'If we had lived in the days of our fathers, we would not have been partakers with them in shedding the blood of these men of God.' You testify against yourselves; you are no different from those who murdered the prophets! Go ahead then and complete the work your ancestors began. You snakes and sons of snakes! You will not escape the condemnation of hell! I will send you prophets, wise men, and lawyers who have a right understanding of the Law. Some of them you will kill, and some of them you will scourge in your synagogues and persecute from city to city. Righteous blood will be on your hands, beginning with the blood of Abel, to the blood of Zechariah, whom your fathers murdered between the temple and the altar, on this very ground! I'm telling you the truth: all their blood will be on your hands in this generation!"

These warnings, these woes, these condemnations had been powerfully spoken. The Master's voice had echoed throughout the temple courts. Anyone in the vicinity had heard them loud and clear. Their message was unmistakable.

Jesus had one more thing to say, and his words were almost the same as the ones that a few of us had heard him speak four days before: his sad lament upon pausing at the crest of the hill during his triumphal entry to the Holy City and looking down on it and its magnificent temple, with tears in his eyes and sorrow in his voice.

"Oh, Jerusalem, Jerusalem! The city which kills the prophets and stones those who are sent to her! How often would I have gathered your children together as a hen gathers her chicks under her wings! But you were not willing. Your temple is left to you desolate, abandoned by God, in ruins! For I say to you, you shall see me no more until you say, 'Welcome, in the name of the Lord.'"

These cringe-inducing denunciations were devastating, and everyone who heard them knew it.

Most, though not all, of the pilgrims agreed with Jesus; but they were too fearful of these powerful men—the lawyers, the Pharisees, and the chief priests—to say what Jesus had said. They were also powerless—or at least they thought they were—to do anything about their entrenched leaders. They felt trapped. Nevertheless, they admired the Master's courage in challenging the unworthy religious rulers, all of whom quickly left Solomon's Portico without saying another word to Jesus. Most of the pilgrims dispersed too, and just the Master and the twelve of us remained.

It was nearing midday. According to tradition, the ceremonial Passover meal would be celebrated at sundown tomorrow—preparation day—all over Jerusalem, all over Israel, and all over the world, for that matter, wherever there were observant Jews. Perhaps we twelve were the only ones in Jerusalem who did not know where we would celebrate this supper; Jesus had not yet said a word about it. We followed him up the steps, through the Gate Beautiful, and into the Court of Women.

In one corner of this court was the temple treasury. Jesus stood a few feet from it, quietly observing those who placed their tithes and other offerings into a receptacle. Several of them were richly garbed men who made a show of depositing large, gleaming coins, one at a time and with quite a bit of noise, into the copper pot. An elderly woman, small of stature and wearing old and worn clothing, then hobbled up and dropped two tiny coins into the container; they were so small, they made no sound at all.

"Did you see what just happened?" Jesus asked. "I'm telling you the truth: This poor woman has given more that all the others combined. Those finely dressed men gave an insignificant portion of their wealth. But this old woman, who lives in extreme poverty, has given everything: all the money she had."

It was now past midday, and we followed Jesus out of the temple courts and up the street that led out of the city and back toward Bethany. In less than half an hour, we arrived at the Mount of Olives, and the Master said we would stop there to eat the noon meal Martha had prepared for us. He chose a place that overlooked the temple, perhaps a mile away.

While we were eating our lunch, Judas offered a comment.

"Master," he said. "Look at the temple and the huge white stones it is made of. Isn't it magnificent?'

Jesus stood up, walked a few feet away from us, and looked intently at the structure. After a few moments, he turned and spoke to us.

"Yes, it is magnificent," he said. "But the time is coming when there will not be one stone of it standing on top of another; they will all be thrown down. The temple will be a ruin."

This was the second time in the past few days that Jesus had made this declaration, but we had refused to believe he was speaking literally. We had interpreted his dire words as coded language—perhaps a metaphor—for something else, certainly something less shocking than the destruction of God's holy temple. This time, however, we were not sure, and we feared he really meant us to take his words plainly.

Peter, James, Andrew, and I walked over to where Jesus still stood.

Peter asked him to move a little farther from our colleagues so that we could speak with him privately.

"Master, are we to take your words about the temple's destruction literally?" Peter asked.

"Yes."

"Well, then, we want to know when this will come to pass. Will it happen soon? Will there be any warning before it happens?"

Jesus asked us to sit down on the grass.

I was glad he did, because his answer was a long one that did not actually answer Peter's simple question until about halfway through it, and, even then, only obliquely.

"Take care that you are not deceived by any man. For many men will come in my name, saying 'I am the Christ,' and they will deceive many people. Do not let them fool you. Likewise, when you hear of wars or rumors of wars, do not be afraid. Such things must necessarily happen first, but the end will not come yet. But be clear: Nation will rise against nation, and kingdom against kingdom, and great upheavals and famines, pestilences, fearful sights, and great signs from heaven will come. Nevertheless, those things will be just the beginning of sorrows. Even before these things occur, evil men will lay their hands on you. Some of you will be persecuted, some of you will be killed, and some of you will be brought before courts of law, denounced in the synagogues, and put into prisons. Some of you will be brought before kings and other rulers, and you will testify of me before them. All of you will be hated. All of these things will happen for my name's sake.

"You will all tell the gospel story, just as you've heard me tell it these last three years—not just here in Israel but in other parts of the world, and not just to Jews but to Gentiles as well. When you are brought before earthly powers, do not premeditate what you will say. That will not be necessary. The Holy Spirit will give you the words to speak; the Spirit will speak through you, and His words will be powerful. He will give you a mouth that will speak wisdom, which your adversaries will not be able to contradict or resist. Some of you will be betrayed by close family members and friends, and some of you will lose your lives for the sake of God's good news. False prophets will arise and deceive many. Evil will abound, and the love of many will grow cold toward you. But, if you endure to the end, you will be saved to eternal life, and not one hair of your head will have perished.

"All these things will require a lot of patience on your part. Nevertheless, the gospel of the kingdom must be preached in all the world for a witness to all nations, and then the end will come. When you see Jerusalem surrounded by armies, then you will know its destruction is near. When you see the abomination of desolation spoken of by the prophet Daniel, then let those in Judea flee to the mountains. They should not waste time gathering up their belongings because, if they do, they will not come out alive. These will be the days of vengeance that all the prophecies have foretold. Many people will die by the edge of the sword or be led away as captive slaves into foreign lands. The Gentiles will level Jerusalem until the times of the Gentiles are fulfilled. Moreover, pray that your flight is not in the winter or on the Sabbath. For in those days there will be tribulation such as has never been seen since the beginning of creation or will ever be seen after it. Unless the Lord shortens those days, no one will survive. However, for the sake of the saved, He will shorten them.

"If any man says to you, 'Here is Christ' or 'There he is,' do not believe it. Because false Christs and false prophets shall arise and perform signs and wonders to seduce, if it were possible, even God's elect. That is why I'm telling you all this before it happens. So, if anyone tells you, 'Look, he's in the desert,' don't go there; or, if someone says, 'He's in some secret place,' don't believe it. For, just as the lightning comes out of the east and flashes across the sky to the west, that is how the coming of the Son of Man will be. In those days after the tribulation, the sun shall be darkened and the moon will not reflect light and the stars will fall from heaven and the powers of heaven shall be shaken. There will be great distress and perplexity among the nations. The seas will roil, their waves crashing to shore. Men's hearts will fail them, for fear of what is happening on the earth; all the powers of earth with be shaken to the core.

"And then the earth's inhabitants will see the Son of Man

coming in the clouds, with power and glory. Many will be fearful; but not God's elect: for He will send His angels, with the sound of the trumpet, and they shall be gathered from the four corners of the earth up to the highest heaven. And when these things come to pass, look up, lift up your heads, for your redemption has come at last."

Jesus then told two parables to illustrate some of the things he had just said to us.

The Fig Tree

Learn a lesson from the fig tree. When it begins to leaf out, you know it is spring and summer is not far behind. When you see the things I have been talking about today come to pass, you will know the judgment of God is near, right at the gates. I'm telling you the truth: this generation shall not pass until all these things come about. Heaven and earth may pass away, but my words will not. Listen carefully now: no man knows the day or the hour when these events will occur, not even the angels in heaven or the Son of Man; only the Father knows. Pay attention; watch and pray, because you won't know the exact time until these things happen. Know yourselves well so that if you are ever overcome by the cares of this life, you will not let them distract you from your preparation for the end times. Do not be a captive of this world. Watch and pray so that you may be worthy to escape all these things that will come and then stand before the Son of Man.

The Returning Master

The Son of Man is like a traveler taking a long journey to a far country; he departs his home and gives certain responsibilities to his servants, along with the authority to discharge them. He commands them to be watchful and alert for his return because they will not know the day or the hour it will occur. It might be in the evening, at midnight, at dawn, or anytime during the day. Therefore, they are to keep a constant watch and not be found asleep.

I would like to tell you that I understood everything Jesus said that afternoon, but I cannot. Some of these prophetic pronouncements would come to pass within months; some would take years; some decades, many perhaps not in my life time.

I would be the only one of Jesus's apostles to live long enough to walk over the ruins of Jerusalem and its once-beautiful temple, where, by that time, not one stone stood on top of another. Just as the Master had foretold.

CHAPTER 31

Jesus led Peter, James, Andrew, and me back to our colleagues. They were still sitting in the same place where we had left them an hour before to speak privately with the Master.

Judas was not among them, and Peter asked the others where he was. No one knew. Judas had excused himself, saying simply that he had a personal matter to attend to and would rejoin us as soon as he could. No one asked any questions about what Jesus and the three of us had talked about.

The Master did not express any concern about Judas's whereabouts and proceeded to relate three new parables: the first about faithfulness, the second about watchfulness, and the third about judgment.

The Faithful and Unfaithful Servants

A certain man, the owner of a large estate, had a faithful servant to whom he entrusted the oversight of his other servants while he was gone on a long journey. He was to manage their work and ensure they were properly fed, clothed, and sheltered. Even though his master's return was delayed, this faithful servant did his duty so well that when the owner returned, he made him ruler over his entire estate. But suppose this servant had been unfaithful. This is what would have happened: When the master's return was delayed, the unfaithful servant became lax in his duties and neglectful of, even cruel to, the servants in his charge. He was frequently absent, fell in with drunkards, and became a drunkard himself. The owner's sudden return resulted in his catching the servant sleeping, which greatly angered the master, who ordered the evil servant's immediate execution.

The Wise and Foolish Young Women

The kingdom of heaven can be compared with ten young women who were members of a wedding party. They each took a lamp and went out to meet the bridegroom. Five of them were wise and took with them extra oil for their lamps; the other five were foolish and took no additional oil. The bridegroom was delayed, and all ten of these young women fell asleep waiting for him.

At midnight, there was a shout: "Look, the bridegroom is coming; go out to meet him!"

All ten jumped up and trimmed their lamps, all of which had used up their fuel supply. The wise added oil to their lamps and lighted them, but the foolish had no oil to add; their lamps were useless. The foolish girls begged the wise ones to share their oil, but they refused, knowing they would not have enough for their own lamps to keep them burning.

"Go and buy more oil from the merchants," the wise girls advised, and the foolish ones went searching.

The wise young women accompanied the bridegroom to the wedding, and the door was closed.

Finally, the foolish girls came and begged the doorkeeper to admit them.

The bridegroom heard the commotion, went to the door, and said to them, "I don't know you; go away."

Be watchful! You don't know the day or the hour the Son of Man comes.

The Sheep and the Goats

When the Son of Man comes in his glory, and all the holy angels with him, then shall he sit on his glorious throne;

before him shall be gathered all the nations, and he will separate them one from another, as a shepherd divides his sheep from his goats. He will put the sheep on his right hand and the goats on his left. Then shall he say to those on his right hand, "Come, you blessed of my Father, and inherit the kingdom prepared for you from the foundation of the world. For I was hungry, and you fed me; I was thirsty, and you gave me water; I was a stranger, and you gave me shelter; naked, and you clothed me; sick, and you cared for me; in prison, and you visited me."

Then those on his right will say, "Lord, when did we see you hungry, and give you food; thirsty, and give you water? When did we see you a stranger, and take you in, or naked, and clothe you? When did we see you sick or in prison, and visit you?"

The king will answer, "I'm telling you the truth: inasmuch as you have done those things for the least significant of my brothers and sisters, you have done them for me."

Then shall the king say to those on his left hand, "Depart from me. You are cursed into everlasting fire prepared for Satan and his angels. For I was hungry, and you gave me no food; thirsty, and you gave me no water; a stranger, and you gave me no shelter; naked, and you did not clothe me; sick and in prison, and you did not visit me."

Then those on his left will say, "Lord, when did we see you hungry or thirsty or a stranger or naked or sick or in prison, and not minister to you?"

Then shall the king answer them, "I'm telling you the truth: inasmuch as you did not do those things for the least significant of these, my brothers and sisters, you did not do them for me."

And so, they shall go away into everlasting punishment. But the righteous shall enter into life eternal.

These three parables encapsulated some of the same warnings, foreknowledge, instruction, counsel, and wisdom that Jesus had just finished imparting to Peter, James, Andrew, and me. To be sure, they were not as detailed or as apocalyptic as what we four had heard. But they were consistent with the themes Jesus had emphasized all week to his friends, his enemies, and those who did not fall into either camp: that is, those who had not yet made up their minds about who or what they thought him to be.

The sun was low in the western sky. Jesus stood up. We had all been sitting near him on the grass, and as we rose to our feet, he looked at us, an expression of great sorrow on his face.

"Tonight, we will celebrate the Feast of Unleavened Bread, the Passover meal," he said. "Tonight, the Son of Man will be betrayed. Tomorrow, he will be crucified."

If we were to share the Passover meal with Jesus, it must be tonight. I will not say I was surprised by his announcement. By this time, none of us who knew him so well or loved him so much expected a different outcome. The events of this Passover week pointed in no other direction than to his death. That one of his own—one of his disciples, one of his *apostles*—would betray him should not have surprised any of us either. More than a year before Jesus had said that one of us was a devil. Anyone who would betray him would certainly fit that description. But who was it?

I remembered that Nathanael had told James and me that he believed the devil among us might not even realize it himself. Hearing that, I had said it meant that it could be anyone of us. But who? I had seen no signs of betrayal in any of my colleagues.

Could it be me? That thought sent a cold chill through my whole being, and I quickly dismissed it. No, I loved Jesus too much for that.

I had been so caught up in these thoughts, I failed to notice that we had begun to move, to follow Jesus as he led the way back down the road toward Jerusalem.

Everyone was somber; not a word was spoken by any of us. This was the opposite of what had happened when we descended the same road on the first day of Passover week. That was only four days ago—*four days!* That day had seen cheering crowds, thousands of happy pilgrims lining the road, spreading cloaks and palm branches in the path of the "son of David." Now? Now, there was no gleeful throng, only eleven silent and somber men following their Master.

I remembered something Thomas, the pessimist, had said a few weeks before, when some of us were trying to talk the Master out of going to Jerusalem: "Let's go with Jesus so we, too, can die."

The Master had made it clear that he was going to die. Would we also die with him?

Just then, seemingly out of nowhere, Judas joined up with us. He was breathing rapidly, as if he had been running. He immediately sensed there was something wrong, but he said nothing, and nothing was said to him.

Just as we reached the city's gates, Jesus stopped and turned to Peter and me.

"I want you two men to go ahead of us, and when you see a man carrying a large pitcher of water, follow him to a house; when he enters the house, I want you to ask its owner to show you to a large upper room, where we will eat our Passover meal tonight. Tell him who you are and that I have sent you. Make sure the room is ready for us, and then return here. We will all go to the house together."

Peter and I followed the Master's instructions. The streets were not crowded, and, since it was unusual for a man to carry water, we spotted him before too long. We followed him a short distance to a large two-story house. He knocked at the door, which was opened, and then he went in. Before it closed, we were on the porch and introducing ourselves to the owner. He was obviously expecting us, and immediately led us up a staircase to a large room. In it was a table set up to accommodate all thirteen of us in the traditional fashion of the Passover meal.

It then took Peter and me only a few minutes to rejoin Jesus and our colleagues. *Jesus* led us to the house and then up the stairs to the room prepared especially for us; he knew exactly where to go.

CHAPTER 32

Jesus invited us all to sit down—or, rather, recline—at table. As I've mentioned, reclining on benches was the custom for more-formal meals; or, in this case, a solemn meal. This supper would be different from the traditional one: there were no servants to attend us, and the only items on the table were flat, unleavened bread, wine, and bowls of olive oil with herbs into which the bread was dipped; absent was the roasted lamb.

The Master offered the traditional prayer said by our ancestors for more than two millennia, after which he had more to say to us.

"I have longed to eat this Passover meal with you before the time when I shall suffer," he said. "I won't eat it with you again until all is fulfilled in the kingdom of God."

He then broke the bread, blessed it, and served each of us.

"Take and eat this bread, which is my body given to you. Do this in memory of me."

He then poured the wine into the silver chalice, gave thanks for it, and handed it to Peter.

"Divide this among yourselves, and drink all of it," Jesus said. "This is my blood of the new covenant, which is shed for you and many others for the remission of sins. Truly, I say to you, I will not drink again of the fruit of the vine until that day I drink it anew, with each of you, in my Father's kingdom."

I was reminded of what Jesus had once told us about eating his flesh and drinking his blood. We had all been puzzled, shocked, and even repulsed by his words at that time. Now their meaning became clear: the bread and the wine were emblems of his body and lifeblood, both of which he was about to sacrifice for our salvation.

Peter drank a portion of the wine and passed it to his brother, Andrew. In like manner, the chalice was passed from hand to hand around the table, coming last to me. No one said a word during this solemn moment.

Jesus removed his outer garment and girded himself with a towel. He poured water into a large basin and began to wash our feet, which he then dried with the towel. As I mentioned earlier, a servant, not the meal's host, always performed this task. However, you will recall that there were no servants present that night.

When he came to Peter, the Master was met with resistance.

"Are you going to wash my feet too?" Peter exclaimed.

"What I'm doing now you won't understand. But, later, you will."

"I will *not* let you wash my feet!"

"If I don't, you will have nothing to do with me."

Peter was aghast.

"Then wash not only my feet but my hands and head too."

"Oh, Peter. If I wash your feet, you will be clean all over. But one of you is not clean."

Jesus paused and then continued.

"Do you understand what I've just done? You all call me *Master* and *Lord,* and you are correct in doing so, because I am. If I, your Lord and Master, have washed your feet, you should also wash one another's feet. I have given you a new precedent that you should do as I have done. I'm telling you the truth: the servant is not greater than his lord. Neither is he who is sent greater than the One who sent him. If you understand these things—the meaning of the bread, the wine, the foot washing—and you carry on doing them, you'll have much joy. I'm not speaking of all of you. I know whom I have chosen. But, that the writings of the prophets may be fulfilled, one of you who is eating this meal with me has already lifted up his heel against me. I'm telling you this before it happens so that, when it does happen, you will believe that I am God's chosen one. This is the truth: he who receives whomever I send, receives me, and he who receives me, receives the One who sent me."

All evening, Jesus had been somber, but he suddenly appeared even more troubled, more anguished.

"I'm telling you the truth: one of you will betray me; he is sitting at this table right now."

We all looked at each other in shock.

Peter, who was sitting near me, leaned over, and whispered that I should ask Jesus who was the traitor.

With no small amount of fear, I did so.

Jesus took some bread from the basket next to him and dipped it into the bowl containing olive oil and herbs. In a low voice that only I could hear, he said that the one he gave the bread to was the betrayer. He then handed the bread to Judas.

I was relieved he had not given the bread to me or to my brother or to Peter or to Nathanael. I was sorry he had given it to any one of us. But Judas! I had not suspected him. To be honest, I had not suspected any of us. It was not that I didn't believe what the Master had just told me; it was just that it was almost impossible to believe that *any one* of us would do such a thing.

Was it too late for Judas to abandon this treachery, or had the die been cast?

Peter touched my arm, and I turned toward him. He wanted to know what Jesus had said to me. Perhaps he was worried that *he* could be the betrayer.

I just looked at him and whispered that he wasn't the one; it was somebody else. His relief was palpable. When I turned away from Peter, I saw Jesus saying something to Judas, but I could not hear the words.

Judas got up, walked across the room, and disappeared down the stairs that led to the front door of the house.

Jesus started speaking again, and we gave him our full attention.

"The Son of Man must die, but woe to him by whose hand he is betrayed. It would have been better for that betrayer if he had never been born."

No one seemed to suspect that the departure of Judas was an

indication that he was the betrayer. I heard several of my colleagues suggest that Jesus had sent him on some sort of errand.

I said nothing.

Jesus asked for our attention again.

"Now is the Son of Man glorified, and now God is glorified in him. Little children, I will be with you only a short time. You will look for me, but where I go you cannot come. Therefore, I'm going to give you a new commandment: You are to love one another as I have loved you. This is how everyone will know that you are my disciples: because you love one another."

"Lord, where are you going?" Peter asked.

"Where I go, you won't be able to follow me now; but you will follow me later on."

"Why can't I follow you now? I will lay down my life for you!"

"Listen to me: All of you will abandon me tonight, because the prophet has written, 'The shepherd will be attacked, and the sheep of the flock will scatter.' But after I've risen, I will go ahead of you into Galilee."

Jesus then looked directly at Peter, but he did not call him Peter, the new name the Master had given him many months before.

"Simon, Simon: Beware of Satan because he has desired to have you, that he may shake you into small bits like grains of wheat. I have prayed for you that your faith not fail you. But your faith will fail you, and when you have recovered from this failure, use your renewed faith to strengthen your brothers."

Peter was distraught and vehemently protested.

"Lord, I'm ready to go with you, both into prison and to death. Even if every other man deserts you, I will not; I *never* will!"

"Peter, listen to me: before the rooster crows tomorrow morning, three times you will deny that you even know who I am."

"Master, I would sooner die than deny you!"

Almost with one voice, the rest of us declared our undying allegiance to Jesus.

Peter looked dejected and confused.

Jesus continued.

"Do you remember the mission journey I sent all of you on two years ago? I sent you throughout Galilee, without money, without extra sandals or clothing. Did you lack anything?"

"Nothing," Peter replied.

"But the circumstances are different now. He who has money, changes of clothing, or sandals should take them; and if he has no sword, he should buy one. I'm telling you that there is much yet to be accomplished in me. As the prophet has written, 'He was reckoned among the transgressors.' The things concerning me have an end, and that end is near."

Both Peter and Simon (formerly known as Simon the Zealot) routinely carried swords.

"Look, Lord! We already have two swords," Simon replied.

Several of us began to argue as to which among us were best able to protect the Master from his adversaries, with or without weapons.

Jesus would have none of it.

"That's enough of that kind of talk! Two swords or two hundred won't be enough to keep me out of the hands of the enemy tonight. Look, the kings of the Gentiles exercise lordship over the Gentiles, and those who exercise such lordship are called benefactors. Nevertheless, it is not to be that way with you. He who is greatest among you, let him be as the younger; and he who is chief, let him be the one who serves. For who is greater: He who is served, or he who serves? Is it not he who is served? Yet, I am the one who served you tonight. You have stayed with me thus far, and I appoint you to my kingdom, just as my Father has appointed me. You will eat and drink at my table in my kingdom, and you will sit on thrones, judging the twelve tribes of Israel."

I was ashamed. Once again, we had argued among ourselves which of us would be the greatest among Jesus's disciples; this time, vying to be his greatest protector. Would we ever learn?

Mercifully, the Master changed the subject. What he said next was one of the most beautiful, wonderful things I had ever heard him say. Given our doubts, our fears, our confusion, and our somber mood, it was the perfect time for him to say it.

"Don't let your hearts be troubled. You trust in God; trust in me too. In my Father's house, there is plenty of room for all of us. If this were not true, I would not say it. I'm going away to prepare a special place for you in my Father's kingdom. I will return for you and take you with me so that we can be together forever. Now you know where I'm going, and you know the way to get there."

"Lord, we *don't* know where you're going, so how can we know the way?" Thomas asked.

"*I am* the way, the truth, and the life. No man comes to the Father but through me. If you know me, you know my Father too. And from now on, you do know Him and you have seen Him, because you know me and you have seen me."

"But, Lord, *show* us the Father, and we will be satisfied," Philip said.

"Philip, you—and all the rest of you too—have been with me almost three years, and yet you still don't know me! Again and again, I have said, 'He who has seen me has seen the Father,' so how can you say, 'Show us the Father?' Don't you believe that I am in the Father and the Father is in me? Every word I speak to you is from the Father, because He lives in me and speaks through me. Those are His words I speak and His works I do. Believe that I am in the Father and the Father is in me. At least believe that my works confirm it. I'm telling you the truth: You who believe in me—the words I speak and the works I do—God will be able to do the same things in you. Your works will even exceed mine, because I go home to the Father. Whatever you ask in my name, that I will do, so the Father may be glorified in the son. If you ask anything in my name, I will do it. If you love me and keep my commands, I will pray to the Father and ask Him to give you His Holy Spirit, who will abide in you forever. He will be many things to you: your comforter, your helper, and, most important, your advocate before the throne of God. The world cannot receive the Holy Spirit because the world does not know

Him. However, you know Him because He lives in you already. I will not leave you alone; I will be by your side through the Spirit of Truth. In just a little while, the world will see me no more. But you will see me because I live in you and you will live in me. That day, you will know that I am in the Father and you are in me because I live in you. He who knows my commands and obeys them does so because he loves me, and he who loves me shall be loved by my Father. I will love and make myself manifest to him who loves me."

Andrew asked, "Master, why do you make yourself manifest to us, but not to the whole world?"

"Those who love me will follow my instructions. Because you love me, you will follow my instructions. The world does not even know me, does not love me, and will not follow my instructions. That is why I tell you clearly what I expect of you. It will then be your work to tell the world about the Father and about me. Some in the world will come to know and love the Father and me because you have told them. You will have assistance to accomplish these things: the Holy Spirit will come to you in my name, and He will teach you everything you need to know; and you will remember everything I've said to you."

Jesus paused, as if giving us time for all this to sink into our minds, our hearts.

He then continued. "Peace I leave with you. My peace I give to you, not the world's peace, but the only real peace that comes from my Father. Do not let your hearts be troubled, and do not be afraid. You have heard me say tonight, 'I go away and will come again to you.' If you love me, if you trust me, you will rejoice in those words. I've told you these things before they happen, so that when they do happen, your faith and trust in me and in my Father will be stronger than ever. I don't have much time left to speak with you, because the prince of this world comes and has nothing in me. But I want you and the whole world to know that I love the Father, and as the Father has given me words to speak, I do the same for you."

As was the custom following the Passover meal, and with the

Master leading us, we sang—or, rather, chanted—one of the praise psalms of our ancient Scriptures. We all knew this psalm by heart.

> Praise the Lord! Praise, O servants of the Lord, praise the name
>   Of the Lord.
> Blessed be the name of the Lord from this time forth and forever.
> From the rising of the sun unto the going down of the same, the
>   Lord's name is to be praised.
> The Lord is high above all nations and his glory above the
>   Heavens.
> Who is like unto the Lord our God who dwells on high?
> Who humbles himself to behold the things that are in heaven and
>   On the earth?
> He raises up the poor out of the dust and lifts the needy out of the
>   Waste.
> That he may sit them with princes, even with the princes of his
>   People
> Praise the Lord!

"It's time for us to leave this place; let's be on our way," Jesus said. "There is so little time remaining, and I have more to say to you as we walk."

I believe that I have quoted everything Jesus said that evening completely and accurately. His promise, that the Holy Spirit will bring his words back to our hearts and minds, has proved true.

CHAPTER 33

It was only a short distance from the house where we had shared the Passover meal with Jesus and the gate through which we had entered the Holy City a few hours before. I supposed it must have been about three hours after sunset and about three hours before midnight. We encountered no one as we passed along the quiet street; the houses were dark, and it seemed as if everyone else had retired for the night. There was always a full moon during Passover week, and it appeared to have reached peak fullness this night. That, along with a cloudless sky, made walking safe and easy, even at this late hour.

We were traveling east, up the hillside and toward the Mount of Olives and the garden of Gethsemane. The eleven of us said nothing, and the Master remained silent as well while we walked the short distance out of the city.

Outside the city, the Master stopped and asked us to sit with him by the roadside.

He then shared his last parable with us.

The True Vine

I am the true vine, and my Father is the gardener. Every branch connected to me that does not produce fruit, the gardener cuts off and takes away. Every branch that does yield fruit, he carefully prunes, that it may yield even more and better fruit. You are to remain connected to me, just as I am connected to you, because the branch by itself cannot produce any fruit. Remember: I am the vine, and you are the branches. If anyone does not abide in me and remain in me, he will be cut off from me and cast out, as a withered branch is cut off the vine, bundled up, and thrown into the fire. But, if you remain in me and I remain in you, you shall ask of me anything, and it will be done. That's how my Father is glorified: that you produce much fruit and are indeed my disciples.

The Master paused, and then continued speaking to us.

"As the Father has loved me, so have I loved you, and you will continue in my love. If you keep my commandments, you shall remain in the Father's love, just as I have kept his commandments and remain in his love. I am speaking these things to you so that my joy might remain in you, and so that your joy might be full. This is my charge to you: that you love one another as I have loved each of you. Greater love has no man than this: that he lays down his life for his friends. You are my friends, if you do whatever I command you. That is why I have never called you my servants, for servants don't understand what their master does. Rather, I have called you my friends, because everything I have heard from my Father, I have shared with you. You did not choose me; I chose you and ordained you so that you should go out and produce an abundance of fruit. Moreover, whatever you ask the Father in my name, He will do. But, first, I command that you love one another."

Jesus stood up, and we continued up the road. We had walked perhaps a quarter-mile more when he stopped and bid us to sit with him again.

"Those who have rejected me will reject you as well. They will not just reject you, they will hate you as they have come to hate me. If you and I were of this world, they would not hate us; but we are not of this world. I will be persecuted, and so will you. Nevertheless, the joy you experience when you pass on my words to those who will listen will far exceed any persecution meted out to you. My words will become your words. Many of the people you teach will believe you, but not all. Those who do not believe do not know the Father or me; nor do they desire to know us. They don't have the faith necessary to believe, and their unbelief has turned to hatred. Their hatred fulfills the words of the prophet: 'They hated me without cause.'"

These were hard things for us to hear, and Jesus could always sense when something he said saddened or distressed or frightened us. Moreover, he usually then said something that would encourage us or dispel our gloomy reactions. Once again, his timing was just right.

"But when the Holy Spirit—the Spirit of Truth—comes, He will testify of me, and He will give you the words, and the courage to use those words, when giving evidence of me to those who will listen. Your witness will be powerful because you have been with me from the beginning. I'm telling you these things so that you will be prepared for them, and then you will meet them with the strength only God, through His Spirit, can give. Here is what you can expect: You will be expelled from the synagogues. But do not let that discourage you, because you will establish *my* church—it will be your church too—and the gates of hell shall not prevail against it! The time will come when you will be persecuted, and some of you will be killed. Those who kill you will think they are doing God a service, but they don't even know my Father or me. They are doing Satan's bidding.

"Now I'm returning to the One who sent me, and the things I've told you about the future have filled your hearts with sorrow and foreboding. I'm telling you the truth: It is necessary that I go away. If I don't, the Comforter, the Holy Spirit, will not come. He will convict the world of sin, of justice, and of judgment. In relation to sin, because those of this world don't believe me; in relation to justice, because I go to my Father, and those of this world will see me no more; in relation to judgment, because the prince of this world is judged. I have a great deal more to say to you, but you cannot bear it right now. However, when the Holy Spirit comes, He will guide you into all truth. He will also be an advocate for you before the Father. And He will reveal to you all things to come."

As Jesus spoke that last sentence, he looked straight at me.

"Yet, in a little while, you won't see me; and then, a little while after that, you will see me again because I go to the Father and will return shortly. Now let's be on our way."

Again, Jesus led the way, and we fell into step a few yards behind him.

"Does anybody understand what Jesus meant by 'Yet, in a little while, you won't see me; and then, a little while after that, you will see me again'? And what did he mean by 'going to the Father'?" Peter asked.

None of us answered him because none of us had understood it either.

Jesus stopped and waited for us to catch up.

Peter asked the Master to explain what had sounded to us like a riddle.

The Master said, "I'm telling you the truth: When I go away, you will be very sad, but those who hate me will rejoice. However, their joy will be turned to anguish. You will be sorrowful at first, but your sorrow will be turned to joy. When a woman is in labor, she has great pain because the hour of the delivery of her child has come. But, as soon as the baby is born, she forgets her pain because her joy has overcome her anguish. Now you have sorrow, pain, and distress. But I will see you again, and your hearts will rejoice; and no man can take that joy from you."

That increased our understanding to some extent, but not fully. We walked on, for perhaps another quarter-mile. Once again, Jesus stopped, we sat with him, and he gave us a more complete answer.

"I'm glad you asked me that question, Peter. However, you won't have many more opportunities like that because, as I have already told you, I'm going home to my Father. When I leave, you will ask the Father, in my name, for the answers to any questions you may have, and also for anything else you need. You will speak to Him the same way I do: through prayer. He will answer your prayers and supply your needs. But, while I am still with you, I will pray to the Father on your behalf, the same as I have done every day we have been together, and even before that. Yes, I prayed for each of you even before I met you. The Father loves you, just as I love you, because you have loved me and you believe I came from God. I came from my Father into the world, and now I leave the world and return to my Father."

"Now we understand what you're saying," Peter replied. "Now we're certain that you know all things, and there is no need for any of us to ask you any more questions because we believe you came from God."

"Are you sure you won't need to ask me any more questions, Peter?"

Well, speaking for myself, I was not so sure.

Jesus continued.

"Look, the hour is coming—yes, it's here now—that all of you will be scattered. You will all desert me, and it will be every man for himself. But I won't be alone because the Father is with me."

Those words horrified me. We—I—would desert Jesus, leave him alone to fend for himself? Never!

The Master then added words of comfort and encouragement, not for himself, but for us.

"These things I have spoken to you, that you might have peace *in me*. In this world, you will be met with adversity and heartache. But be of good cheer: I have overcome the world, and through me, you will overcome the world too!"

Jesus knelt where he had been sitting. He was going to pray to his Father. We all knelt with him.

"Father, the hour has come. Glorify Your son, that Your son may glorify You. You have given me authority over everyone so that I can give eternal life to everyone You have given to me. This is life eternal: That they might know You, the only true God, and me, Your son, whom You have sent. I have glorified You on earth; I have finished the work that You gave me to do. Now, oh Father, glorify me alongside Yourself, with the glory that I shared with You before the

world existed. I have made manifest Your name to these men whom
You have given me from out of this world. Yours they were, You gave
them to me, and they have kept Your word. Now they have come to
know the truth and that all things, whatever You have given me, are
of You and from You. Moreover, I have given to them the same words
You gave to me, and they have received them and have known surely
that I came from You, and they do believe that You sent me. I pray
for these eleven men, not for those of the world, but for those whom
You have given me, for they are Yours. All of mine are Yours, and all
of Yours are mine. And I am glorified in them. Now I am no more in
the world, but they are in the world, and I come to You, Holy Father,
and ask that You keep these You have given me, that they may be of
one accord, just as You and I are of one purpose. While I was with
them in the world, I kept them in Your name; those whom You gave
me I have guarded, and none of them are lost but one: the son of
destruction, that the Scriptures might be fulfilled. Now I come to
You, and these things I speak in their hearing: That they may have
their joy fulfilled in You, Father. I have given them Your word, and
this world has hated them because they are not of this world, even
as I am not of this world. I do not pray that you should take them
out of this world but that You keep them from the evil in it. Make
them holy in Your truth: Your word is truth. As You have sent me
into the world, even so I also send them into the world. For their
sakes, I sanctify myself, that they may also be sanctified through
the truth. I am praying not only for my disciples but also for those
who come to believe in me because of their witness. I pray that they
all may be one, as You, Father, and I are one, united in our belief of
Your gospel of salvation. I in them, and You in me, that they may be
made perfect and that the world may know that You have sent me,
and You have loved them as You love me. Father, I pray that these
You have given me be with me, that they may see the glory, which
You have given me, for You have loved me from the foundation of
the world. Oh, righteous Father, the world has not known You, but
I have known You, and they know that You have sent me. And I

have declared to them Your name and will declare it again: that the love with which You have loved me may be in them and that I may always remain in them."

Jesus had prayed to his Father for my fellow disciples and me! Not only tonight, not only every day since we had followed him, but before he had even met us! I could not then and cannot now describe in poor mortal words what that meant to me then and what it means to me now.

The prayer finished, we rose to our feet, and continued on our way. In a few minutes, we reached what was to be our destination: the Mount of Olives. Jesus opened the gate, and we all entered the garden of Gethsemane.

CHAPTER 34

The garden of Gethsemane was one of Jesus's beloved places. Every time we visited Jerusalem, he would spend hours there—usually alone, but sometimes with us, his twelve apostles. It seemed to be his special place of prayer, and I have no doubt that the garden was where he had gone to pray each of the last four nights of this Passover week, walking there from the home of Lazarus, Martha, and Mary. In all our previous times with him there, he seemed to be more relaxed and happy than anywhere else, with the possible exception of the home of our dear friends in Bethany. It was in this garden that we had found Jesus, unharmed, after he had mysteriously absented himself from the angry chief priests, lawyers, and Pharisees earlier this same week. However, tonight was different, very different.

Jesus had often told crowds, large and small—and he had also told us privately many times—that we should cast our cares, our burdens, on him, and that in so doing, *he* would carry the load and give us rest. This had always had a positive effect on us and on many others as well. Nevertheless, tonight it was as if he were shouldering the cares and burdens of the whole world. He seemed to be weighed down in a literal sense: he walked slowly and with great effort, sometimes even groaning audibly. None of us knew what, if anything, we could do to lift his spirit, to lighten *his* load. He stopped, turned, and, as if he had read our minds, told us there was something we could do.

"You men stay here while I go a little way farther to pray. You should pray too. Pray that God will strengthen you for the trials and temptations that lay ahead."

The Master then motioned to Peter, James, and me to accompany him. He walked only a short distance—perhaps ten yards—turned to the three of us, and, in barely audible, labored words said, "My soul is overwhelmed with grief, even unto death. Wait here, and pray for me."

There was no question he was deeply distressed. We had never seen him like this before. He was our rock, our strong leader; he always knew what to do, when, and how best to do it. He now seemed repelled by the coming ordeal, almost fearful of it. By now, we all accepted as inevitable that he would soon die, but we could not begin to imagine exactly how or exactly when or exactly why this terrible thing would happen. He walked just a few feet from us—he was too weak to go farther—collapsed on his knees, and began pouring out his heart to his Father. He was close enough so that I could hear some of what he said.

"Oh, Father. ... With You, all things are possible. ... If it is Your will, may this moment pass from me. If there is any other way for Your purpose to be accomplished, may I not have to drink this bitter wine. ... But, if I must drink it, I will."

I glanced at Peter and James. They had dozed off and had not heard Jesus's pleas. I looked in the direction of our other eight colleagues; all of them lay still and quiet, fast asleep on the ground. I, too, was exhausted, both physically and mentally. My eyes were heavy; I could hardly keep them open. I began to drift off.

And then, suddenly, although my eyes were closed, I was aware of light. When I opened my eyes, I saw a large, luminous angel bending over Jesus, who lay prostrate on the ground. The angel appeared to be speaking to him, but I could not hear what he said. Now, I had never seen an angel before; I had only heard of them and read about them in our ancient Scriptures, and this being certainly fit the description of them therein. I glanced at James and Peter, both of whom were still fast asleep. I was on the verge of waking them so that they, too, might see this celestial sight, but just then, quite suddenly, the heavenly visitor disappeared.

Jesus seemed strengthened by the angel's visit. He was back on his knees, fervently pouring out his heart to his Father.

Unfortunately, once again, my eyelids grew heavy, and struggle as I might, I fell back to sleep. I awoke to the sound of the Master's voice. Opening my eyes, I saw him gently nudging Peter. The three of us roused.

"Could you not pray with me for just one hour? Be vigilant. Your spirits are willing, but your flesh is weak."

Even in the pale moonlight, it looked to me as if Jesus had been weeping; his face was streaked with the tears. He walked back to where he had been praying, knelt down, and continued speaking to his Father. He repeated the same plea as before: to be delivered, if possible, from the anguish he was suffering.

Peter and James were again slumbering, and, despite my efforts to stay awake, I quickly joined them. Sometime later, all three of us were stirred to partial consciousness by the sound of Jesus's voice.

"Sleep on now; you need the rest," he said.

My brother and Peter remained in their semiconscious state.

And then, suddenly, all of us, including the others several yards away, bolted upright from our prone positions and got to our feet.

"Get up! Let's go!" Jesus's shout awoke us all. "My work is done, and my hour has come."

He paused and then pointed into the surrounding olive trees. "Look! The Son of Man is betrayed into the clutches of evil men, and the one who betrays him is in the lead."

We all looked in the direction he was pointing, and what we saw sent chills up and down my spine. We could see no one, but we did see dozens of torches and lanterns bobbing up and down among the trees and advancing on us. We eleven were paralyzed with fear, but not Jesus. He seemed to have regained his usual strength and composure; he did not flinch or cower as this silent band walked straight toward us. There must have been at least fifty men, many of whom were heavily armed with swords and clubs. Most were temple guardsmen, not Roman soldiers; there was not a Roman among them. There were even a few priests, lawyers, and Pharisees in their midst. Every one of these men was a Judean. And the man leading them was Judas.

Because of what I had witnessed earlier that evening, I was not shocked to see Judas in the forefront of this company, but my colleagues were. They were dumbfounded and confused.

How did Judas know Jesus would be in the garden of Gethsemane? Probably because it was the most likely place for him to be, given his affection for the place.

Judas approached Jesus, called him Master, and kissed him on the cheek. Witnessing that devious gesture made me sick to my stomach. It was the signal he'd chosen to use to identify Jesus to those he led.

I was standing close to the Master, and I noticed something about Jesus's face that I had not been able to see in the waning moonlight. Now, in the bright glow of blazing torches, I saw what appeared to be dried blood on his cheeks. I was puzzled by this, as he had not been struck by any of those carrying clubs. Could it be that his tears had somehow turned to blood?

"Judas, do you betray the Son of Man with a kiss?" Jesus asked him.

The traitor did not answer.

The Master then asked a question of the officer in charge, the captain of the temple guard.

"Whom do you seek?

"Jesus of Nazareth," the man replied.

"*I am* he."

Upon hearing the words "*I am* he," not only the captain but also several of the men standing just behind him staggered backward as if pushed by an unseen hand, lost their balance, and fell flat on their backs. They were briefly dazed and immobilized. When they regained their strength and stood up, Jesus asked the captain again whom he was seeking.

The officer, this time in a weakened, barely audible voice, repeated that they were looking for Jesus.

"I have already told you that *I am the one* you are looking for. Let my friends go."

Hearing this, the officer ordered two of his men to seize Jesus and bind his hands behind his back.

Seeing what was about to happen, Peter, drew his sword.

"Master, shall we drive these men away by the sword?"

Regrettably, he did not wait for Jesus's answer, but immediately made a wild thrust at one of the men preparing to bind our Master. He severed the man's right ear, and it fell to the ground. Peter's bizarre and irrational act shocked everyone, and all of us present— except Jesus—froze in our tracks.

Jesus placed his left hand on the right side of the man's head, where his ear had been just a few seconds before. When Jesus removed his hand, the ear had been restored. The severed ear remained on the ground; the Master had fashioned a new one.

The man, who had been writhing in pain, went quiet. He reached up and touched his new ear, and the look on his face cannot be described.

There was no conversation among anyone present. Everyone was perfectly still, and it was eerily quiet.

Jesus looked at Peter.

"Peter, put your sword away!" he said "Those who live by the sword will die by the sword. Stop and think! Don't you know that if I wanted to be spared from the fate that awaits me in Jerusalem, I could ask my Father to save me from it? Don't you know that He could send twelve legions of angels to destroy my enemies and deliver me from them? But that is not His plan. I must drink the bitter wine my Father has given me to drink. That's the only way the Scriptures concerning me can be satisfied."

Jesus then turned to the officer in charge, who had not said a word or made a move since Peter's foolish swordplay. The Master asked the captain a simple question, which was also directed to the priests, lawyers, and Pharisees who were present among the company.

"Why did you come all the way up here in the middle of the night, carrying torches, lanterns, swords, and clubs to arrest me now? For the past four days, I have spent many hours in the temple, right under your noses, teaching and healing the people. You were there every day too. Why didn't you arrest me in broad daylight? It would have been easier on you. Why do you come in the darkness of midnight? Go ahead; do your evil deed."

As with so many of Jesus's questions put to those who hated him, there was no answer; no one said a word. They bound his hands and led him away.

What did *we* do? We his closest friends; we his disciples; we his apostles; we the ones he had chosen—what did *we* do? We the ones he had prayed for every day we had been with him; we the ones he had prayed for before we even met him; we the ones he had taught how to pray; we the ones he had trained to preach the same gospel he preached—what did *we* do? We the ones he had empowered to heal as he healed; we the ones he had prepared for the hardships that lay before us; we the ones he had promised to send his Father's Holy Spirit to guide and encourage—what did *we* do? We the ones whose feet he had washed that very evening; we the ones whom he had poured out his heart in prayer to his Father, a prayer we had all heard, just a few hours before—what did *we* do?

What did *we* do? We abandoned him and ran for our lives.

CHAPTER 35

There was only one way in and one way out of the garden of Gethsemane, and all eleven of us ran in that direction, putting as much distance as possible between the arresting party and ourselves.

As I was the youngest and swiftest of the disciples, I got to the gate first and stopped momentarily to think about what I should do next: run toward Bethany and take refuge in Lazarus's house? For the time being, I decided to hide behind a large bush across the road from the garden gate. From that position, I heard and then saw several men emerging from Gethsemane: In the waning moonlight, I recognized nine of my colleagues, led by my brother, James. Peter was not among them. They turned up the road toward Bethany.

A few moments later, I saw the glow of the torches and lanterns. The silent company then came into view: the captain of the temple guard in the lead, and right behind him, Jesus, bound and surrounded by four large guardsmen. They turned down the road toward Jerusalem, passing only a few yards from where I cowered in silence, hardly breathing. I am not sure why I made the decision to follow them, but I did—at a relatively safe distance, to be sure. They passed through the gate to the Holy City, into its deserted and quiet streets, turning first left and then right, and arriving in front of a large house. A gate led to the grounds of the house. Someone on the other side of the gate opened it, and the company filed in.

At this point, I was about fifty yards behind them. I was not sure what to do next; I had no plan. I heard footsteps behind me, and my heart nearly leaped into my throat. I was afraid to turn around. Next, I heard a familiar voice whispering my name. It was Peter. He was alone; none of the others had accompanied him.

Afraid of being overheard, we walked several yards away and spoke in whispers. Neither of us could explain to the other what had possessed us to put ourselves in harm's way. I told Peter that I wanted to get closer to see and hear what was going on. That was a foolish ploy, and Peter looked dubious. I was adamant, though, and explained that, because of my youth—I was nineteen now but could easily pass for fifteen—I thought I could safely enter through the gate, which had been left ajar, without dire consequence. Peter was not about to accompany me, and I could not blame him. Because of his foolish assault on one the high priest's guards, if he were recognized, he would be arrested immediately.

I walked gingerly toward the gate and, with no one guarding it, pushed it open, closed it quietly behind me, and entered upon the scene: a large courtyard that sloped down toward the house in the fashion of an amphitheater. It was the home of the former high priest, Annas. I knew that because I recognized him. I also recognized his son-in-law, Caiaphas, the current high priest and, as you may recall, my father's cousin. There were perhaps fifty or sixty men sitting on the grassy slope overlooking what was, in effect, a courtroom. Many of the onlookers had been in the company of those who arrested Jesus. It was dark, and torches had been placed around the courtyard. There were ten chairs arranged in a single row, facing the spectators. Standing in front and facing them was Jesus, who, hands still bound behind his back, was guarded by two large men. Annas occupied the large, more elaborate middle chair. On his right was Caiaphas; on either side of them were chief priests, elders, and Pharisees. These men just sat there, silently staring at Jesus. I was perhaps forty feet from the Master. I turned and looked back up the slope and over the low wall. There was Peter, standing alone in the shadows about twenty feet from me.

Annas began speaking; he was calling the court to order. That is what it amounted to: a court, and this was to be a trial.

Annas began with a question for Jesus.

"Don't you have some close followers? I think you call them disciples."

"Yes."

"Where are they? They deserted you, didn't they?"

The former high priest did not wait for an answer, immediately asking another question.

"I want to know about your teachings; tell me about them."

Jesus spoke firmly but with respect.

"I have always taught openly and publicly to gatherings large and small, all over Judea and Galilee, often in the synagogues. Every day this week, I've been in the temple openly, never in secret. My teachings are well known. Many Judeans have heard me speak, including some who are here tonight. Why do you ask me? They know my beliefs and my teachings are based on God's eternal truth. Why don't you ask them?"

Annas was not accustomed to being spoken to in this manner, and his expression clearly conveyed his displeasure.

One of the guards standing by Jesus got the message. He slapped the Master hard across the face.

"How dare you speak to the former high priest in this manner!" the guard shouted.

"If I've said something untrue or disrespectful, tell me what it is. But if I have spoken the truth respectfully, why did you strike me?"

For several moments, Annas, Caiaphas, and the others conferred quietly among themselves.

While this lull in the trial continued, I turned to see if Peter was still behind me. He was. The last time I checked, he was standing alone, but now there were perhaps twenty other people standing in the outer area of Annas's residence. Word of what was happening had spread, and these newly arrived observers wanted to see and hear for themselves what was happening. It was cold, and someone had built a small charcoal fire. Peter and several others were warming themselves around it. He was facing in my direction but had not noticed me looking at him. A servant girl approached and stared at him. I was close enough to hear their short conversation and two more that followed.

"You're one of his disciples, are you?" she asked.

"No, I'm not."

"You're from Galilee, just like the man on trial. I can tell by your accent. You must be one of his friends," a man standing next to him said.

"I've never even met him."

"Look, don't tell me you don't know him! I was with the company that came to arrest your leader not more than two hours ago. You were the one who tried to kill Malcus with your sword."

"Man, I don't know what you're talking about, and I'm telling you, as God is my witness, *I don't know that man!*"

Peter said those last five words with such emphasis that everyone present in the area heard them; even the former high priest and those still conferring quietly with him turned to look up the slope.

Just at that moment, a rooster crowed. Suddenly, I remembered what Jesus had said to Peter during our Passover meal: "Before the rooster crows tomorrow morning, three times, you will deny that you even know who I am."

It was obvious that my friend remembered those words too. His shoulders slumped, and so did his face. He saw me looking at him. He glanced past me, down the slope, and I turned to see what had gotten his attention. The Master was facing Peter, and their eyes met. The expression on Jesus's face was not one of condemnation or even disappointment, but, rather, sadness.

One of the soldiers guarding Jesus realized he had turned around and roughly spun him around back toward Annas and the other dignitaries.

I looked at Peter; he was devastated that the Master's prediction of his denials had come true. He was beginning to sob softly and hastily walked away into the darkness.

I felt sorrow for my friend and wondered what would become of him.

The attention of the assembly retuned to Annas when he began to speak. His announcement was short: The prisoner would be taken to the high priest's home, where the examination of Jesus would continue. Those in attendance were invited to proceed to Caiaphas's house.

It looked as if everyone who had attended the first trial was en route to what would be the second trial of Jesus. Caiaphas and Annas led the way, followed by the captain of the temple guard, the Master, and the same four soldiers I supposed were charged with preventing his escape. If Jesus had wanted to escape, nothing could have stopped him; only days before, he had vanished from the temple when leaders of the Judeans had threatened his life. Everyone else fell in behind, and I brought up the rear. I glanced over my shoulder to the east and up to the Mount of Olives, and above it was the first hint of dawn. I heard another rooster crow, and it immediately made me think of poor Peter.

In a few minutes, we all arrived at Caiaphas's home. The grounds on which it stood were level. The onlookers, with me among them, assembled on his spacious lawn. Above it was a large porch, and on the porch, arrayed in five rows of ten each, were fifty chairs. Caiaphas led his father-in-law, Annas, and the eight other men who had formed the "jury" in the first trial up the steps to the porch. These ten men occupied the first row of chairs, and members of the Sanhedrin, the Jewish Judicial Council, already occupied the remaining four rows. As high priest, Caiaphas was the president—the presiding officer—of the Sanhedrin. It was obvious this had all been planned out. There were seventy-one members of the Sanhedrin. They came from all over Israel and were always in the Holy City during Passover week. Of the forty chairs provided for them, three were unoccupied. The quorum for a legal proceeding was *twenty-three*. I wondered why nearly half the members were absent.

I stood near the back of the onlookers. However, because I had not been recognized in the crowd at Annas's house, I was emboldened to inch my way nearer the front, to where I could better see and hear what would transpire at this second trial.

Caiaphas called the Sanhedrin to order and then proceeded to call the witnesses one by one. Every single one of them would testify against Jesus; no one would come to his defense. However, it was soon clear that things were not going well for the prosecution. Witness after witness contradicted earlier witnesses, or gave evidence so unbelievable, so ridiculous, that it was almost laughable. It was obvious that whoever rehearsed these men had not done a good job. Members of the Sanhedrin began to look at each other, some shaking their heads in disgust. Caiaphas began to look nervous and worried.

Finally, the last witness came to his rescue. He pointed to the Master and spoke with great force and dripping sarcasm.

"I heard this man say, 'I will destroy the holy temple made with hands, and within three days, I will build another made without hands.'"

This was a gross distortion of the truth. I was there, and I'd heard exactly what the Master said: not Jesus, but *Gentiles* would destroy the temple.

Caiaphas looked relieved. The words of the witness provided exactly what Caiaphas wanted to hear; this set the stage for a capital charge, and for what happened next.

"Don't you have *anything* to say to those who gave evidence against you?"

The Master did not answer.

"I put you under sacred oath before the living God of heaven and earth. *Are you the Christ, the Son of God?*" Caiaphas was nearly screaming.

Jesus looked straight at the high priest and, in a clear and firm voice heard by all present, spoke.

"*I am.* And you will see me sitting on the right hand of power, coming in the clouds of heaven."

Caiaphas tore his outward priestly robe from top to bottom, turned toward those seated behind him, and shrieked.

"Why do we need any more evidence? *This man has blasphemed against God.* What is your verdict?" the high priest demanded.

With one voice, the thirty-seven members of the Sanhedrin present cried, "Guilty!"

"What punishment do you propose?"

"Death!" they all shouted.

"So be it," Caiaphas declared.

Jesus stood silent, with his head held high.

The captain of the guard ordered Jesus to be blindfolded. The two large guards who stood next to him began to spit on him, strike him in the face, and curse him. The profanities directed at the Master were so vile that I could hardly bear listening to them. They continued to handle him roughly, punching him in the face, back, and abdomen with their fists. Three of them took turns hitting him, spinning him around and challenging him to prophesy: to tell them the names of those who had struck him. When he ignored this challenge, they told him he could not be a prophet; if he were, he would know their names.

All the while this was happening Caiaphas, Annas, the chief priests, elders, members of the Sanhedrin, and audience looked on. There was not an ounce of decency in any of them. No one tried to put a stop to this barbaric display. Regrettably, *I* did not say a word on his behalf; *I* did not lift a finger to help him.

There was one problem with the guilty verdict and sentence of death pronounced by the Sanhedrin: the sentence could not be carried out. Jesus had been convicted and sentenced to death for blasphemy against the God of the Jews. Rome cared nothing for the God of the Jews, and did not recognize the judicial authority of the Sanhedrin or their verdicts. Only Rome could execute a man for a capital offense, and blasphemy against the God of the Jews meant nothing to the Romans. In their eyes, this trial was nothing; it would be as if it had not even happened. No, Caiaphas, Annas, and their coconspirators would have to convince *Rome* that Jesus was worthy of death because he had committed a capital offense against the *Roman Empire*. And, in Jerusalem, the Roman Empire was personified in the Roman governor of the Roman province of

Judea. His name was Pontius Pilate. Caiaphas announced to the crowd that Jesus was to be taken to Pilate's residence immediately.

But what good would that do? Jesus had committed no capital crime recognized by the empire. He had not murdered, robbed, or committed treason against Rome. Of course, he had not committed blasphemy either, but a lying witness had said that he had, and the Sanhedrin had chosen to believe it. If Jesus's enemies could create a false witness for the trial just concluded, perhaps they could do the same in the next trial.

CHAPTER 36

Pontius Pilate spent most of his time in the city of Caesarea Maritima, Rome's administrative capital for the province of Judea. Situated on the coast of the Mediterranean Sea, it was purported to be the most beautiful city in Judea. Its construction was commissioned by the Romans, carried out during the reign of Herod the Great (some fifty years before), and named in honor of the Roman emperor of that time, Caesar Augustus. Pilate made two or three visits to Jerusalem every year, usually during our festivals. He brought with him most of the contingent of soldiers stationed in Caesarea Maritima, and when combined with those of the smaller Roman garrison in Jerusalem and augmented with several hundred more from other military posts throughout Judea, Galilee, and Samaria, the troops in Jerusalem that Passover week numbered four thousand or more. They were here to keep the peace and to put down quickly any attempts to overthrow their imperial rule. Pilate himself had a military background, rising through the ranks to the point of being given the administrative role of prefect (or governor) of Judea. He was probably a better soldier than politician. When in Jerusalem, his residence was the praetorium, an impressive, large, and much-hated building not far from Caiaphas's house, where the second trial of Jesus had just concluded. It was also near the holy temple. Pilate and Caiaphas were well acquainted, and rumor had it that their relationship was a reasonably good one, characterized by mutual respect for, and mutual influence over, each other. One of the Roman governor's duties was to appoint the high priest. Upon his arrival in Judea five years earlier, he had named Caiaphas to that honored office and had reappointed him every year since.

It was the sixth day of the week, preparation day. More than that, it was the day of the Passover meal. That evening, shortly after sunset at the beginning of the Sabbath, Jews all over Jerusalem would eat this special meal—the same meal Jesus and the twelve of us had eaten the night before. On this day, Jews were forbidden to enter any Gentile home, and any other Gentile structure, for that matter. To do so would defile us, thereby preventing us from celebrating the final ritual of Passover week.

When the trial procession reached the praetorium, Caiaphas asked the guard at the entrance to the Hall of Justice to inform Pilate of his arrival and that he wished to speak with the governor as soon as possible. In a few moments, the governor emerged; he understood that Jewish law prohibited Caiaphas from entering the edifice. Seeing the governor with the high priest, the crowd went silent.

I was standing within earshot of what transpired between the two of them.

"What brings you to the Hall of Justice so early in morning, Caiaphas?" Pilate asked.

The governor was toying with the high priest; his spy network had kept him well informed since late the evening before. He knew of the movements of the temple guard, the arrest of Jesus, the scattering of his followers, and what had transpired at the two previous trials. He knew Caiaphas would bring Jesus to him, and Caiaphas knew that he knew. Pilate continued, pretending to know less about Jesus than he actually did.

"I see you have brought a prisoner to me. What are your charges against this man? I assume you are accusing him of doing something wrong."

"If he wasn't a malefactor, we wouldn't have brought him to you!" The high priest's tone was sharp, and Pilate was not pleased.

"You take him and judge him by your laws. I haven't got time to deal with this."

"He has committed a capital offense, and we have no authority to carry out the sentence of death."

"Yes, I know you have accused and convicted him of blasphemy against your God, but what is that to me? I'm not going to sentence him to death for that."

Annas, who was standing next to his son-in-law, spoke up.

"This man has committed *two* capital offenses against *Rome*. First, he told Jews not to pay the imperial tax; second, he said that he, not Caesar, is the true king of the Jews. He deserves to die because he has violated your own laws."

I had expected something like this.

Pilate had no choice now; he would have to investigate further. He looked at Caiaphas, who nodded agreement with his father-in-law, and then he looked at Jesus, who stood quietly, with no discernible expression.

The governor ordered two of the Roman soldiers flanking him to seize Jesus and bring him into the Hall of Justice.

Without thinking of the possible consequences, I fell in behind them. The thought that I was defiling myself by going into this place did not enter my mind. I just wanted to be near my Master; I wanted to see and hear what was about to happen. For some reason, no one seemed to notice me; if anyone did notice me, he didn't care that I was there.

The governor, now in his role of chief magistrate of the province, ascended several steps that led to a regal chair. Seating himself on the chair, he peered down at Jesus, who was flanked, this time, by Roman soldiers who had escorted him into this large and stately room. Pilate stared silently at my Master for several moments.

"Are you the king of the Jews?" Pilate finally asked.

"If you say so," Jesus replied.

"The chief priests of your own country—your own religion—have delivered you to me, asking me to condemn you to death. What have you done to deserve their condemnation and the penalty of death?"

"I am a king, but my kingdom is not in this world. I did not come from this world. If my kingdom were of this world, my followers would have fought for me; they would have kept me from being taken by the Jews and brought before you. I came into the world that I should bear witness to the truth, and those who live according to the truth hear my voice. Today, I will do what I was born to do."

Pilate said nothing for several moments. He appeared to be trying to absorb, to understand, what Jesus had said.

"You speak of truth. What is truth?"

The chief magistrate did not wait for an answer. Just at that moment, a messenger entered the room through a side door, ascended the steps, bowed to Pilate, and handed him a small sealed scroll. Pilate broke the seal, opened the scroll, and read what must have been a very short message. He immediately left his chair and exited the hall, offering no explanation. He was gone perhaps a quarter of an hour, and then he returned to his seat, a troubled expression on his face. He sat there for several minutes, saying nothing. He then abruptly descended the steps, motioned the soldiers guarding Jesus to follow him, and proceeded out the door to the courtyard, where the high priests, elders, and the crowd—now larger than it had been half and hour before—waited in silence for him and his decision.

I stood in the shadows behind the chief magistrate, the soldiers, and Jesus.

Pointing at my Master, and in a raised voice that could be heard by all present, Pilate spoke.

"I find no fault with this man Jesus. I'm going to have him flogged, and then I will release him."

A murmur of disapproval rose up from the throng.

Annas and Caiaphas simultaneously began to protest Pilate's decision. The high priest yielded to his father-in-law, who began a broad denunciation of Jesus, making all kinds of wild and untrue accusations against him. Finally, he finished.

Pilate looked at my Master and urged that he defend himself against these charges.

"Don't you have *anything* to say to refute these charges?"

Jesus remained silent.

Pilate was astonished.

However, now Caiaphas had something to say.

"This man has traveled all over Galilee and Judea, stirring up the people and inciting them to rebel against Rome."

The mention of Galilee got Pilate's attention. I was sure he knew Jesus was from that province, but he must have forgotten it. Galilee was in King Herod's jurisdiction, and Herod was in Jerusalem for Passover. Pilate seemed to be considering that perhaps there was a way for him to extricate himself from this predicament.

"I order that the man, Jesus, be taken before King Herod for questioning," Pilate declared.

He told one of his soldiers to hasten to Herod's Jerusalem residence and inform him that he was sending Jesus of Galilee to him for interrogation. And then he sent Jesus off with a cohort of soldiers to Rome's puppet ruler, the same man, you will recall, who two years before had ordered the execution of John the Baptist.

I followed close behind.

Herod's residence was not far, and it took only a few minutes to reach it. It seemed as if the entire company that had been present in the courtyard of the praetorium was behind me. As had been the case there, the throng would have to remain outside the residence of the so-called king, but not for the same reason. Herod was a Jew, and entering his residence would not be defilement; rather, there was simply no room inside for hundreds of people.

Jesus, led by a small contingent of Roman soldiers, entered a stately but not capacious hall. I was right behind them and, again, had no difficulty in gaining entrance. Only Caiaphas, Annas, and a few of the chief priests entered as well.

At the far end of this hall was an elevated platform, and on it was an elaborate throne upon which Herod sat. His retainers, probably a dozen of them, stood below him, to his right, and to his left. It sickened me to be in the same place with this adulterous murderer. He was smiling broadly and seemed pleased that Pilate, with whom he had had a strained relationship of late, had sent this important prisoner to him; he took this gesture as an acknowledgment of his own stature. I assumed that Herod would question Jesus about the charges brought against him by the Sanhedrin. He, as did Pilate, had a spy network and certainly knew what had taken place in the last twelve hours.

I was wrong.

Herod wanted Jesus to entertain him with some miracles. Jesus ignored his repeated requests to do so, which angered the petulant monarch.

Herod then turned toward Caiaphas and Annas, asking them if they had anything to say about Jesus.

They repeated the same charges they had brought before Pilate an hour before.

And, just as he had in the presence of Pilate, Jesus said nothing in his own defense.

Much to the consternation of the high priest and the chief priests, Herod, too, refused to condemn my Master. In addition, just as the governor had done, the king ordered the prisoner to be beaten. He then directed that Jesus be returned to the praetorium.

Once again, the Roman prefect emerged from his residence. Once again, he told the chief priests that he could find no fault with "this man."

"You've made many charges against him, and I don't believe any of them. I have already told you I will not condemn him to death, because he has committed no capital offense against Rome. Your own Jewish king, Herod, does not agree with your charges either; he, too, found nothing worthy of death. You people have a Passover tradition that I have honored every year since I became governor. Each year, I pardon and release one Jewish prisoner held in our praetorium jail. I am going to have Jesus flogged again, and then I will release him. That will fulfill my obligation to you."

"No! We want you to release Barabbas, not Jesus!" It was

Caiaphas, speaking loud enough to be heard by many in the courtyard throng.

"Barabbas!" Pilate shouted the well-known name. "Barabbas is a convicted murderer and a convicted insurrectionist against Rome. He is going to be crucified this afternoon!"

I could hear this name, Barabbas, being repeated throughout the courtyard. Unlike Jesus, Barabbas had actually committed murder—of a Roman soldier—and had advocated the overthrow, by violence, of Roman rule in Israel. Not all Jews admired his zeal or his tactics, but many did. However, it was beyond the pale to advocate the release of that man and the execution of Jesus. I could not imagine the Roman governor agreeing to such a gross miscarriage of justice.

Next, I heard Pilate speak to one of his soldiers. He ordered the man to fetch Barabbas from his cell and bring him there. In short order, the heavily guarded, heavily chained prisoner arrived. He was a large, muscular man, seething with hatred and defiance.

The crowd began to chant his name, "Barabbas! Barabbas!"

Roman soldiers pushed their way into the throng and quickly quieted them down.

Pilate had their respective guards position Jesus on his right and Barabbas on his left. The contrast between these two men could not have been greater. Apparently, the prefect had given up on reasoning with the high priest, because he now spoke directly to the crowd. He looked at my Master.

"Shall I release this man, the king of the Jews, the man named Jesus? "Or," Pilate glanced at Barabbas, "shall I release this man, Barabbas?"

"Barabbas! Barabbas! Barabbas!" they screamed.

"Then what shall I do with this man Jesus?"

"Crucify him! Crucify him! Crucify him!"

"Why? What crime has he committed? I have found this man innocent. I have no cause to issue a death sentence, and I'm going to let him go."

Caiaphas turned to the crowd and raised his arms to silence them. They instantly complied, and he turned back to Pilate and pointed at Jesus.

"This man claims to be the Son of God. He has blasphemed against *your* God, as you, and all Romans, believe Caesar to be the son of God."

Pilate turned ashen. Once again, he retreated into the praetorium, taking Jesus with him. I was close behind them. Pilate ordered the chief of his personal guard to muster several hundred additional soldiers to control the crowd, which had suddenly become more unruly and potentially violent. He ascended the steps to his judgment seat for the third time that morning.

Jesus stood before him, with a look of peaceful resignation.

Pilate looked down upon him for several moments, saying nothing. He looked troubled, almost desperate.

"Where did you come from?"

Jesus just looked at him and said nothing.

"Man, what is wrong with you? Why will you not speak up in your own defense? You know you are innocent! I know you are innocent! Don't you know I have the power to crucify you or to make you a free man?"

"You would have no power over me at all unless it was given to you from above," Jesus replied. "Therefore, those who have delivered me to you, especially their leaders, have greater guilt than you."

Jesus had finally broken his silence, and Pilate was astonished at his words. He said nothing in response for several moments. He then ordered Jesus to be flogged, yet again, and dressed in a royal robe. My Master was taken into a side room, and I could hear the leather straps of the whip being applied to his already lacerated back. He was returned to the trial chamber, wearing not only the robe but also a crown—not a regal crown, but a crown fashioned of thorns. It was pressed down upon his head, and the blood from his wounds flowed freely down his face. I was reminded of the bloody sweat that I had seen on his face the night before in the garden of Gethsemane.

I wondered why Pilate, who obviously believed Jesus to be innocent of *any* crime against Rome, had ordered him to be flogged twice and then humiliated like this.

The governor led my Master back out to the courtyard and the waiting multitude, now larger than ever, which instantly fell silent. Jesus stood on his right as Pilate spoke.

"Behold the man—the man in whom I find no fault."

The crowd exploded. "Crucify him! Crucify him! Crucify him!"

Again, the high priest raised his arms to silence them. Their obedience was instant.

Caiaphas turned back to Pilate.

"If you let this man go, you are not Caesar's friend. This man has made himself a king, and he does not recognize the authority of Caesar. You will be disloyal to Caesar if you let this man go free."

The blood drained from Pilate's face. He stood silent for several moments. The throng waited anxiously for his response to this reckless challenge. Finally he spoke, his voice softer, less confident than it had been before this moment.

"Behold your king. ... Shall I crucify your king?" Pilate said.

Caiaphas shouted the answer to his question.

"We have no king but Caesar!"

With one voice, the multitude repeated the same sickening phrase.

"We have no king but Caesar!"

Once again, the high priest motioned for the crowd to be silent.

Pilate turned to one of his soldiers and whispered something to him. The man disappeared into the praetorium. Everyone remained silent, waiting to see what would happen next.

Two men returned, one carrying a basin containing water; the other, a stand to place it on. The governor dipped his hands in the water. One of the men handed him a towel, and he dried his hands on it.

"I am innocent of this man's blood," Pilate asserted.

Someone in the crowd shouted, "His blood is upon us and upon our children!"

The onlookers did not respond to this ghastly pronouncement.

The look on Pilate's face was one of utter shock. He walked slowly back into to the Hall of Justice, his head bowed, his shoulders slumped, my Master, accompanied by two soldiers, following behind him. The governor ascended the steps to his judgment seat once more. Jesus stood before him. Barabbas was led in and placed beside my Master. In a voice so low that I could hardly hear it, Pilate issued his rulings. He found Jesus guilty of unspecified capital offenses and sentenced him to death by crucifixion. The sentence would be carried out that afternoon. He pardoned the convicted murderer and insurrectionist, and ordered his immediate release.

I watched as Barabbas walked swiftly to the exit, where he was greeted warmly by the chief priests, received by the cheering crowd, and hoisted on their shoulders. I learned later that he had been carried triumphantly from the praetorium grounds to the holy temple and that he had been the guest of honor at that evening's Passover meal in the home of the high priest.

I followed Jesus and his soldier guards to a side room, where they beat him yet again. They mocked him, bowing and calling him "king of the Jews," placing a reed representing a scepter in his right hand, and then taking it from him to strike him in the face with it. His back was lacerated with a whip containing sharp pieces of metal imbedded in the cords, which cut deeply into his already bleeding skin. I hated to see this, but I wanted him to know that someone who loved him was there. I saw him look at me more than once, and I hoped he found some comfort in my presence.

CHAPTER 37

He was wounded for our transgressions; he was bruised for our iniquities; the chastisement of our peace was upon him; with his stripes we are healed.

—The Prophet Isaiah

When the Roman soldiers finished mocking and beating Jesus, they removed the "royal" robe and placed his own brown outer garment on him. They left the crown of thorns on his head. It took two of them to hoist the heavy horizontal crossbeam onto his shoulders. The weight of it forced his neck to bend forward, and he used his hands and arms to balance it. The crossbeam was about five feet long and six inches thick. The journey to the place of execution then began.

I followed as closely as I could; none of the soldiers objected to my presence or even seemed to care.

Two criminals would be crucified with my Master: Each had been convicted of plotting the overthrow of Roman rule. Ironically, they had been part of Barabbas's rebellion.

Jesus struggled to carry the crossbeam—and, no wonder! He had not eaten since the evening before, had had no water or anything else to drink since then, had been beaten severely three times, and had lost a lot of blood. He fell three times under his heavy load, but he somehow struggled back to his feet and kept going. When he collapsed for the fourth time, the beam pinned him to the pavement, and he was unable to stand.

The Roman soldier closest to him seemed to recognize that Jesus could not go on like this and commandeered one of the bystanders, ordering him to carry the heavy burden. The man looked familiar to me, but I couldn't quite place him. (I would later learn that he was Simon, a pilgrim from the Roman province of Cyrene, in North Africa, and the father of Alexander and Rufus, also pilgrims. All three of these men had become followers of Jesus during this Passover week.)

The procession moved very slowly. It was a short walk—perhaps a quarter-mile—from the praetorium to what was then called *calvaria,* just outside the western wall of the Holy City. Calvaria was a small hill—a rocky knoll—on which the crosses of execution were erected. Many thousands of Jews had been crucified there since the beginning of the Roman occupation nearly a century before. The route to this dreadful place was called, appropriately, The Way of Suffering. Hundreds of onlookers lined the route. It was a mixed multitude: Most shouted insults, some offered words of sympathy or encouragement, and a few thanked my Master for healing them or teaching them the good news of God's kingdom. Many of the female observers were crying.

At one point, Jesus stopped momentarily and spoke to them.

"Don't weep for me. Weep for yourselves and your children. The day will come when it will be said, 'Blessed are those who have no children.' They will pray for the mountains to fall on them and save them from their misery."

These words to the onlookers reminded me of the words the Master had spoken just a few days before: dire warnings about the future of the temple, Jerusalem, and the fate of Jews.

We arrived at the place of execution at midmorning. A lot had happened in the past twelve hours: the conclusion of our Passover meal; the walk to the garden of Gethsemane, with several stops along the way, where Jesus counseled, encouraged, and prayed for us; Jesus's agony in the garden; his arrest; his first trial, before Annas; his second trial, before Caiaphas and the Sanhedrin; his third trial, before Pilate; his fourth trial, before Herod; his fifth trial, again before Pilate; his numerous floggings; and, ultimately, his sentence to death, as pronounced by Pilate.

The twelve-inch-thick vertical beams on which the condemned were hung were a permanent fixture on this knoll. There were at least ten of these vertical beams—much larger than the crossbeams carried by the condemned—all of them sunk deeply into the ground and rising about twelve feet above it. Only three of the beams would be used this day.

It soon became obvious that the Romans, who had invented crucifixion, had become experts at crucifying men. The soldiers assigned to this grim task carried out the various components of it with cold military precision. Jesus was stripped naked of his outer and inner garments. They pushed him to the ground, his shoulders on top of the crossbeam that had been carried, first by him and then by Simon of Cyrene. They stretched out his arms and hammered a large iron spike through each of his wrists, deep into the wood. They then tied a length of heavy rope around each arm to fasten him more securely to the beam, in the event his flesh should tear. Two very tall, very burly soldiers brought Jesus to his feet. It was their duty to position the crossbeam in a slot cut into the top of the vertical beam. Each of them used a strong wooden device in the shape of a Y. Placing this instrument under the crossbeam to which Jesus was secured, in unison they lifted it and him up, and then dropped their burden securely into the slot. They then drove an even-larger iron spike through his feet and into the vertical beam. His feet were about two yards above the ground, and just below them, one of the soldiers affixed a sign that in Latin, Greek, and Hebrew read, "The King of the Jews."

Jesus's cross was at the top, the very pinnacle, of the hill.

He has poured out his soul to death. He was numbered with the transgressors.

—The Prophet Isaiah

Simultaneously, additional executioners nailed, tied, and raised the other two convicted men into position, one on each side of Jesus.

All that remained for them to do was wait. I had heard that some of those crucified died slow deaths, sometimes taking many hours or even days. Besides the executioners, there were another hundred or so ordinary soldiers standing guard, making sure the crowd of onlookers remained orderly.

I noticed that many of the soldiers and all the executioners were drinking wine, a lot of wine. I supposed its purpose was to dull their senses, to take their minds off this gruesome duty. They also offered wine to the three slowly dying men: my Master and the man on his right refused; the man on his left accepted the offer.

I saw one of the executioners pick up the outer garment he had removed from Jesus just a few minutes before. It was without seams, fashioned from one piece of fine linen dyed a dark brown. He held it up, admiring it. Three of his comrades also examined the garment. An argument ensued: each of them wanted it. One suggested the cloak be divided four ways; another suggested they cast lots for it, and they all agreed.

They parted my garments among them and upon my apparel they did cast lots.

—The Psalmist

The eldest of my sisters, Sarah, had spun the flax for the linen and then fashioned that tunic especially for Jesus.

Just at that moment, one of the chief priests present approached the cross on which my Master hung and looked closely at the sign that had been placed below his feet. He rejoined the other priests present, and after a short conversation that I could not hear, they departed, passing near Jesus, who looked down and spoke to them.

"Father, forgive them. They don't know what they're doing."

As was the case with the journey from the praetorium to calvaria, the spectators here were a mixed crowd: some were followers of Jesus, some were his enemies, some—the Romans—were just doing their frightful duty. The followers were quiet, some of them—the women—sobbing softly. The detractors—mostly lawyers, priests, and other religious leaders—were more vocal; not a few of them mocked and derided my Master.

"He saved others. Let him save himself, if he is the Christ, the chosen one of God," said some.

"You, who would destroy the temple and rebuild it in three days, save yourself and come down from the cross!" said others.

"He trusted God; let God deliver him now. Let's see if God will save him. He said he was God's son," still others said.

"If you really are king of the Jews, save yourself!" said the last of the lot.

Even one of the two men on crosses beside Jesus participated.

"If you really are the Christ, save yourself, and save us with you!" the man said.

"Don't you fear God? You and I are also condemned," chided the other. "We are both guilty; we deserve to die. But this man has done nothing to deserve death."

Turning to my Master, the second man pleaded, "Lord, remember me when you do become king."

"I'm telling you the truth," Jesus replied. "You will be with me in paradise."

Since arriving at the place of execution, there had been three women standing close to me. I easily recognized two of them: one was Mary, the wife of Cleophas, one of Jesus's outer-circle followers; one was Mary Magdalene, the woman who had washed Jesus's feet with her tears, dried them with her hair, and then anointed them with expensive ointment. The third woman, who was standing right next to me, looked familiar, but I could not place her.

Jesus looked down into my eyes, and then, slowly, he turned his head slightly and looked into this woman's eyes.

"Mother, behold your son."

He turned to look at me.

"John, behold your mother."

Mary, the mother of Jesus, and I looked at each other. Now I knew why she looked familiar. I had seen her and her other sons and daughters—brothers and sisters of Jesus—in Capernaum more than two years before. Both she and I knew exactly what Jesus meant. I took care of her from that moment on.

By now, it was midday, and the sun was high in the heavens. However, within minutes, thick black clouds covered the sky from one end of the horizon to the other. Strangely, there was no rain, no thunder, no lightning, and no wind.

It was so dark, the Roman soldiers lighted their torches. They were prepared to stay the night if the men on the crosses lingered on this side of death as long as they usually did.

A mood of fear soon descended on the spectators.

And then an unexpected and mournful lament was heard. It was from Jesus.

"My God, my God! Why have You abandoned me?"

He spoke these words in Hebrew. In that language, it sounded as if he might have been calling out to Elijah, one of our ancient prophets.

One onlooker misunderstood and retorted sarcastically, "Let's see if Elijah comes to save him."

It shook me greatly to hear my Master utter these shocking words. Did he really believe God, his Father, would forsake him in the hour of his greatest need?

Jesus's breathing became more labored as the afternoon wore on. I had never witnessed a crucifixion before, but others had told me that most men (women were never crucified) executed in this manner died of asphyxiation: The longer they were on the cross, the more their bodies sagged, until their lungs were compressed, and then they simply stopped breathing. This seemed to be what was happening to Jesus.

"I thirst," he said in a barely audible voice.

In response to this plaintive request for water, the soldier closest to him soaked a sponge in vinegar, affixed it to his staff, and pressed it against Jesus's lips.

Jesus refused to drink or even taste it.

This was one of the cruelest things I had ever seen. There was a pail of water nearby that the soldiers had been helping themselves to all day.

It was midafternoon. Jesus had now been on the cross for six hours. He spoke again.

"Father, I commit my spirit into Your hands. My work is finished."

I heard him groan. His head slumped forward. The breath remaining in his body was slowly expelled. My Master was dead.

The three Marys standing with me also knew he was gone. They all sobbed openly.

Jesus's mother began to collapse, and I lowered her into a sitting position, sat down with her, and steadied her, my arm around her shoulders.

The nearby soldiers did not seem to realize that Jesus had died. I supposed they thought he had merely fainted. Both of the men crucified with him were still very much alive.

As I sat with my Master's mother, I remembered something John the Baptist had said the first time I set eyes on Jesus that day three years before, when he and I had been baptized by John in the Jordan River. When he saw Jesus, he said, "This man is the Lamb of God. He will take upon himself the sins of the whole world." In that instant, I knew that Jesus had not died of asphyxiation. He had not died from his physical wounds, as terrible as they were. No. It was the sins of the entire world that had crushed out his life. In that one terrible moment, he had taken upon himself all the sins of all the people who had ever lived in this world, or ever would. Those sins—my sins, your sins, all our sins—had killed him. The weight of the entire world's evil had descended upon Jesus. Sin had separated him from his Father; sin had made him feel abandoned and alone.

Immediately, darkness descended upon calvaria—over the whole world, for all I knew. It was as if the sun had stopped shining on the other side of the thick black clouds. It began to rain hard; lightning flashed across the skies; thunder rolled through the heavens; the wind began to howl. There was an earthquake. Most of the civilians present began to flee. The soldiers, who could not leave, were unable to conceal their fright. There was one exception among them: a centurion.

The centurion walked closer to Jesus's cross, looked up at him, and said, "Truly, this man was the Son of God, and he was innocent."

I was astonished to hear a Roman say such a thing, and I looked at him closely. I had not noticed him before, but now I recognized him: Jesus had healed *this* centurion's servant nearly two years before in Galilee!

A few moments later, one of his executioners thrust the tip of his spear into my Master's right side. Blood flowed from the gaping wound, confirming his death. This soldier and several of his comrades looked up at Jesus's body.

> *They shall look upon him whom they have pierced.*
> —The Prophet Zechariah

The rain ran down Jesus's lifeless body, carrying his precious blood with it. When it reached the ground, it formed tiny rivulets, which flowed down the hill in all directions. That precious blood was shed for everyone on that hill that afternoon: the chief priests who had plotted his death, the soldiers who had crucified him, those who had mocked him, and all of us who had loved him.

Meanwhile, back in Jerusalem proper, as I would learn later, the high priest, Caiaphas, was starting to worry. In just three hours, the Sabbath would begin, and it would not do for Jesus and the other two Jews to remain on their crosses during its holy hours. Something had to be done. The high priest went to the praetorium and demanded to see Pilate, who came into the courtyard to meet him.

Whenever condemned men took too long to die, the Romans, for their convenience and to hasten death, broke the men's legs.

Caiaphas insisted this be done immediately in order to protect the sanctity of our holy day. Furthermore, he wanted the bodies removed and disposed of by the soldiers. Unless friends or family claimed the body of a crucified man, the corpse was simply thrown into a common grave. The high priest requested that this be done with Jesus's body.

Pilate informed Caiaphas that he had already authorized, in writing, the removal and burial of my Master's body by someone he knew and trusted. The high priest was astonished and asked him who it was. Pilate refused to tell him. The governor did, however, dispatch one of his aides to calvaria, with the order that the legs of the convicted men, all believed to be still alive, be broken.

In less than fifteen minutes, the aide returned, stating the order had been carried out, but that one of the men, Jesus, had already succumbed; there had been no cause to break his legs.

Not a bone in his body shall be broken.

—The Psalmist

A second time, Caiaphas asked Pilate who would be claiming my Master's body; a second time, the governor refused to tell him.

By this time, the rain had ceased, the black clouds had dissipated, and the lightning and thunder were no more. The sun was setting in what had been transformed into a beautiful western sky.

Almost all the civilians had left calvaria, but the soldiers remained, many of them quite intoxicated.

My mother and father, who had witnessed the execution from the edge of the crowd, joined my Master's mother, the two other Marys, and me near the foot of the cross.

Mary had made clear to me that she would not leave her son until she knew what would happen to his body, and I promised her I would stay by her side. Jesus had given me a solemn duty, and I was determined to carry it out.

Just at that moment, two finely dressed men arrived, accompanied by several servants. One of the men approached the centurion I mentioned previously, handing him a small sealed scroll.

The centurion broke the seal and read what was written upon the scroll. He turned to the chief executioner and gave him an order I could not hear. The executioner then gave orders to the same two soldiers who had lifted Jesus upon the cross some six hours before. Carefully, much more carefully than they had placed him on the cross, they lowered my Master's lifeless body into the waiting arms of two other men. These men carried the body a few feet away, to a waiting donkey cart. Gently, they placed him on a blanket inside the cart and covered him with a white sheet. Inside the cart were several bolts of fine white linen and containers filled with spices used in the burial custom.

I had not been able to see the faces of these men until this moment, and when I did, I recognized them both. One was the owner of the donkey Jesus had ridden into Jerusalem five days before. The same donkey would now transport him to his place of rest. The other man was the owner of the house where we had celebrated the Passover supper the previous night. I would learn later that both these men were members of the Sanhedrin. Neither of them had been present at Jesus's trial before Caiaphas earlier that day. They were Joseph of Arimathea and Nicodemus. In touching my Master's dead body, neither of them would be able to celebrate the Passover meal later that evening or participate in Sabbath rituals the next day. I doubted either of them was concerned about such comparative trivialities at a time like this. Joseph, the donkey's owner, took the rope tied around the animal's neck and began to lead him away.

Mary Magdalene and Mary, the wife of Cleophas, insisted on following them to see where they were taking Jesus. The two Marys said they would report to us later, either that evening or the following morning. But where would they find us?

My father suggested that Jesus's mother stay at the house he and my mother always rented in Jerusalem during Passover. Of course, I would stay there too; Jesus had appointed me her guardian. Father gave the two Marys the location of the house, and they assured us they would come no later than the next morning to give us a full report.

Fortunately, the house my parents had rented for this week was just inside the western wall, only a short distance away. Jesus's mother was exhausted, both physically and emotionally. She was no longer sobbing, but she looked as desolate as anyone I had ever seen. My mother prepared a simple meal, but none of us had much of an appetite. Mother put Mary to bed, and the three of us (my sisters were spending the night with close family friends) stayed up a while longer, talking about the events of this terrible day. None of us had any idea where James was—or, for that matter, any of the other apostles. As far as I knew, none of them had been present at Jesus's crucifixion.

CHAPTER 38

It was the Sabbath, but none of us had any thought of participating in the usual Passover-week activities for that particular holy day. Even though I had gone to bed exhausted, I did not sleep well; the horrors of the previous day kept me tossing and turning. It didn't take the rising sun and its light penetrating the window of my room to wake me. I arose, dressed, and went into the sitting room. It was quiet; no one else was up and about. I sat in a chair, wondering what might happen next. Jesus's life had ended; would this to be the end of his story, too?

There was a faint knock at the door. Who could it be at this hour? And then I remembered the two Marys had promised to let us know what had become of the body of my Master. I opened the door just a crack, to see who was there, and, indeed, it was these two women. The three of us conversed quietly, so as not to awaken the others.

Before long, my father and mother emerged from their room, and my mother asked that the report of the women be delayed until Jesus's mother joined us. When putting her to bed the evening before, Mary had insisted that she wanted to know what had been done with her son's lifeless body. We did not have to wait long.

Mary opened her door, and I hastened to her side and assisted her to a chair. She looked weak and worn and as if she had been crying all night.

Mother looked at Mary, and then at the other two Marys, and nodded her consent.

The elder of the two Marys, the wife of Cleophas, told us what had transpired the evening before.

They had followed, at a little distance, Joseph and Nicodemus.

From calvaria, they'd traveled north, perhaps a quarter-mile. By that time, the sun had set, and the full moon was their only light. Most residents and pilgrims were celebrating the Passover meal, and the sad procession encountered very few others; the ones they did meet showed no interest in them or what they were doing. Of course, they all knew they were breaking the Sabbath by performing this somber duty, but at that moment, showing regard for the crucified Master seemed more important than man-made restrictions. In a few minutes, the cortege reached its destination: a beautiful garden near the Damascus Gate on the north side of the city. One of the servants opened the gate, and the silent company entered. They traveled only a short distance, to an area of the garden with a large solid rock outcropping. A tomb had been hewn out of the rock, and a large round stone covered its entrance. Four of the servants rolled the stone away. At that moment, one of the attendants noticed the two Marys, who were standing several yards away. He pointed out the women to his master, Joseph, who motioned them to approach. He introduced himself and Nicodemus to them and asked who they were. They told the two men their names, said they were followers of Jesus, and offered to assist in the preparation of their Master's mortal remains for burial. The men agreed and thanked them.

I looked at our Master's mother. Her sadness was obvious—from time to time, she brushed tears from her eyes—but she seemed to be listening carefully to the older Mary, with some semblance of relief that good and loving people had taken care of her son's burial preparations.

Mary continued with the story.

One of the servants lighted a torch and carried it into the tomb. Two others removed the baskets of spices and placed them inside the chamber. Joseph and Nicodemus, assisted by two other the servants, carried the body of Jesus into the crypt. Joseph emerged and invited the two Marys to enter. The tomb was new; Jesus's body was to be the first to occupy it.

At this point, Mary wisely chose to omit the details of the embalming process.

When their work was finished, Joseph ordered the stone, which contained an etched inscription, rolled over the entrance. On account of the lateness of the hour, Nicodemus, who lived nearby, just inside the city's north gate, invited the two Marys to stay at his and his wife's home that night. They gratefully accepted his offer, arose early in the morning, and made their way to my parents' house.

The mother of Jesus thanked the women for their kindness and then excused herself. I escorted her back to her room.

My mother offered to bring Mary bread, fruit, and something to drink, and she agreed. Mother quickly prepared these items and took them to Mary's room. She invited the other Marys to join us for a light breakfast, and they both accepted.

None of us had much of an appetite. Our meal finished, my mother invited these women to stay with us the rest of the day and even overnight.

They politely declined. The younger Mary was staying with friends nearby, and the elder Mary would join her.

After the women departed, I sat quietly with my parents, none of us saying much. What was there to say? My Master—our Master—had died on a cruel cross. He was now lying on a cold, hard slab of rock, in a tomb just outside the city he had entered in triumph six days earlier; the city in whose temple he had spent four of those six days teaching and healing everyone who desired to be taught or healed. He had barely escaped death by stoning at the hands of his tormentors in the temple. It was the same temple in which he had saved a woman accused of adultery from being stoned to death by her accusers—the same accusers who walked away in shame when he challenged those of them without sin to throw the first stone—and then told her he didn't condemn her either.

Now these same men had succeeded in killing our Master.

My reflections were interrupted by another knock at the door. I looked at my silent parents. Who could this be? Perhaps it was the temple guard, searching for followers of Jesus.

I opened the door a crack and was relieved to see the sad but friendly faces of Joseph and Nicodemus. They both called me by name. I invited them in and introduced them to my parents. My father asked them to sit down. I briefly related to them the recent visit of the two Marys and their description of the disposition of Jesus's body in Joseph's tomb. We thanked them for their kind act. My mother added that Jesus's mother was in one of the bedrooms, resting, and that she, too, had heard what these men had done and was greatly relieved to know that her son's body had not been desecrated, but honored with a proper Jewish burial.

Both men told us they had been secret followers of Jesus for some time. I was not surprised and had, in fact, speculated that, considering what had happened the evening before; something along those lines had to be the explanation for their merciful act. In so doing, they had put their lives at risk, and their bold behavior would ruin their reputations among the chief priests, elders, and other leaders. (Both would soon be expelled from the Sanhedrin. Both would eventually lose their earthly possessions. Neither would have any regrets.)

I asked Joseph and Nicodemus to tell us how they had managed to obtain permission to claim and take the body of Jesus for burial.

Joseph said, "As soon as I got word that Jesus had died, I went straight to the praetorium to see Pilate. He knows me and came out to greet me. He looked very tired and troubled, almost distraught. I told him I wanted his written permission to remove the body of the Master from calvaria and transport it to my own tomb for burial. I was afraid our Lord's body would be desecrated unless Pilate granted my request, and he replied that as soon as Jesus died, he would authorize me to claim the body. I told him Jesus was already dead. Pilate looked surprised, even skeptical, and ordered one of his soldiers to hasten to the place of execution, confirm Jesus's death, and report back to him immediately. While the soldier was gone, Pilate invited me inside the praetorium and was surprised when I accepted. He said, 'This is a nasty business. I tried to save your king, but your high priest, Caiaphas, forced my hand. There was nothing more I could do.' He looked and sounded like a man trying to convince himself. I said nothing. Then he told me that earlier that afternoon, Caiaphas himself had come to him, demanding that the sign I had ordered placed on Jesus's cross be changed from 'The king of the Jews' to 'He said he was the king of the Jews.' Irate, Pilate had refused, telling the high priest, 'What I have written, I have written.' Within a few minutes, the soldier returned and confirmed that Jesus was dead. The governor wrote out the order, signed his name to it, stamped it with his seal, rolled up the parchment, and handed it to me. He then directed the soldier and three others to accompany me to calvaria. Nicodemus was waiting for me outside the praetorium, and we walked to the crucifixion site. You know the rest."

"Sir, how did you become a follower of Jesus?" I asked.

"Perhaps you should hear first how Nicodemus became his follower. He's the one who introduced me to the Master," Joseph replied.

Nicodemus then told us his remarkable story.

"A year ago, during Passover, I stood on the edge of the crowd in the temple when Jesus was teaching and healing. At first, I was shocked, then angered, by his denunciation of me and my fellow Pharisees. I could not abide what he was saying, almost all of which directly contradicted what I had always believed. I left in a huff and went to my home—the same home in which you, John, your fellow disciples, and Jesus celebrated the Passover meal two nights ago. While I didn't like what Jesus said that afternoon, I could not stop thinking about him. I went to my study and began to pour over the ancient Scriptures, especially the prophecies concerning the Messiah. I read all night, and my perspective began to change. I decided to have an open mind about Jesus and what I had heard him say. His criticisms no longer seemed like the rantings of a heretic. I resolved to seek him out privately; I wanted to have a personal conversation with him, to satisfy myself one way or the other. Could he actually be the Promised One, the Messiah? Or was he just another imposter? However, I couldn't be seen with him in public, where I might be recognized. I was afraid of losing my position, my reputation. I am embarrassed now to admit that I even thought such things.

"So, I sent a trusted emissary to discreetly deliver a sealed message to Jesus. He replied in writing that he would meet me at midnight the next evening in the garden of Gethsemane. I came alone and arrived at the appointed hour. I found him praying, and I waited in silence until he had finished. Nearby were two benches which faced each other, and he led me to them, motioning me to sit opposite him. He had yet to say a single word, leaving me to start the conversation.

"'Rabbi,' I began, 'I know you are a teacher sent by God. And no one can do the miracles you do unless God is with him.'

"He paid no mind to this compliment, but said simply, 'I'm telling you a solemn truth: unless you are born from above, you will never see God's kingdom.'

"I was speechless for a moment, not knowing what to say. When I finally did respond, my words sounded ridiculous, even to me. 'How can I be born, when I'm old? Are you telling me I can go back into my mother's womb and be born a second time?'

"Jesus sighed. 'Nicodemus, listen carefully. I'm telling you the most important truth you will ever hear. Unless you are born of *water* and the *spirit,* you will not enter God's kingdom. You are talking about *physical* birth; I'm speaking of a different kind of birth—a second birth, a new birth. Flesh gives birth to flesh. However, God's Holy Spirit gives birth—a new birth—to a man's inner being, his heart and mind. Don't be surprised that I'm telling you that you must be born from *above.* The Holy Spirit, who comes from above, is on the move in Israel. He is like the wind that blows: You cannot see it; you never know where it comes from or where it is going. You hear only the sound it makes and see the results of its movements. That's what it's like when you are born of the Spirit.'

"I wasn't sure I fully understood what Jesus was saying, and so I asked, 'How can this be true, and how does this happen?'

"'You're a teacher of Israel, and you don't understand how

this works?' Jesus countered. 'I know what I'm talking about; I'm speaking God's truth. Nevertheless, you are having a hard time even considering the evidence: not just my testimony but also the testimony of our ancient prophets. Look, if I speak of earthly matters, and you don't understand or believe what I say, how will you understand or believe if I speak of heavenly matters? Will you ignore them? Nobody has gone up into heaven except the one who came down from heaven: the Son of Man.'

"With my own ears, I had heard Jesus refer to himself as the *Son of Man* in the temple. Now he was saying that the Son of Man—he himself—had come to earth from heaven. I was stunned, to put it mildly. I thought of ending the interview at that moment. But I'm glad I didn't. We continued our conversation, and Jesus explained his mission on earth: To begin a new family, a spiritual family, in which ordinary birth was not enough. The members of this new family would also be born of water—the baptism performed by John, and since his death, now carried out by Jesus's own disciples—and by the Holy Spirit of God, who would live in us, producing a new life inside our hearts and minds.

"'When would God's Spirit manifest among us?' I asked.

"'In God's appointed time,' he answered.

"'Will I live to see it, to receive Him into my life?' I inquired, with no small amount of fear.

"'You will,' he said.

"That is the story of how I came to Jesus. How I came to believe he is the promised Messiah."

Thus, Nicodemus concluded his story.

We all looked at Joseph. We wanted to hear his story.

Joseph and Nicodemus had become close friends during the time they served on the Sanhedrin. In the past year, their social friendship had taken on a deeper meaning: Together, they began to study more carefully the Scriptures, especially those passages that pointed toward the coming of the Anointed One, the Messiah. During the first few months of their research, Nicodemus did not reveal his nighttime visit with Jesus to his friend. However, when he thought the time was right, he told Joseph the story—but not the whole story—of their encounter. Of course, Joseph knew about Jesus, about his teachings and his miracles. Gradually, Nicodemus provided more details about his interview with the Master, until Joseph knew all that had transpired. He told Joseph that he had come to believe that Jesus was indeed the Messiah and that he was now a secret follower of the man from Galilee. At first, Joseph was taken aback by this news. But, over time, he, too became convinced. Only a few days before, during this Passover week just ending now, he and Nicodemus had met privately with the Master, in the same place in the garden of Gethsemane where Nicodemus had first met Jesus the previous year. This interview had cemented Joseph's commitment to Jesus.

Before seeing these two men the afternoon before at the foot of the cross of our Lord, I had no knowledge that anyone so high up in the ecclesiastical hierarchy had become a follower of Jesus. I was astonished, and so were my parents.

Just at that moment, there came another knock at the door. Again, I opened it only a few inches and recognized one of the servants of Joseph who had been with him at calvaria the previous afternoon. He asked if his master was there, and when I answered affirmatively, he asked to speak with him.

Joseph came to the door and stepped outside. In a few moments, he returned, telling us that he thought we, too, should hear the news the servant had brought.

My father quickly agreed, and the servant joined us. He had three pieces of intelligence to report. First, Judas had gone to the home of Caiaphas earlier that morning. Several other chief priests were there in conference with the high priest. Judas, apparently distraught, had burst into their meeting shouting something about his betraying innocent blood. Caiaphas, nonplussed, had retorted that Judas's feelings meant nothing to him or to the others present. Hearing this, the betrayer threw a handful of silver coins onto the stone floor, and fled. The high priest dispatched one of his servants, with instructions to follow the disgraced former disciple of Jesus and report back on his movements. Within an hour, the servant returned. Judas had gone outside the city, taken a length of rope apparently concealed inside his tunic, fashioned a noose at one end of it, tied it to a low-hanging branch of a tree, and hung himself to death. No one else witnessed this gruesome event, and the servant had left his lifeless body hanging there. The high priest and the others looked pleased, and Caiaphas ordered that the body remain in place until the end of the Sabbath and that Judas's remains be buried in a potter's field the next day.

We were all horrified to hear this grisly news.

I asked the servant how he came to learn this news. He told us that all his fellow attendants had become secret followers of Jesus (so had Nicodemus's servants) and that there were even covert adherents of the Master among the servants of the high priest himself. It was a kind of underground movement through which information sometimes traveled fast.

Hearing this, my father, mother and I were amazed.

Next, the servant told us about the second piece of news: an incident that had occurred in the temple during the midafternoon of the previous day. The thick and heavy curtain that separates the Holy Place from the Most Holy Place had been torn completely asunder, from top to bottom. The priest closest to it at the time had collapsed and died. The third item he reported was something that had happened just this morning. Some of the chief priests, along with several Pharisees, went to the praetorium and asked to see Pilate. They requested his permission to seal the tomb of Jesus and place a contingent of temple guards around it. The governor wanted to know why they thought that necessary. He laughed when they told him they feared Jesus's followers would steal his body and claim he had risen from the dead. Nevertheless, he agreed to let them proceed.

My father invited Joseph and Nicodemus to stay for a midday

meal. They declined, saying their families were expecting them at their respective homes. They departed, with our gratitude.

Mother prepared a light meal and knocked softly on Mary's door. She opened it and said she would join us at the table. We told her about our visitors and most of what they had said, omitting the report about Judas. She was surprised that her son had exerted such influence on these high-ranking officials.

As soon as we had finished our meal, there was another knock at our door.

CHAPTER 39

For the fourth time that day, I opened the door slightly to see who was calling. It was a woman who looked familiar to me but I could not quite place when or where I had seen her. Her name was Esther. She said she had met Jesus more than a year before, at Jacob's Well, a notable landmark situated on the outskirts of the town of Sycar in Samaria. Of course, I remembered her now. I invited her in and introduced her to my parents and our Master's mother. She was overwhelmed to meet Mary. Esther was heartbroken by the crucifixion of Jesus; she had been among the throng observing his journey to calvaria and had witnessed his death on the cross. I asked her to share with us her life-changing encounter with Jesus.

For the sake of my parents and Mary, I set the scene.

"It was just after last year's Passover. Jesus and the twelve of us were returning from Jerusalem to Galilee. Jesus decided that we would travel by the most direct route, straight north through the heart of Samaria. By noon of the second day of our journey, we had reached Jacob's Well. We had run low on food, and Jesus asked us to go into the village and purchase bread for our midday meal. He was tired and said he would wait in the shade of a tree a stone's throw away from the well until we returned."

Not knowing what had occurred during our absence, I asked Esther to tell us what happened while we were in the village.

"It was my custom to draw water from the well at midday, when there was usually no one else there," she began. "When I saw John and the other disciples walking toward the village, right in my path, I stepped away from the road until they had passed. I didn't think they saw me, and I did not want to be seen, certainly not by Judeans or

Galileans. I'm sure you understand that. When I arrived at the well, I lowered my bucket into its depths, filled it with water, and drew it up. Just at that moment, I heard a man's voice. I had not seen anyone else and was startled. Turning around, I saw a man sitting nearby.

"'Please give me a drink of water,' he said.

"Looking at him carefully, I replied, 'Aren't you a Jew? Why would you ask me, a *Samaritan woman,* to give you a drink of water?'

"His reply only deepened my confusion. 'If you only knew God's gift and who is asking you for a drink of water, you would have asked him, and he would have given you living water.'

"'But, sir, you haven't got a bucket or even a cup for water! The well is deep; how could you get water out of it, anyway? Are you greater than our father, Jacob, who gave us this well and drank from it himself: he and his sons and his animals?'

"'All those who drink this water will get thirsty again. But the water I offer to you and everyone else will be a spring welling up into eternal life.'

"I wasn't sure what he was talking about, but his words were so gentle, so inviting, that my response, I would soon learn, was rather foolish.

"'Sir, give me this water! Then I won't be thirsty any longer, and won't have to come to this well every day.'

"Jesus didn't answer this silly question. He changed the subject completely, much to my embarrassment.

"'Go and fetch your husband so that he can join us.'

"'I don't have a husband.'

"'You're right about that. In fact, you have had five husbands, and the man you are living with now is not your husband. You're speaking the truth when you say you don't have a husband.'

"I nearly fainted from shock and shame, and for a moment, I couldn't speak. Then *I* changed the subject.

"'Sir, I can tell you are a prophet.' I pointed to Mount Gerizim. 'Our ancestors worshipped on that mountain, but you believe Jerusalem is the place people should worship.'

"'Believe me,' Jesus responded, 'the time is coming when you won't worship God on this mountain or in Jerusalem. You worship what you do not know. We worship what we do know. Salvation, you see, is from the Jews. However, the time is coming—indeed, it's already here—when true believers will worship the Father in spirit and in truth. Yes, that's the kind of worshippers the Father wants. God is Spirit, and those who worship Him must worship in spirit and in truth.'

"'I know that the Messiah—the Anointed One—is coming someday,' I said. 'When he comes, he will tell us everything.'

"Jesus responded to what I said—and I will never forget his exact words: '*I am* the Messiah. Yes, the one who speaks with you now.'

"John, just at that moment, you and your fellow disciples returned, and I departed for the village. I was so excited to tell everyone I could about Jesus and what he had said to me, and, in my haste, I forgot my water jar! All of you looked surprised to see the Master and me in conversation."

"Yes, we were," I replied. "Right away, we all noticed something peculiar in Jesus's appearance. He looked different to us; it was as if he had been freed of the weariness of travel. Of course, as he had requested, we brought bread to satisfy his hunger, and we encouraged him to eat. And then he said the strangest thing: 'I've had food to eat that you don't even know about.' Confused, we looked at each other, and Peter asked him if someone else had brought him something to eat. His response was puzzling: 'My food is to do the will of the One who sent me and to finish His work.' Those words now remind me of something he said yesterday on the cross as he was dying: 'Father, I commit my spirit into Your hands. My work is finished.' At that moment, I believe he was relieved of the weariness of all the sins he bore on behalf of all mankind."

There was silence for a few moments, and then Esther continued her story.

"When I arrived in the village, my excitement caused an instant stir. I began to tell anyone who would listen about my encounter with Jesus. A crowd gathered around me, and I entreated them to come with me to the well and see a man who knew everything about the life I had lived. I believed he was the promised Messiah. More and more people crowded around, and they followed me! I doubt many believed my story but at least their curiosity was aroused."

At that point, I had something to interject.

"Shortly before you returned to the well, Esther, our Master said to us, 'The other day, I heard some of you men talking about the next harvest, saying that it would come in late summer, a few months from now. Well, let me tell you: look over there.' He pointed in the direction of your village, Esther. We turned and saw you coming toward us, leading a large throng. As we turned back to face Jesus, he continued. 'You won't have to wait months! The fields are ready for harvesting right now! The sower earns his reward by planting the seeds of eternal life. The reaper gathers the crop produced by those seeds. This is where the expression "one sows and one reaps" comes from. Now you will be able to reap what that woman sowed. And you will all rejoice together over the results.'"

Esther was deeply touched to hear what Jesus had said, and she concluded her story.

"The crowd gathered around our Master, and he began to teach the good news of God's kingdom on this earth, and to heal the sick and infirm. The mayor of Sycar was among them, and he implored Jesus to come into our village. Jesus and his disciples stayed with us for two more days. Many believed and became followers of our Master, and continue to believe in him to this day. Jesus proved to the whole village that his gift of the water of life is freely given to all who will accept it, regardless of their race, their religion, or their sinful condition. As for myself, my life is completely changed. I am no longer an embarrassment—an outcast—in my own community. He died on the cross, bearing my sins, and I will always be grateful to him."

While Esther was telling of her encounter with our Master, from time to time, I glanced at Mary. At the beginning of the story, she appeared to be overwhelmed, not only with grief but also with fatigue. Considering the circumstances, it would have been strange if she had looked—and felt—any other way. However, as Esther's narrative continued, Mary's mood seemed to lighten. Hearing of her son's tender regard for this lost soul, a woman whom most people would scorn or at best ignore, seemed to lift Mary's spirit. It was not unlike what our Master said about having food to eat that we, his closest friends, knew nothing about: the spiritual nourishment of saving a lost soul.

Mary, understandably, had hardly spoken a word all day. Now she wanted to talk. She wanted to tell us about the life of her son: from his birth—and even before—until the time he left home to begin his ministry.

I knew as much as anyone about the last three years of his life, the ministry part. But, strangely, I now realized that I knew nothing at all of his early and middle years.

CHAPTER 40

Mary began with a brief description of her background. She was born and raised in Nazareth. Her father was a farmer; her mother had died when she was a small child; she had four brothers and no sisters. At the age of sixteen, she was engaged to marry Joseph, a twenty-one-year-old furniture- and cabinetmaker, also of Nazareth. He was a deeply religious and well-respected man, noted for excellent work in his chosen craft. He was also a direct descendant of King David, Israel's most famous and beloved king, who had ruled many centuries before.

"Shortly before my scheduled wedding, I was sleeping soundly in my bedroom one night when I was suddenly awakened by a bright light. I was frightened to the point of screaming but could not open my mouth. The light was the aura of an angel.

"'Greetings, favored one, the Lord is with you,' he began. 'You are blessed among women. Do not be afraid, Mary, for you have found great favor with God. You will conceive a child in your womb and give birth to a son and you will name him Jesus. He will be a great man and will be called the *Son of the Most High,* and the Lord shall give him the throne of his ancestor, David. He will reign over the house of Jacob forever; his kingdom will never end.'

"The angel, who had told me his name was Gabriel, paused, and somehow I gathered the courage to ask him a question. 'How can this be? I have never had sexual relations with any man!'

"He answered, 'The Holy Spirit shall come upon you, and the power of the Highest shall overshadow you. That holy child who shall be born of you shall also be called the *Son of God.* Your cousin, Elizabeth, has also conceived a child in her old age. She is no longer barren; she is now in her sixth month. With God, nothing is impossible.'

"'I am the Lord's servant,' I responded. 'May this happen to me, according to your word and the will of God.'"

Mary's description of the conception of Jesus was the most astonishing thing I had ever heard. I'm sure my parents and Esther thought so too. As fantastic as it seemed, it made perfect sense to me when I thought about all the other singular characteristics of our Master. For instance, his miracles: creating thousands of meals from a few fish and loaves of bread; casting out demons; calming an angry sea; reading people's thoughts; changing ordinary water into rich wine; raising Lazarus from the dead; and hundreds more.

Mary continued, and her story became even more fascinating.

"Within a few days of the angel's appearance, I felt compelled to visit my cousin, Elizabeth. I suppose I wanted to confirm that she, as the angel had declared, was also pregnant. This was before I had said anything to my betrothed, Joseph, about my condition. One of my brothers accompanied me on the journey, which was more than a hundred miles and took six days. Elizabeth's husband, Zacharias, was a priest in their village synagogue. They were both very old. When we reached their home, I knocked on the door. A servant girl opened it, and I told her I wanted to see her mistress. I asked my brother to remain outside; I wanted to see my cousin alone. Elizabeth heard my voice and came immediately into the sitting room. She dismissed the servant, and the first thing she said to me was that, when she heard my voice, her baby leaped in her womb. Then she said, 'Blessed are you among all women, and blessed is the fruit of your womb.' Those were almost the same words the angel had spoken to me. She then said with great joy and excitement, 'Why has this happened to me? Why does the mother of my Lord come to visit me?' Then she told me her story. Six months before, she and her husband were in Jerusalem. It was the time of his annual duty to serve in the holy temple for a fortnight. One day, when he was alone in the Holy Place, the same angel, Gabriel, appeared to him, telling him that his wife would conceive a child who would grow up to be one of Israel's greatest prophets. This child was to be named John, and he would grow up to be a great prophet of God, preparing the way for the Messiah—the Anointed One. Zacharias was dumbfounded: He and his wife were too old to have a child; Elizabeth had been barren all her life. The angel rebuked him and said that because of his doubt, he would not be able to speak until after the child was born. He left the temple and communicated this information to his wife in writing. Soon she was pregnant; now she was in her sixth month. Our conversation had taken an hour, and my brother was still waiting for me outside the house. I said farewell to Elizabeth, and my brother and I traveled back to Nazareth. My brother wanted to know what my cousin and I talked about. I simply told him that he would know soon enough."

So, John the Baptist and Jesus were cousins, born six months apart and under similar circumstances: Both births miraculous, but in different ways. John had indeed become a great prophet, the one who prepared the way for Jesus's kingdom message.

Mary continued her remarkable story.

"Now, I had to tell Joseph. Would he believe me? If not, would he keep his commitment to marry me, regardless? Or, more likely, would he break the engagement? If he did, what would I tell my father? Would my father believe my strange story? Nevertheless, I had to tell my betrothed, and thinking about that made me almost frantic. I prayed, asking God to give me the right words to say to Joseph, and the strength to say them. I also prayed that Joseph would believe me and that we could go forward with our wedding. I met him at his home, the house he had built, the next afternoon, and we sat on his porch, on chairs that he had made with his own hands. He asked me about my journey south to visit my cousin. The Lord had calmed my spirit, and I was able to tell him the whole story in a clear and steady voice, including the details of Elizabeth's unexpected pregnancy. He listened without discernable emotion, and when I had finished, he asked me no questions. He said simply that he wanted to think about what I had told him. His response gave me no comfort, but at least he did not immediately break the engagement. He said we would meet again the next day. Early the next afternoon, there was a knock at the door. My oldest brother answered it and invited Joseph in. He asked that I come outside and sit with him. We walked away from the house and sat on the grass under a sycamore tree. Joseph told me that, after our conversation, his first thought was indeed to end our engagement. He had gone to sleep in that frame of mind. He knew he was not the father of my child—if indeed there was a child. He wondered if my imagination had conjured up the whole story. My heart sank. He saw my desperate expression and quickly added that something strange had happened to him during the night. The angel Gabriel had appeared to *him* in a dream! This heavenly visitor had said, 'Joseph, son of David, don't be afraid to take Mary as your wife. The Holy Spirit conceived her child. She will give birth to a son, and you and she will name him Jesus, for he will save his people from their sins. Now, all this will be done, that the Lord's word through the prophet might be fulfilled: Look, a virgin shall be with child and shall give birth to a son, and they shall call his name *Emmanuel,* which means God with us.'

"Our wedding, scheduled for the coming week, would go on as planned. We would not have marital relations until after the birth of Jesus.

"Joseph and I—and Elizabeth, of course—were the only ones who knew the circumstances of my son's conception. I moved into my husband's house, and we both eagerly awaited Jesus's birth. Neither of us knew what it would be like to be the parents of such a special child. When I was well into my eighth month, a Roman soldier came to our house, telling us that the emperor, Caesar Augustus, had issued a decree: Every inhabitant of Israel must return to his place of birth to be registered and taxed. Joseph had been born in Bethlehem, the City of David, more than a hundred miles to the south. It would take many days to travel there. We left the next week, with little prospect of my son being born in Nazareth. Fortunately, Joseph had a sturdy, gentle, and reliable donkey. My husband walked the entire route, and I rode most of the way, walking only occasionally. We spent most nights at inns along the way. However, when we finally arrived in the small village of Bethlehem one evening, the only inn was completely occupied. Seeing my condition, the innkeeper offered to let us stay in a small stable behind the inn, at no charge. At least we would have a roof over our heads. I was relieved to see there were no animals in it that night. There was fresh straw in abundance, and with it, Joseph made a comfortable bed for me. Shortly after I lay down, I went into labor. My husband placed straw into a feeding trough—it would be a cradle for Jesus—and within an hour, Joseph delivered our son. He looked no different from any other healthy and normal newborn baby I had ever seen. About two hours after I had given birth, we had three visitors. It must have been midnight by that time, but my husband and I were still awake, and Jesus was sleeping peacefully in the cradle. They were shepherds who had been standing watch with their flocks on a hillside overlooking Bethlehem. Joseph asked them why they had come.

"They told an extraordinary story. An angel had appeared to them and said, 'Don't be afraid. I bring you good tidings of great joy for all people! Born this day in the City of David is the Savior, Christ the Lord. You'll find him there, lying in a stable with his mother.' Then, suddenly, they saw a host of angels, singing praises: 'Glory to God in the highest and on earth, peace and goodwill toward men.' So, they had decided to go into Bethlehem and see with their own eyes if what the angel had said was true. And, it was true, just as he had said.

"I have thought about that evening, about those humble shepherds—the first visitors my son had received—many times."

We all listened with rapt attention to this story of Jesus's birth, told by the woman who bore him, and we were anxious to hear more.

Mary continued.

"Joseph and I agreed that I would not be ready to travel the great distance back to Nazareth for some time. The innkeeper told

Joseph he owned a small house in Bethlehem that we could rent. When he learned my husband was a carpenter, he offered it to us at no charge if Joseph would repair several chairs, tables, cabinets, and beds in his inn. There was a synagogue in the village, and we made an appointment with the priest for our son to be circumcised on the eighth day following his birth in accordance with the requirements of our law. It was then that he was formally named Jesus. Three weeks later, we traveled the short distance—less than six miles—to Jerusalem, to dedicate Jesus to the Lord in the holy temple. We presented the appropriate sacrifice of two turtledoves, and the priest performed the short dedication ceremony.

"As we turned to leave, an elderly man approached us. He told us his name was Simeon, and he looked closely at our son. He asked our permission to take Jesus in his arms, and we agreed. He said that the Holy Spirit had revealed to him that he would not die until he had seen the Lord's Christ and that the Spirit had led him to the temple that day. As he looked at our son, with tears of joy flowing down his cheeks, he said, 'Lord, let me depart this world in peace, for my eyes have seen your salvation, which you have offered to all people: A light for the Gentiles and a light for your glory and for your people, Israel.' Then Simeon looked at me and said, 'This child is set for the fall and rising of many in Israel, and for a sign: A sword shall pierce through your own soul, that the thoughts of many hearts may be revealed.'

"I didn't understand the meaning of the last few words he said to me that day until yesterday."

Mary began to cry softly, and my mother, who was wiping away tears of her own, gave her a handkerchief. We sat quietly until Mary had regained her composure. There was still much she wanted to tell us, and it seemed that sharing her memories of Jesus's childhood provided some respite from her grief.

"We returned to our rented house in Bethlehem. Jesus was now a month old, growing bigger and stronger every day. In addition to his work for the innkeeper, word of Joseph's carpentry skills had spread around the village, and he was kept quite busy.

"On a Sabbath afternoon a few weeks later, my husband, with Jesus in his arms, and I were sitting on our porch when three finely dressed men accompanied by several servants rode up on camels. They all dismounted, and the three men approached us. Joseph rose, placed our sleeping son into the cradle he had made, and greeted them. They introduced themselves, and we invited them to sit and rest—Joseph brought three additional chairs from the house. They had a story to tell, and what a story it was! Their names were Melchior, Gaspar, and Balthasar. They had been friends for many years and had traveled together from Persia, far to the east. Melchior—the one who did most of the talking—had had a dream several weeks before. He shared the content of the dream with his two friends. Now he would share it with us.

"The dream was simple and straightforward. An unusually bright star would appear low in the heavens. It would come from the east and would be visible only at night. When it appeared, he was to follow its path wherever it led. It would lead him to a child who would someday be the greatest king the world had ever known. Since he was a young man, he had developed a keen interest in the stars. Over time, he began to chart them, learning which ones appeared at certain seasons of the year. He was sure he could discern any new or unusual heavenly body that might appear. His two friends did not share his passion for the firmament, but they always listened with interest whenever he told them of his latest celestial discovery. So, he decided to tell them of the dream. Their looks betrayed skepticism. He said that, if the star did appear, he was determined to follow it wherever it led. They looked dismayed, but their dismay turned to incredulity when he asked if they would follow it with him. He looked at his friends and smiled, and they returned his smile with grins of their own. He slept during the days and stayed awake each night, peering into the sky. Within a few days, his persistence was rewarded: A bright star, more brilliant than any he had ever seen, appeared low in the eastern sky. It tracked very slowly, and near dawn, had traveled perhaps ten degrees. The next morning, he sent a servant to each of his friends' homes, with invitations to have dinner with him that evening. Both accepted. They dined on the east-facing terrace of his home as the sun was setting in the west. He sat on one side of the table, across from his friends. As they were enjoying the meal and one of their deep philosophical discussions—all three of them fancied themselves to be philosophers—he could see the star rising in the east two hours earlier than it had the previous evening when he first saw it. Melchior could hardly contain his excitement but said nothing until the meal was finished and the table cleared. The servants retired, leaving the three of them alone. His friends could not see the phenomenon, thanks to the seating arrangement. He rose, dimmed the torchlight—he wanted his friends to see the full effect of the star's brilliance—and asked them to stand up and turn around. They both gasped in awe. All three gazed at it for more than an hour, and during that time, it moved westward several degrees. As they were preparing to leave, he stated that when the star passed over his house on its westward journey, he was going to follow it. Would they join him? They looked at each other and then at him, and each said that they would.

"They began to make preparations the next day. In ten days' time, the star was directly over Melchior's house as the sun set, and they began the journey. That sojourn brought them to our country, to our house, and right to my child. But I'm getting ahead of the story. They traveled by night and slept by day. The star's brightness made traveling safe and easy; it was their faithful guide every step of the way. By their reckoning, it was a journey of nearly nine hundred miles, and it took them forty nights to reach us. The star's light never failed them; every evening, it would be directly over their heads. Early one morning, as they were descending the Mount of Olives to our Holy City, the star shone directly over the residence of Herod the Great. They thought they had reached their destination. Perhaps a king, whom they had never heard of and of course knew nothing about, was the father of the child-king they were seeking. They waited until midday, left their servants and camels outside the city, and sought an audience with

Herod. He received them, and they told him the purpose of their visit: They were here to see the child who would someday be the King of the Jews. They had followed his star from the east and had come to worship and pay homage to him. On hearing this, Herod excused himself, saying he had an urgent appointment with some of his advisors but promised to return presently. In half an hour, he reentered the room. The child they sought was not there, but he was anxious to know more about him. He asked them to return when they had located him so that he, too, might go and worship this child who would become king. They thought it strange that the present king did not know anything about his likely successor.

"They left the city, returned to their campsite, and wondered what would happen next. As the sun was setting, there it was again: The star was shining brightly and directly over them. It began to move south. Well before midnight the previous night, it came to rest above our house. They pitched their tents in an open field just a few hundred yards from our home, and for the first time in over a month, slept at night and waited for a proper time to visit us. They did not want to disturb us in the morning, thinking we might be in synagogue.

"Joseph and I were astonished. They were thrilled to find the child who one day would be king. All three men looked at Jesus; all three had big smiles on their faces as they each held him in their arms. Melchior said that they had now seen with their own eyes the greatest king the world would ever know. He then motioned to one of the servants who, along with two others, brought three beautiful sandalwood chests and handed one to each man. All three stood, walked to Jesus's cradle, bowed and knelt before him, and presented their gifts, which consisted of frankincense, myrrh, and gold coins. When they rose, they told us they would be returning to Persia but would be stopping in Jerusalem to honor Herod's request that he be told the whereabouts of the future king."

Mary was right: that was an amazing story. These men were not Jews; nor did they know much about our religion. However, for some reason, God had chosen them to be a part of the story of Jesus's birth. The three philosophers also strengthened Mary and Joseph's confidence that their son was indeed the Messiah.

Mary went on with her account.

"That very night, Joseph had a dream. He awakened me and said an angel had appeared to him and told him that we were to take our child and flee to Egypt immediately. We were to remain there until the same angel returned in another dream to tell him it was safe for us to return home. We left in the middle of the night, Jesus and I riding the donkey. Several days later, we crossed into Egypt, journeyed a few miles to a tiny village, and found a small cottage to rent. Joseph could not find work there, but thanks to the generosity of our foreign visitors, we had enough money to live modestly during our one-year sojourn. And then, one night, the same angel appeared to my husband in a second dream. We were to return to Israel. Nevertheless, we were to avoid passing through Jerusalem, and so we proceeded to Nazareth by another route. First, we went to the home of my family. They were overjoyed to see us. They did not know what had become of us, had never seen our son, and knew nothing of our flight to Egypt. They told us of the appalling slaughter of every child under the age of two years that had occurred in Bethlehem, apparently just after we had fled that village. They asked why we had gone to Egypt. I told them just enough of the story to satisfy their curiosity. We returned to Joseph's home, the house where our son would grow up, along with his younger brothers and sisters. My husband continued in his trade as a maker of good and sturdy furniture. He taught Jesus the skills of his trade, and by the time our son was eleven years old, he had become quite good at it.

"Every year, it was our custom to travel to Jerusalem in the spring to attend Passover. The year Jesus was twelve, something unusual happened. We journeyed to and from the festival in a large company of our relatives and neighbors. As he got older, Jesus seemed to take more and more interest in these yearly visits. His love of our Holy Scriptures also grew deeper with every passing year. When he wasn't helping his father make furniture, he would go to the synagogue and read the scrolls for hours at a time. He would ask Joseph and me questions about certain passages in the prophecies concerning the promised Messiah. As time passed, he seemed to know more than either of us knew, and we began to ask *him* questions. He astonished us with his deep understanding of the Scriptures. The day after Passover week ended, we departed in a company of our loved ones and friends, some fifty people. Jesus had several young companions among this group, and he usually walked with them for much of the time. When we had finished the first day of what would be a three- or four-day journey, we could not find Jesus. We assumed he was with his friends, but none of them had seen him that day. We panicked and knew we must return at once to Jerusalem to look for him. We entrusted the care of our other children to my father and struck out for Jerusalem. However, it was getting dark, and we had to stop for the night. Early the next morning, we hurried on to the city, reaching there at midday. We searched frantically for two days but found no sign of him. On the third day, we went to the temple. We discovered him in one of its courts, speaking with a number of the elders, most of them priests and lawyers. We were relieved that he was safe and well, and listened to their conversation for a few minutes. Joseph and I were both astounded. He was not only asking questions of these learned men, he was answering their questions too. Finally, he noticed our presence, excused himself, and came to our side. Joseph took him by the hand, and we left the temple. We were both relieved but angry with our son. Moreover, we were angry with ourselves for not being more responsible and watchful parents. I chastised Jesus, telling him we had been searching for him for three days; how could he cause us so much anxiety? His response was simple and puzzling. 'Why were you looking for me?' he asked us, 'Don't you know I must be about my Father's work?' Neither of us responded to this strange reply. We thought we knew our son, but we did not really know him at all. Of course, I understand now exactly what he was saying. He wasn't speaking of his earthly father; he was speaking about his heavenly Father. In the last two days, I have come to understand that truth more deeply than before."

So, Jesus had begun astonishing the religious leaders when he was just twelve years old!

"Joseph was concerned that our son would no longer work with him in the furniture shop. Nevertheless, Jesus continued to be a faithful and hardworking apprentice. His younger brothers and sisters loved and looked up to him. He was well regarded in our village. When he entered his early twenties, he built his own small house near ours but continued to work with Joseph. When my husband died a few years later, Jesus took over his business and provided for me and the younger children who remained at home. He and my second born, James—who was two years younger—worked side by side for three years, up until the time he left Nazareth to begin his ministry.

"Several months later, he returned to our village with his disciples. That was the first time I saw you, John. As I'm sure you remember, he went into the synagogue on Sabbath and read from the Holy Scriptures those passages that tell of the coming of the Messiah. When almost everyone present realized that he believed he was the fulfillment of those prophecies—that he was the Messiah—there was an outburst of uncontrolled anger. They were ready to kill him right then and there, and probably would have, had he not somehow eluded their murderous intent. After that, our family was shunned: We lost all our friends, and even our relatives would have nothing to do with us. James had to close the furniture shop for lack of business. He was so bitter that he tried, with some success, to turn the rest of us against Jesus. Then I remembered the things about his conception, his birth, and his early childhood: They were all signs from God. I knew in my heart that he must be the Anointed One, the Messiah sent from heaven to earth. What I have heard today from the two Marys and Esther has served to increase my belief that my son is indeed the Savior of the world."

I thought it interesting that Mary had used the present tense when referring to Jesus, as if he were still alive and not in the tomb of Joseph of Arimathea. I supposed it was probably just a slip of the tongue.

Esther excused herself; she would rejoin friends from her Samaritan village who had traveled with her to the Passover festival. Festival? There had been nothing festive about it.

Mother prepared fruit, bread, and wine for our evening meal, after which, my mother and father went to bed.

Mary retired to her room too.

I sat alone in the front room. It had been a bittersweet day: lamenting our Master's death and celebrating his life. I contemplated visiting the tomb where Jesus's body lay. Perhaps I would go there tomorrow. My reverie was interrupted by what sounded like a faint knock at the door. It was nighttime. I wouldn't be able to see who it was unless I opened the door wide enough for the candlelight inside to illuminate who was outside. There was a second soft knock, and I opened the door. It was Peter! I put a finger to my lips and let him in. He looked desolate, fearful, ashamed, and faint. He was breathing hard, as if he had been running. We spoke in hushed tones, so as not to wake the others.

"Where have you been? Have you seen any of the other disciples?" I asked.

No, he had not seen any of our close colleagues. He had witnessed the crucifixion and death of Jesus from a distance, alone. He had spent the day walking about the countryside, alone. I asked if he'd had anything to eat or drink. He had not, so I led him into the tiny kitchen, sat him at the table, and gave him bread, fruit, and wine. His strength was slowly restored. I related to him, in a summary fashion, the events of that day, including the location of the tomb where our Master was buried. When I told him Jesus's mother was in one of the bedrooms, he was alarmed, saying he must leave immediately; he could not face the mother of the man he had denied. I told him I doubted Mary knew about that; none of us had said anything to her about it, nor would we. I told him he was not going anywhere. There were two cots in my room, and he would sleep this night in one of them.

CHAPTER 41

I awoke with a start; someone was shaking my arm. It was Peter.

"I think I heard a knock at the front door," he whispered.

It was very early; the window in my room admitted so little light, I could barely see. With Peter following me, I went to the door, opened it slightly, and saw Mary Magdalene. She said nothing and motioned for us to come outside.

"They have removed the Lord's body from the tomb, and we don't know where they've taken him," she said, sobbing.

"Slow down Mary. What do you mean by 'we'? Did someone else go with you to the tomb, and why did you go there?"

"Last night, after the Sabbath, Mary, mother of James the Younger, Salome, [not my mother, a different follower] and I purchased more spices, and we went to the tomb early this morning to care for the Master's body. We found the chamber unsealed and the stone rolled away. When we looked inside, his body wasn't there. It's been stolen!"

Hearing this ominous news, Peter bolted out of the house and ran toward the garden.

I took Mary Magdalene into the house and told her to wait there, instructing her that, should my parents or Jesus's mother awaken before I returned, she was to say nothing about the body of our Master until we all knew more about what had happened. I took off running, and within a few minutes—about halfway to the garden—caught up to Peter.

Just at that moment, coming from the direction of the garden tomb, James's mother and Salome met us. They had more news.

Salome said, "Shortly after Mary Magdalene left us, we went

back into the tomb. We saw a young man dressed in white, as white as snow. We think he was an angel. There were two more men dressed in the same dazzling white clothing standing next to us. One of them said, 'You seek Jesus of Nazareth, who was crucified.' We were so frightened, we fell on our faces. 'He has risen; he's not here,' the angel said. 'Look at the empty place where they laid him. Don't you remember what he said to you in Galilee? "The Son of Man must be delivered into the hands of evil men, be crucified, and the third day, rise again." *This* is the third day!' Of course, we remembered! And then he said, 'Go and tell his apostles, especially Peter, that he will go ahead of you into Galilee. You will see him there, just as he promised. But before that, you will see him here in Jerusalem *today!*'"

I desperately wanted to believe what these women had just told us.

"Mary Magdalene is at my parents' house," I told them. "Go there and knock softly. Ask her to come outside, tell her what you saw, and remain there until we return. If anyone else in the house is awake, don't say anything about what you've seen. Just tell them I'll return as soon as I can."

Peter and I hastened to the garden.

Again, I outran him, reaching the tomb a few moments sooner than he. I stooped down to look into the chamber. It took a moment for my eyes to adjust to its semidarkness. I saw the white linen grave clothes neatly folded on one side of the ledge. There was no sign of our Master's body.

Peter arrived and entered the tomb. He, too, noticed the neatly folded grave clothes and one other thing I had missed: the shroud that had covered Jesus's face.

"John," he said, "who would steal our Master's body and take the time and trouble to fold the grave clothes?"

We looked at each other, and it was at that moment that we both believed. Jesus was *not* dead! He *had risen!* There was no point remaining in an *empty* tomb. But where was our Master? How would we find him?

And then I remembered what Salome had said: The angel had told her we would see Jesus today! Perhaps he would find us.

It was time the other apostles knew about this, and Peter and I set out to find them. Peter would search the tiny villages surrounding Jerusalem, and I would search inside the city. We agreed to meet back at my parents' house at noon, which would give us several hours to find them. My search was fruitless; I returned to the house and waited outside for Peter. Within a few minutes, he arrived; his search had also been in vain.

My father said that Mary and my mother had left a few minutes before to go for a walk.

There was no sign of Mary Magdalene, and my father did not mention seeing her. Before I had a chance to ask him about her, there was a knock at the door, and my father opened it. It was Mary Magdalene. She was out of breath and very excited about something. She asked for a cup of water, which I fetched for her. She had just caught her breath and was beginning to tell her news when she was interrupted by rapping at the door.

I opened the door this time, surprised to see eight of our fellow apostles—only Thomas was missing—and several other followers of our Master. I would not know until later how they had found us or what had induced them to come. They were all in mourning: the men stoic, the women sobbing.

After everyone had quieted down, Mary Magdalene spoke.

"When I heard the news from Salome and Mary about their encounter with the three angels at the tomb and what one of them had said about Jesus's resurrection, I ran back to the garden."

You can imagine the stir this caused among our newly arrived colleagues: They were all incredulous. When they heard the rest of her account, their skepticism deepened.

She continued.

"I stood for a moment outside the tomb. Suddenly, there were two angels standing in front of me. One of them said, 'Woman, why are you crying?' Before I could answer, for some reason, I felt compelled to look behind me. A man was standing there. Because of the tears in my eyes, I did not recognize him at first and assumed he was the gardener. He asked me who I was looking for and why was I crying.

"'Sir,' I said, 'if you have carried away the body of Jesus, please tell me where you have taken him.'

"And then he called me by my name. The way he said 'Mary' opened my eyes, and I knew it was our Master. I ran to him, falling at his feet.

"'Don't detain me, Mary,' he said. 'I have not yet ascended to my Father. Go and tell my brothers that I must go to my Father and their Father; to my God and their God.'"

None of the eight believed her. But Peter and I did, because we had more evidence than they possessed: that is, the evidence of the folded grave clothes and what that had implied to us.

It was now early afternoon. I was fearful that my mother and Jesus's mother might return from their walk at any moment and that the presence of a large number of people—there were at least twenty-five in the small house—would unnecessarily shake Jesus's mother. I suggested that everyone leave and then we reconvene elsewhere later in the day. But where?

Once again, someone was knocking on the door. It was Nicodemus, come to tell us about how the stone had been rolled away from Joseph's tomb. Quickly, I explained that our large party must find another place to gather, as we anticipated the imminent arrival of Jesus's mother. He understood and invited us all to his home, not far away. We left immediately, traveling in smaller groups of three or four so as not to draw undue attention to ourselves. The streets were not crowded, as most of the pilgrims had departed earlier in the day. We reached his home without incident. Entering it, we followed him up the stairs to the large upper room, the same room where three nights before we had celebrated the Passover meal with our Master. Servants brought several more chairs, and everyone sat down.

Few in the room knew Nicodemus, and only I knew he was a follower of Jesus. I briefly explained that he was a member of the Sanhedrin, which caused quite a stir among those present. I quickly added that he had become a secret follower of Jesus a year before and so had his friend Joseph of Arimathea, also a member of the ruling council. These men had provided Jesus with a proper burial in Joseph's own garden tomb.

Nicodemus then proceeded to tell to us how the huge stone covering the chamber's entrance had been removed.

"In addition to Joseph's servants and my own servants, some of the servants in the household of Caiaphas are also secret followers of Jesus," he began. "Early this morning, one of Caiaphas's servants told my chief steward that the temple guard sent to monitor the tomb where Jesus's body was buried had failed in their mission. Shortly before sunrise, the guards reported, an earthquake had rocked the garden, throwing them to the ground. They then saw an angel descend from the heavens and roll the large round stone away from the chamber's entrance. The angel then sat atop it. The soldiers fainted from fear, and as soon as they gathered their wits about them, they ran to report the strange occurrence to Caiaphas. They had not looked inside the tomb because they feared the angel. The high priest told them to wait outside while he thought about the matter. Within the next hour, several elders arrived at Caiaphas's residence. Two hours later, the guards were summoned back before the high priest, who told them to keep their mouths shut. They were to tell no one what they had seen. Moreover, if word of this incident spread and anyone asked them about it, the soldiers were to say that Jesus's disciples had come and stolen his body. Caiaphas bribed them all, giving each a great deal of money. They would not be dismissed or punished if they followed his instructions."

This report only served to deepen the puzzlement of everyone there except Mary Magdalene, Peter, and me.

It was late afternoon now. The sun would soon set. Everyone present was physically and emotionally exhausted. It had been a trying three days for all who loved Jesus. Although he had appeared to Mary, no one but Peter and I believed her story, and even we were reluctant to say so.

Would the Master appear to anyone else?

Nicodemus invited us all to eat supper with him and his wife. Everyone accepted this generous invitation, and we were served bread, wine, and baked fish. The sun had set an hour before. It was time for us to leave, and we descended the stairs to the first level.

Someone was knocking on the front door. One of the servants opened it, and I was surprised to see Cleophas and his wife, Mary.

Nicodemus, who recognized Mary, invited them both to come in. They were brimming with joy and excitement, and wished to share their news with us. We went back upstairs.

This couple lived in Emmaus, a small town west of Jerusalem, about seven miles away. Earlier in the day, they had departed Jerusalem for their home. As they walked along, they discussed the events of the past three days. Both were grieved by the death of their dear friend. Mary told her husband that she'd heard Jesus might have been resurrected. He did not believe a word of it. Within a few minutes of their departure, a stranger joined them.

"The stranger asked us what we were talking about, and why we were so downcast," Cleophas said. "Without looking at him, I said, 'You must be the only man in Judea who doesn't know about the events of the past three days.' He asked me what events I was talking about. I told him, 'They concern Jesus of Nazareth, who was a prophet, mighty in deed and word before God and all people. We were among his close followers. On the preparation day, the chief priests and rulers condemned him. Pilate sentenced him to death, and he was crucified on calvaria that afternoon and buried in a tomb that evening. We had expected him to redeem Israel. Today is the third day since he died. One of our friends, Mary Magdalene, went to the tomb this morning and told us it was empty, that someone had stolen his body. This is much more than our loss. His death is the loss of all Israel. We are left desolate.'

"And then he said, 'Don't you believe—don't you understand— what all the ancient prophets have said about Jesus? Didn't he have to suffer all these things you've described before he could enter into his glory?'

"For the next two hours—until we had reached Emmaus—this stranger told us everything about the mission of Jesus. He began with Moses, and then he discussed each of the prophets who had foretold all things about the Messiah. Just as we approached the turnoff to the side road that led to our house, he continued on the main road a few steps. We both implored him to come with us to our house; it was already late afternoon, and we hoped he would stay the night. He agreed. Mary prepared a meal of bread and wine. The stranger broke the bread, blessed it, and gave us each a piece. Suddenly, as if our eyes were opened, the stranger was no longer a stranger. We recognized him; it was Jesus himself! And then he vanished from our sight. How, we don't know; he was just gone. Jesus is not dead! He is alive! He has risen from the grave! Our hunger for the bread and wine disappeared, and we immediately hurried back to Jerusalem. We stopped at the house of James and John's parents'. Their father told us where to find them and all of you. But, of course, you, Mary, and you, Peter, already know what we have said is true, because Jesus told us he had appeared to each of you earlier today."

We all looked at Peter. Everyone else in the room had heard—or heard of—Mary Magdalene's claim of seeing our Master, but what was this about Peter seeing him too? And, if it were true, why hadn't he told us of it? It was not like him to keep silent about something so momentous—or about anything else, for that matter.

Before Peter could say a word, Jesus himself was standing in our midst. No one had heard him approach; no one had seen him arrive. He was just suddenly standing among us. We were stunned into shocked silence.

"Peace be with you," he said, with a broad and inviting smile on his face.

Many in the room were visibly fearful, looking as if they had seen a ghost. The exceptions were those of us who had seen him and a few of us who had believed him to be alive, even though we had not seen him. We believed he had been restored to life by the power of God early that morning. Now the proof was standing before us.

"Why are some of you fearful?" Jesus said. "Look at the scars on my hands and my feet; look at the wound in my side. Touch me and see that I have flesh and bones. A ghost doesn't have flesh and bones."

Everyone was overjoyed. Our Master was alive and well, and he had returned to us!

"I'm hungry," he said. "Do you have anything to eat?"

Nicodemus practically flew down the stairs and returned shortly with bread, baked fish, a honeycomb, and wine. He brought enough for Cleophas and Mary, who had left their supper uneaten in Emmaus.

All three ate heartily. The somber mood had turned to joy. Everyone looked at Jesus with awe and wonder.

After the meal, our Master asked everyone to sit down. He had some things to tell us.

"My dear brothers and sisters, everything that has happened these past few days had to happen exactly as it has happened. None of these events should have been unexpected, because I spoke of them often. And they were all foretold in the Scriptures: first in the writings of Moses, then in the Psalms, and ending in the prophecies of Zechariah."

He then repeated some of the things he had said to us during our years together: that he would suffer before his death; that he would be crucified; and, glory to God, that he would rise from the dead on the third day, this day! He charged us with preaching, in his name, the good news of his gospel: repentance and remission of sins, beginning here in Jerusalem and then extending to the whole world.

"You have been with me for years, some of you from the beginning of my ministry," he said. "You have witnessed these things. You are equipped to tell anyone and everyone, anywhere and anytime, about the gospel of the kingdom of God. Peace be with you. As my Father has sent me, so I'm sending you."

Of course, we had all heard these same words before. But now their force seemed stronger, and this time we would never forget them or their true meaning. Jesus had never seemed more alive, more vital. He looked the same; his voice sounded the same. Nevertheless, there was something different about him that I could not explain.

He asked all of us to stand with him.

"Receive the Holy Spirit," he said. "The sins of those who accept the salvation I offer through you are forgiven. The sins of those who reject the salvation I offer through you will remain."

And then, just as he had done in the home of Mary and Cleophas, Jesus simply vanished. Would we see him again? Of course, we would. He had sent word through Mary Magdalene— whose credibility among us apostles had increased immeasurably— that he would see us in Galilee. We would leave the next morning on our journey home to meet him there.

As we were leaving Nicodemus's house, Thomas arrived. We told him we had just seen Jesus. He was doubtful, telling us he would not believe any such thing until he had seen the nail imprints in our Master's hands and feet and touched the wound in his side. He would not have long to wait.

CHAPTER 42

We left Jerusalem the next morning, on our long journey north to Nazareth in Galilee. As we had done with Jesus, we traveled by the most direct route, through Samaria. In our company, which numbered about thirty, were the eleven apostles and a few other close followers, including James's and my parents and sisters. We were also joined by Esther, the woman at the well, and a few of her friends from Sycar, and, of course, Mary, Jesus's mother. Before we departed, Joseph of Arimathea gave his donkey—the one Jesus had ridden into Jerusalem at the beginning of Passover week—to Mary. It would take Mary and me five days to reach our destination.

Our Master's triumphant resurrection had unburdened our hearts, which made for a happy and pleasant journey. Near noon on the third day, we passed Jacob's Well, on the outskirts of Sycar. Seeing it and drinking its water made the day special. It was there that we bid farewell to Esther and her friends. I would accompany Mary due north to Nazareth; the rest would travel northeast to Capernaum. The eleven of us agreed that would be the most likely place to await our Master's promised return to Galilee. We wanted to spend as much time with him as possible before he returned to his Father in heaven.

Late in the afternoon of the fifth day of our sojourn, we reached Nazareth. It was the preparation day, and I would spend the Sabbath there. We arrived at Mary's home, and who should open the door but Jesus himself! Of course, his mother knew he was alive, but this was the first time she had seen him since his death on the cross, just about this time of day one week before. Mother and son rushed into each other's arms, our Master smiling and laughing, and Mary weeping, this time for joy. Their embrace lasted for several moments.

Mary's youngest daughter was there; she, too, was overjoyed to see her mother, and relieved she had made the journey safely. She left to tell the rest of her brothers and sisters that their mother had returned. In a few minutes, the whole family was there, and it was quite a happy occasion. The three sisters prepared the evening meal, while Mary, Jesus, his brothers, and I sat on the front porch, talking. Jesus had been home for two days—his mode of travel clearly faster than ours—and had visited extensively with his family. It was obvious that the breach between them had been closed. All would become active in the new church he was establishing, and one of them, James, the second-oldest sibling and the one who had been the most alienated from Jesus, would become one of the most prominent of his evangelists.

Jesus had already explained to his brothers and sisters that he had charged me with the responsibility to care for their mother for the remainder of her life. I assured them all that I would bring her to visit them as often as possible and that they were always welcome to visit her in Capernaum.

Two days later, Mary and I departed for Capernaum, making the journey in one day. Jesus had remained in Nazareth; he said he would join us—the rest of his apostles and me—in a few days. Mary and I went to my parents' house, where she was warmly received. It was good to be back home in Galilee.

The day after I arrived, Peter and Andrew came to our house and asked if we had seen Jesus. I of course had, and told him the story of our Master's reunion with his mother and siblings. I added that Jesus had simply said he would see us all in a few days but specified no certain time or place.

Peter, always the man of action and not one to idly sit and wait, suggested we all go fishing together. To him, fishing had not been just an occupation; he loved it. He wanted to go that very night. He'd always thought night fishing produced better results, probably because most men fished in the early morning and so there was less competition in the hours well before dawn. We were all rested from our journey and agreed to join him. Peter invited James's and my father to join us, but he declined, protesting he was getting to old for such nocturnal exertions. Later that afternoon, Thomas, Nathanael, and Philip arrived at Peter's house, and he invited them to join us too. Peter's boat was large and would easily accommodate the seven of us. My mother and Peter's wife, Concordia, and her mother prepared a large food basket for us to take along. My family would look after Mary during my absence.

We met at the lakeshore after sunset, and cast off. The sky was clear, the half-moon provided adequate light, and the lake was calm. We had a great time together, not because we caught any fish—they were not biting—but because we were all good friends and enjoyed each other's fellowship. We had been through good and bad times together, and now, with our best friend and Master miraculously resurrected from the dead—well, words cannot describe our unbounded joy and the anticipation of taking our Lord's gospel message wherever that should lead us. The one exception was Thomas. He was the only one of the eleven who had not yet seen the risen Jesus. He wanted to believe, of course, but he had not yet been able to achieve that level of faith; he wanted to see our Lord in the flesh.

For hours, Peter's large net had been alternately let down several feet into the dark water of the lake and pulled back up, without a single fish being caught. All seven of us knew how to cast, drag, and haul, and we took turns all night long, but we had nothing to show for our efforts. Finally, the eastern sky began to glow faintly with the first sign of dawn.

Nathanael asked Peter if he was disappointed.

"No," he said. "We have a new vocation: Jesus has taught us how to fish for men."

He added that God's grace and the power of the Holy Spirit would give us success in our new full-time occupation.

Peter turned the rudder, the sail caught a light eastern breeze, and we slowly headed back to shore. About two hundred yards from the beach, we noticed someone standing next to what appeared to be the glow of a charcoal fire. When we got a hundred yards closer, he cupped his hands to his mouth and called out to us.

"Children, have you caught any fish?"

"No," Peter shouted, "not a single one."

"Cast your net over the right side of the boat, and you will."

That sounded pointless, but we had nothing to lose.

Andrew helped Peter drop the heavy net over the right side of the boat. Within moments, it was filled to capacity, so much so that it was too heavy to lift into the boat. We secured it and let the boat drag it toward the beach.

As we got nearer the shore, I looked more closely at the man and then shouted to my friends, "It's the Lord! It's Jesus!"

Hearing this, Peter took off his outer garment, dived into the water, and swam to shore faster than the boat would go.

Andrew and James secured the boat, and we all gathered around our Master.

There were several fish already on the grill, and a large basket of fresh bread.

Jesus asked me to bring a few more fish from the net—which contained well over a hundred—a load so heavy, I was surprised the net was still in one piece. I prepared them for cooking and took them to Jesus.

"Sit down, bothers," Jesus said.

While he served us, he added, "It's good that we can eat together again. Do you remember that it was in this very spot three years ago that I first met you, James, and you, John? I had already known Peter and Andrew for a few weeks, and John, although we had seen each other at the Jordan River before that, we hadn't yet met. Three years ago, we enjoyed our first supper together. John and I gathered firewood for the same meal we are having today; only this time, we're having breakfast."

The rest of us joined in this comfortable and lighthearted conversation, and we all enjoyed it immensely—all but Thomas, doubting Thomas, who said nothing. I was sure he was convinced that this was really Jesus, in the flesh and risen from the tomb, who now sat among us. I supposed he was feeling sheepish about his incredulous reaction when we tried to convince him of this fact two weeks before.

Jesus stood up, and the rest of us stood up with him. He then walked over to Thomas.

"Thomas, look at my hands. Do you see the nail imprints? Look at the scar in my side; touch it with your finger. Is it real?"

Thomas fell on his knees. "My Lord and my God."

"Because you've seen me, you believe. Blessed are those who have not seen me and yet have believed."

Our Master then turned and looked at Peter.

"Walk with me a little while, Peter," he said.

The two of them walked down the beach together. I do not know what compelled me to follow them; I shouldn't have, but I did. I stayed close enough behind to hear their conversation.

"Simon, son of Jonas, do you love me," Jesus asked.

I had not recently heard our Master refer to Peter by his original given name, except once or twice at our last Passover meal, and I was curious as to why he did so now.

"Yes, Lord. You know that I love you," Peter replied.

"Feed my lambs."

They walked several yards in silence before Jesus repeated the question, word for word.

"Simon, son of Jonas, do you love me?"

Peter repeated his answer, word for word.

"Yes, Lord. You know that I love you."

Jesus's response was only slightly different.

"Feed my sheep."

Again, they walked on without speaking for a few minutes.

Again, Jesus stopped, looked at Peter, and for the third time asked, "Simon, son of Jonas, do you love me?"

Peter looked wounded, distraught, and confused. Why had our

Master asked him the same question three times? His reply was a mixture of frustration and grief.

"Lord, you know *everything* in my heart. You *know* that I love you."

"Feed my sheep," the Master said, yet again, and then added, "While you are young, you dress yourself and go where you please, when you please. But, when you are old, you will stretch out your hands, and other men will dress you and carry you to where you don't want to go. Follow me."

To me, this was a riddle, and it would be years until I fully understood its meaning.

But Peter seemed to understand.

Up to this point in their conversation, Peter had not noticed me close by. When he did, he nodded in my direction and asked Jesus, "What about John? What will happen to him?"

"If I decide that he should live until I return, what is that to you?"

The three of us walked back and rejoined our colleagues.

Matthew, who lived nearby, had arrived, and he invited us all to spend the afternoon at his house.

Arriving there, we settled in, sitting together in his large front room.

Peter was quiet, apparently still shaken by our Master's questioning his love and loyalty.

Jesus, too, was silent.

Finally, I spoke up.

"Master, I've wanted to ask you a question about something for a long time, ever since James and I met you on the beach three years ago."

"All right, John, go ahead," he replied.

"A few months before that day, you and I had both been baptized by John the Baptist. You walked away into the desert, and I followed you. I was close to catching up to you when you passed behind a large rock outcropping, and when I rounded it, you were nowhere in sight. I searched for you for over an hour but couldn't find you. What happened to you? Where did you go?

"I had a rendezvous with Satan," he said quietly.

If jaws made a sound when they dropped, there would have been several thuds on the stone floor. Rather, in the silence that ensued, you could have heard a pin drop. We all wanted to hear *this* story.

"I was led by the Holy Spirit deep into the wilderness east of the Jordan River," Jesus began. "I was directed there by the Spirit specifically to be put to the test by the Devil himself. Before the encounter, I fasted and prayed for forty days and forty nights. I petitioned my Father to strengthen me for this ordeal so that I might be able to resist any temptations the Evil One might throw at me. Aside from my crucifixion, it was to be the biggest challenge of my life on this earth. On the forty-first day, Satan confronted me. He knew I was famished, and his first appeal regarded my hunger.

"Pointing to the large round stones that littered the ground around us, he said, 'If you really are the Son of God, turn these stones into bread. Surely, your Father doesn't want you to starve to death.'"

Jesus interrupted this story by asking me a question.

"John, do you remember what happened at my baptism—the voice from the heavens and what was said?"

Of course I remembered.

"This is My son, the one I love. I am delighted with him," I replied.

"So, the first words out of Satan's mouth called into question my relationship with God, my Father. My reply to him was to quote our Holy Scriptures: 'Man does not live by bread alone but by every word that comes from God's mouth.' His first temptation had failed, and the look on his face betrayed disappointment. But, of course, he was not finished with me.

"In a matter of mere moments, the tempter and I were standing atop the pinnacle of the holy temple. 'If you really are the Son of God,' he repeated, 'throw yourself down. After all, your Holy Scriptures say that God will command His angels protect you. They will carry you in their hands so that you won't be injured in the least way.'

"I responded to him by saying, 'Yes, but the Scriptures also say, 'No one should try to tempt God; not try to make him prove Himself.' Again, he looked dismayed, but he persevered.

"Momentarily, we were standing on the peak of the highest mountain in this world, which, by the way, is three thousand miles from here. Before me appeared a panoramic view of all the great kingdoms of the world, some of which you have never heard of and don't know anything about. 'I will give you all of these kingdoms, now under my control, on one condition: Fall down and worship me,' he demanded.

"My response was quick and unequivocal, and it terrified him: 'Get away from me, Satan! The Scriptures say, "Worship the Lord your God and serve only Him."'

"He fled the scene. Moments later, I was back in the wilderness, and my Father sent angels to care for me; they gave me bread and water to sustain me. Shortly after that, I began my public ministry, and in a few months, all of you joined me."

"Were you ever tempted by Satan again?" Nathanael asked.

"Oh, yes, many times. Satan has thrown every temptation imaginable at me. But, by my Father's grace and with the help of the Holy Spirit, I never succumbed. Since my rising from the tomb, he has made no further efforts to tempt me. However, he isn't through with you. All of you must be constantly on your guard against his temptations and traps."

"Why do you think the Devil hasn't tried to entice you to sin since your resurrection? Andrew asked.

"I want you to listen carefully to my answer to Andrew's question, and never forget it. My resurrection doomed Satan; he has been utterly defeated. His fate is sealed, and he knows it. When I arose from the grave, I conquered death. This is the greatest truth of the gospel: My blood was shed for everyone who has ever lived, or will ever live, on this earth. Those who accept my sacrifice, confess their sins, and live in my grace will inherit eternal life. Their mortal bodies will die, just as mine did. Nevertheless, just as I did, they will rise on the last day. Their bodies will no longer be corruptible, just as mine was changed from mortality to immortality.

"Do you remember what I said at the Passover supper we shared a few weeks ago, specifically, about the next time we would share such a meal?"

"I do," said Peter. "You said you wouldn't drink of the fruit of the vine until the day you drink it with us in your Father's kingdom."

"That's right, Peter. However, you will not be the only ones at my table. No, *everyone* who accepts the truth of the gospel and lives by it will be there too. You all are responsible to spread the good news of God's kingdom to everyone who will listen. It will be your full-time occupation. It will take all your strength and courage to fulfill your mission. Just remember, you will not be alone; the Holy Spirit will guide, protect, and strengthen you."

The Master paused and then said, "Now, I have a question for you. Why were all of you so surprised by my resurrection?"

"We shouldn't have been surprised," Philip said. "There should have been a vigil at your tomb. All eleven of us should have been there, waiting for you to come out. You told us you would rise on the third day, but I suppose our faith wasn't strong enough to sustain our belief in your plain words. And I think we were all afraid of being caught by the Romans or the temple guard. That is why we all abandoned you the night of your arrest. We're all ashamed of that; I know I am."

Simon, one of the least talkative of our Lord's apostles, had something to say. "If I hadn't found you, Lord, I might have been among Barabbas's motley crew of insurrectionists. I might even have been its leader, so misguided was I before I found you."

"You didn't find me, Simon. I found you. It was I who found each of you."

Our Lord was right, of course. It was his personal invitation to each of us, and our acceptance of that invitation, that made us his followers.

"Why did you appear to Mary Magdalene first after your resurrection?" my brother wanted to know.

"Because, of all my followers, she was the most heartbroken. I could not wait to comfort her. And speaking of Mary Magdalene, why didn't any of you believe that she had seen me alive?"

We all looked down in silence.

Finally, I said, "One of our traditions is that women are not reliable witnesses. I suppose that's why."

"Well, that's another *man-made* tradition isn't it? It needs to be abandoned. There will be no man-invented traditions in my church."

Thomas spoke next. "Everyone here has told me that since your resurrection, you have been able to appear and disappear quickly and that you even seem to have the ability to pass through solid objects like doors and walls. Although I haven't witnessed this myself, I believe it. I want to know how you can do that."

Jesus smiled broadly. "Dear Thomas, that is a mystery you will understand only when you are resurrected to eternal life on the last day."

It was late in the evening. It had been an exhilarating day but, having spent the previous night fishing, we were all tired and ready for rest. Peter and Andrew went to their home nearby; James and I to our parents' house. The others, including Jesus, stayed with Matthew. We would all meet at his house for breakfast the next morning.

CHAPTER 43

During breakfast, Matthew told Jesus that he was going to sell his house and reserve the proceeds of its sale for the support of our Lord's new church. Jesus commended him for this sacrifice; we apostles thought it a fine idea. Our Lord then told us he would be away for a few days and that he would meet us at the top of Mount Tabor early in the morning, seven days hence. He would absent himself in this manner from time to time during our last days with him. We never asked him where he had gone or what he had done. He bid us good-bye and walked out the door, closing it behind him.

Peter jumped up to follow him, telling us he wanted to ask Jesus a question. He returned in a few moments, saying our Lord was nowhere in sight, and invited me to take a walk with him. He then asked me the question he had planned to pose to Jesus.

"John, you heard the conversation between Jesus and me yesterday."

"Peter, I'm sorry. I shouldn't have eavesdropped on your private conversation like that," I said sheepishly.

"No, that's all right. I'm glad you did, because maybe you can help me understand why Jesus asked me the same question, 'Do you love me?' not once, but three times."

"Well, Peter I was puzzled by that too," I said. "But I have thought about it, and I think it might have something to do with what happened during our Lord's first trial, the one before Annas."

From the look on his face, I could tell Peter knew exactly what I was referring to: his three denials of Jesus.

"Oh yes, that must be it. I will carry that burden with me for the rest of my life." Peter was crestfallen.

"You don't have to! Remember what our Lord said to us and to a lot of other people too: we were to cast our burdens on him; he would bear them for us."

"Thank you for reminding me of that. What do you think he meant by telling me three times to feed his sheep, his lambs?"

"I've thought about that too. I think that was his way of telling you that, not only had he forgiven you, but he also still wants you to be the leader of his church—a kind of recommissioning: feeding and caring for his flock, his new church."

"I'd like to believe that, John."

"Well, you can always ask him about it privately. Now I would like to ask you a question. When you and I and several other followers of our Lord were in Nicodemus's house late in the afternoon of the resurrection day, Cleophas told us that when he and his wife, Mary, finally recognized Jesus, he told them he had already seen you earlier that day. I've been meaning to ask you about that ever since."

"On the resurrection morning, when you and I were together and we realized that Jesus was indeed alive, we went to look for our brother disciples. We separated and searched in different places but had no success. That's when the Lord appeared to me. I had gone up to the garden of Gethsemane in search of him. We all know how he loves that place, even though that is where he was betrayed. I went to the spot where he prayed that last night before his crucifixion. I looked about, and, seeing no one, I turned to leave. And there he was, standing right in front of me. I was both overjoyed and embarrassed, ashamed about my denials of him. He put his arm around my shoulders and invited me to sit with him on a nearby bench. I asked him to forgive me, and he did."

"Well, Peter, his forgiveness is all you need. There is no reason for you to condemn yourself over a forgiven sin, no reason at all," I said.

He looked reassured.

"Let's go back to Matthew's house and rejoin our friends," he said.

While we were away, the last two of the apostles—James the

Younger and Thaddaeus—had arrived. The others had already told them of Jesus's request that we meet him on Mount Tabor in seven days' time. The eleven of us passed the remainder of that day at Matthew's house, and we met there often until it was time to depart for our appointment with the Lord early in the morning of the sixth day. (Mary stayed with my family during my two-day absence.)

We traveled southwest, thirty-six miles to the mountain, which is situated in the Jezreel Valley. We reached its base as the sun was setting, and we spent the night there. At sunrise the next morning, we began our ascent, taking the winding trail that led to the mountain's peak. Mount Tabor is cone-shaped and rose nearly two thousand feet above the flat plane surrounding it. It took us less than two hours to reach the summit.

The Lord was already there, waiting for us. He received us warmly and then asked us to look back down the mountainside.

We saw an amazing sight: Hundreds of people were ascending the mountain by the same trail we had used. Traveling as we had, single file up the narrow path, their train must have been a half-mile long.

"Who are those people?" Thaddaeus asked.

"When they draw nearer, you'll recognize many of them. Some are your relatives. Most are followers from the days of our ministry. Some are people we encountered during those days. Some you will not know. However, they all have one thing in common: they are my disciples. You, as my apostles, will work closely with them: teaching them, training them, encouraging them, and correcting them when needed. You, they, and the generations that follow will take this gospel of mine to every corner of the world. They have been led here today by the Holy Spirit."

We did recognize many of them. People Jesus had healed— lepers, cripples, and the no-longer-blind Bartimaeus. Those out of whom he had cast demons—the Gadaran man on the eastern shore of the Sea of Galilee and the young man at the base of Mount Hermon. People he had raised from the dead—the widow's son in Nain, and Lazarus. The Roman centurion who had watched Jesus die on the cross, former religious leaders, Nicodemus, Joseph of Arimathea, Esther, the Samaritan woman at the well, and the woman taken in adultery all were there too. And, pushing his way to the front of the multitude so he could see Jesus, was diminutive Zacchaeus. Some of these folk had never seen Jesus before; they had come because of the witness of friends or family.

Our Lord stood atop the gently rounded pinnacle of the mountain. We stood nearby, facing him, the throng behind us. All of us knelt as one and worshipped him. There was no doubt in anyone's mind that the man who stood before us was more than the Messiah. He was the Christ, the Son of God, the Emmanuel, which in our Hebrew tongue means "God with us." He was not only fully human; he was fully divine. God the Son, clothed in the flesh of mankind, come down from heaven to earth to sacrifice his life for the redemption of anyone and everyone who would accept that sacrifice.

"All authority has been given to me in heaven and earth," he announced. "Go out, all of you, and invite the people of all nations to join with you as my followers. Baptize them in the name of the Father, in the name of the Son, and in the name of the Holy Spirit. Teach them to observe all things I have taught you: to love God supremely, to love your neighbors as you love yourselves, to forgive others as God has forgiven you. I will be with you every day, even unto the end of the world."

It was a short but powerful exhortation. Our Lord then asked everyone to stand, and he waded into the large assembly. He spent the next five hours speaking individually to everyone there, encouraging each one for the task that lay ahead.

The five hundred disciples departed in midafternoon. They had been given their charge. They were ready to do the work our Lord had assigned them.

Jesus asked us to remain with him a little longer.

"I will not see you again until two weeks from today. I will meet you in Bethany, at the home of Lazarus, Martha, and Mary," he said. I will return to my Father a few days after that. Until we meet again, I ask all of you to pray together, to contemplate, and to discuss with each other what you have heard me say today. Until then, peace be with you all."

With that, he vanished from our sight.

CHAPTER 44

As we made our way back down the mountain to the valley below, I could not help thinking about how many times mountains had played a significant role in our Lord's ministry. There was the Sermon on the Mount, where Jesus laid out the fundamentals of his kingdom-of-God message. There was the encounter Jesus had with Moses and Elijah on Mount Hermon, which Peter, James, and I witnessed. There were the mountainsides where Jesus preached and miraculously fed thousands of people. There was his descent from the Mount of Olives at the outset of his triumphal entry into Jerusalem at the beginning of the most challenging and fateful week of his life. And, this day, there was the commissioning of the five hundred disciples, also on a mountainside. There was one other day too: The day he was transported to the highest mountain in the world to be tempted by his archenemy. It was on that very mountain that Jesus won the final victory over Satan. Yes, mountains had figured prominently in the life of our Lord, and in our lives too.

Because we had departed Mount Tabor late in the afternoon, we would spend one night on the road before reaching Capernaum the next day. We stopped in a tiny village and purchased bread for our evening meal. As we sat around a fire that night, Peter suggested that, in accordance with our Lord's parting words to us, we spend the time between now and when we were to meet Jesus in Bethany praying together and deliberating about the work that lay before us. We all agreed, and before we slept, each of us prayed aloud that we would be worthy of the sacred charge our Lord had given to us.

The next day, as we approached Capernaum, Matthew told us that he had sold his house to Jonah, a man we knew. The most successful fisherman in Galilee, Jonah owned a small fleet of boats and was one of the richest men in the area. He would take possession of Matthew's large home as soon as we departed for Bethany.

We all commended Matthew for the sacrifice he was making.

"What is that compared with the sacrifice Jesus made for me?" Matthew replied.

He was right, of course. None of us ever would, or ever could, match the sacrifice of our Lord and Savior.

Until we departed for Bethany, we met daily in Matthew's house. We prayed together, and we also talked about many things. We acknowledged Peter as our leader. Our Lord had commissioned and recommissioned him, and Peter would never abuse the authority Jesus had given him. He was a changed man: humble, and no longer impetuous or overconfident. We all looked up to him and respected his leadership. For his part, Peter always sought our counsel before making decisions, and he respected our ideas and suggestions.

One of the matters we discussed was the replacement of Judas, the betrayer. Our Master had said nothing to us about a successor for Judas, and we wondered if he should be replaced.

Peter proposed that we ask Jesus what, if anything, we should do. Perhaps our Lord would choose someone before he departed the earth.

After ten days, we said farewell to our families and friends, and set forth on the eighty-five mile journey to Bethany, two miles east of Jerusalem and near the peak of the Mount of Olives. As she was in my care, Mary joined us, riding the faithful donkey.

As we ascended the pathway between Jerusalem and our destination late in the afternoon of the day before we were to meet Jesus, we passed through the village of Bethpage. The home of Joseph of Arimathea was along that route, and as we approached his house, he came out to greet us. His friend, Nicodemus, was at his side. We had seen them both at Mount Tabor two weeks before, and we were delighted to see them again. We explained we were on our way to Bethany. Joseph invited us to stay in his house overnight, and we happily accepted. It was nearly suppertime, and we enjoyed a good meal, and even better fellowship, with these two dedicated disciples of our Lord.

During the meal, Peter informed Joseph and Nicodemus that we were to meet Jesus at the home of Lazarus and his sisters the next day. The mention of this name prompted Nicodemus to tell us about a murderous scheme against the man our Lord had raised from the dead.

"One of the members of the Sanhedrin told me that the high priest had hatched a plot to have Lazarus killed," he said. "That Jesus had restored this man to life was more than Caiaphas could stand. I immediately told Joseph about this hateful plan."

"Nicodemus and I went to Lazarus's home to tell him his life was in grave danger," said Joseph. "I insisted that he and his sisters stay with me until the danger passed. After our Lord's resurrection, word came to me that the high priest was no longer interested in Lazarus."

Joseph paused and then continued. "Things are tense and unsettled in Jerusalem. The high priest, the leaders among the Pharisees, and the whole Sanhedrin all are in an uproar over the events of Passover week. They have tried mightily to suppress the reports of our Lord's resurrection. They have concocted all sorts of alternate stories as to what happened to his body."

"Of course, their original lie—that his body was stolen by his disciples—is at issue, as they have presented no evidence of it," Nicodemus said. "In fact, word of the temple guard's harrowing experience with God's angels at the tomb has somehow leaked out and become common knowledge."

Nicodemus grinned as Joseph went on with the story.

"And," Joseph said, "the rending of the veil between the Holy and Most Holy Places in the temple at the very moment of Jesus's death is now common knowledge too, despite the vehement denials of Caiaphas. Word of Judas's paid betrayal of our Lord has spread like wildfire. There have even been demands from some members of the Sanhedrin that Caiaphas be replaced. But I don't expect that will happen."

"What about Pilate?" I asked. "How has he faired since he condemned Jesus to death?"

"No one really knows," said Nicodemus. "Two days after the resurrection of our Lord, he went back to his villa in Caesarea Maritima. But I will tell you this: rumor has it that during Jesus's trial—that part of it inside the praetorium and out of public view—Pilate's wife told him she had been vexed by a dream she'd had about our Master and that her husband would be well advised to have nothing to do with him."

"So, that's what happened," I said.

Everyone looked at me.

"Let me explain. I haven't told anyone about this, but I witnessed every one of our Lord's four trials; actually, there were five, counting both sessions before Pilate. During Jesus's second appearance before Pilate inside the praetorium in the Hall of Justice, he was interrupted while questioning Jesus. A messenger handed Pilate a small, sealed scroll. After reading what was written on the scroll, Pilate left for several minutes. When he returned, he looked quite troubled. Maybe that's when his wife told him about her dream."

"That seems quite possible," said Nicodemus.

"It makes sense to me," Joseph added.

"You must have been the only one of us who witnessed all the sad events of that day," James said.

"I suppose so," I said. "But I do know this: it was the worst day of my life; and the worst day of our Lord's, for sure."

There was silence for a few moments, and then Nathanael asked me a question.

"Do you think you defiled yourself by entering the praetorium? Jews aren't supposed to enter a place like that during Passover week."

"You don't think our Lord was defiled by entering it, do you?" I countered. "That may be another instance of what Jesus referred to as *man-made law*."

"Why do you think the Romans allowed you to be present in their Hall of Justice?" Nicodemus asked.

"I don't know why. I wondered about that at the time, expecting to be thrown out at any moment. It was as if they couldn't even see me."

The next morning, we walked the short distance to Bethany and arrived at the home of our friends. Our Lord greeted us at the door; we were overjoyed to see him. Lazarus, Martha, and Mary were there too, of course, and we were very happy to see them as well. We all sat down and had a most enjoyable conversation.

It was midmorning when Jesus announced that we were to accompany him on a walk to the garden of Gethsemane. Martha produced two baskets filled with bread and baked fish. It was only a ten-minute walk from Lazarus's house to the garden. On the way, Jesus told us he had arranged for Joseph to accommodate all of us each night, and we would spend each day in the garden together.

We passed through the gate, and our Lord led us to the same spot where he had been betrayed a few weeks before. How different things were this time! There was no pall of gloom descending upon Jesus or us. We knew he would soon leave to return to his Father, and we knew we would miss him. But we also knew he would forever be in our hearts. Moreover, we knew that he would send the Holy Spirit to encourage and guide us. To be sure, we did not yet understand exactly what that would be like, but we trusted his word.

Those last few days with our Lord were marvelous. He reiterated and reinforced many of the things he had said to us during the past three years.

On that first afternoon he said, "After I ascend to my Father, I want you all to go into Jerusalem and wait. You will stay with Nicodemus during that time. Ten days from now, the Holy Spirit will come upon you, and you will all receive His full power. That power will embolden you; you will preach my kingdom message forcefully, without hesitation or fear."

"Lord," asked Thomas, "will that be the time you will restore God's kingdom to Israel?"

"Thomas—and rest of you—it's not your concern to know about times and dates. The Father has placed those matters under His own authority. Your concern is that the Holy Spirit will fill you with power to be my witnesses: first in Jerusalem, then in all Judea and Samaria, and after that, to the very ends of the earth. God's kingdom will encompass much more than Israel. Moreover, it is a spiritual kingdom, not an earthly one. Israel will not rule the world; God will. John baptized you with water. The Holy Spirit will baptize each of you in just a few days. That is when you will be filled with power. In my name, you will cast out demons; you will lay hands on the sick, and heal them. When you speak in your own language, those who don't speak or understand it will hear you as if you were speaking in *their* language. They will understand everything you say, and many will believe. That will greatly increase the effect of your witness of me everywhere you go."

I especially liked what our Lord said about God's kingdom reaching beyond Israel, about its being spiritual and not of this world, about God, not Israel, ruling the world. For most of the last three years, my fellow apostles and I had thought of Jesus as a type of David, whom I've described many times as Israel's most beloved king. God had anointed David as king years before the death of King Saul, David's deeply flawed predecessor. Of course, Jesus had told us many times that *his* kingdom was not of this world. But, for some reason, we had failed to fully understand what our Lord had meant by that. That misapprehension would no longer cloud our minds.

Late in the afternoon, Peter asked our Lord if he wanted Judas to be replaced.

"I *do* want him replaced," Jesus said. "But as to how the choice is made, I will leave that up to all of you."

Too quickly, the final day arrived. It was forty-two days since Jesus's resurrection. That morning, after Jesus had said good-bye to his mother, Lazarus, Martha, and Mary, we walked with our Lord to the crest of the Mount of Olives. It was a magnificent day: the sky was azure, with not a cloud to be seen. Olive trees covered much of the mountain, and there were numerous burial sites, some containing the remains of our most prominent prophets: Zechariah, Haggai, and Malachi among them. It was the place where David worshipped God before fleeing from his own son, Absalom, who was determined to murder him. It was where Ezekiel stood and saw God's glory. And it was where Zechariah, in a vision, beheld YHWH (the never-spoken name of God) standing on its summit.

We knew our Lord was going home to his Father. We knew his Father's home was in heaven.

"Lord, where exactly is heaven?" Peter wanted to know.

"Wherever the Father is, that's where heaven is," Jesus replied.

"Is heaven very far from here?" James asked.

"It's not far at all."

"Then why can't we see it?" James persisted.

"Because heaven is a spiritual place and cannot be seen by human eyes."

"Well, if we can't see it, how can it be real?" Thomas asked.

"Oh, it's real, all right, Thomas. It is more real, more beautiful, and more permanent than anything else, anywhere else. When I return, I will create *this* world anew. Heaven will cover this earth, including this spot right here. In fact, when I come back, this will be the place—this very spot—I will return to."

We reached the top of the mountain. The eleven of us stood in a circle around Jesus. He spoke to each one of us individually, beginning with the eldest, Peter, and finishing with the youngest, me. He blessed each of us saying, "God the Father bless and keep you until we meet again."

And then he slowly began to rise from the earth.

We all fell to our knees and looked up into his face, worshipping him. God the Son was going home to God the Father.

In ten days' time, God the Holy Spirit would come upon us. Someday—none of us knew when—God the Son would return to this very place.

Our Lord continued to rise, and when he was, perhaps, two hundred feet in the air, a small white cloud enveloped him, and he disappeared from our view. As we rose to our feet—still staring at the cloud—we became aware of two angels dressed in dazzling white robes standing next to us. Before our Lord's resurrection, such a sight would have terrified us, but not now. One of them spoke to us in a clarion voice.

"Galileans," he thundered, "why are you standing here gazing into the sky? This same Jesus who was taken from you into heaven to sit at the right hand of God will come back down to you again in the same way you have seen him go into heaven."

The robed ones then departed as swiftly as they had arrived.

As we walked toward Jerusalem, Nathanael, the apostle most knowledgeable on the subject of our ancient Holy Scriptures, said something interesting in light of what we had all just witnessed.

"When our Lord entered that low cloud—the only cloud in an otherwise cloudless sky—I was reminded of other times God used clouds to shield His dazzling divinity. A white pillar of cloud guided the children of Israel when they escaped from Egypt. When God was in the Most Holy Place in the temple, He was shrouded by a white cloud. When we heard what the man in white said about our Lord entering heaven to sit at the right hand of God, I thought about what the prophet Daniel said: 'I was watching in the night and I beheld one like the Son of Man coming with the clouds of heaven. He came to the Ancient of Days and sat down at His right hand.'"

It had been forty-two days since the crucifixion of Jesus. It was high noon that day when a black cloud descended on calvaria—descended over the whole earth, as far as I knew. Jesus was dying a painful death upon a cruel cross. I was there; so was Peter. But even the other nine apostles, though they were not eyewitnesses to that horror, knew what was happening that afternoon. That darkness penetrated deeply into our very beings. We could not escape it, not that day. Now, just six weeks later, as we stood atop the Mount of Olives, from which we could see calvaria in the valley below, everything had changed. It was a stunningly bright day; no blackness marred the sky. The only cloud we had seen all day was pure white. Our Lord, our Savior, had ascended into that cloud, and he was now seated at the right hand of his Father. We longed for the day when we would see him again.

We returned to Lazarus's home and, joined by our Lord's mother, we made our way to Jerusalem. We would stay in the home of Nicodemus, and we would wait. In ten days' time, we would be filled with God the Holy Spirit, and we would enter upon the next great adventure of our lives.

EPILOGUE

You may question why I have entitled this story *The Man Nobody Knew,* when it becomes obvious, as the narrative unfolds, that tens of thousands of people knew of Jesus. However, knowing *of* a person is not the same thing as truly knowing him or her—and this proved even more true with Jesus than an ordinary mere mortal. As I have described, my fellow disciples and I traveled and lived with Jesus for three years, had hundreds of intimate conversations with him, and observed how he related to all sorts of people in all manner of circumstances. During the course of those three years, as I've further described, we also marveled at his healing powers, were frightened by his power over nature, were spellbound by the profound simplicity of his teachings, and were frequently amused by the way he confounded self-assured religious scholars and so-called legal experts. Nevertheless, we, his closest friends and confidants, did not really *know* him until after his resurrection. How could that be? Because Jesus was *the* unique man in history: the Son of Man and the Son of God, fully human and fully divine. It took three years for us, his apostles, to understand that. No one can really know Jesus unless he or she understands that preeminent truth. It is to serve the Truth that I have told this story.

> In the beginning was the Word. The Word was close beside God, and the Word was God. In the beginning, he was close beside God.
>
> All things came into existence through him; nothing that exists came into existence without him. Life was in

him, and his life was the light of the human race. The light shines in the darkness, and the darkness didn't overcome it.

There was a man called John [the Baptist] who was sent from God. He came as evidence, to give evidence about the light, so that everyone might believe through him. He was not himself the light, but he came to give evidence about the light.

The true light, which gives light to every human being, was coming into the world. He was in the world, and the world was made through him, and the world didn't know him. He came to what was his own, and his own people didn't know him. He came to what was his own, and his own people didn't accept him. But to anyone who did accept him, he gave the right to become God's children; yes, to anyone who believed in his name. They were not born from blood, or from physical desire, or from the intention of man, but from God.

And the Word became flesh, and lived among us. We gazed upon his glory, glory like that of the father's only son, full of grace and Truth.

—John 1:1–14

"Don't let your hearts be troubled," Jesus continued. "Trust God—and trust me, too! There is plenty of room to live in my father's house. If that wasn't the case, I'd have told you, wouldn't I? I'm going to get a place ready for you! And if I do go and get a place ready for you, I will come back and take you to be with me, so that you can be there, where I am."

—John 14:1–3